Praise for Lisa Hall

'... addictive ... brilliant!'
B A D...

'A classic twisting mystery from the
Queen of Suspense, Lisa Hall'
Woman's Own

'Brilliantly plotted ... a gripping read'
Alice Feeney

'An uneasy creeping feeling followed me through
the book – I was never quite sure who I should be
trusting... I read this book in one sitting because
I had to know what was going to happen next. An
excellent thriller that had me hooked from the start'
Katerina Diamond

'This is an unrelenting and scarily plausible
story weaved expertly around some very real
characters. Good luck putting it down...'
Heat

'Relentlessly pacey and brilliantly written'
Phoebe Morgan

'An addictive read'
Closer

Lisa Hall loves words, reading and everything there is to love about books. She has dreamed of being a writer since she was a little girl and, after years of talking about it, was finally brave enough to put pen to paper (and let people actually read it). Lisa lives in a small village in Kent, surrounded by her towering TBR pile, a rather large brood of children, dogs, chickens and ponies and her long-suffering husband. She is also rather partial to eating cheese and drinking wine.

Readers can follow Lisa on Twitter @LisaHallAuthor.

Also by Lisa Hall

Between You And Me
Tell Me No Lies
The Party
Have You Seen Her

The Perfect Couple

Lisa Hall

ONE PLACE. MANY STORIES

HQ
An imprint of HarperCollins*Publishers* Ltd
1 London Bridge Street
London SE1 9GF

This paperback edition 2020

1
First published in Great Britain by
HQ, an imprint of HarperCollins*Publishers* Ltd 2020

ISBN: 9780008356453

MIX
Paper from
responsible sources
FSC™ C007454

This book is produced from independently certified FSC™ paper
to ensure responsible forest management.

For more information visit: www.harpercollins.co.uk/green

This book is set in 12.3/16 pt. Bembo

Printed and bound in Great Britain by
CPI Group (UK) Ltd, Croydon, CR0 4YY

To my lovely Mum

Prologue

How well do you really know the people in your life? The person closest to you – the one you live with, share a bed with, have children with… have made an entire *life* with? The one person you think you know every little detail about, the one you choose to let in – your *significant other*. It's a question we rarely have cause to ask. You think you know it all – you know that he can't play football anymore because he's ruined his knees, that he has high blood pressure, that sometimes he laughs in his sleep, that he's a good dad and a hard worker. You know that she tells everyone she is allergic to mushrooms but really she just hates them, that she can't tolerate liars, that sometimes when she's tired stupid things make her laugh so hard, she cries. You notice gestures, gait, intonations that are exciting at first, until they become part of everyday life, things that are as familiar to you as your own movements. But do you know what lies underneath? The secrets that hide beneath the skin, burning and branding their way into that person until they're indelible. Until they are a part of them, hidden from view, but still there, waiting to be exposed.

And then, how well do they know you? You let slip little details as you sit over dinner, sipping wine on the perfect first date, and then as time goes on, more is uncovered. Accidentally, you reveal little bits of yourself on romantic weekends away, holidays, and then snatched moments on the sofa in the evening after a long day at work.

You think you know them inside out and you let them think the same about you, but do they really? Have you told them every little detail of what makes you, you? Do they know what really drives you? The things you keep hidden, tucked inside yourself, too ashamed to ever let them see the light of day?

Secrets. We all have them. They are the things that turn the ordinary everyday into an enigma, sometimes exciting, sometimes explosive. But some secrets are so shocking, so devastating, that you'll do anything to keep others from finding out. So, I'll ask you again. How well do you know the other person in your life?

Chapter One

It's time you got yourself sorted out. Sadie's words echo in Rupert's ears as he drains the last of the red wine from the bottle into his glass, grubby with greasy fingerprints. He greedily swigs at the purple liquid, shuddering slightly at the furry film it leaves on his teeth. Can he really be blamed for letting things slide? He's been on his own for months since Caro died; surely everyone is allowed some sort of mourning period, in which they don't have to wash the dishes every night, and red wine is allowed for dessert?

He pushes himself upright from the depths of the sofa, a struggle in his mildly inebriated state, and glances around the living room, in the house he used to share with Caro. The cushions – ridiculously expensive electric blue Wolf & Badger cushions, which he'd had to bite his tongue over when Caro brought them home – are saggy and squashed without anyone to plump them. Two empty pizza boxes sit on the marble coffee table, although he hasn't had pizza since he worked late into the evening last week. An empty white wine bottle sits alongside the now empty red wine bottle on the floor by the sofa and

Rupert knows for a fact that his recycling bin is crammed full of more. He gets to his feet, stumbling slightly, almost sloshing red wine all over the cream rug in front of the open fireplace.

As he walks into the kitchen, past the pile of unopened post that sits on the worktop, the dishes that are stacked in the sink even though the dishwasher sits empty beneath the counter, cornflakes welded to the rim of the crockery, he catches sight of himself in the reflection of the kitchen window. Outside is pitch black, and his face in the glass is a stark, white oval. His hair falls over one eye, and dark circles ring his eyes. He peers into the glass, squinting at the purple stain on his lips from the wine, and bares his teeth, the purple carrying over to the enamel. It's been a long day. Moving to the sink, Rupert tips the wine down the drain, watching as it swirls away before running the cold tap and refilling the wine glass. Sadie's voice nips at the back of his mind, and he has to concede that maybe she does have a point, but did she have to choose today to voice her opinion?

Rupert slides into a kitchen chair, weariness infusing his bones. Today was not the best day for Sadie to tell him to get his act together. Today was Caro's memorial. He closes his eyes and takes a sip of water, the liquid cold on his tongue and leaving his mouth full of a sharp, metallic taste.

The death knock, he believes that's what they call it. That hard, fast knock that signals the beginning of the end of something for a family. When that knock came at Rupert's door, on a miserable, wet January evening, the bare branches of the trees bending and swaying in the wind as rain began to lash at the windows, Rupert knew he would open the door to the police. He'd been waiting for the knock for three days. He knew what they would tell him, and his stomach had rolled as he pulled the door open, slowly, as if to delay the moment.

'Mr Osbourne-Milligan?' They'd stood there, grim-faced, before he'd nodded and let them into the house, and they'd told him that they'd found her car, that it was found not far from the Severn Bridge, with her purse and a card with a single word scrawled across it – 'Sorry' – on the passenger seat inside. That given her state of mind and previous history, they were in no doubt about what she had done.

Nothing has been the same since those two police officers stood on Rupert's doorstep, with their serious faces and grave voices, and told him that his life was about to change forever. Everything is washed out, faded, blurred by a persistent tug of guilt every time he lets himself think of her. More so today, the day they held a memorial service in Caro's name. Everything is over for Caro, she is at peace. He has to keep on going, guilt balanced on each shoulder.

The church had been freezing cold earlier this morning despite the weak sunshine outside, as they all shuffled in and sat, straight-backed, waiting for the vicar to start his speech. All except Michael, Caro's father. His shoulders were rounded, hunched, grief scored into his face as he finally took his seat next to Esme, Caro's mother. The tip of Rupert's nose was cold, meaning he had to keep sniffing, inhaling the cat piss scent of the lilies that adorned the aisles. Thinking he was crying, Esme turned to pat his hand, a tissue pressed against her own nose, and he was grateful when numbness overtook him as the vicar stood to give Caro's eulogy. A man who barely knew her – Caro hadn't attended church for years despite Esme's requests – standing talking about Rupert's wife, telling the church how loved she was, how generous, how kind, how caring. Rupert felt disconnected, removed from the moment as the voice of the vicar boomed around the echoey chambers of the church, as though they weren't talking about Caro. As though the vicar was talking about someone Rupert couldn't recognize, someone he'd never met before. Then he'd had to endure drinks and a buffet at Caro's parents' house, as strangers – Caro's people, not his – told him that they were sorry, but at least he could move on now. He expects this kind of thing from them, but not from Sadie.

'Rupert? Are you OK? Well, I know you're not OK, of course you're not. It's just, you don't seem to have spoken to many people. I'm just a little worried that you're… oh, you know what I mean.' Sadie appears beside him in the dining room of Michael and Esme's home, thinner than ever in her black dress, her collarbones jutting out white and bony above her neckline. She holds a glass of white wine in one hand and Rupert wonders if it would be crass to ask her to get him one.

'I know what you mean. I can't speak to them, Sadie. They're Caro's friends, not mine. I didn't want a memorial, you know that. I did it for her mother more than anything.'

6

Rupert resisted the idea of a memorial for almost a year, but when Caro's mother had cried on his last visit to her, telling him she needed a memorial before she could let Caro go, he didn't have the heart to deny her any longer. Now, he tries to temper his tone; Sadie is – *was* – Caro's best friend after all. She is feeling the loss of Caro today just as much as she did a year ago. Sod it, he needs a drink. 'Where did you get the wine?'

'Someone handed it to me in the kitchen. Here.' Sadie thrusts the glass towards him, and he takes it. The wine is warm, sour on his tongue, but he swallows it down anyway.

'I don't even know who half these people are. I don't even know if Caro would know who half these people are,' Rupert says. There is a heavy lump in his stomach, weighing him down. Sadie is right, he hasn't spoken to many people here at all, just accepted their condolences, letting Sadie and Miles brush them away. People mill about in the spacious living room, keeping their conversation to a respectable low level, as Caroline stares out from the huge framed wedding photo on the mantelpiece, her face alive, eyes sparkling, a glass of champagne in her hand as bride and groom beam into the camera.

'I bet she could tell you the name of every person in here. She was very popular,' Sadie says, her eyes roaming over the crowd that fills the room. 'Everyone loved her, you know that. She was... God, Rupert, I'm so sorry.' Her eyes fill with tears and Rupert has to look away. 'Shit.' She dabs at her eyes with a tissue. 'I thought it was getting easier – it's been a year.'

'Old chap.' Miles appears beside Sadie, giving her a peck on the cheek, his hand sliding around her waist as he aims a thin smile in Rupert's direction. 'People are starting to leave. Do you want to say goodbye?'

'Do I have to?' The wine has gone to his head, after he necked it on an empty stomach. Caroline would never have approved.

'Well, not if you don't want to…' Sadie starts to say, before Miles interrupts.

'Best if you did,' he says. 'It'll only take a few minutes, and then they'll all be gone. Just show your face.' Subtly reminding Rupert that that's what you do, when you're upper-middle class like Miles. Show your face, keep up appearances. It's what Caro would have wanted. Rupert hauls himself to his feet, ready to shake hands, hug, kiss cheeks until the last of the stragglers depart, and at last he's able to think about leaving.

Finally, Sadie and Miles drive Rupert home, and they stand in the chilly living room of the house Rupert once shared with Caro. The house that still holds hints of her scent, catching him unawares, as though she is still here, a ghost that roams the rooms. He is hoping that Sadie and Miles will be leaving straight away, but Sadie shrugs off her jacket and heads through to the kitchen, and Miles starts to lay a fire in the hearth.

'I poured you some more wine.' Sadie comes back in carrying three glasses and a bottle on a tray, and Rupert thanks her even though he doesn't want any more wine, the

8

first sip feeling like acid as it burns its way down his throat. 'You did so well today. Caro would have been proud.'

'You did bloody well, mate.' Miles slaps Rupert a little too firmly on the back in his attempts to sound like a regular bloke, instead of a trust-fund-supported, slightly-too-posh corporate lawyer. Which he is. 'Cigar?' He offers one out, a fat, juicy Cuban, and Rupert shakes his head. Where he comes from, a cigar is only for celebrations, not an everyday occurrence. 'Mind if I…?' Miles nods towards the door, still respecting Caro's wishes about not smoking in the house, even though she isn't here anymore.

'Go ahead.' Rupert watches him leave and when he turns back Sadie is stood beside him, so close he can feel the warmth of her breath on his face.

'Rupert. Are you sure you'll be OK on your own? It's been a rough day.' She cocks her head on one side, a sour tang of alcohol like a cloud around her. Her eyes are rimmed with red, her face pale. There is a faint smudge of mascara at the corner of her left eye, but her lipstick looks freshly applied.

'Of course.' He's had a year without Caro beside him already. 'I'll be fine. You two should probably go. It's been a long day, shouldn't you be getting back to the twins?' Blanche and Barclay – a fraternal nightmare, and Rupert and Caro's godchildren. *Rupert's* godchildren, now.

'They're fine. They're with the nanny.' She looks away, running a finger around the rim of her wine glass. 'Rupert, if you need to talk, you can call me any time, you know that? You've shut us out since Caro's been gone. You can talk to me about her – I won't fall apart. She was my best friend, part of my life since I was eleven years old. We did everything together. I know what you're going through. I know how it feels.' Her words slur slightly, and Rupert realizes she's a little drunk. She leans towards him, laying a hand on his arm, and he focuses on the gap between her two front teeth, the tiny mole that sits just above her top lip and prepares to push her away. 'It's been a rough year for all of us.'

'I know. Thank you, Sadie. I promise I'll call you if I need to talk. But you really should go now, it's getting late.' He places his hand on her shoulder, just firmly enough to make her start and pull away.

'At least now we've had the memorial service you can start to move on, Rupert.' Any inhibitions Sadie may have about speaking her mind have disappeared with the alcohol as she looks around the room. 'It's time you sorted yourself out. You know, get this place tidied up, start taking care of yourself – it can't be good for your mental health, living like this. Caro's gone, Rupert, but you aren't. You're still here.'

'Like I said, it's getting late. You should go.' Rupert doesn't want to talk about it, he never wants to talk about it.

'Of course.' She puts her empty glass on the low coffee table, jumping slightly as the front door slams closed and Miles appears, rubbing his hands together against the cold and stinking of cigar smoke, thick and heavy in the air. 'Miles, we should leave Rupert in peace. It's been a long day.' Parroting Rupert's words back to him as she reaches behind her for her coat, her leopard print scarf, then reaching for Rupert himself, pulling him towards her as she kisses his cheek leaving a dark red stain from her lipstick. And then they go, and he is completely alone.

Any buzz that Rupert might have got from the wine is long gone now, as he shifts in the chair, a chill settling over him despite the warmth blasting from the radiators. He feels clear-headed suddenly as he looks around the kitchen, taking in the dust that thinly coats the kitchen table, the window sill and even parts of the worktop. He let the cleaner go after Caro died. Tea stains litter the floor around the waste bin and Rupert feels a sudden surge of nausea. Sadie is right. This is not who he is. He needs to sort himself out. Caro would be appalled to see the way he's been living since she's been gone. He shakes his head at the thought of Caro and reaches for the bottle of whisky on the kitchen counter. He pours a healthy measure and opens up his laptop, tapping his fingers impatiently as he waits for the browser to open. He's going to do what Sadie said – he's going to sort himself out and get things back on track. He can't change what happened, but he can start to move on. She's right, it's been long enough.

An hour later, he rereads what he has written and presses the submit button, a fluttering in his stomach making the nausea rise again, as he waits for the confirmation email. It's done.

Chapter Two

I heave a sigh of relief as I let myself into the flat, dragging Tiny behind me. I dread walking her most of the time, my heart sinking as she dances in circles whenever Mags gets the lead out. Tiny has no idea how to behave in public, having taken to peeing on things she shouldn't and barking at every single person who crosses our path, but the alternative is to sit in the flat all day while Mags smokes joint after joint, and sometimes I just can't bear the thought of it; I have to get out, get some fresh air.

The strong smell of weed in the hallway tells me that Mags is awake, and she hasn't left the flat yet. I unclip Tiny's leash, wincing as the little dog rushes into the kitchen, barking her high-pitched, ear-splitting yaps.

'Your dog is a psychopath,' I say to Mags as I walk into the kitchen, heading straight for the fridge. I pull out a carton of orange juice, drinking deeply and ignoring my flatmate making a fuss of her socially inept chihuahua.

'Well, there's a reason why I ask you to take her for a walk, and it's not just because you're not paying me any rent at the moment.' Mags resumes her position, sitting on the table top, and peers through the smoke curling from the end of her joint to where Tiny has tucked herself into a ball and promptly gone to sleep.

'I am looking for a job, there just doesn't seem to be much out there,' I say quietly, a fizz of irritation burning low in my belly. No 'thank you' for taking the dog out, just a dig about my finances. I turn to the sink and start washing the glass out, letting the cold water run over my wrists.

'Oh, you know I don't mean it,' Mags snorts, stubbing her joint out. 'Take as long as you need, I can make the rent. I know you've had a tough time. It was just a joke.'

Secretly, I think that perhaps Mags needs to take a second look at her 'jokes' because they're really not very funny, but I don't say anything, instead just keep drying my glass until it squeaks under the pressure of my hand.

'I like having you here, you know that.' Mags jumps down off the table and pulls me into a musty, patchouli-scented embrace. 'I don't mind looking after you.'

'I don't need *looking after*,' I pull away, resisting the urge to wrinkle my nose. I'll never get used to the incense that Mags burns day and night. Mags has been kind to me after what happened with Harry, but honestly this was only ever meant to be a temporary thing. I didn't envisage myself still living here six months on.

'Well, clearly you do.' Mags's voice takes on a snippy tone. 'Not being funny, Emily, but you didn't exactly have people beating down the door to take care of you when Harry treated you the way he did. It's not like you had anywhere else to go, and your mum didn't really rise to the occasion, did she? Too busy sunning herself.'

I squash down a sigh. It's not the first time that Mags has thrown back in my face how she was the only one who helped me when I was literally on my knees, and once again, I wish I hadn't revealed to Mags how I felt about my mum, after two bottles of wine in front of the telly one Friday night. 'I know, Mags, and I do appreciate it, you know I do.'

And I do appreciate it, I'm not lying. I still remember the fear that gripped me every time the buzzer rang, or the neighbours banged on the wall, when I first arrived – how the blood would speed around my veins, making my breath come short in my throat, believing that Harry had found me. And I remember the way Mags didn't mind me leaving the chain on twenty-four/seven, even when it meant that she missed her dealer dropping off her gear one Saturday evening. The way Mags would sit with me for hours, watching old movies with one arm looped over my shoulders, so I didn't have to be alone, even though she probably had a thousand and one better things to be doing. But I don't want to live like this anymore. I'm ready to get back to the old Emily.

'Did I get any messages?' I ask. I handed my CV to a recruitment company in Swindon town centre last week, and they'd said they'd call but they haven't.

'Nope.'

'I might call them. I just think it's time I got back out there, you know. Properly out there, working, not just taking Tiny out for a walk twice a day. I can't hibernate in here forever.' I move towards the clothes airer in the corner of the kitchen, even though there is barely any laundry on it and start to fold the few things that hang there.

'You don't have to, Em, you know that.' Mags follows me, standing close behind me as I fold and smooth the fabric. I can feel her breath on the back of my neck, a grass-scented huff raising the wispy hairs that don't reach my ponytail. 'I like you being here, and it honestly doesn't matter about the rent; you know my dad pays it anyway.'

I realized this not long after I moved into the flat. I had answered Mags's Gumtree advert, taking the flat without even looking at it in my desperation to get away from Harry before he carried through the threats he hurled at me daily, and when after the third month of living there I had run out of money and couldn't pay the rent, Mags had waved me away and said not to worry.

'I think I need to look for a job though.' I worked in IT before everything went so horribly wrong with Harry, but now I think I'd take any job, just to get back on my feet. 'I don't want to sponge off you forever, I have to be able to take care of myself,' I say again gently, as Mags takes my hand and leads me through to the sitting room. She pulls me down next to her on the grubby couch, an overflowing ashtray on the ring-stained coffee table in front of three dirty mugs – one with a layer of mould sitting on the surface – and once again I have to resist the urge to sigh.

'Listen. You don't, Em, not if you don't want to.' Mags looks at me earnestly as she puts a fresh joint to her mouth, inhaling sharply as she lights it. 'We can manage here, just the two of us. I like it being just the two of us.'

'I do, too, I promise,' I say, wanting to cross my fingers. 'You've been so brilliant, Mags.' I slide my phone out of my pocket. 'Help me look for something suitable? You've always got such a good vibe about things; you'll know if something feels wrong.'

Ego massaged; Mags nods her head slowly. 'Yeah. You're right. I got a good vibe about you, didn't I?' She nudges me and laughs. 'And this place. I suppose… if you get a job, then we can maybe do something in here? Decorate, maybe. Get some fancy cushions or something.'

I paste a smile onto my face, but my heart sinks a little. I want to get a job so I can move on – much as I am grateful to Mags (and I *am*, God only knows what would have happened to me if Mags hadn't let me move in), this place is stifling, and Mags, although she means well, is more than a little suffocating. 'So, let's see…' I pull up Safari on my phone and type in the name of a local job search site. 'Bar staff?'

'Ugh, no,' Mags shakes her head, 'coming home stinking of booze every night?' Despite smoking an immense amount of weed, Mags is completely teetotal. 'And what about dealing with pissed-up losers every night? You had enough of that with Harry, didn't you?'

She has a point. I swiftly move on, not wanting Mags to start talking about Harry again. It makes my stomach swoop when I think of him, and not in a good way.

'What about this one? The money is a bit crap, but you

probably get a discount on the clothes.' Mags points to an advert for a shop assistant in a well-known clothes shop. I read through it, trying not to frown. I like the shop, wear their clothes even, but I'm not sure that that's the kind of job I want. Plus, it's right in the centre of Swindon.

'I don't know,' I say, as Mags's mouth curls at the corners into a tiny smile. 'It's right on the High Street… I'd feel a bit safer in an office somewhere, or at least somewhere where there isn't so much traffic. What if Harry came in? What if he saw me?' I blink, and Mags grabs my hand, her fingers crushing mine even though there aren't any tears.

'I told you, you don't have to do this. I can… take care of you,' Mags looks down at our joined hands, 'you could be Tiny's dog walker, I could pay you for that if you wanted.'

I shake my head, gently disentangling my fingers from hers. That would be my worst nightmare – people already cross the road when they see the two of us out walking, thanks to Tiny being an actual maniac. I turn back to my phone, scrolling on, my finger swiping gently at the screen when I see it.

'Oh. What about this one?' I turn the screen so Mags can see it. 'Housekeeper wanted for large property in Somerville. Duties to include general housework, ironing, some garden maintenance, light cooking, plus some additional admin duties. Immediate start and competitive salary. Please send CV to…' I feel my cheeks warm as a flush spreads across my skin from my neckline. This is just the kind of thing I was thinking of. 'Mags, look, this could be perfect!'

'Is it a live-in position?'

'No, I don't think so, but don't you think something like that would be perfect?' A flicker of excitement lights a spark in me, and I get to my feet, already thinking what I might wear if I get invited for interview. 'Can I borrow your laptop?'

'Are you sure you want to apply?' Mags tucks her dirty bare feet up onto the couch, making no move to go to her room for her computer. 'I mean… I'm not really feeling the *vibe*… and Somerville is *far.*'

'Well, I am.' I have to temper my tone as I resist the urge to snap the words at Mags. I'm not sure I buy into all this 'vibe' thing that Mags has going on, and now I'm so impatient to get my CV over for the job that I don't have time to pretend I do. And Somerville isn't *that* far. Half an hour maybe, if I jump on the train with my pushbike. 'Come on, Mags, this is perfect. And it says the money is "competitive", just think what we could do in here.' Mags could probably get her dad to pay for redecorating, but I don't want to remind her of that, not now. 'We could get one of those massive, squashy sofas, and get rid of this old thing.' I toe the stuffing that leaks out from the bottom of the couch, like some sort of grim, grey lava.

'Hmmm.' Mags gets slowly to her feet, and disappears into her room, emerging five minutes later with the battered Mac.

'Thank you, you're amazing.' I grab the machine, giving Mags a huge smile that makes her cheeks flush pink. 'Right, here goes.'

'Are you really sure?' Mags blurts out, one hand raised as if to take the laptop back from me. 'I mean, think about it, Em, it's really just a glorified wife. That's all this guy wants. You'll be doing all the cooking and cleaning, with none of the benefits.'

'I'm pretty sure I'll be OK without having sex with him,' I say, raising an eyebrow as I turn away and place the laptop out of reach. 'And anyway, he might already have a wife, the advert doesn't say.'

'I'm just saying, that's all…' Mags gestures to the flat around us, to the clutter that sits in piles in the corners, 'it's not like housework is your favourite thing to do, let's be honest. Like I said, you'll just be a wife – but doing all the shit bits but without getting any of the good stuff. And Somerville is far, you'd spend an hour every day commuting there and back. You'll be exhausted.'

I open up my Hotmail account, noticing a message from the recruitment company. A quick read tells me they have called and left a message, and they are awaiting my response to a temp job they have. I look over at Mags, who is watching me closely, and there is a stutter in my chest. Maybe she missed their call. I open up a new email and attach my CV, blocking out Mags as I hit send on the email. 'There, I've done it. We'll just have to wait and see now – if it's meant to be, then it's meant to be.'

It takes me a long while to fall asleep that night, my mind returning over and over to the job advert, as I try to picture the house, whoever placed the advert and what this could mean for me. I think if I get an interview, I'll print the advert and add it to my scrapbook to document the next stage of my journey. I tuck my hand between the mattress and bed frame, my fingers searching out the comforting feel of the book's spine, and I imagine myself smoothing the advert into place, before dressing to impress at interview. Smiling, I roll over in an attempt to get comfortable. I can hear Mags's music through the wall – something slow and turgid that really should help me fall asleep – and I finally doze off around two o'clock in the morning.

I've barely begun to dream when something jolts me from sleep, an unknown noise breaking into my conscience. Keeping my eyes closed, I count to ten under my breath before I open them, my heart thudding painfully in my chest as I try to get my bearings and I listen hard to figure out what it is that has woken me. *Breathing.* That's what has dragged me from sleep. The sound of another person breathing in my room.

'Fuck.' Whispering the word, I push myself up on shaky arms, frantically casting my mind over what is on the bedside table that I could use as a weapon, stifling a shriek as I see the figure standing at the end of my bed, illuminated by the thin shaft of moonlight that streaks through the gap in the curtains. For one moment I think my heart has stopped dead in my chest before the figure takes a step towards me and I realize that it is my flatmate. It's only Mags.

'Shit, you scared me. Shhh, Mags, come on, back to bed.' I push back the duvet cover and gently take Mags by the arm, shivering slightly as the night air meets the sweat on my body. Mags mumbles something, something about not letting go, and I shush her again before guiding her back to her room on legs that feel like jelly, making sure the door is firmly closed when I leave. I pad silently back to bed, taking deep breaths to get my heart rate back to normal. It's been a while since Mags has sleepwalked, and she's never actually walked into my room before. I let out a shaky laugh of relief at it being Mags, and not someone more sinister – feeling foolish now I know I'm not under any threat. I won't miss this part of living with Mags when I leave. If I manage to leave.

The job floats into my mind again as I climb into bed and I hug myself tightly, sending up a prayer to whoever is up there that I get called for an interview. I turn the pillow over to the cool side, Mags's voice sniping in my ear, *'you'll just be a glorified wife'*, and as I drop off the edge into sleep, my last thought is that perhaps that wouldn't be the worst thing in the world.

Chapter Three

I try not to gawp as I hop off my pushbike and wheel it up the path to the house, making out as though houses this huge, this imposing, are part of my world. There is a sweeping gravel drive, leading to the front of a huge, double-fronted house, with a double – maybe even triple – garage nestled to the side. I try to keep my eyes on the front door ahead of me, two stone lions flanking the porch, and take a deep breath.

Although the house is imposing, and clearly my potential employer is doing OK for himself, there are tiny signs of neglect. Weeds sprout up in the tubs that house straggly-looking topiary bushes on either side of the windows, there is a recycling box in front of the garage that looks as if it is about to overflow with empty bottles, and the window sills look as though they could do with a scrub. Despite what Mags says, I am actually very house-proud, having been brought up with a mother who couldn't abide dirt. I've just given up in the flat, because Mags doesn't have the same outlook. *I could take a picture,* I think, *once it's all clean and tidy. I'll stick it next to the job advert in my book.* I finger the outline of my phone in my pocket, resisting the urge to take a 'before' picture.

Smoothing my hair down, I make sure the waistband of my skirt hasn't twisted round – after what happened with Harry, I lost nearly a stone that I haven't put back on yet – before taking a deep breath and lifting the brass knocker, letting it fall with a loud bang. There is a long pause, where I think for a moment that perhaps there is no one home; that the guy, Rupert, has forgotten I'm coming, before the door is wrenched open.

'Yes?' The man in front of me is tall, over six feet, with floppy dark hair in a style that reminds me of old Hugh Grant movies. Even though it is Saturday morning, he is wearing jeans with a smart shirt, as if he is about to go to work. That is, if he'd actually tucked it in and he had shoes on his feet. My stomach gives a tiny flip.

'Hi,' I smile, holding out a hand. 'I'm Emily Belrose. I'm here for an interview?'

'Oh. Of course.' He runs his hand through his hair before standing to one side and ushering me in. 'I'm so sorry, I'm running a bit behind this morning. You can see why I need a housekeeper.' His mouth tugs up into a small smile and I let out a laugh.

'It happens to the best of us.' I follow him along a light, airy hallway into the kitchen, and have to resist the urge to let my mouth hang open. It is *huge*. It's also untidy, with mugs and dishes in the sink, a dying houseplant on top of the fridge and an overflowing bin.

23

'Sorry about the mess.' Rupert looks a bit sheepish, and I smother another smile.

'Well, isn't that what I'm here for?' I discreetly run my eyes over the kitchen, over the thin layer of dust that sits on the counter top, the pile of post that has been shoved to one side.

'Can I make you a cup of tea?' Rupert is already rummaging in the cupboard above the kettle for mugs. 'Milk? Sugar?' I say yes to both, and wait as he fills the kettle, water splashing over his shirt as he turns the tap on too high.

'Can I get the milk?' I ask, as he swipes ineffectually at the damp patches with a tea towel, but when I open the fridge, the shelf is bare. 'Black is fine,' I say with a smile, my nerves dissipating as I see that Rupert is possibly just as nervous as I am. 'Here, shall I finish this off while you get dry?' I reach for the now boiling kettle as Rupert scrubs at the fabric of his shirt.

'So, Emily, I suppose I should actually interview you, not just let you make me tea.' Rupert smiles as I pass him a mug. 'Why did you apply for this job? You're not really what I was expecting.'

'Really?' I turn to him. 'What were you expecting?'

'Well, someone more… Mrs Danvers, I suppose. Or Mrs Doubtfire.'

My heart skips in my chest. Not only is Rupert easy on the eye, but he *reads* too. I choose to ignore the reference to Mrs Doubtfire. 'I'm definitely not Mrs Danvers. I suppose I'm just looking for something different. I've had a bit of… bad luck, I guess you could say, so I'm trying to turn things around.' I wrap my cold fingers around the warm mug, staring at the dark tannin patches left on the china by the black tea, buying myself a few seconds. 'This seemed like the perfect job for me, right now.'

'You're certainly making a good impression,' Rupert says, with a quirk of his eyebrows. 'Can I show you the rest of the house?'

'Yes, please.' I dry my hands and he leads me through double doors from the kitchen towards a large orangery, where sunshine streams in through big windows, onto the stylish Italian-tiled floor. I pause in the doorway. Two huge sofas fill the space, and bi-fold glass doors open out onto what must have been an immaculate garden at some point, although now the lawn needs mowing, and the shrubs are looking a little wild. Despite the cosy, comfortable vibe this space gives off, there is something slightly dead about it – a thin layer of dust sits atop the small glass table next to one of the sofas, and the air is thick and stale, as though the doors haven't been opened for a long time.

'Wow. This space is incredible.' I venture closer to the window to peer out into the garden. What I'd do for a garden this size – you don't get a lot of outside space with a flat over a takeaway in the centre of Swindon.

'I, er… I don't really use this room much,' Rupert says stiffly, appearing beside me and taking my arm to walk me through the rest of the house. 'Let me show you upstairs.'

We go upstairs via the living room, another huge space, occupied by a large open fireplace. Floor-to-ceiling book-shelves line one wall, and a piano is strategically placed, giving that whole part of the room a calm, quiet feel, like a library. 'Do you play?' I ask Rupert, but he shakes his head.

'No, not me.' He doesn't elaborate and I wonder who does play – his wife, maybe? He hasn't mentioned anyone else living here yet, and I have to squash down the question on the tip of my tongue. I follow him up to the first floor, where he quickly shows me the bathroom (huge, freestanding claw-footed tub, dusty Jo Malone bottles of bath oil on the window sill), first one small spare room, the master bedroom and en suite and then into another, larger spare room, where his phone starts ringing. Rupert sighs as he glances at the screen.

'I'm so sorry, I need to take this... Will you excuse me for just a second?'

There is no time to answer before he steps out of the room, pulling the door gently closed behind him. I wait a moment, his voice a low mumble along the corridor, feeling the slight sink of the lush, thick-piled carpet under my feet. There are a couple of prints on the walls, arty-looking pictures that give me the feeling I should probably know who they are by, but I don't. A heavy French oak wardrobe sits in the corner, a slip of peacock blue fabric peeping out from between a small gap in the doors. I step forward, the rumble of Rupert's voice in the background, letting my fingers brush over the silky fabric, and before I know what I am doing, the wardrobe door is open, just enough for me to see it is filled with clothes – a woman's clothes, dresses, jackets, trousers, all hanging neatly on wooden hangers – the expensive ones that I can never afford. Some are covered in plastic, as if just back from the dry cleaners, others – expensive-looking gowns, something sparkly with sequins – hang uncovered, so many of them that the hangers are rammed tightly together. The slip of fabric belongs to the sleeve of a silk jacket in a vibrant blue, and I stroke it gently, the feel of it like cold water under my fingers, wondering who the clothes belong to and more importantly why are they in here, instead of the master bedroom. Before I get a chance to let my imagination run riot, Rupert's voice gets louder as he approaches the bedroom, saying his goodbyes to whoever was on the other end of the phone. The buzz of curiosity dies away, and I close the wardrobe door, moving to the middle of the room, as if I have done nothing but wait patiently for him to return.

'Sorry about that.' He stands by the door, waiting for me to slip past him. 'I think that's just about it for the grand tour.'

'Very impressive,' I say, before wincing on the inside, hoping I haven't come across as a bit crass. 'It's a lovely house, Rupert. A lovely home.'

A look I can't quite read crosses his face. 'Yes, well. You can see that it needs a bit of sprucing up here and there. That's why I'm on the lookout for a housekeeper. It's a big house for me to take care of, especially with the hours that I work.'

I take that as an opportunity to learn a bit more about him. 'What is it that you do?'

'I'm the Contracts Director for a construction company. It's quite intense – the hours are long, especially if I have to go out and visit sites, and it's quite stressful. I'm mostly based at the Swindon office, but I commute into Paddington several times a month. That's why I need a bit of help here.'

I follow him down the stairs, back into the vast sitting room. 'Is it…' I pause for a moment, not wanting to appear rude. 'Is it just you living here? I mean… will I just be looking after you, or is there anyone else who might need me to do things?'

'No, er… it's just me.' Rupert swallows, and rocks back on his heels a little. 'I lost my wife just over a year ago.' The words creak out, as though they are too big for his throat and he gives a tiny cough. 'Hence the reason why things have gone to pot a bit.'

That explains why there aren't any perfumes or fancy shampoo in the en suite. 'I'm so sorry,' I say, looking down. I hope I haven't offended him – the more I've seen of this place, the more convinced I am that this could be just what I'm looking for. The perfect escape route from Mags's weed-ridden flat, and back to standing on my own two feet again.

'Look, Emily, I'm not going to beat about the bush.' Rupert's cheeks colour slightly, and my heart does another little flip. 'If you want the job, I'd love for you to come and work for me, if the state of the place hasn't put you off. We can even just do a trial period for a month or so, if that would work better for you?'

'Oh, no,' I exclaim, before putting my hand over my mouth, 'I mean, yes, please. But don't worry about a trial period… unless you want one, I mean. I'm quite happy to come and work for you.' I stop talking before I make a complete idiot of myself. 'Thank you.'

'Brilliant.' The stress melts away from Rupert's face, his shoulders lowering, and I realize that he really was more nervous than me about the whole job interview scenario. 'When could you start?'

I have to resist the urge to squeal as I hop on my pushbike and ride down the driveway, before turning onto the main road. *I got the job!* And yes, it does seem a little daunting, putting that huge house back to its rightful state, but I am in no doubt that I can do it. Plus, I'm pretty sure I didn't imagine that fiery spark that shot through my skin when Rupert shook my hand to say goodbye – and I'm ninety-nine per cent sure he felt it too. Now, all I need to do is tell Mags. My raised spirits dampen slightly at the thought of breaking the news to her. I know she's going to make some snippy comments about being a glorified wife, that the village is too far for me to go there and back every day, and she'll try to make me feel guilty about leaving her in the flat on her own all day, but we can't all live off our father's money. I don't even know where my dad is, and I doubt my mum does either. I let myself turn back at the end of the road, to glance towards the house, a shiver of excitement running through me. Yes, this is definitely the start of something big.

Chapter Four

Humming under my breath I breathe in the scent of laundry detergent and softener as I fold Rupert's pyjamas and tuck them carefully under his pillow, pushing away the thought of him lying in bed wearing them, his hair tousled and rumpled from sleep. Not that I've seen him like that, of course. Pressing my lips together, I neatly fold his socks into a ball, praising myself for thinking about him wearing the pyjamas, instead of lying in bed *not* wearing the pyjamas. I feel my cheeks flush and I shake my head, picturing instead the dishes that wait to be stacked in the dishwasher downstairs.

I've been working at Fox House (the house not only has a beautiful sweeping drive, but a *name* too!) for a little over a month and I can't lie, it's not just the incredible house that has me skipping into work every day. Rupert is... well, Rupert is just about the perfect man from what I've seen of him so far, which to be fair isn't a huge amount, but enough to make me not mind the commute into work every day. He's good-looking, that goes without saying, but he's also a nice guy. He doesn't leave too much of a mess (no more than a typical guy, and nothing like the scale of untidiness that I saw when I first came), he's polite (he leaves me notes with lots of 'please' and 'thank you' dotted through them when he wants me to do certain things), and judging by the letters he leaves lying on the kitchen worktop he donates to charity a lot, especially to a children's charity, which made my heart skip a beat in a good way. The only tiny, little thing that makes me feel a bit awkward is the idea of his wife.

He hasn't mentioned her again since the day I came for my job interview, and I don't feel as if I can ask about her. There are no photos of Caro anywhere in the house, something that strikes me as odd. I could understand that perhaps Rupert doesn't want her photos on display downstairs, that maybe it is too painful, but I thought that he might have one in his bedroom, but there's nothing. All he keeps on the bedside table is a small lamp, a water glass and a battered copy of Dan Brown's *The Da Vinci Code*. On the other side of the bed – Caro's side – the nightstand is bare, apart from a matching lamp.

Stealthily, even though I know I am the only one in the house, I perch on the side of the bed and give in to the hum of curiosity that buzzes through me when I think about her, taking care not to rumple the pristine white duvet as I slide open the drawer on Caro's side. It is crammed full of things, and I hold my breath as I dip in and pull out a slim date diary. I gingerly open the cover, flicking through the expensive cream pages but they are all blank. I put it on the bed next to me and turn back to the drawer.

Pens, hair clips and the plug from an iPhone charger lie jumbled among tiny perfume sample bottles and I lift one out and raise it to my nose. It smells of nectarines and sunshine and has 'Jo Malone' written down the side of the bottle. Pushing it back into the mess of the drawer I see a half-empty packet of contraceptive pills, and something low in my stomach flips, the idea of Rupert and Caro tumbling around together, naked, right here in this bed makes me feel hot and uncomfortable. I stand, fumbling with the handle of the drawer, when a sharp ring pierces the air, making me slam the drawer closed with a bang.

'Shit,' I whisper under my breath, raising a trembling hand to my hot cheek. Taking a deep breath, I glance round the room, satisfied that I haven't left anything out of place. 'Coming!' I call, as the shrill doorbell rents the air again, and I hurry down the stairs to the ornate, oak front door.

There is a woman standing on the doorstep, chic and glamorous, and clearly not expecting to see me answer the door.

'Hi,' I smile, 'can I...'

She pushes past me with barely a glance, calling down the hallway towards the kitchen. 'Rupert? Darling, are you home?'

I wait a moment, letting the fizz of irritation in my veins cool a little before I follow her into the kitchen, my bare feet silent on the Italian tiled floor. 'He's not home. Can I help you?'

'Oh.' The woman turns to me, and I catch an expression that I can't read flit across her face. It's definitely not friendly though. 'Where is he? It's Saturday, I thought he'd be home.'

'I'm sorry, I'm not too sure,' I say, even though Rupert left me a note yesterday, asking me to make sure his rugby kit was clean, as he was planning on playing this morning. 'Is there something I can help you with?' I fix a smile on my face.

'Who are you?' She flicks her eyes over me in an attempt to look me over without me noticing. I fight the urge to smooth down my blonde hair, to tighten my ponytail and brush the dust from my jeans. Instead I smile at her, showing off my perfect white teeth (they cost my mother's second husband a fortune), and apologize for not introducing myself.

'I'm so sorry – how rude of me. I'm Emily.' I hold out a hand, but she ignores it, instead tapping her chin as if thinking.

'Emily? Oh, of course.' She smiles at me now, and I get the feeling I imagine a tiny gazelle feels when a lion is sizing it up, ready to pounce. 'You must be Rupert's new cleaner.'

'Housekeeper,' I say, keeping my tone neutral, 'well, Rupert isn't home, so if you wanted me to pass on a message…' I trail off, hoping she'll take the hint.

'Oh, just tell him that Sadie was here. I'll catch up with him later, it wasn't anything important.' She runs a hand over her already immaculate black bob and tucks her Hermès bag under her arm. Everything about her oozes money – from the tight-fitting designer jeans to the expensive scent that follows her. It reminds me of the nectarine perfume I found in Caro's drawer. 'How are you getting on here? Are you enjoying the job?' Her tone is distinctly warmer now she knows I'm just the housekeeper.

'Fine, thank you.'

'Oh, good. Rupert did need someone to take care of him after Caro... died. We were all so worried about him; I'm just so thankful that he took my advice and got you in. He isn't very good at taking care of himself – he was just devastated after what happened with Caro.' Sadie throws herself dramatically into a kitchen chair, and I realize that she isn't planning on leaving anytime soon.

'Can I get you a cup of tea?' I ask. 'Although if you're planning on waiting, I'm not too sure how long Rupert will be.'

'Oh, OK. Peppermint,' she says and I turn to the kettle, mustering up the courage to mention Caro's name. 'This place looks marvellous now you've given it a once over. Caro was always very house-proud.'

There. She's dropped Caro's name twice already in the past two minutes. Surely it won't look odd now if I ask her about Caro? I'm itching to know about the woman who lived here, and I don't feel I can ask Rupert.

'She's made a lovely home. Caro, I mean,' I say, placing a steaming mug in front of Sadie.

'Yes. She had a wonderful eye for interiors, and I always told her she should do something professional with it, but she was more about saving the world than decorating.' Sadie lets out a little laugh, tinged with pain. 'Caro was very lucky – she had it all really. Such a waste.' She looks down at her cup, and I think for a moment she might burst into tears.

'I'm so sorry for your loss. It must be very hard on all of you.'

'Yes, it is. Especially Rupert, obviously. They were the perfect couple. I wasn't at all sure that he'd cope without her, and it was touch and go for a while, but he's been so brave. I'm not sure he'll ever move on, though. Caro was the only one for him.'

'I'm sure.' I get the feeling that Sadie is warning me off, even though I am just the housekeeper. 'I should get back to work. I'll let Rupert know that you stopped by.'

Sadie opens her mouth as if to say something, before thinking better of it and getting to her feet. 'It was nice to meet you, Emily. I'm sure I'll see you again.'

Relief floods through me as Sadie closes the front door behind her and I am alone again. I head back upstairs, intent on putting away the last of the laundry, but pause outside the spare room. Sadie's words ring in my ears, 'they were the perfect couple', and my heart aches for Rupert. Caro may have been the only one for him, but I wonder if he ever gets lonely. Silently, I push open the door to the spare room, my body gravitating towards the huge wardrobe that houses Caro's clothes. Her scent wafts out as I open the door, and I suppress a shiver. It feels as though she is in the room with me, a ghost of what was before. I glance down at the row of shoes that sit neatly under the hanging dresses, a mix of Converse trainers – still a brilliant white, unlike the faded grey-white pair of my own that sit at the bottom of the stairs – and flat gladiator sandals that must have been a favourite as the ends bear the faintest imprints of her toes, an oddly intimate glimpse into her life that makes me feel vaguely sad, and finally several pairs of sparkly sandals, with heels so high she must have barely been able to walk in them.

Sinking down onto the plush carpet, I pull out a pair with silver straps and a dragonfly buckle on the side. Hardly daring to breathe I slip my feet into them, the straps pinching as they are ever so slightly too small. I stand, wobbly on the spindly heels, and steady myself as I am assaulted by a flashback – myself, at around ten years old, trying on my mother's high heels as she prepared to go out for the night with the man who would eventually become my stepfather, and her second husband.

'Look at me, Mum! I look just like you!' I wobble towards her, as she slicks red lipstick around her mouth, pouting and smacking her lips together in the mirror.

'Hey, be careful!' Finally, my mother turns to look at me as I stagger my way across the threadbare carpet towards her, arms outstretched. 'Don't you snap those heels. I want to wear those tonight.'

I slip the shoes off and hand them to my mother, unsure as how to she could possibly manage to spend the whole night upright while wearing them. I blink back tears at her harsh tone, and when she hears me sniffing, she turns to me, her face softening.

'Silly thing, don't cry.' She pulls me towards her, and I snuggle into her shoulder, the silky fabric of her dress cool against my skin. I breathe in her heavy perfume, something thick and cloying but it doesn't matter, she smells like my mum. 'I just need to wear those killer heels tonight. John won't know what's hit him, and before you know it, we'll be a proper family.' She spins around with me in her arms and kisses my face until I shriek and giggle. 'Honestly, little one,' she sobers now, sitting me down on the bed as she puts the finishing touches to her make-up, 'you don't want to live here forever, do you? If John and I get married we can get out of here, go and live in his big house, all of us together. You want Mummy to be happy, don't you?' She shoos me into bed, and then I hear the click of the lock on the front door and the clacking of her heels down the path towards the man she thinks will turn our lives around.

Now, I slide the shoes off and place them back exactly where they were, not wanting Rupert to know that I've been in here. My mother did snare John, but that was years ago, and now she's living in Florida with her fifth or sixth husband – I forget which number she's on now – but she lives in a huge house and doesn't have to think about money. Just like Caro. From the little that Sadie said about Caro earlier, she lived a charmed life right from when she was young. I stroke the arm of a fur coat, the pelt thick and glossy. It feels remarkably real – if it's a fake, then it's a good one. How would it feel, I wonder, to have all of this? To live the life that Caro lived?

The thunk of a car door closing outside brings me back

to myself, and I slam the wardrobe door closed, half of me regretting that I didn't take the time while I could to quickly try on the silky fur, the seductive feel of it luring me in, even though I am against real fur, while the other half of me feels grubby at the very thought of trying on a dead woman's clothes. Peering out of the landing window, I see Rupert getting out of his car, his face ruddy and his hair sweaty as he pulls his gym bag from the boot.

'Hi.' I stop at the bottom of the stairs, as he bursts through the front door.

'Oh, sorry. I thought you would have been gone by now.' His face flushes and my heart skips a beat.

'I just had a few things to finish off. I'll get off now, get out of your hair. If you leave that bag by the washing machine, I'll get it sorted on Monday.'

Rupert pauses for a moment, as if he wants to say something, before he gives me a small smile. 'Thank you. For today, I mean, not the gym bag. I really appreciate you coming in on a Saturday.'

'It's no bother.' I slide my feet into my trainers. 'A woman called Sadie came over earlier – she said she'll catch up with you later.' I smile, even though the thought of Sadie and her chilly manner is like grit under an eyelid. 'I'll see you on Monday.'

'Emily…' Rupert says, and I wait, my heart thudding hard in my chest. 'Oh, never mind. Have a good weekend.'

I nod and make my way down the path towards the gate, sure I can feel his eyes on me every step of the way.

Chapter Five

Rupert finds himself sliding out of the office on time a week later, something he hasn't done for months since Caro died. He tells himself that it's Friday night, of course he should be leaving on time, that it's the weekend and no one else is doing any overtime – in fact, Michael – Caro's father and Rupert's boss – left at lunchtime, as he often does on a Friday.

An hour later, Rupert drives through the gates of Fox House, and is relieved to see that there are still lights on inside. Emily must still be here, even though she is usually finished by four. Adrenaline fires through his veins and he has to take a deep breath before he gets out of the car. He can't lie, he is looking forward to seeing her, in a way that he hasn't looked forward to seeing anyone since Caro died. He takes his time getting out of the car, giving himself time to get his breathing back to normal – it's ridiculous, the idea that he feels nervous at the thought of seeing his housekeeper. As he puts his key into the lock and twists the door open, his heart stops in his chest. *Music*. He can hear music, something that hasn't happened in his house in over a year.

Slowly, he closes the door behind him, the hairs on the back of his neck standing to attention. Someone is playing the piano. Caro's piano. The sound of Tchaikovsky's 'Swan Lake' filters out into the hallway and Rupert has to lean against the wall to steady himself. He knows if he looks into the living room, he will see Caro sat on the tiny piano stool, her back straight and her attention fully focused on the keys as she runs her hands over them. Tchaikovsky was always her favourite, and 'Swan Lake' was the tune she played whenever she'd had a bad day or felt less than happy. She'd play it right through to the end, as Rupert waited patiently, letting the music run over him like water. When she'd finished, he would go to her and pull her into his arms, trying his hardest to make her feel better, to let her know that whatever she thought, whatever she was feeling, she mattered.

Don't be ridiculous. Caro is dead.

As the music dies away, Rupert pushes himself away from the wall and forces himself to walk on leaden feet into the sitting room. As he enters, Emily jumps up from the piano stool, a flush turning her cheeks a hot red.

'Rupert!' Her eyes are huge in her face, and she covers her mouth with both hands. 'Oh, Rupert, I'm so sorry. I wasn't expecting you home yet.' She turns to the piano and closes the lid, pushing the stool back into place, keeping her back turned to him.

'I didn't realize you played the piano,' Rupert says, not taking his eyes off her.

'I learned at school. I've tried to keep up with it, but

I'm very rusty. I don't have a piano where I live now,' Emily replies, brushing her hair away from her face and looking anywhere but at him. 'I couldn't resist it. I'm sorry, I should go.'

She trails her fingers over the closed lid before she moves past him, and Rupert catches her by the arm. 'Emily, there's no need to apologize. It just caught me by surprise, that's all. Caro used to play, and the piano hasn't been used since she died. I should have called and told you I would be leaving work on time.'

'Oh no, you don't need to do that.' Emily shakes her head, smiling slightly. 'I should get going. I've left you dinner in the oven.'

Rupert realizes now that he can smell something delicious on the air, and his stomach gives a low growl.

Emily laughs and her whole face lights up. 'You're hungry, then? I've made a beef bourguignon. There's a bit too much for one person, but if I leave you a tub, you can just pop the rest in the freezer.' She is leading him along the hallway towards the kitchen as she speaks, her bare feet silent on the tiled floor. Rupert breathes in the scent of meaty stew, a clean lemony scent beneath it, and feels a pang, as though finding something he didn't realize he had lost.

'There's enough for two?' he asks.

'Well, yes.' Emily pulls the dish out of the oven, and Rupert notices that there is an open bottle of red wine breathing on the kitchen counter. 'It's a bit difficult to make a beef bourguignon for one. But like I said, you can just freeze whatever is left over…'

'Why don't you stay?' The words are out before Rupert has even had a chance to think through the consequences. He looks down, worried that Emily might think he's over-stepped the mark.

'Stay?'

'Yes. Only if you want to, of course. It would be nice to have some company for a change. It gets pretty lonely eating on my own every night. Oh, unless you're busy, that is?'

'No. No, I'm not busy.' Emily smiles, and Rupert's stomach does another flip. 'That would be lovely, if you're sure?'

'Of course. Here, let me.' Rupert takes the hot dish from her and places it on the table, as Emily brings out plates and cutlery. Rupert grabs two wine glasses and the open bottle of red and pours them both a large glass.

'Cheers.' He leans forward and chinks his glass against hers. 'So, Emily Belrose, housekeeper extraordinaire. How about you tell me a little bit about yourself? You're in my house every day and I feel as though I barely know you.'

'There isn't much to tell.' Emily ladles a spoonful of stew onto his plate. 'I live in Swindon, not far from the High Street, with my flatmate. Above a kebab shop, believe it or not. It's not my dream home, but it'll do until I can find somewhere better.'

'Oh?' Rupert's heart sinks in his chest a little – does she mean flatmate, or boyfriend? He tries not to think that way, but this is the first time he's had any flicker of interest in anyone else at all since Caro died.

'Yeah, Mags and I have lived together for about a year now – I had a bad break-up and Mags kind of saved me.' Emily gives a tiny laugh, but there is a strange expression on her face, half sadness, half fear.

'I'm sorry.' Rupert sips from his wine, holding the stem of his glass tightly so he doesn't lay his hand on hers. 'It sucks, doesn't it? I always thought I liked my own company, but now I guess not so much.'

'It does suck a bit.' Emily looks down at her plate as she pushes the meat round and round without eating. 'My break-up is nothing, though, compared to what you must have gone through.' She looks up at him expectantly, and Rupert clears his throat.

'It's been tough, yes. It came as a huge shock when Caro died, that's for sure.' He pauses for a moment, unsure whether to say what he really wants to. 'It was partly a relief too, though.'

Emily says nothing, just tilts her head on one side.

'Caro was… she was difficult to live with.' Rupert lays his fork down, his appetite gone. 'She was bi-polar. I never knew which Caro would be here when I got home. That's why the piano playing took me by surprise. Caro would always play that song when she was low. I knew if she was playing that, I was in for a bad night with her.'

He is quiet for a moment, as he is assaulted by the memory of Caro crying, her mascara smudged black around her swollen eyes, the slamming of the bathroom door before the lock rammed home and he had no choice but to wait outside, murmuring through the door that he loved her, that if she would just come out… or the times he would come home from work, the house cold and dark as she lay huddled under the duvet, refusing to speak to him.

'Oh my God, Rupert. I had no idea. I'm so, so sorry.' Emily lays her hand on his, and squeezes, the warmth of her palm scorching his cold fingers. Rupert looks up to see she has tears in her eyes.

'It's not your fault – you couldn't have known.' Rupert keeps dead still, not wanting her to take her hand away. It's been a long time since he's been touched by anyone other than Sadie or Miles, or his family. 'When Caro died, I was devastated, I didn't know how I would go on. But there was the tiniest part of me that felt relief, that there would be no more pain, no more suffering for either of us. Does that make me a terrible person?'

'God, no. Rupert, you must have been a wonderful husband to be able to cope with her mood swings. I had a stepfather who was bi-polar; I understand exactly what you mean.'

'I miss her dreadfully,' Rupert says, 'but I think I'm finally ready to start living again. Sadie told me I needed to move on, get myself sorted out, and if I'm honest, the best thing I could have done was to take you on.'

Emily nods, but slides her hand away. 'I am very much enjoying working for you, Rupert. If you must know, I feel like working for you has given me a second chance. Now, pass me your plate.'

Rupert hands her his plate, a deflated feeling pushing all the breath out of him. He came on too strong. Emily

44

clearly just looks at him as an employer; she hasn't been having the same kind of thoughts he has. And why should she? He's the one who has got used to coming home to a cooked meal, a tidy house, a lemon-fresh scent filling every room after Emily's hard work. He's come to enjoy arriving home, knowing that even if Emily has finished for the day there will be a small lamp left on so that he doesn't come home to a cold, dark house.

He feels like he has to break the awkward silence that fills the room, as Emily stands in front of the sink, running the tap, her face reflected in the glass of the window that looks out into the back garden. 'Leave those,' he says, 'you're off the clock now. I invited you to stay – the least I can do is wash the dishes.'

Emily laughs, raising her eyes from the bubbly water to the window, when she lets out a gasp, the plate in her hands falling into the sink with a crash. 'Rupert!'

Rupert crosses the room in two strides, standing close behind Emily, who is looking out into the garden, her face pale. 'What is it?'

'There was someone out there, in the garden.' Her voice wobbles and Rupert wrenches open the back door, the security light pinging on and illuminating the lawn down towards the trees at the bottom fence. The damp February air is chilly as he steps out, causing goosebumps to rise on his forearms through his thin shirt. At least, he tells himself it's the cold air, not the sinister shadows at the bottom of the garden. He quickly scans the garden, but he can't see anybody lurking in the bushes. 'There's no one out there.'

'I saw someone,' Emily says, her arms folded tightly across her body. 'I'm sure there was someone standing at the bottom of the garden, watching us.'

'A fox, maybe?' Rupert says, not taking his eyes off her. Her shoulders shake a little as she tries to stop herself trembling.

'I don't think so. It looked like a figure, a person.'

'It really scared you, didn't it?' Rupert steps closer, blocking Emily's view of the garden.

'Yes. Sorry. I... I definitely thought I saw something. Someone.' She swipes at a stray lock of hair with a shaking hand.

'There's nothing out there now. I promise. How about I pour us some more wine? If that's all right with you?'

'I'd like that. I don't really feel comfortable riding my bike home just yet.' Her eyes flick towards the darkened window and Rupert wonders if she's still imagining someone lurking in the thick, inky shadows. 'Maybe we could move into the sitting room? No offence, but these kitchen chairs aren't exactly designed for comfort.'

Rupert laughs, squashing down the memory of the argument he and Caro had had over the chairs – his argument being the exact same as Emily's, that the chairs were a statement rather than something designed to be sat on in comfort, but it was Caro's money that was paying for them, so he didn't really have much of a choice.

Emily scoops up the half-empty wine bottle and their glasses and makes her way towards the sitting room, as Rupert plucks another bottle from the wine rack and follows behind, suddenly nervous. It's been a long while since he spent any time alone with a woman who wasn't Caro. He tells himself that it's just a bottle of wine, and even if it wasn't, Caro wouldn't want him to be lonely. He hesitates for a moment, giving Emily the chance to change her mind, but when he steps into the room she is already snuggled into one end of the sofa, and she gives a thin smile as she pats the seat next to her invitingly.

'I'm sorry,' she says, 'for freaking out a bit in there. I really thought I saw something.' She looks down at the ruby liquid in her glass, giving it a swirl before she takes a deep breath. 'I had a really bad relationship last year. It's left me feeling... jumpy, I guess.'

'And vulnerable?' Rupert asks, aware of his hand lying close to her thigh. He knows that raw, flayed feeling only too well. 'I can relate.'

'Vulnerable. Jumpy. Unsafe.' She pauses. 'Alone.'

Giving in to impulse, Rupert lays his hand gently on her wrist, his fingers wrapping around the delicate bones as he seeks out the pulse that jumps under her skin. Emily looks up at him, and Rupert gives in to impulse again, leaning down and pressing his lips to hers. She freezes for a moment, before he feels her mouth soften under his and he can taste wine on her lips and smell the light floral scent that she wears.

'Oh.' Emily pulls away and her face is no longer pale. She presses her hand to her mouth and Rupert thinks for a moment that he might have just fucked up monumentally.

'I'm so sorry, Emily.' He turns away, scrubbing his hand

through his hair. 'I didn't mean… I don't know what came over me.'

'It's OK.'

'I haven't done anything… I mean, I haven't even been on a date with anyone since Caro died, let alone kissed anyone. I'm so sorry, I've had too much wine. I completely understand if you think this was a huge mistake, and you want to leave. Not that I want you to leave…' He's rambling, but he's quite sure that he doesn't want her to go yet.

'Rupert, I said it's OK.' Emily puts her hand on his shoulder, turning him to face her. 'Honestly, I'm not at all offended.' She gives him a shaky smile, before drinking the last of her wine. She reaches for the new bottle, shifting around so that her thigh lies against his. 'I think we need more wine, don't you?' He smiles at her, waiting as she tops him up and as her fingers linger on his as she passes him the glass, Rupert thanks his lucky stars he left work on time this evening.

Chapter Six

'Don't go.' His voice is quiet, barely a whisper, and I have to strain to hear him. 'Stay the night.'

I smile in the darkness, before rolling over to face him. In the six weeks since he asked me to stay for dinner, we have spent every evening together, talking, laughing, and having some of the best sex I've ever had. But each evening, I slip away, riding my pushbike back to the flat by the light of the streetlamps, sneaking my way in so as not to wake Mags. 'Really? You want me to stay?'

'Don't you want to?'

Rupert's voice is husky, and he reaches out to lazily roll my nipple between his finger and thumb, a sharp pang of desire slicing through me. I let out a gasp, and nip at his wrist. 'Of course I want to stay.' I don't ever want to leave, if the truth be known. Rupert rolls on top of me, and then for a little while I stop thinking about going home, or staying, or anything else except him.

Later, as he snores softly, his hair ruffled and the sheets tangled around his waist, I doze next to him, my limbs feeling heavy and contentment flooding my veins. Everything is so different with Rupert than it was with Harry. I picture the last time I laid in Harry's bed, waiting for him to come home. The way his face had twisted with anger and hate as he staggered into the bedroom, the sour, sickening smell of old whisky on his breath as he'd crouched over me, tugging away the duvet and dragging my naked body to the floor. Shaking the image away, I tug the sheets over me and burrow down, the scent of sex and Rupert's aftershave emanating from the bed.

Finally, I feel as though I have found what I have been looking for my whole life, the elusive thing that my mother assured me was out there as she chased after it herself. I sigh, snuggling against Rupert, when something – a noise outside – jolts me from sleep, my heart racing. For a moment I am confused, thinking I'm at home, and I slide naked from the bed ready to guide Mags back to bed, before I remember where I am. Pausing, I listen hard but all I can hear is the sound of Rupert's breath. Silently moving to the window, I peer out from between the slats of the blinds. I'm sure I heard something outside, and I remember that I left my bike out there, not bothering to bring it into the hallway as I thought I'd be leaving.

Trying to look down into the front garden, I can see the back wheel of my bike poking out of the porch and I breathe a sigh of relief, ready to head back to the warmth of the bed as I realize how cold my bare feet are. *Maybe I imagined it*, I think, Harry on my mind making me hear things that aren't there. As I turn away from the window a movement in the corner of my vision makes me stop, and I turn back, my breath catching in my throat. There is someone there, just as I thought. The figure of a person stands under the dim glow of the streetlamp across the road, a hooded top pulled up over their head, making it difficult to distinguish whether it is a man or a woman. Holding my breath, afraid to make a sound, I watch as they raise their head to the window and I get the unmistakable feeling that they know I am here, that they are watching me.

'Rupert!' I hiss his name, turning to the bed, 'Rupert, wake up!'

Rupert rolls over, mumbling under his breath.

'Rupert, wake up, please! There's someone outside, they're watching the house!'

Remembering the face I saw at the bottom of the garden a few weeks ago, my hands start to shake, and I turn back to the window with my heart in my throat, only to see that the street is empty. There is no one there.

Creeping into the flat, I jump as Tiny rockets out of the kitchen, snarling and yapping. So much for sneaking back home without waking Mags up. I was hoping that it was early enough on a Sunday morning for me to sneak in, grab a quick shower again and creep back out before she got up, but not anymore. Not now Tiny is awake.

Despite a sleepless night, the faceless figure outside the house appearing in my dreams every time I managed to drop off, I feel remarkably chipper. Rupert thinks perhaps I either imagined the person outside – being half asleep and having Harry on my mind – or it was just someone waiting for a lift or something outside the house. Either way, my bike was still there, and even though I am tired, there was something magical about last night, about staying the whole night right through, sleeping in the space in Rupert's bed that Caro used to occupy. I thought things might be awkward this morning when we woke, but it wasn't at all. It was like it was meant to be. Only now, I have to face Mags, and any trace of my magical night with Rupert is washed away by her appearance in the doorway to her bedroom.

'You came home then.' Her voice is flat, and she looks exhausted, her orange hair stuck up on one side. She's wearing my T-shirt, the old Happy Mondays one I got from a charity shop, but judging by the look on her face now isn't the time to mention it.

'Sorry.' I pull an apologetic face and wrinkle my nose, while trying to calculate whether I have time to wash my hair before it's time to meet Rupert back at his house.

'I bet,' Mags sniffs. 'Do you have any idea how worried I've been about you?'

'Worried? Why would you be worried? I thought you knew where I would be.' Mags is acting like my mother, not my flatmate, and I feel a flicker of uncertainty as I try and offer up a smile. 'I didn't think you'd even notice if I wasn't home.'

'Of course, I would notice. You've been home after midnight practically every night for the past few weeks – I can't sleep until I know you're home. You didn't even bother to let me know you weren't coming back, you didn't respond to any of the text messages I sent you.'

I pull my phone out, to see six missed calls and seventeen text messages, all from Mags. *Seventeen*. 'Jesus, Mags. How many texts? My phone died, OK? I gave it a quick blast this morning before I left – in fact, I need to put it on charge now.' After last night, this is too much. I push past her and head for the sanctuary of my own bedroom.

'Harry threatened to kill you, Emily! Ever since you've lived here you've been terrified of him tracking you down – what was I supposed to think? I thought he'd found you, hurt you! You can't just not reply to my texts and expect me to not be concerned…' Mags follows, Tiny circling her feet in an attempt to remind her to feed her. 'Don't get cross, I was just worried, that's all. I've hardly seen you recently.'

I pause in pulling my T-shirt over my head. I've been so used to being on my own, looking after myself since Mum did a runner with her latest husband, that it didn't occur to me that Mags would be concerned. And she does have a point – I have hardly seen her lately, but that's only because I've been trying to avoid a lecture. Immediately I feel like a bitch. 'I'm sorry, Mags, I didn't think. I'm fine. I promise. I'm actually really happy.' I sit on the bed in my underwear as Mags leans against the doorframe, a frown on her face.

'So, you are seeing this Rupert then?'

'It looks like it.' I can't stop the huge grin that spreads across my face. 'He's amazing, Mags, honestly, he's kind, he's funny… he treats me like I'm special, you know?'

'I'm sure Harry did in the beginning too.' Mags's tone is sour.

'What? What's that supposed to mean?' I tug the hair bobble from my ponytail and throw it onto the bedside table.

'Nothing. Just… you're rushing into things a bit, aren't you? This was supposed to be a job, you said. A chance to "get yourself back on your feet".' She makes quote marks in the air with her fingers. 'What if it all goes wrong? You'll be back to square one.'

'I thought you'd be pleased by that,' I snap, grabbing my towel and heading for the door, before Mags steps in front of it.

'Don't be like that, Em!' Her tone changes, and I am surprised to see tears in her eyes. 'After everything that happened with Harry, I'm just concerned for you, that's all. I wouldn't be a very good friend, would I, if I didn't worry when you didn't come home?'

Not wanting an argument, I sigh, conscious that I am supposed to be meeting Rupert in just over an hour, when he says he's going to introduce me to his brother. My stomach gives a flip at the idea of being introduced to the most important people in his life. 'No, OK, I do understand that. I'll call in future, if that will stop you worrying. And I *am* sorry – you know I'm not used to having people worry about me.'

'It's OK. Maybe we can do something together today?' She taps her chin, thinking. 'We could go to Coate Water, go for a walk round the lake?'

'No, Mags, I'm sorry.'

'No, you're right. It's still a little bit chilly out there, even if the sun is out. What about shopping? We could go to that vintage place you like on the High Street.'

'I can't, Mags,' I feel a twinge of guilt, 'I'm meeting Rupert. I only came home to get showered and changed. Let's do something in the week – I'll take you out for dinner after work.' And if I'm honest, if I wasn't meeting Rupert, I still don't think I'd want to spend the day with her. Much as I do appreciate what Mags has done for me, I can't get used to having someone fuss over me the way she does, and twice since I started working for Rupert I've woken up to find her at the foot of my bed, having sleepwalked there, her shadow making my heart stop in my chest every time.

'Fine. I've been waiting to go to that new vegan place.' She injects a breezy note into her voice that doesn't match the expression on her face, before it passes and she smiles, letting me past to the bathroom. 'I've got things to do today anyway. People to meet. *Old friends.*'

'Right.' I manage a smile, and close the bathroom door, locking it behind me before sinking onto the toilet and scrubbing my hands over my face. Hopefully the promise of dinner will keep Mags happy – I don't want to upset her; after all, I still have to live with her.

Chapter Seven

'Are you sure I look OK?' I pull down the sun visor and peer into the tiny mirror for the fifth time since we left Rupert's house half an hour previously. I push my tongue over my teeth to remove any rogue lipstick marks before flipping the visor back up and running my hands over my dress, easing away any creases.

'Beautiful. As always. Come on, we're late as it is. Plus, we're sitting in their driveway, so that looks weird.' Rupert opens his car door and I think that maybe I detect a hint of irritation in his voice, or maybe it's just nerves. Rupert is about to introduce me to his family and friends for the first time, after all. I met his brother, Will, a couple of weeks ago, but I've yet to meet the rest of them, although Rupert assures me they know all about me. When he comes round to my side and opens my door – ever the gentleman – there is a smile on his face and I think maybe I imagined it.

'Ready?' Rupert holds his hand out and I take it, easing myself gracefully out of the car. I straighten my shoulders and mentally gird my loins, ignoring the flutter of nerves that bounce around in my stomach. Today is A Big Deal.

It's Sadie and Miles's annual Easter party – and thanks to Easter coming late, the weather means a garden party, which means I am about to be introduced to every important person in Rupert's life in one go.

'Finally, I thought you were never going to make it.' Sadie appears in the front doorway, looking as though she's about to step onto the catwalk in a clinging, green silk dress, just as glamorous as I remember her. I try not to feel underdressed in my white linen shift dress, resisting the urge to smooth out the creases again. 'Rupert, darling, it's so good to see you. It's been absolutely *ages*.' She kisses his cheek warmly and then turns her attention to me. 'Emily. How nice of Rupert to bring you along.' There is a hint of coolness in her tone, that I am sure only I can hear. 'Come through, both of you. Everyone is already here.'

Sadie turns and walks down the long, light, narrow hallway, not waiting to see if Rupert and I are following. Rupert obviously knows the way and leads me through a spacious kitchen and then out through bi-fold doors into an impressive landscaped garden, like nothing I have ever seen before – it makes Rupert's garden look tiny.

'Rupert! And this must be Emily! How lovely to meet you. I'm Miles, Sadie's better half.' The portly man with the rosy cheeks standing in front of us as we step onto the patio is more welcoming than Sadie, and I feel my shoulders drop down from somewhere around my chin. As I listen with one ear to Rupert and Miles's conversation, I let my gaze roam across the grounds, taking in the structured landscaped borders, the small orchard of apple trees that cluster at one side of the expansive garden, and if I crane my neck discreetly I'm pretty sure I can see the glint of water, a swimming pool, tucked away behind the pagoda. It's a far cry from John's three-bedroom detached house in Surrey. Even further from the tiny council flat Mum and I lived in before that.

'Emily?' Sadie appears beside me, a flute of sparkling wine in her hand. 'Would you like a drink? I brought you a glass of champagne.'

Of course, I think, *of course it is champagne.* I am beginning to realize that Sadie and Miles – and to some extent, Rupert – occupy another level of income entirely from anything I have ever been used to.

'Come and meet everyone – those two will be chatting for ages.' Sadie gestures to where Rupert stands with Miles, both of them laughing. She picks her way delicately across the lawn in her heels, and I follow, thankful that I wore wedges.

'Amanda, this is Emily, Rupert's…' there is a pause, 'girlfriend. Emily, this is Amanda. She's married to Will, Rupert's brother.' Amanda is beautiful, that's the only word I can think of to describe her. Slanting green eyes, flawless dark skin and hair carefully styled into a huge afro, with a figure to die for.

'Nice to meet you. Sorry I couldn't make it when Rupert introduced you to Will.' Amanda holds one hand out and I shake it limply, taking a sip of champagne to hide my awkwardness. 'So, you're the one who's brought Rupert back out of his shell. We all thought he'd be in mourning forever.'

'Oh, um… thank you?' I flounder for a moment, not sure how to respond. I wasn't expecting anyone to reference what happened to Caro quite so quickly. 'I'm glad he's, errr… back out of his shell.'

'He looks… much better. Although I'll be honest, when I met you at the house, I wasn't expecting Rupert to end up bringing you here as his… girlfriend,' Sadie gives a brisk smile, 'but then our Rupert has always been full of surprises.'

I blink, taken aback by her comment, and before I can muster up a response she's talking again.

'Emily, tell us a bit about yourself. Rupert has barely told us anything, he's been hiding you away from everyone.'

'There's not much to tell really.' I find my eyes are drawn back to Rupert every other minute, desire tugging at the pit of my stomach every time I see him. He seems to be having a good time, surrounded by Miles and Will and an older gentleman who looks so much like Sadie he can only be her father. 'I applied for the job Rupert posted, and we just hit it off, I suppose. I feel incredibly lucky to have found him.'

'Lucky indeed. Although I'm sure Rupert must be feeling the same,' Amanda says. 'Have you been married before? Children? Sorry.' She glances towards Sadie, who raises an eyebrow. 'Rupert is like a brother to me… I could say I'm just protecting him, but the truth is I am unbelievably nosy. Feel free to tell me to mind my own business.'

Glad that Amanda is trying to engage me in conversation, I smile gratefully at her, as Sadie says nothing, sipping at her wine. 'Never been married, and definitely no children.' Before I can ask Amanda to reciprocate, Sadie pipes up.

'So, Rupert has told you all about Caro, has he? What happened to her?'

'Sadie!' Amanda widens her eyes.

'What?' Sadie's voice has a defensive tone to it, and my skin prickles uncomfortably. What can Rupert and Miles possibly be talking about for so long? 'I just wondered if Rupert had told her everything. It's only fair that Emily knows the situation.'

'Yes.' Giving up hope that Rupert will rescue me anytime soon, I shift on my feet slightly, my wedges feeling like they might start sinking into the damp grass below. I'm half wishing the ground would just swallow me up and get me out of here. 'He told me she died. We spoke about it when I went for the job interview.' I want them to know that Rupert hasn't hidden anything from me.

'Poor Caro. So beautiful, and so young. I still miss her so much.' Amanda lets her eyes fill with tears and I stare down into my rapidly emptying glass, not knowing where to look.

'Amanda, go and splash some water on your face, you don't want Rupert to know you've been upset. Emily, let me get you another drink, and I'll introduce you to some of the others.'

Sadie leads me towards another group of people, making

introductions, names spilling from her lips as I try frantically to remember who is who, and what their relationship is to Rupert, fighting back a wave of anxiety at being thrown in at the deep end. As I half listen to someone – I think it is a friend of Miles's father – talk about rising share prices for some company or another, I find myself wondering about how Caro felt when she was first introduced into this circle of friends. I doubt that Caro would have felt overwhelmed, the way I do. Feeling eyes on me, I look up to see Rupert watching me, as Miles continues to talk at him. He smiles and drops me a slow wink that shoots a lightning bolt straight to my groin. I look away, a smirk playing on my lips as I try to focus on what the man next to me is saying.

'Sorry, say that again?' Sadie still hasn't returned with my drink and I twirl the empty glass in my hand.

'I was just saying, it's nice to see Rupert out again. We haven't seen much of him, not since the night of his party.'

'His party?' I am still distracted, my eyes sliding back to where Rupert stands now with his back to me, his shoulder muscles outlined through his shirt.

'Yes, the party he and Caro held that night.'

I open my mouth, about to ask what he means about 'that night' but before I can say anything, a tipsy Amanda stumbles over her own feet slightly as she approaches us. '*There* you are! Oops… I've been looking for you everywhere.' Her eyes go to my empty glass. 'Oh, Caro, you're empty. Let's go and top you up.'

There is a deathly silence as Sadie, who has finally returned with a fresh champagne bottle, and I realize Amanda's Freudian slip before she does.

'I'm just going to pop inside and use the bathroom.' I walk away quickly, trying to quell the sick feeling that settles in my stomach. Maybe she didn't really mean to say it – she has been knocking the champagne back pretty quickly, and the canapes Sadie has provided don't really fill you up – but that doesn't stop me feeling off kilter. Neither does the fleeting hint of a smile that I thought I saw cross Amanda's lips before she spoke.

I step into the cool kitchen, relieved to be out of the unseasonably warm sunshine, and make my way into the hallway, looking behind me as I step off the tiled floor onto carpet, entering the living area. The room is immaculate, with no sign that two boisterous twins live here. Rupert told me about his godchildren, and I realize that I haven't seen any sign of the children for the entire afternoon. I can only assume that Sadie has a nanny, that they are tucked away out of sight, another reminder that this is a whole different world to the one I inhabit. I wonder for a moment if that's how it would have been, had Rupert and Caro had children together, before allowing myself to imagine for the briefest of seconds how it would be if Rupert and I had children together.

Casting my eyes around the room, I notice that a lot of the furniture in here is remarkably similar to the stuff Rupert has in his own living room, and I wonder whether Caro had extended her influence to Sadie's house, or whether Sadie gave direction to Rupert after Caro died – or maybe they just had similar taste. Years of being best friends might do that to you, I suppose. I wouldn't know, having not had a best friend since primary school. It's things like these that I don't feel ready to ask Rupert yet. There is a piano at the end of the room, and as I approach it, I see that the top is littered with framed photographs, most of them depicting Caro in some form or another. Caro holding a baby – presumably one of the twins – as Rupert stands to one side looking a little awkward, Caro and Rupert on their wedding day, Sadie and Miles either side of them, all four of them grinning madly at the camera. Sadie and Caro on a beach in bikinis, definitely a few years ago, I think slightly bitchily, their arms slung around one another's shoulders. Sadie and Rupert grinning into the camera, faces smashed together, a party hat at a rakish angle on Rupert's head. I fight down the envy that rises in me, at years of memories on display.

'Em? I wondered where you'd got to – I thought you might have headed for the hills.' Rupert appears in the doorway, looking a little rumpled and tipsy.

'Don't be daft.' I cross the room in three steps, pushing myself into his arms and lifting my face. He kisses me, his tongue sliding into my mouth and I groan slightly against his lips. He pushes against me, his thumb flicking over my nipple through the thin fabric of my dress.

'Follow me,' he says, pulling me into the hallway and into the downstairs cloakroom, which is at least as big as mine and Mags's bathroom at home.

'Rupert,' I whisper, feigning shock, 'we can't! Not here.'

'We can.' He turns me away from him, unzipping my dress as I lean against the square ceramic sink. He kisses my neck, his hands running over my breasts, before I hear a zip drop and I gasp as he enters me from behind, watching our reflections in the mirror above the sink the whole time.

After, as I pull my dress back on, conscious of my flushed cheeks and wayward curls, Rupert zips me back up, kissing the back of my neck tenderly, before wrapping his arms around my waist.

'Has everyone been OK with you? I'm sorry I abandoned you; it's been a while since I saw everyone.'

I turn to face him. 'Everyone has been absolutely lovely. I've been made to feel very welcome.' I can't quite meet his eyes as I say it, but I'm not going to tell him that his sister-in-law called me by his dead wife's name. 'I just came in to use the bathroom.' We both suppress a giggle, leaning against each other, our breath coming in tiny gasps as we try to keep quiet.

'Meet me outside in five minutes.' Rupert kisses me again, more deeply this time. 'Make sure you grab some more champagne on the way out too.' He winks.

I take my time to freshen up in the bathroom, fixing my hair and pouting into the mirror as I slick on some more lipstick. The wine has gone to my head a little, and I run my wrists under the cold tap to cool down. As I approach the kitchen to refill my glass, I see Amanda and Sadie at the counter, heads together, oblivious to my presence.

'What do you think of her, honestly?' Amanda is saying.

It looks as though they are both cutting fruit for Pimms. I hold my breath, waiting to hear Sadie's response.

'She seems all right, I suppose. Not really the type I thought Rupert would settle for.' Sadie pauses for a moment. 'He seems happy, though.'

'You don't think she's just after his money? She's a lot younger than him and she hasn't exactly got a career, has she?'

'Well, neither have I, if you're really honest.' Both women snort with laughter, as if the idea of Sadie working for a living is a huge joke, which I suppose it is really, with that kind of money behind her. Despite the sharp sting of hurt, I wait for a moment, curling myself around the doorframe so that if either woman turns they won't see me, unsure of whether to announce my presence or wait and see what else they say. My mother always said an eavesdropper never hears good of themselves, but part of me wants to hear what they'll say next.

'No, I don't think she is after his money,' Sadie says eventually, 'she does kind of light up when she talks about him and it's pretty hard to fake that.'

'But don't you think…' Amanda breaks off, laying the knife she's using back down on the counter gently. 'Don't you think she's the absolute spitting image of Caro?'

As I rush along the hallway, Amanda's words echoing in my ears, I almost collide with Miles.

'Oops. Steady on, old girl.' He reaches out to stop me from tripping, snagging my empty wine flute as he does

65

so. 'This needs topping up, doesn't it? Rupert is waiting for you, out by the pagoda. Hurry along and I'll bring this out.' He carries on towards the kitchen without giving me a chance to respond.

As I cross the lawn to the pagoda, I see Rupert standing waiting, his own glass of champagne in one hand, the other shoved into his pocket. I resist the urge to rush to him, to beg him to take me home, instead stepping lightly across the grass keeping a smile fixed on my face. Will stands next to him, and there seems to be a small cluster of people around them. Slowing my pace, I frown in confusion at Rupert as I approach him, but he just beams back at me, pulling me into his side as I reach him.

'Have you had too much to drink?' I force out a laugh, as he kisses me in front of everyone. Rupert doesn't give in to public displays of affection very often from what I know of him, and I shrug off a sense of awkwardness as I feel the eyes of all Rupert's friends on us.

'Absolutely not,' he says, before pulling away. I watch as he digs in his pocket, and then in front of all the party-goers, all of his family and friends – all of them strangers to me – Rupert goes down on one knee.

'Emily…' A gasp ripples through the small crowd, and I find I have pressed my hands to my hot cheeks, my breath sticking in my throat, as my heart rate takes on the speed of a galloping horse. 'Emily Belrose… I know this has been a bit of a whirlwind, and we've both been a little swept off our feet, but, Emily… will you do me the honour of becoming my wife?'

For a moment the word sticks in my throat, and I can't help it, tears spill over my cheeks, before Rupert nudges me, announcing into the shocked silence that I have to say it out loud.

'Yes, yes I will,' I say, and he slides the ring onto my finger. It's a perfect fit.

Chapter Eight

Rupert was drunk on something last night, and he's not one hundred per cent convinced that it was just champagne. He hadn't mentioned his plans to propose to Emily to anyone, not even Will, just in case things didn't pan out – in fact, he wasn't even a hundred per cent sure himself that he was going to do it – but once he'd seen Emily with his friends, the way she'd smiled and chatted, even though he knew that she probably felt a little overwhelmed, he knew the timing was right. She fits, the way he used to fit with Caro before. He fights to keep the smile from his lips now as he glances across the pillows in Miles and Sadie's spare room, to where Emily still slumbers on. Once she had said yes, the party had really started, and he'd had far too much to drink to be able to drive them both home. He stretches, thinking about the previous evening.

On one knee in front of the pagoda, Rupert looks up as Emily says yes, letting him slide the ring onto her finger before she smashes her mouth against his and after a pause that is heavy with its silence, Miles starts to clap and the others join in. Miles comes over to them both, leading

Sadie by the hand, and kisses Emily on the cheek before pumping Rupert's hand in a brisk handshake.

'Congratulations,' Sadie says with a tight smile.

'Mate, this is brilliant – sudden, but still brilliant. You kept it very quiet – worried she might say no, eh?' Miles nudges Rupert with a wink, his cheeks florid and ruddy with booze. Rupert hates it when Miles gets like this.

'Well, more a case of wanting to do it at the right time – without any of you lot giving the game away.' Rupert forces a laugh, relieved when Will approaches, Amanda not far behind him.

'Congratulations, bro. And err… welcome to the family, I suppose, Emily.' Rupert watches his brother kiss Emily awkwardly on the cheek, Emily – his fiancée, it feels strange to say that after Caro – flushing pink with what Rupert hopes is joy. 'Bit of a shock but we're pleased for you, aren't we, Amanda?' Will lowers his voice, and steers Rupert slightly to one side as Sadie and Amanda coo over the engagement ring. 'Wow, Rupert, this is a bit unexpected. I can't believe you never mentioned anything – I mean, we only knew you were dating someone a couple of months ago. Don't get me wrong, if you're happy then I'm over the moon for you. It's great that you're moving on after what happened to Caro, and Emily seems like a nice girl, but it's just a bit of a… shock.'

'She is great.' Rupert lets his gaze wander back to Emily, her hand outstretched to show off her ring. 'She's exactly what I was looking for; I just didn't know that until I found her.'

Will looks at him for a moment without speaking, before he draws in a breath. 'I am pleased for you, Rupert, honestly… but it's a bit sudden, isn't it? You're definitely sure you want to do this?'

Rupert resists the urge to snap at Will to make his mind up – either he wants Rupert to move on or he doesn't. Instead he says, 'Look, Will, I love – loved – Caro, but I've been on my own for over a year. I'll always miss her, but I don't want to be on my own anymore. I'm lonely.' Rupert swallows hard, trying to dislodge the lump in his throat.

'Oh God, mate, I get it, I do,' Will says, 'but you know you don't have to marry her. You can just be together; you don't need to rush into anything.'

Rupert feels a wave of anger, as his fists clench by his sides. Of course, Will doesn't get it. How could he understand how Rupert felt after Caro died? How could any of them? 'If it feels right, then why wouldn't I ask Em to marry me? I did what you all wanted – I did what Sadie *told me to do.* She said I should move on, get myself sorted, and I have. Emily is perfect, and I know I'm doing the right thing. Don't put a downer on it.'

'I'm not, really I'm not,' Will says quickly, before he pulls Rupert in for another man hug. 'Sorry, Rupe, I didn't mean to upset you. If you're happy then I'm happy too. For both of you.'

Once the ring has been admired and congratulations have been showered over Rupert and Emily, Sadie reveals that she has booked a band for the evening. Fairy lights that have been strung across the garden are lit, and Rupert sees that a marquee has been set up at the end of the garden. Despite the chill that settles now that the sun has gone down, everyone is happy to spend the night dancing in the marquee, and Sadie makes sure that the champagne carries on flowing. For a moment Rupert wonders if Sadie had an idea about what he was planning, before Sadie announces that she also has news – Miles has been promoted, and she makes a point of saying that this is the real reason why she has arranged the party, even though this is the first Rupert has heard about it.

Finally, at around two o'clock in the morning, the band retires, and Rupert realizes he is ready for bed too. He turns to Emily, who has matched him dance for dance tonight, dancing with not only him, but Will, Miles and a few of Miles's colleagues as well. She looks flushed and rosy-cheeked, a grin plastered across her face as she tries to get her breath back.

'Hey,' Rupert stops her in her tracks as she passes, 'ready to go up?'

'Absolutely,' she smiles up at him, 'ready when you are. Oh, Sadie—'

Sadie has appeared beside them, a glass of what looks like water in her hand. Rupert remembers that Sadie is always the sensible one, the first to start combatting her hangover before she's even gone to bed.

'Are you sure it's OK for us to stay? We can always get an Uber home.' Emily looks down quickly as she says the words, and Rupert realizes that when she says 'home', she means his house.

'Of course, Rupert and Caro always stay when we have a party,' Sadie says, a boozy red flush creeping up her neck as she carries on regardless. 'It's no problem for the two of you to stay. There's plenty of room. *Mi casa es tu casa.*'

Rupert is mortified as Sadie gives a shrill laugh and knocks back the contents of her glass. Maybe it isn't water after all. Emily says nothing, and Rupert admires her restraint.

'Thanks, Sadie,' Rupert finally manages to get the words out, breaking the cloud of tension, 'I think we'll just go up.' He grasps Emily's hand firmly in his and they make a quick escape, managing to get upstairs without bumping into anyone else. Rupert closes the door to the spare bedroom quietly, and turns to Emily, who is very quietly reaching behind her neck to unzip her dress.

'Are you OK?' he asks, as she fumbles with the zip. 'Here, let me.'

Emily's arms fall to her sides. 'It's all right, Rupert. It's not the first time this evening someone has referred to me as "Caro". It'll take people some time to get used to me, I suppose.'

Rupert turns Emily to face him, lifting her chin with one finger so he can look directly into her deep blue eyes. Eyes that remind him of Caro's. He blinks away the vision of Caro's face that swims briefly in front of his eyes, and kisses Emily. Her face is set, but he feels her mouth soften under his as he gently slides the shoulders of her dress off, letting it fall to the expensively carpeted floor. He breathes in her scent, floral and by now familiar, and rests his chin on the top of her head.

'They don't mean anything by it, you know. It's just a slip of the tongue. Like you say, it'll just take time for them to get used to saying "Emily". Caro and I were together for a long time.' Emily stiffens slightly in his arms, and he strokes her back, until he feels her start to relax.

'Of course, I do understand,' she says eventually, the words so quiet she is almost speaking under her breath. 'It was just a shock to hear her name in place of mine. But you're absolutely right, time is all we need. And we have plenty of that. I'm not going anywhere.' She looks up at him now, her blue eyes serious. 'I mean it, Rupert. I said yes. It's not to be taken lightly. I've made a commitment to you. After Harry… well, you know it took me a long time to get over happened with him.' Emily has told Rupert some parts about her relationship with Harry, how it scarred her.

'And I couldn't be happier that you said yes.' Rupert means it too; he really does feel like he has been given a fresh start. He kisses her again and reaches round to unclip her bra as she sighs and leans into him, letting his fingers wander over her skin.

'Wait.' Emily freezes, her hand against his now bare chest. 'Did you hear that?'

'Didn't hear anything.' Rupert reaches for her again, nuzzling into her neck. Now that the champagne has worn off, he doesn't want to waste another minute of the evening.

'Listen.' Emily pulls away and goes to the door, pressing her ear against it. 'There's someone outside, Rupert.'

'Em… don't be silly, come here. It's probably just Miles or Sadie going to bed. Or one of the others. They've got more than one spare room, you know.' He tries to keep the testiness from his voice, but honestly, he just wants to get into bed. And not to sleep. He walks up behind her, turning her to face him. Emily relaxes back into his arms and he starts to edge her towards the bed, planting tiny kisses all over her face, her neck, his hands running over her body.

'Wait.' She freezes again, pushing him away from her, and he groans in frustration. 'Listen. Can you hear it?'

Rupert strains his ears, and thinks maybe, *maybe*, he hears the tiniest of knocking sounds. 'It's nothing, Em. Come on, you're just feeling jumpy because you thought you saw someone outside the house the other night. There was nothing then, and there's nothing now.'

As soon as the words leave his lips there is a sharp bang, as if someone has slapped their hand against the bedroom door, and Emily lets out a little shriek, her hands flying to her mouth.

'Please, Rupert, will you just go and look?' Emily turns to him, her face pleading. 'That was definitely someone outside our bedroom door. I feel weird enough staying here tonight; I'll never sleep if I think someone is spying on us.' Caro's name hangs unspoken in the air between them.

Rupert sighs, although his heart is racing. 'OK. If it'll make you feel better. It's probably just someone staggering to their room – you saw how drunk everyone was. I won't be a minute.' Emily gives him a roguish grin, and he pulls his shirt back on and heads downstairs.

★

I wait for fifteen minutes or so, the sheets artfully arranged around my naked body so that my shoulders and chest are bare. I fidget, running my fingers through my hair, giving it that sexy, tousled look that Rupert loves and glance impatiently at the bedside clock. How long does it take to check if there's anyone outside? The champagne is wearing off now, leaving me with the thick thud of a headache beginning at my temples, and I am starting to get cold, goosebumps rising on my arms as I wait for Rupert. I wait another five minutes before I tug the sheets away and pull on Rupert's discarded sweater and slip my knickers back on. Rupert will surely be on his way back and I'll bump into him on the landing, and then we'll slide back into the warmth of the bed. Grinning to myself at the thought, I let myself admire my ring one more time before I open the door and peep out. Part of me is still jumpy, and I half expect a face to loom out of the darkness... but there's nothing. Not even any sign of Rupert.

Maybe he's gone to get some water? My temples throb in sympathy and I decide that I'll go down and get some anyway. Rupert can't have gone far. I creep silently down the stairs, not wanting to wake anyone, a reassuring yellow glow of light spilling from the entrance to the kitchen. As I get to the bottom stair, I pause, unable to comprehend what I'm seeing at first. I was right, Rupert did go to the kitchen, but he's not alone. Sadie sits on the high bar stool in front of him, her head resting against his chest, as his arms go around her shoulders and she clasps him about the waist. Rupert is murmuring something, and she raises her head to look at him, pulling away.

I watch, hardly daring to breathe, my ears straining to pick up what they might be saying but I can't hear anything, just the low mumble of their voices. Rupert takes her hands in his now, holding them tightly as she says something and he nods, leaning down to kiss her on the cheek. It feels intimate, private, and I turn and quietly hurry back up the stairs to the safety of the bedroom, sliding back into bed and tugging the sheets up around my neck. A few minutes later, I hear the door open, and Rupert's light breaths as he gets into bed beside me. I can feel him leaning over me, so I regulate my breathing as if I have fallen deeply asleep and he pauses for a second, before dropping a light kiss on my hair and rolling over. I lay there, my mind replaying the two of them together, until fingers of light filter through the blinds and finally, I fall asleep.

Emily stirs, and Rupert smiles as he watches her go from dozy to full wakefulness, slowly, like she's making the most of the morning sunlight that slants across the room.

'Morning, sleepyhead.' Rupert has been awake for what feels like hours, waiting for Emily to wake up.

'Ouch.' She struggles into a sitting position, one hand clutching her head. 'Champagne head. Sorry for falling asleep on you last night.'

Rupert laughs and kisses her, not wanting to talk about it. He had been a little relieved when he got back to the room and Emily had been fast asleep in bed – his brief conversation with Sadie had left him feeling unsettled. But a good night's sleep and waking up to Emily's smile has just made him even more convinced he's doing the right thing. Emily is definitely the one.

'Coffee?' Emily says, as she wriggles away from him and pushes back the covers. Her face is pale, and Rupert thinks she looks tired. 'And I should probably text Mags and apologize for not letting her know I wouldn't be home last night. She'll be annoyed with me again, I expect.' She swings her legs out of bed and rummages amongst the pile of clothes left on the bedroom floor. 'Have you seen my phone? I thought… no, it's not here.' Emily frowns, her crumpled dress in one hand.

'Maybe you left it downstairs?' Rupert gets out of bed, pulling on his jeans and yesterday's shirt. 'I'll come down with you.'

They head downstairs, Emily making it clear she feels out of place dressed in last night's clothes. The others are already in the kitchen when they make their appearance, Sadie and Amanda knocking up pancakes while Miles and Will sit at the kitchen island, not helping.

'Morning, you two lovebirds,' Sadie says, a smile on her face. 'Pancakes? Coffee?'

'Lovely, thank you.' Emily slides onto a stool as Rupert helps himself to two cups of coffee, pushing one in front of his fiancée. Emily wraps her fingers around the cup and takes a sip, before grimacing and adding sugar.

'Emily, do you want to borrow something to wear?'

Amanda says, looking her up and down. 'I keep a few bits here for nights like last night – I think we're about the same size? Caro used to borrow my stuff all the time.'

Rupert feels his stomach flip at the use of Caro's name, watching Emily for signs that she is upset, although it's a little unreasonable for her to expect his friends to never mention Caro by name ever again, but Emily nods and smiles, jumping down off the stool and following Amanda to the second spare room. Rupert feels himself relax a little, taking a sip of coffee.

'Hangover?' Will asks, a huge stack of pancakes in front of him. 'I feel as rough as a badger's arse.'

'I'm not too bad,' Rupert says, reaching over and pinching a piece of pancake doused in syrup.

'It'll be young Emily, keeping you up all night, getting the booze out of your system,' Miles scoffs, and Rupert avoids Sadie's eye as his neck prickles uncomfortably. 'What are your plans for today?'

'I should imagine you'll be visiting Emily's parents, won't you?' Sadie asks, wiping her hands on the apron she wears before whipping it over her head and smoothing her short bob back into place. 'She'll want to break the news to them, won't she? And of course, you'll want to let your parents know.'

Rupert says nothing for a moment. 'I think we'll just take the day to keep it to ourselves, for now. Get used to the idea, you know?' He doesn't want to admit to Sadie that he hasn't met Emily's parents yet – that she barely talks about them, if he's honest. 'Has anyone seen Emily's phone, by the way? She couldn't find it in the bedroom this morning.'

'Here. Is this it?' Sadie hands him an iPhone, and when he presses the side button his own face appears on the lock screen, smashed against Emily's in a selfie they took on a day trip to Stonehenge a couple of weeks after they started dating.

'Thanks.' Emily reaches over his shoulder and takes it, kissing his cheek and making him jump. 'Sorry, didn't mean to startle you. Amanda lent me a dress.' Rupert turns and she gives a little twirl. 'I'll launder it and give it back,' she says to Amanda, who flaps a hand in her direction. 'I better just call Mags and let her know I'm still alive.' She flits out of the room, leaving Rupert to his breakfast.

Later, Emily is quiet on the drive home, and Rupert wonders if she still feels a bit rough, or whether she might be regretting saying yes.

'Are you OK?' He takes one hand off the steering wheel to rub her knee, as she gazes silently out of the window.

'Did you see anyone last night after I asked you to check if someone was outside our room?' she asks.

'No,' he says, 'there wasn't anyone outside, and no one on the stairs either. I'm sorry, I should have told you that first thing this morning.'

'You didn't see anyone at all?'

'No. I just told you that. Emily, is there a problem?' Rupert feels a little irritated. If there is something wrong he'd rather Emily just came out with it, not beat around the bush. Caro used to do the same thing and it drove him mad. The traffic slows and crawls to a stop, typical M25 gridlock, even on a Sunday morning.

'Not even Sadie?' Emily's mouth is turned down and she fiddles with the phone in her hands.

'Sadie?'

'Yes, Sadie.' Emily turns to look at him, her eyes searching his face and Rupert feels a flicker of alarm, even though he knows he hasn't done anything wrong. 'She was our host after all; it stands to reason that she might still be up after we'd all gone to bed.'

'Nope.' He lies smoothly, edging the car forward as the traffic starts to move. 'I didn't see anyone at all. I told you there was no one there.'

Chapter Nine

I haven't been able to stop looking at the ring on my left hand since Rupert slid it onto my finger at Sadie's party. Of course, I am happy – who wouldn't be? – but a little part of me, every time I look at it, sees Rupert and Sadie standing close together in the kitchen, holding hands, as I strain my ears and try but fail to hear what they are saying, before hearing Rupert's voice in my mind saying, '*No, I didn't see anyone.*' The whole idea of it makes me feel odd, even though I know they have over twenty years of shared history, while Rupert and I have only been together for a few months. I don't feel able to challenge Rupert on it. He lied, but it is only a white lie, and maybe he said it just to make me feel better? Perhaps Sadie was upset over Caro – she had had a lot to drink, and she did look as though she might have been crying. Maybe. I couldn't see too well. Rupert has been nothing but his usual attentive self since the party, and I don't want to cause a row with him over something that I may simply have read too much into. It wouldn't be the first time. The first time I asked Harry about his ex-wife, it had ended with me sitting in the dark, alone, nursing my hand where Harry had slammed the door on it. Not that Rupert would behave like that, but it makes a girl wary.

Speaking of causing rows, I twist the ring around on my finger, hiding the small diamond out of sight as I push open the door to the vegan restaurant that Mags has been so keen to try. I was half hoping she would be busy when I texted her to see if she was free for the lunch I had promised her, but she messaged back with an enthusiastic 'YES' within seconds of me sending it.

'Hello, stranger.' Mags stands from a table in the corner, holding her arms outstretched. I walk into them, breathing in her familiar scent of weed and patchouli. She's lost weight, her orange hair now dyed bright blue at the tips. I haven't been back to the flat properly for weeks.

'Mags.' I let her squeeze me tight for a moment before gently pushing her away and taking a seat at the table.

'I thought you were never coming home.' She smiles, but her voice is laced with an accusatory tone.

'Sorry... I just... I was staying at Rupert's.' I duck my head, letting my hair fall over my face as a blush scorches my cheeks, and I pick up a menu, pretending to read it. I know I've neglected Mags, been a terrible friend, but I've just been so caught up in the excitement of a new relationship, in the idea of no longer being on my own.

'Yeah, I gathered that, you dirty stop-out,' Mags snorts, deftly rolling a joint and spilling flakes of tobacco over the table. 'So, things are going well then?' Her voice softens and I think that perhaps she isn't going to give me a hard time over abandoning her after all.

'Really, really well.' I paste on a smile. *Things are going well*, I tell myself, trying not to think of the shadows over my shoulder. I shove the image of Rupert and Sadie stood close together to the back of my mind.

'Right, well, that's good then,' Mags pauses for a moment. 'It's been quiet without you. A bit boring, actually. I always thought you were just a pain in the arse, but it turns out it's quite shit living on your own.' She gives a sharp huff of laughter, and blinks rapidly before she picks up the menu, picking at the peeling laminate on the corner.

I say nothing, trying to choose my words carefully. Anxiety makes my stomach clench at what I have to tell her, at how she will react to my news. 'Actually, I have something to tell you.'

'Oh?' She drops the menu now and fixes her gaze on me. 'What? Although I think I already have a good idea.'

'You do?' I don't know whether to feel relieved or not.

'You're going to move in with him, aren't you?'

'Well… seeing as he asked me to marry him and I said yes, then that does seem to be the next logical step.' I try and fail to stop the smile from spreading across my face, but it soon fades when Mags opens her mouth to speak.

'Are you fucking kidding me?'

'Mags…'

'No, seriously, Emily, is this a fucking joke?' A harsh bark of laughter escapes her lips, as she folds her arms across her chest.

'No, it's not a *fucking joke*.' A hot bubble of anger bursts in my chest. 'Really, Mags? This is how you're going to react? Believe it or not, I am happy to be engaged to Rupert, and I thought you of all people would be pleased that I'm moving on with my life after Harry.'

'Harry is exactly my point!' Mags bursts out. 'Have you forgotten everything I've done for you?'

Really? 'Is that what this is about?' I blink in shock at Mags's reaction. 'What you've done for me?' Wearing my clothes without asking? Buying the same food as me, reading the same books as me, telling me I have no messages when people have called the house, *standing at the end of my bed in the middle of the night*?

'I took care of you after you and Harry split up.' Mags almost spits the words across the table at me. 'You were a mess when you turned up on my doorstep, so convinced that Harry was going to kill you, you made me keep the chain on the door twenty-four/seven. You were covered in bruises; you had nothing – you didn't even have a suitcase. You didn't step foot outside the flat for the first two weeks – who was it who bought you food? Took care of you?'

'Jesus, Mags.' I shake my head, ready to get up and leave. I know she doesn't want me to leave but this is a massive overreaction. 'I am grateful to you, you know that. I've told you enough times. You've been a good friend to me, and of course I'm sad to be leaving the flat. It's been my home, too; we've had some good times there. Just because I'm moving out doesn't mean we don't have to see each other anymore… but if this is how you feel maybe I should just go and collect the rest of my things.' I push my chair back, but Mags shoots out a hand and grabs my wrist. I stare down at her hand, her pale, freckled skin, the dirty fingernails and say nothing.

'I saw him,' she whispers, her eyes never leaving mine.

My stomach does a slow roll and I have to swallow hard, as I sink back in to the hard, plastic chair. No soft leather chairs for the vegans. 'Who?' But I know who she's going to say.

'Harry,' she says, still leaning in close to me, so close that I can feel her breath on my cheek. 'I saw him.'

'When? Where?' A flutter of panic makes my words tumble out. I can't believe he would have found me; I've been so careful. I think of the figure under the streetlamp outside Rupert's. Could it have been him?

'He was in The Savoy.' Mags's favourite pub. 'It was not long after you started working for Rupert. I knew it was him from the pictures on your phone.'

'Did you speak to him?' I feel hot, uncomfortably so, and it's as if all the air has been sucked out of the room.

'No. But he sort of raised his pint to me, you know?' Mags makes the motion with her hand. 'So, I got the feeling he knew who I was, at least. I would have told you if you'd bothered to come home.'

The nausea is getting worse and I have to get outside, get some fresh air before I think I really will throw up. 'Mags, I have to go. I'm sorry.'

'What? Why? Because of him? This was supposed to our time. Please, Em, don't go.' Mags gets to her feet, but I am already moving towards the restaurant door. 'At least let me give you your mail before you run off.' She reaches into her bag and pulls out a small sheaf of envelopes, stuffing them into my bag. 'I can look after you, Em, you know that. I'm your best friend. Aren't you worried that if he knows who I am he might have followed me to the flat? He might have followed you from the flat to Rupert's, did you think about that?'

I stare at her, not sure what to say. 'Shit. Do you think...? Oh, God.' The image of the figure stood under the street-lamp outside Rupert's house looms large in my mind and I scrub my hands over my face. I need to get out, to suck down great lungfuls of fresh, cold air. 'Sorry, Mags, I do have to go. Thank you for telling me about Harry – you did the right thing. Just... if you see him again, don't talk to him, don't engage with him at all. OK? Promise me.' Impulsively I lean forward and kiss her on her cheek before I hurry away.

Later that afternoon, I sip at the champagne Sadie hands to me as we sit in Veronica's Bridal Boutique – an upmarket bridal outfit that I would have no chance of patronising if it wasn't for Sadie's influence. She and Amanda have dragged me out to help me choose a dress, even though after my meeting with Mags I tried to cry off; dress shopping was the last thing I felt like doing. I could have told them I would be happy with something from the Next bridal range, but I would have been lying. In all honesty, up until I met Mags earlier, I was excited to be able to choose literally any dress I want – and relieved that Sadie and Amanda seem to have accepted me as Rupert's partner.

'What about this one?' Amanda holds up a slinky Vera Wang and I groan as I run my hands over it, shaking off all thoughts of Mags.

'It's gorgeous – shall I try it on?' I hand Sadie my glass and glide into the fitting room, slipping the silky fabric over my head. Moments later, I pull back the curtain and await their reaction. I feel like a princess, and the heaviness on my shoulders since meeting Mags earlier lifts slightly, just for a second. Until Amanda speaks.

'It's lovely, Emily, but it just makes you look a bit…'

'Fat,' Sadie says bluntly, and I look down at the teeniest, tiniest bulge of my belly. It's almost that time of the month and I am bloated, despite not eating any lunch earlier.

'Fat?'

'Not fat, as such,' Amanda tries to reassure me, but the damage is done. I can't wait to get the dress off now.

'Just a little bit… poochy,' Sadie says, before turning to the rail beside her and pulling another dress off, one that is decidedly more shapeless than the one I'm wearing. 'Oh, don't look like that, Em, girlfriends are supposed to tell you how it is. Try this one on.'

I try on dress after dress, none of them quite right, and eventually we call it a day. Amanda stands talking to Veronica, as Sadie hands me my bag.

'Are you OK?' she asks. 'I'm sorry we couldn't find you anything today. It's not just that, though, is it? You seem a bit quiet.'

'It's nothing,' I say, shaking my head, 'nothing important anyway.'

'Listen,' Sadie says, with a glance to where Amanda is air-kissing Veronica, 'how about you and I go dress shopping next week, just you and me? I know a lovely little place in Chelsea – I know it's a bit of a trek into London, but it's pretty exclusive.'

'Really?' Something warm glows in my stomach at Sadie's invitation – finally, I'm starting to feel properly accepted. 'What about Amanda?'

'Oh, she'll be too busy. She's got her interior design stuff to do. It'll be fun just us… although we can wait till she's free, if you'd rather?'

'No, that's fine,' I say quickly. There is so much to do that time will fly before the wedding, and I feel as though I can relax a little if I have my dress.

'Excellent.' Sadie smiles, all perfect white teeth on show, and I make a mental note to see about having my own teeth whitened before the wedding. 'I must dash – I'll call you.' She waves to Amanda, leaving me feeling as though maybe I don't need Mags after all.

Back at Rupert's, I tug the sheaf of envelopes out of my bag and dump them on the pile that has grown again on the kitchen counter, reaching into the fridge for a cold bottle of wine. As I cross the kitchen for a clean glass, the pile snags my attention and I give a small smile. Who could have known that when I first saw that bundle of post, on the day of my interview, that a few short months later my own mail would soon be added to it. A bubble of happiness bursts in my chest as I reach out for the pile with the aim of sorting it all out, but my hand catches the edge and the envelopes scatter over the floor.

'Shit.' I stoop down, the blood rushing to my head as I collect them up and move to the table, bringing my wine with me. I sift them into two piles – junk and the ones with Rupert's name on. Most of my post is still going to the flat, so I pause when I come to an envelope with no postmark, just my name written in Sharpie across the front. I hesitate for just a moment, before sliding my finger under the flap and pulling out a single sheet of white paper. There is one word written in block capitals.

BITCH.

I drop the paper to the floor with a gasp, as if it is on fire, before I bend to pick it up, laying it gingerly on the table. The block writing is thick and dark, and I imagine I can smell the hate oozing from the page. Who could have sent it? I see Mags in my mind's eye shoving envelopes into my bag, but I can't recall whether this one was in there, or whether it was in the pile already stacked in the kitchen. I have no idea who sent it, or whether it was sent to me here, or to the flat.

I gulp at my wine, realizing my hands are shaking. Would Harry have sent this? It wouldn't be the first time he'd used that word in relation to me. Could Mags have told Harry where I was? I remember her words when

I told her I couldn't go out with her that day, her saying she was meeting 'old friends', then seeing him in the pub. Was it really a coincidence? I hear her voice in my ear, *He might have followed you from the flat to Rupert's, did you think about that?* Another thought strikes me, one that makes my blood run cold. She said she recognized Harry from the pictures in my phone, which means she must have been snooping as I have never willingly showed them to her. I knew Mags was clingy, and she's always helped herself to my things and copied my style – I was flattered by it at first – but I didn't think she would go so far as to snoop through my phone. I get to my feet, pacing the floor, the wine making my cheeks hot and flushed, before I snatch up the paper, running my eyes over the word again, as the paper trembles in my hands.

Hearing the scratch of Rupert's key in the lock, I hurriedly tear the paper and the envelope into pieces and shove them deep into the bin without thinking. *Out of sight, out of mind.* A knot of fear and anger sits in a heavy ball in my chest as I force a smile on for Rupert.

'Everything all right?' He reaches for me, pushing my hair away from my face, and kissing me. 'Mmm, wine. That kind of a day? How did the dress shopping go?' He releases me and pours himself a glass.

'Yeah, a bit. Oh, it didn't really. I'm going to go to town with Sadie another day,' I say, grateful that he's turning his attention to the wine and away from me. I start fussing in the fridge, pulling out steak and butter and garlic, the word **BITCH** etched into my brain.

★

Later, after the rest of the wine and a steak that Rupert declares worthy of restaurant fare, we are snuggled together on the sofa, something mindless playing on the television. The events of today stick under my skin like a splinter, and I find my gaze is drawn repeatedly to the darkness outside the still open blind in the sitting room, almost expecting to see the blurred white oval of a face peering in.

'Are you sure you're OK?' Rupert asks, his stubble rasping against my hair, and I give a little sigh of near contentment. Even though we haven't been together very long, he knows that something isn't right. It's been a long time since I've been in tune with anyone to that extent.

'I met Mags.' The words spill out, and I shift from where I am leaning against Rupert so I can look at him.

'Yeah?' Rupert raises an eyebrow at me. 'You don't seem too happy about it. You've been a bit jumpy since I got home. Did she say something to upset you?'

'It wasn't…' I flounder, the words sticking in my throat. 'She said she saw Harry.' I blink, hot tears burning behind my eyes.

'Harry? Where?' Rupert frowns and twists to face me, as he reaches out and nips a stray hair from the shoulder of my jumper. I can smell his aftershave, and my heart rate starts to slow.

'In town. I'm worried, Rupert. Do you think it was him? Outside the house that night?'

'God, Em, we talked about this. There's no way it could

be Harry – Mags doesn't even know where I – we – live, so even if she did see him, she couldn't tell him.'

'But if he knew where the flat was… he could have followed me.' Part of me knows I am being ridiculous; another part is half convinced that Harry will find me and follow through on his threats.

'Don't be so paranoid – I told you, it was just someone waiting for a lift or something. Nothing has happened since, has it? So, don't be ridiculous. If seeing Mags is going to upset you, then maybe you shouldn't see her anymore.'

I let him pull me into an embrace, his chin resting on my hair, as I blink back tears. I'm not paranoid – I know I'm not – and I know that Rupert had bad experiences with Caro's paranoia, so I don't press the matter. I'm glad I pressed the torn letter deep down into the bin so Rupert wouldn't see it. But maybe he has got a point about not seeing Mags for a while.

Chapter Ten

I let myself back into the flat – for what I realize will be my final visit – and start packing the last of my things into a holdall, when the sound of someone clearing their throat makes me jump, and I turn, one hand pressed against my mouth as my heart threatens to burst out of my chest.

'Shit, Mags. You scared me.' It's a stifling hot August day and I have thrown open all the windows in the stuffy top-floor flat in an attempt to flush out the smell of Mags's weed. Thanks to the sounds of passing traffic and the gas men digging up the road outside, I don't hear Mags enter the flat.

'So, this is it then? You're officially leaving.' Mags stands in the doorway, her orange hair piled up on top of her head in a haphazard bun, one hand picking at the nail varnish on the other. She wears a green and purple maxi dress that clashes horribly with her hair, and once again her feet are grubby and bare.

'Yeah,' I say quietly, turning back to face the overfull holdall. 'This is the last of it.' Much as I am happy to be moving into Rupert's place properly, my chest feels tight at never being here again. Even though I'm pleased to be moving on, it feels like the end of an era. I won't sit on the sofa with Mags, stuffing cheesy popcorn, while we watch a marathon of Eighties movies. I won't be making terrible margaritas, that Mags and I neck almost as a challenge, they are so awful. Equally, I won't have to hold Mags's hair back, as she vomits them back up either.

Mags sniffs, and I feel a wave of guilt. 'Come on, Mags, you knew it was coming.'

I tried to time collecting the last of my things with Mags being out, but now part of me is glad I get to say goodbye to her properly.

'I know,' Mags says, her mouth downturned. 'I suppose I thought maybe it wouldn't happen. Sorry.' She gives a rueful grin, and I breathe a sigh of relief. Perhaps this won't be so bad.

'End of an era,' I say, forcing a smile onto my face. Now I have my things, and I've said goodbye, I'm ready to leave. 'But it's the start of a new one, that's how we have to look at it.'

'I saw the announcement his parents put in *The Times*. The engagement is announced… blah blah blah.' Mags screws her face up, like a child who has just taken a spoonful of medicine.

'There's no need to be like that,' I say, slumping down onto the bed. 'Mags, you always knew it was a temporary thing, me living here. I thought you wanted me to be happy after Harry.' I look down at the scarf I'm holding, worried for a moment that I won't be able to hide my emotions from Mags. That I won't be able to hide the fact that part of me is relieved to be leaving the flat, and Mags, behind. That I'm looking forward to the space Rupert's house can afford me, instead of these tiny, cramped four walls that make me feel so claustrophobic at times it makes my chest hurt. That *Mags* makes me feel claustrophobic.

'Yeah, I did always know that.' Mags smiles but her words have bite to them. 'Are you sure you're doing the right thing? I mean, it's a bit quick, isn't it? Aren't you worried about what people might say?'

'What do you mean?' I go cold, the word **BITCH** flashes in neon in my mind.

An emotion that I can't read flickers across Mags's face. 'Well, it's just that you barely know each other. There are bound to be people saying that you're not quite the genuine article.'

'We love each other, Mags. I feel incredibly grateful to have found Rupert after the horrendous time I had with Harry. If people think I'm some sort of…' I pause for a moment, my eyes on Mags, looking for a reaction, '*bitch* then that's their problem. I just hoped you at least would be happy for me.'

'I am, I promise.' Mags leans over to hug me, and I force myself to relax. 'I'm sorry, OK? I didn't mean to upset you.'

'And I'm sorry I'm leaving you, OK?'

'I'll live.' Mags pulls away, the tension easing as she says, 'What the fuck are you wearing, anyway?'

I look down at my outfit. Instead of my usual cut-off denim shorts and cheap vests, I'm wearing linen shorts, with a silky Karen Millen top, gold sandals on my feet. Rupert had bought me the outfit at the weekend, and it was perfect, or so I had thought. Now, under Mags's scrutiny, I just feel a bit uncomfortable. 'Don't you like it?'

'Not really my style. Or yours.' Mags raises an eyebrow and gives a little laugh. 'Do you want another bag for that stuff?'

'Yes, please.' I smile as Mags bustles from the room to get me another holdall. At least I won't be leaving under too much of a cloud – although I'm not sure how Rupert will feel if I invite her to the wedding. I still haven't sent her an invite. Even I'm not too sure how Mags will fit in with Rupert's friends – my friends now too, of course – and I find myself hoping that Mags won't be able to make it.

I pull out my scrapbook, turning to the last page where I smooth over the newspaper cutting I clipped from *The Times*.

The engagement is announced between Rupert, eldest son of Mr and Mrs Eamonn Milligan, of Norfolk, and Emily, daughter of Mrs Janice Walden, of Boca Grande, Florida.

I smile as I run my fingers over the print, careful not to smudge the wording. Rupert insists on still calling himself 'Osbourne-Milligan', the double-barrelled surname that he and Caro agreed on when they were married, but it makes me feel a little odd, the idea of my name becoming entwined with Caro's. Still, at least they didn't put it in the engagement notice. I read over the words again, still feeling that fizz of excitement every time I see it. I should try and get another copy, one to send to my mum in Florida, so she knows I'm finally on my way to true happiness.

'Here—' Mags appears in the doorway and throws an empty duffel bag towards me. 'You might as well keep it; I'm not going to be going anywhere.' Mags perches on the end of the bed as I carefully place the scrapbook into the bag, stuffing the last of my things on top.

'I haven't had any more mail, have I?' I ask, my breath catching in my throat. I'm half expecting Mags to pull out another envelope, but she shakes her head.

'Only circulars and junk. I threw it out, like you asked.'

'OK. Good. Well, that's the last of it.' Breathing out a sigh of relief, I sling the holdall over one shoulder, careful not to wrinkle my expensive top. 'I suppose I'll be off.'

'Come here.' Mags gets to her feet, pulling me into a hug. 'Sorry for being arsey. I will miss you, though, you know that? And you know if it all goes tits up with Rupert, you can just move back in.'

I let Mags hug me, the scent of patchouli oil tickling my nose. 'It won't go tits up. I know it won't. But thank you – for everything.'

I won't let it, I think as I let myself out of the flat, out into the hot, sticky heat of summer in Swindon. This is the beginning of my new life. In just two short weeks I will be Rupert's wife, and everything is going to be perfect.

★

One week later, I am dancing, my hair sweaty and stuck to my forehead, a gaudy sash tied across my body proclaiming me as the 'bride-to-be'. I am in Bristol with Sadie, Amanda and a few others in their circle on my hen night, and I feel on top of the world. Sadie grabs me by the arm and tugs me towards the bar, intent on getting me another cocktail.

'No, no,' I laugh, my head already starting to spin from the alcohol.

'It's your hen do, and I'm in charge. I say drink.' Sadie grins, and shoves a lurid pink drink into my hand. 'Are you having fun?'

'Yes, I really am,' I give a drunken nod, 'thank you so much for organizing this.'

'It's my pleasure – I am your Matron of Honour, after all.' Sadie raises her glass to mine and we clumsily clink together.

Yes, Sadie is my Matron of Honour. Hence the reason why Mags has somehow ended up not being invited. Some might think it a bit strange, the best friend of my fiancé's dead wife being so involved, but Sadie has been helpful, despite us getting off to a shaky start. And there wasn't really anyone else I could ask to do the job. My mind flickers briefly to Mags, and I shake the thought away. Mags wouldn't fit in with this crowd, the new set of friends that I've worked hard over the past couple of months to make my own. Thinking of Mags sobers me up, and I realize that it's two o'clock in the morning and I really just want to go to bed.

'I'm going back to the hotel,' I shout into Sadie's ear, 'Amanda already left and I might be able to catch her up.' I slink away before Sadie can persuade me to change my mind.

Outside, the air is cool and refreshing. We are in the midst of a heatwave, but it feels tonight as if the weather might break. I take in a huge gulp of fresh air, hoping that it might revive me and sober me up a little. I feel weird, a bit spacey and off kilter, and I wish I hadn't let Sadie and Amanda ply me with so many cocktails. Glancing down the street I get my bearings and start to walk the short distance back to our hotel.

It's only once I've crossed the road and am passing a darkened strip of shops that I first think that perhaps I can hear footsteps. I slow, and glance across the street, too scared to look over my shoulder. I strain to listen, but I can't hear anything, only the hard, fast thump of my pulse in my ears. Muttering under my breath, I shake my head, feeling like an idiot, but still I start to walk faster, the lights of the sign for our hotel visible in the distance. The clack of my heels rings in my ears as I realize that I can hear something; I *can* hear a second set of footsteps behind me and I step up the pace, my heart thundering in my chest and my breath coming loud in my ears as my ankle rolls in my stupidly high shoes.

I stop, my mouth dry and my palms sweaty as I hurriedly slide my shoes off and sprint the last couple of hundred metres to the hotel, shoving my key into the outside lock and tumbling through the doors into the dimly lit reception. I sink into a chair there, the night receptionist glancing towards me with a frown, and a few minutes later the door creaks open and Amanda walks in, looking decidedly cooler than I do.

'Amanda.' I get to my feet, my shoes dangling from one hand, phone in the other.

'Emily. Are you OK?' Amanda raises an eyebrow. 'You look a bit… hot?'

'Sorry, I got freaked out. You didn't see anyone out there, did you?'

'No?' Amanda looks at me questioningly. 'Em, are you sure you're OK? You look ever so pale. I didn't see anyone out there, not even you.'

'Right. Sorry. I think I must have been imagining things. Too much booze.' I am unable to raise anything more than a thin smile and I gesture towards the lifts. 'I'm going to go up, if you don't mind. I'm exhausted now.'

I walk slowly towards the lifts, feeling like an idiot. There was no one out there, Amanda said so. There was no dark shadow chasing me. I give a little laugh as I get out of the lift and reach my room, sliding my key into the lock as my phone buzzes. It's probably Rupert, I think, he'd asked me to text when I was back at the hotel to let him know I was all right. But when I look at the screen it's an unknown number. I swallow, an inexplicable ripple of fear running through me. I haven't had anything since the letter calling me a bitch, and Amanda said herself there was no one following me just now, so why do I feel so apprehensive about opening the text message? Maybe it's

Sadie, texting from one of the other's phones – she said she was almost out of battery earlier. I'm being ridiculous, I think, but when I open the text message there is a photo. Me, in the dim light of the streetlamps, looking across the street with fear etched into my features, one hand gripping the 'bride' sash that lays across my shoulder. There is one word under the photograph.

BITCH.

I give a cry of horror, my hand flying to my mouth, before I jab a finger at the delete button, erasing my image for good.

Chapter Eleven

It's the first Saturday in September and I am getting married in approximately three hours. It's only been nineteen weeks since Rupert proposed in Sadie's garden – much to Sadie's horror, she was under the impression that the perfect wedding would take at least a year to organize – but the day has arrived. Originally, I had thought that we wouldn't tie the knot until the following summer, but Rupert was keen to make things official and once I had come around to the idea of a quick wedding, I had set my heart on September – my favourite month. Other people didn't seem quite so keen.

'September? Really?' Sadie says, as I tell her and Amanda over lunch once Rupert and I have it confirmed. 'Well… I suppose September is a nice time to do it.'

'You do know Rupert and Caro got married in September?' Amanda says, a frown creasing her brow.

'I… Rupert said they were married at the end of the month. We'll be getting married on the seventh,' I say, my heart sinking. Once I had discovered that little fact, I wasn't at all sure about getting married the same month as Rupert and Caro, but Rupert had told me I was being silly. That it didn't matter what month we were married in, just that we did it soon, because he doesn't want anyone else to snap me up. I had laughed, although if I am really, truly, honest with myself, I would have preferred a little more time. Deep down I know I am doing the right thing, but what happened with Harry has left me battle-scarred.

'I suppose you must do what you feel is right,' Sadie says, 'if *you* think September is OK, then September is OK. Although personally, I always thought April was the perfect month for a wedding.' I remember feeling relieved, as though she had given Rupert and I her blessing.

Now, I am in a hotel room, mere hours away from saying, 'I do'.

'Hold still, let me shove these pins in.' Sadie stands behind me in the mirror, her mouth full of bobby pins that she pokes relentlessly into the back of my up-do. 'There. God, Em, you look stunning.' Sadie holds a small hand mirror up to the back of my head to show me, and I preen this way and that, secretly a little amazed by the transformation I've undergone.

Sadie has been a godsend helping with the wedding plans, and while I am so grateful to her for agreeing to be my Matron of Honour, I can't help but feel a little bit odd that my Matron of Honour is a woman who I've only known for six months. As a child, I always thought that my wedding would be made up of family and life-long friends, but that was before my mother moved us from pillar to post, always in search of bigger and better. I think of her last wedding, the photos she had emailed over of herself in yet another ivory gown, a greying, older man at her side. I had offered to fly to Florida, to be there when she said her vows, convinced that she has finally found THE ONE, but she told me not to worry, that it was too expensive. I feel a pang of guilt when I think of Mags, the only proper friend I've had in recent years, before I push the thought of her away.

'Sorry you had to make do with my hairdressing skills.' Satisfied her job is done, Sadie sits on the edge of the bed and pours us both a glass of champagne. 'I can't believe your hairdresser let you down at the last minute. How are you feeling? Nervous?'

I take a cautious sip, careful not to smudge my make-up. The hairdresser being a no-show, and then telling me via text that *I* had cancelled the booking when I had done no such thing, had my blood pressure through the roof this morning but thank God for Sadie and her willingness to help. It's not quite how I envisaged my hair on my big day, but it's better than anything I could have done myself. 'No, not really. Surprisingly *un*-nervous, if the truth be told. That must mean I'm doing the right thing, eh?'

'It's not too late to back out,' Amanda pipes up from where she lounges on the bed, pillows piled up behind her as she puffs on a vape, a glass of champagne in her other hand. A cloud of sickly-sweet smelling smoke surrounds her thick dark hair as she smiles, but there is a touch of something caustic in her tone.

'She's got a point. You could call it off now, there's still time,' Sadie says, and I think she's joking, only she's not smiling. 'Only kidding, Rupert and Emily are perfect for each other, aren't you, Em?'

'Absolutely.' I let out a laugh, something made up of relief and nerves, before I take another, larger sip of wine, trying to quell the sudden fluttering in my stomach. 'This is everything I've ever wanted. *Rupert* is everything I ever wanted.' I honestly can't wait until one o'clock, when I will become Mrs Milligan.

'Shame your parents couldn't be here, Emily,' Amanda says, swinging her legs round so she is sitting up. Her hair and make-up are perfect as always, and I haven't seen her even pick up a mascara wand since she got here. 'We were looking forward to meeting them.'

'They live in Florida,' I say, trying not to let Amanda's words get to me, not today. Amanda made a few comments the previous evening as we had dinner together, mentioning Rupert and Caro's wedding a couple of times as she got more and more drunk, but I refused to react. 'Unfortunately, they just couldn't make it over. They had already booked a cruise.' I had sent my mother and – Jim? Jack? I couldn't remember his name – the clipping of my engagement from *The Times* but hadn't heard anything back. I had no idea if my mother was on a cruise or not, although chances were, she was. But I didn't want to confess that to Rupert's family, so it was just easier to tell a white lie.

'Oh, gosh. So, they booked this cruise before you even met Rupert then?' Sadie says, her eyes widening.

I turn my gaze back to the mirror under the pretence of checking my lipstick, and pretend I haven't heard Sadie's comment, my eyes flicking towards Amanda's reflection in the glass. I think back to the image of myself in the street in Brighton, fear written all over my face, and I shake it away. This is supposed to be the happiest day of my life.

'Em, you should probably think about getting into your dress. Shall I give you a hand?' Sadie takes one last sip of champagne and places her empty glass on the bureau, as Amanda gets up and stretches.

'I need to get dressed. I'll be next door if you need me. Emily, I'll see you at the church.' She stalks away, her legs even longer than usual in her tiny hotel dressing gown. I say nothing, but watch her leave, feeling myself exhale as the door closes behind her.

'Now.' Keen to dissipate the tension that thickens the air, Sadie bustles over to the wardrobe to where my dress hangs – the dress it has taken us hours to decide on. It's a simple, elegant Grecian style dress that would be better suited to a beach wedding – at least that's what I thought at first glance, but Sadie was adamant I should try it on – and I fell in love with it as soon as the silky fabric pooled over my body. 'Let's get you into this dress. You're going to look amazing – Rupert won't know what hit him.'

The ceremony goes off without a hitch, even though I am nervous all the way through that I'll stumble over my words or call Rupert by the wrong name. The butterflies in my stomach only fade away when the vicar announces that Rupert 'may now kiss the bride' and Rupert turns to me, bending me backwards from the waist in his arms as he presses his mouth to mine. I am flushed and laughing when he pulls me upright, my bouquet almost tumbling out of my arms. I grin at him, mouthing the words, 'I love you,' relieved that it is done, that our fate together is sealed. My legs turn to jelly as Rupert smiles back at me, his arm snaking around my waist and pulling me close. When the vicar turns to the congregation and says, 'May I present to you, Mr and Mrs Milligan,' the church full of family and friends cheer, and Rupert raises my hand in his in a gesture of celebration.

But as we descend down the steps into the aisle, I can't help but feel a sharp pang as I realize that I don't have a single person there just for me. No family, and without Mags, no friend. I blink back the tears that spring to my eyes, telling myself they are 'happy tears', because I finally found what I've spent my life searching for, and I follow my husband out into the bright September sunshine.

Later, after a meze meal – I didn't want to force our guests into a three-course dinner, not in the prolonged heat that means glorious wedding day weather – Will makes a speech, welcoming me into the family, which moves me to tears. Knowing how close they all were to Caro, I am aware that some people thought Rupert might be making a mistake, moving too fast, but there is no sign of that, not today, and I feel the warm arms of acceptance around me. Gathering up my dress so I don't trip, I stand, a hush falling over the room. I see Rupert's mother glance at his father – quite clearly, the bride making a speech isn't really the done thing.

'I know this is unusual, but in my father's absence I thought perhaps *I* should make a speech. Rupert,' I look down at him, a fond smile creeping across my face, 'Mr Milligan. My *husband*.' I press my hands to my face in glee as a ripple of laughter fills the room. 'Today is the start of the rest of our lives together, and it honestly couldn't have been more perfect. The sun came out, you look adorable, and all of our family and friends are here to celebrate with us. It's no secret to the people in this room that you have been through some hard times, and we haven't known each other for as long as is perhaps expected, but I want you to know that I adore you. I am so ready for our life together. This is all I've ever wanted, and after kissing a few frogs, I finally met my prince. I'm so glad I applied for that job – even if I'm not quite as good at cleaning as I made myself out to be.' Another swell of quiet laughter. 'To us, Rupert, and our perfect life together.' I clink my champagne glass against his and lean down to kiss him, feeling giddy with happiness. The room erupts with applause and as I sit back down, I see Sadie discreetly dab at her eyes with a napkin.

'Ladies and gentlemen, the band are here, and I think it's about time I took my bride onto the floor for our first dance.' Rupert stands and holds his hand out to me. 'What do you say, Mrs Milligan?'

'Definitely time,' I laugh up at him and get to my feet, kicking off the tiny heeled pumps that Sadie picked out for me to wear. Following Rupert onto the dance floor as someone, somewhere, dims the lights, I loop my arms around his neck before stiffening as the first strains of music reaches my ears.

'What?' Rupert stops, frowning as I tug my arms away, my hands flying to my mouth as my brow creases. The song is 'Tiny Dancer' by Elton John.

'This isn't our song,' I gasp in confusion, looking up at Rupert. His face is like thunder as he gestures to Will to get the band to cut the music. 'Rupert, did you ask them to change our song?' The music carries on, as Will is forced to mount the stage and physically tap the singer on the shoulder.

'No, Emily, I wouldn't do that. I take it you didn't either?'

'No, of course I didn't.' I press my hands against my stomach, each chord striking my skin like a thousand tiny needles. Finally, the music changes, the first notes of 'At Last' by Etta James fill the room and Rupert pulls me back into his arms. I try to go with it, but although my feet are moving, I am stiff, my joints like cardboard.

'Darling, try and enjoy it. This is our first dance, everyone is watching. I'm sorry about the mistake, I don't know what happened,' Rupert murmurs into my ear, and to anyone watching it looks as though he's whispering sweet nothings.

'Relax?' I whisper back, pinning a smile onto my face, even though smiling is the last thing I feel like doing. The moment has been spoiled now. 'That was the song you had your first dance to with Caro, wasn't it?' I try to swallow down the tears that make it difficult to speak. 'Amanda mentioned it when we were discussing what song we were going to have over lunch one day.'

'Oh, Em, I really am sorry. I have no idea how this happened. You must know I would never have changed the song, not without talking to you, and certainly not to that song.'

'No. No, of course I know that.' I take a deep breath, trying to push away the anger that bubbles beneath the surface. 'But if you didn't change it, and I didn't change it, then who did? Someone here must have done it deliberately to upset me. You. Us.'

I haven't told him about the letter, or the text message I received in Brighton, worried as I am that it might be Harry trying to get in contact with me, but now I'm regretting it. I should have showed him – maybe then he would realize just why I'm so upset now.

'No one would do that – they're our friends, Em! It's more likely the band got us mixed up with another couple. It's the end of the wedding season, darling, there are bound to be a few hiccups. Please, let's just forget it, and enjoy our day. Yes?' He nuzzles into my neck as he whisks me across the floor and I can't help but melt a little. I don't want to argue with him, especially not on our wedding day and in front of our guests, so I just nod in agreement, forcing a smile and giving our guests a little bow at the end of the dance.

Once I see that Rupert is busy talking to some old university friends, I take a moment when the band are on a break to snag the singer and ask him about the song change.

'You asked me to change it,' he says, slightly belligerently.

'No, I didn't.' I inject a note of steel into my voice, one hundred per cent certain that I never requested for the song to be changed.

'You did,' the singer argues, 'you left me a note on top of the speaker. Here.' He fumbles in his pocket, bringing out a crumpled piece of paper that looks as though it has been torn from a notepad, the kind I remember my grandmother using to send airmail letters to her sister in Canada. As he unfolds the pale blue sheet, I see the words:

CHANGE OF PLAN! PLEASE PLAY 'TINY DANCER' – ELTON JOHN AS FIRST DANCE! SORRY FOR THE SHORT NOTICE. E.

The writing is all block capitals, and although I don't think I can recognize it, I know it isn't mine and while I can't be certain, I'm pretty sure it's not Rupert's.

'Right. Thank you. I'm sorry for the confusion.' Ignoring his puzzled look, I take the note from him and plastering yet another fake smile on my face, quickly cross the dance floor, stopping to snag my shoes from under the top table, and march out into the evening.

I lock myself in the posh block of portaloos in the garden, my hands shaking slightly as I slide the lock to the cubicle closed. I thank God silently that Rupert had insisted on the most expensive block, the ones with mirrors and cubicles and actual tiny sinks with jars of pot pourri on top of them. Alone, I open the note again, my eyes scanning over the words as I rack my brains to think who could have done something this cruel. It was intentional, there's no doubt about it, but I think that hopefully, Rupert and I reacted in such a way that everyone else must have thought it was an error on the band's part. I am so engrossed in trying to work out who requested that the song be changed, that I don't realize I am no longer alone in the portaloo until I hear my name.

'That must be Emily's idea.' A woman's voice, thin and reedy with that plummy undertone that all Rupert's friends seem to have, but I'm not sure I recognize it.

'Oh, of course. Why else would Rupert drop the Osbourne? Becoming Osbourne-Milligan was Caro's idea, wasn't it? And Rupert carried on being Osbourne-Milligan after she died. Definitely Emily's idea.'

I sit bolt upright on the closed toilet seat, tucking my dress out of the way and drawing my feet up so the cubicle appears empty. I hold my breath, afraid of giving myself away.

'What do you think of her anyway? It's all a bit quick, isn't it?' A smacking sound, like someone is refreshing their lipstick.

'Rupert on the rebound, do you think? Or maybe she's just after the money. Caro left him at least a couple of mill, I'm sure.' A spritz, and then a sickly-sweet perfume wafts on the air, catching in the back of my throat. **BITCH**. The word floats through my mind and I have to bite down on my tongue, to tamp down the fury that rises as I listen to the women tear me apart just feet away.

'Of course, Rupert is very attractive. He was bound to move on sooner rather than later. Although he was devastated at what happened with Caro. I was at the party that night, you know.'

I hear a gasp of delicious shock from the other woman, and I shift slightly, my nerve endings singing. *The party.* Someone else had made mention of a party just before Caro died. I lean forward as far as I dare, trying to hear what they say next.

'Really? What happened? Can you tell me?'

'Well, they had a blazing row, right there in front of us all. And then Caro stormed out. We got the call a few days later to say that she was gone.'

'Oh gosh. Do you think…?'

'Ladies.' A new voice butts in, and this time I am sure it is Sadie. A flutter of nerves stirs in my belly as I wait to hear what Sadie will say. Will she let slip anything about the party? Or will she join in their spiteful bitching about me? I almost feel sick, waiting. 'Even if Emily is after Rupert's money, is it any business of yours? And how dare you gossip about Caro? You're supposed to be friends of Rupert. I strongly suggest you watch what you're saying, seeing as you're enjoying a night out on his dime.' There is a pause, footsteps as the bitchy women hurry outside, and then a tap on the cubicle door. 'Emily? It's OK, darling, you can come out now.'

I wipe my face with a piece of toilet tissue and slide the door open, peering out cautiously. 'Well, that was refreshing.' I try to laugh, but as I catch sight of my reflection in the mirror, the mascara that smudges under my eyes, I want to cry.

'Oh, ignore them. They weren't anyone who matters, trust me. They're just jealous that you snagged Rupert and not them.' Sadie gives a brittle smile before turning to the mirror and swiping more bright red lipstick over her mouth. 'Are you OK? That wasn't the song you chose earlier, was it?' My eyes meet Sadie's in the mirror, and any chance I had of asking her about Caro and the night of the party slips away. 'What happened?'

'No. It wasn't our choice. The singer said I left him a note but… I don't know. It was just a silly mistake, no big deal.' I lick my finger and wipe away the black smudges of make-up from under my eyes, so I at least look presentable.

'Well, it gave me a jolt, so goodness knows how it made Rupert feel.' Sadie eyes me closely. 'They played that for Caro and Rupert's first dance.'

'I know. Amanda mentioned it when we went for lunch together a few weeks ago, you know when all three of us went to that new place, near the station?'

'Oh, Emily. I didn't realize that you knew. Are you sure you're OK?' Sadie's face is creased with concern, her lip-sticked mouth turned down as she gently squeezes my arm.

'Honestly, it's fine.' I blink. 'I think I'd like to just forget about it, you know? Whatever happened I don't want to let it put a shadow over our day.'

Sadie pulls out a tiny hairbrush from her clutch bag, running it over her already immaculate bob. 'Well, as long as you're feeling all right. Let's get you back out there before people start talking.'

I follow her out into the garden, back towards the hotel. 'Sadie, those women, what they were saying… do people really think that? That I'm just out for Rupert's money?' *Does someone want to scare me off?* For a moment, I wonder whether to tell Sadie about the text message, the letter, the feeling of being watched.

Sadie stops, the shadows from the wooded area to the left of us hiding one side of her face. 'No. Of course not. But Rupert was a very eligible widower for a while – you're bound to have some people – some women – who are jealous. And things happened so quickly. Obviously, we all know you two are very much in love.'

'I meant what I said in my speech, you know. That I want to live the perfect life with him. He told me that he knew immediately that I was the one for him, that he knew straight away we were meant to be together, that we're twin souls…' I trail off as I catch sight of someone lurking in the entrance to the woods.

'Emily?' Sadie turns to me, frowning. 'Are you OK?'

'Yes… you go on back, I'll be in in a minute. Just need some fresh air.'

I give her a quick smile, waiting for her to move off before I turn my gaze to the woods. The figure still stands there, watching me, and a ripple of unease snakes up my back. *It's the same person,* I think for a moment, *the same person who was watching the house. Isn't it?* With a quick glance towards the hotel, where warm light spills out of the windows and I can make out the shadows of people dancing and drinking, I take a deep breath and turn back towards the trees, fully intending on finding out who is there and what they want from me, even though I feel as if my knees are quaking like some cartoon character. But as I step forward, the grass soft under my feet, I find there is no one there. But there was. I am sure of it. A dark silhouette watching me walk across the garden with Sadie. I rest a hand on my chest in an attempt to stop my heart from racing. Someone was definitely watching me, the only question is, *who?*

Chapter Twelve

Rupert watches from his comfortable position sprawled across their huge king-sized bed in their ocean view bedroom, complete with balcony, as Emily gets ready for dinner. They are on their honeymoon in an exquisite hotel in Hastings, Barbados, still another two weeks of bliss ahead of them. Rupert isn't too sure how he feels about the hotel, despite the luxury they are surrounded by. He had left the honeymoon decision up to Emily and had been partly horrified when she had announced that Coconut Court was her first choice. He'd tried to dissuade her at first, but she had been adamant that she wanted to stay here – that she'd heard only good things, and she was only planning on ever having one honeymoon, and besides, she had already booked it. He couldn't find it in himself to tell her that he and Caro had honeymooned on the island, albeit at a different hotel. That he had proposed to Caro on a beach not five miles away from where she was suggesting they spend their honeymoon. Sadie had told him he was mad when he mentioned it.

'Bloody hell, Rupert... are you sure about this?' Sadie

had looked at him in horror, then at the confirmation email on the screen of his phone. 'What if Emily finds out you went to Barbados with Caro? That you bloody proposed to Caro there!'

'She won't… not if you don't tell her. Please, don't tell her, Sadie. She's got her heart set on it, and I don't want to disappoint her.'

'She'll be more than disappointed if she ever finds out the truth.' Sadie shoved the phone back in his direction, and he fumbled, almost dropping it. 'You'd better hope that someone doesn't let it slip.'

'She doesn't need to know,' Rupert implored. 'Please, Sadie. I did try to tell her in a roundabout way. I tried to persuade her that Thailand would be nice, but she wouldn't listen, and it was too late. She'd already booked it.'

Sadie had just looked away, changing the subject, but Rupert hadn't missed the look on her face. Now, he pushes the memory down, out of sight, convinced that despite Sadie's disapproval, he has made the right choice. The hotel is one hundred per cent high-end luxury, and he's determined to make new memories here with Emily over the next fortnight.

'So, what do you think of the honeymoon so far?' he asks Emily, as she pins her short curls up into some complicated hairstyle in front of the mirror. Her skin already glows with the beginnings of a light tan.

'Beautiful.' Emily meets his eyes in the mirror and smiles, a tiny lifting of her lips. 'Everything I hoped it would be.'

'What made you decide on this place? Apart from the reviews, obviously. I thought you'd be more... I don't know, India, or Peru. Somewhere... less relaxing.' Rupert genuinely is curious about Emily's decision. The fact that he's even had to ask her just shows how much they still have to learn about each other. He could have told you that Caro would have picked the Caribbean every time, thanks to fond memories of childhood holidays (Rupert's childhood holiday memories were more Cornwall than Caribbean), and a love of long days stretched out on the sand soaking up the sun.

'Someone recommended it.' Emily pouts into the glass, pressing her lips together and checking her lipstick hasn't gone astray.

'Someone?' Rupert frowns.

'Yes, Sadie or Amanda, it might even have been Will. I don't remember who exactly.' Emily spins on the stool to face him, satisfied that she is finally ready to go down to the restaurant. 'We were talking about honeymoon destinations and one of them recommended Barbados. Hastings. They said that you had been to the island before and you loved it, that if I wanted to make the honeymoon really special, Barbados was the place to go. And then when I found this hotel, I thought it looked perfect – the ideal place to relax after the wedding. It was pretty stressful.' A cloud crosses her features.

Why would Sadie or Amanda recommend coming here to Emily? It's true, he does love the island, always has done ever since Caro brought him here the first time they went away together, but he'd rather have gone somewhere different, somewhere where there was no ghost of Caro looking on. Now he'll feel on edge for two weeks, worried he'll upset Emily by letting something slip about being here with Caro.

'I'm sorry again about the song cock–up. I really don't have any idea how it happened.'

'It's fine, Rupert. Just a silly mistake.' Emily closes her eyes for a moment. 'I'd rather not think about it anymore, to be honest. Let's concentrate on now, on being happy and making the most of our beautiful honeymoon together.'

'As long as you are happy, Mrs Milligan.' Rupert scoots to the end of the bed to kiss her, worried that the look on her face means she *isn't* happy.

'Of course I am.' Emily gives him a smile, and turns to the mirror, her hands going back to fiddle with her hair again. 'Now, are you going down to the restaurant like that, or are you going to get dressed?'

The restaurant is quiet when they arrive for their meal. Theirs is one of the tables on the edge of the restaurant floor, closest to the sea. There are no walls or windows, just a space that opens out onto the sand. A warm breeze ruffles Rupert's hair as they wait to be seated. Tiny lights are strung across the ceiling and it is the perfect setting for romance. Rupert blinks away the vision of Caro sitting in a restaurant very like this one, just before they took a stroll onto the beach and Rupert went down on one knee in the sand, under a full moon. There is a pain, somewhere close to his heart. He still misses her, even though things weren't perfect between them. He must be careful this evening, he thinks, not to let anything slip that will let Emily know that he's been here before. He could kill whoever it was who recommended Barbados – why not let Emily make up her own mind about their destination?

'Mr Milligan? How lovely to see you again.' The maître d' appears beside him, and Rupert recognizes him from the last time he was here, his heart leaping into his throat. He glances towards Emily, who is gazing out towards the ocean and doesn't seem to have heard. 'Let me show you to your table.'

Emily looks amazing this evening. She's wearing a semi-sheer, off-the-shoulder Diane Von Fürstenberg dress in shades of green that accentuates the colour of her eyes. Rupert almost feels underdressed in his cargo shorts and pale blue Ralph Lauren polo shirt. He watches as several other guests turn to look at the pair of them as they cross the room to their table, feeling a little burst of pride that Emily, the woman all the other men in the restaurant wish was with them, is with him.

'Have you been here before?' Emily eyes him closely as Rupert takes his seat opposite her.

'Errr… no, I don't think so.' He makes a big deal of fussing with his napkin, adjusting his cutlery so it sits dead straight on the pristine tablecloth.

'I thought he said it was lovely to see you again?' Emily's brows are knitted together, and she doesn't take her eyes off him.

'You know how these places are, Em, they welcome you like an old friend, and then you spend more money with them. He'll probably ply us with wine all evening.' He feels a bead of sweat gather at the corner of his temple. Why hadn't he just told Emily they were going somewhere else for their honeymoon, or even just confessed that he'd been there with Caro and let Emily make up her own mind? It's too late now. He changes the subject, keen to avoid any confrontation. 'Hungry?'

'A little.' Emily's voice is quiet. She's been subdued since they got on the plane yesterday morning, the morning after the wedding. Rupert had thought that perhaps she was hungover, that's why she'd been so quiet, but now it's two days since the wedding. No hangover lasts that long, and surely she can't still be annoyed about the mistake with their first dance song, can she? After all, it was only the first few bars of music, and none of the other guests even seemed to notice it.

'Maybe we should start with a cocktail?' Rupert suggests, waving over a waiter and ordering two rum punches before Emily can respond. 'We are on holiday after all.'

'Rupert...' Emily starts to speak, before the waiter returns with menus, giving them both a run-down on what the specials are. Rupert orders for them both – salted cod – and when the waiter finally leaves, he waits for Emily to speak. She looks a little pale under her tan, but that might just be the lighting; Rupert isn't sure. He feels a tiny wave of panic rise in his chest. Is she about to tell him they've both made a terrible mistake? He can't let her go, not now, not after he's finally found what he's been looking for.

'Rupert—' Emily clears her throat, then sips at her cocktail, wincing at the burn of rum on her tongue. 'There's something I should probably tell you. I wanted to wait until after the wedding...'

'What is it?' Rupert puts his cocktail down and leans across the table, avoiding the strategically placed candle, to grasp her hand in his. 'Emily, whatever it is, it's OK.'

Her face is serious as she lets him squeeze her fingers, before sliding her hand delicately away, her right hand going to her wedding ring to twist it on her finger. 'It's quite a big deal, Rupert. I'm not sure how you're going to react.'

Rupert's first instinct is to reply that of course she doesn't know how he's going to react, if she won't just bloody tell him what it is that's got her so worried. But he bites the words back, reminding himself that she's not Caro. She can't read him like a book, the way Caro used to. Not yet anyway.

'I don't know, maybe I'm just being silly... but I really don't think I am.' Emily shifts in her seat and looks away. 'I am a bit worried that... well, that someone isn't very happy about the two of us being together.'

'What do you mean, someone isn't happy about us being together? This isn't about Mags, is it? She hasn't upset you again?' Rupert feels a familiar prickle of annoyance. He thought they were done with all of this. He was relieved when Emily hadn't invited her trouble-making friend to the wedding.

'No, it's just…' A deep red flush is staining Emily's cheeks, and she fidgets in her chair, clearly uncomfortable. 'I'm worried that people think I'm only after you for money – which I'm not – you know that, right?'

Rupert nods. 'Of course I know that, but who cares about what anyone else thinks?'

'I got a letter,' Emily blurts out, 'calling me a bitch. I don't know who it was from, but it was in a bundle of post. I don't know if it was sent to me at the flat or sent to the house. Our house.'

'Jesus.' Rupert sits back and shoves a hand through his hair. 'Why didn't you tell me? Have you still got the letter?'

'No,' Emily shakes her head, 'I threw it away. I didn't want to worry you, that's why I never said anything. Harry called me that once or twice.' She looks down and Rupert sees a tiny damp spot on the tablecloth where a single tear has fallen. 'I got a text message, the night of my hen party, saying pretty much the same thing. And then some hideous woman was in the loos at the wedding, saying I was basically a gold–digger. I love you, Rupert, I just want to be with you. I don't understand who would want to say these awful things to me.'

'It sounds to me like someone is a bit jealous, that's all.' Rupert takes her hands in his. 'It's nothing to worry about, and I certainly don't care what other people might think. We know this is the real deal. You and me, we're the only people who matter.'

Emily nods, but says nothing.

'And you certainly don't need to worry about Harry, or

Mags, or anyone else who might want to stick their oar in. I'm here to look after you now and I won't let anyone hurt you. Em, you're safe with me – if I see any sign of Harry, I'll send him packing. We're a team. Does that sound OK?'

Emily is quiet for a moment, before she says, 'That sounds absolutely perfect.'

They spend the next few days soaking up the sunshine, Emily arranging herself prettily on a sun lounger each morning, while Rupert pulls his slightly to one side into the shade. He burns easily and doesn't want to look like a lobster when they both look back on their honeymoon photos. He is frantically checking emails – trying to keep up with all the work that still floods his inbox even whilst on holiday – tapping quietly at his phone screen while Emily dozes. She wants to try scuba diving later, and he absolutely has to get these figures back before lunchtime. She has still been a little subdued since their conversation over dinner, and Rupert can't shake off the nagging feeling that there is still something bothering her. He'll bring it up tonight at dinner, he thinks, just double-check that she is OK. He goes back to his figures, not noticing when Emily stretches and sits up, reaching over for the suntan lotion and smoothing it into her legs. He doesn't notice when she shifts on her sun lounger, rolling over so she is propped on one shoulder, facing him.

'Rupert.'

Rupert holds up one finger, his eyes running down the column of figures in front of him. 'One minute, Em,

I really need to get this checked and back to the office. Grab a cocktail if you want, I won't be long.'

'Rupert, I wanted to ask you something.' Emily sits up, sprinkles of sand clinging to her ankles and feet.

'Just give me a minute, please? I promise, I won't do any more work today once this is done.' Rupert reaches out a hand and strokes her thigh, as he saves the document and attaches it to an email. 'There, done.'

Emily shakes her head and lowers herself back down onto the sun lounger, a frown drawing her brows together as her words come out in a rush. 'Rupert, tell me about Caro.'

'Caro?' Rupert stalls, his heart rate speeding up. Glad he is wearing sunglasses, he risks a glance towards where Emily lies, but she has her eyes closed as she waits for his response. 'What… what do you want to know about her?' He supposes it was inevitable that Emily would ask questions about Caro eventually.

'What happened?'

'You know what happened. She died.'

'No.' Emily turns to him and props herself up on one elbow. 'I mean what *happened*? I know she died, and I know it's hard to talk about, but I just want to understand.'

'Understand what?' Rupert gives a shaky laugh. 'There's nothing to understand.' He reaches for her, stroking from behind her ear and tracing a line down her neck and along her collarbone in the way he knows she loves.

Emily shivers, and leans down to kiss the back of his hand. 'Who she was. Why she did the things she did.'

'You already know that.' Rupert sighs. 'She was bi-polar, her moods were all over the place. The police knocked on the door and said they'd found her car close to the Severn Bridge, along with a note. It was pretty obvious what she'd done.'

'It must have been devastating for you.' Emily grasps his hand tightly, and presses it to her lips. 'I can't even begin to imagine it, how it must have felt.'

'Yeah,' Rupert nods slowly, 'it was devastating. But you know, you can't let things like this make time stand still, you have to keep going, move on. I took the time to heal and deal with things and then you walked into my life and look at us now.'

'Did you have any idea, though? That she would go that far? I mean, lots of people are bi-polar, but they don't do what she did.'

'Emily...' Rupert sighs, closing his eyes for the briefest of moments as the warm sea breeze rustles his hair. 'No. I didn't have any idea. It was a total shock, and now I'm just glad I have you, and our life together ahead of me.'

'Yes, but...' Emily starts to say something, but Rupert silences her with a kiss, a proper kiss that takes her breath away as he slides his tongue into her mouth, his hand stroking her nipple through her bikini top.

'Come on,' Rupert pulls Emily to her feet and leads her gently towards their hotel room, any other unasked questions sliding right out of Emily's mind, forgotten as Rupert lays her down on the huge white bed and covers her body with his own.

Chapter Thirteen

Something's not right. The thought crosses my mind the minute I step foot inside the house, goosebumps rising on my tanned forearms as Rupert bumps our heavy suitcase into the hallway behind me. I can't put my finger on it, as I walk past the living room into the kitchen. Nothing is out of place, not that I can tell, and nothing seems to be missing, but there is a feeling in the air. As though someone has been in the house, and recently too. Walking back, I pause at the foot of the stairs, almost unwilling to go up them.

'Em? What's the matter?' Rupert appears beside me, his face flushed pink with exertion from wrestling with the heavy bags.

'Nothing,' I say quietly, and start to climb the stairs, heading towards our bedroom. As I open the door it gets stronger, the feeling that someone has been in our house while we have been away. I sniff the air delicately, wondering if I can really smell a faint hint of perfume or whether I'm imagining it. Rupert appears behind me, wrapping his arms around my waist and nuzzling against my neck.

'Straight to the bedroom, eh? I like your style, Mrs Milligan.'

'Rupert, stop.' I pull away, a ghostly draught washing over my skin and I wrap my arms around myself, unable to stop the shiver that ripples through me. 'Does it feel weird to you?'

'Weird? Does what feel weird?'

'The house.' I reach out a hand and smooth the already immaculate duvet, not sure what it is that I'm looking for.

'The house?' Rupert shakes his head. 'Sorry, Em, I have no idea what you're talking about.'

'It feels… odd. Like someone has been in here. You know like, when you come home and you know that I'm here, just by that feeling in the air. You know that there's someone home, right? That's how it feels. Like someone just left.'

'Em, please,' Rupert sighs, reaching out for me. I let him pull me into his arms, even though I feel as though I need to look under the bed and check in the wardrobes. 'Not this stuff again. I told you, no one is interested in us. There wasn't anyone watching the house, and I certainly don't think anyone has been in here while we've been gone. And if they have, it'll only be Amanda – I asked her to keep an eye on the place.'

I stand there, silently, wishing I could believe him.

'Is this about the messages you received?' Rupert holds me at arm's length and looks into my eyes, making me feel as though I'm under a microscope. 'I told you, I'll look after you. Whoever it is, they're no threat to us, to our marriage. I swear to you, Em, no one has been in the house. It's been a long day.'

I nod and pull away, tiredness tugging at my bones. We've been travelling for over twelve hours and with a five-hour time difference, jetlag is already starting to kick in. 'OK. I expect you're right.' And he probably is. I haven't lived here for very long, and I don't know every creak, every groan of the house like I did in the flat. I feel a sudden wave of longing for my tiny, cluttered bedroom, the thud of Mags's terrible music coming through the wall. *No, Emily*, I think, *this is who you are now. This is what you chose.*

'I'll make us some tea.' Rupert kisses me on the forehead and I feel that tickle of irritation toward him dissolve a little. I'm sure he is right – I'm just overtired and thinking things that aren't really there. 'Why don't you get into bed? It's nearly one o'clock, and I have to be up at six for work in the morning.'

As Rupert leaves the room, a chilly draught settles over my skin again and I shiver more used to the warm Caribbean breezes of the past two weeks, than the autumnal September air we've come home to. Shivering, I move towards the en suite, intent on running a cleansing wipe over my tired face and brushing my teeth, when I see where the draught is coming from. The window in the en suite is open a little, not wide open, but pushed to as though someone has forgotten to latch it. It's not a huge window, but it's long and wide and potentially someone could get through it if they wanted to. Which means the fact that it is open doesn't make any sense. Neither Rupert nor I would have left this window open, not when we were leaving for two weeks. I rack my brains, thinking back to the morning after the wedding. I definitely remember shutting all the windows upstairs because I had thought to myself how I never had to worry in the flat, being above the takeaway.

Now, I tiptoe across the bathroom floor, the underfloor heating warming my toes as I reach up and peer through the crack in the window. Just as I thought, the large recycling bin is under the window, to the left of the orangery, right where I left it, only… I push the window wide open and look out as far as I can. The recycling bin is on its side, a small spillage of plastic and a couple of glass bottles on the patio beside it. *That doesn't mean anything*, I tell myself, my breath coming fast in my throat. *A fox could have knocked it over. Maybe there was a storm.*

I slam the window closed, latching it tight and sit on the cold toilet seat, rubbing my hands over my face. Just because the bin is on its side doesn't mean that someone used it to stand on, to climb up onto the orangery roof and then force their way into the house through the bathroom window. It doesn't mean that when they heard our taxi arrive they climbed out of the bathroom window and tipped the bin on its side in their hurry to get away. It doesn't mean *anything*.

'Em? Are you in there?' Rupert's voice rouses me, and I move to the sink, quickly scrubbing at my face with a wipe before pulling open the bathroom door. He hands me a steaming hot cup of tea, and gestures towards the bed where he has pulled back the duvet and plumped my pillow.

'Thanks.' I gratefully take the tea, wrapping my cold hands around the mug. 'Rupert, the recycling bin. It's on its side out there, some of the rubbish has fallen out. The bathroom window was open too.' I wait, watching his face to see what his reaction is.

'Oh bugger, really?' He pauses in stripping his T-shirt over his head. 'You don't want me to go and sort it out now, do you? It's just started raining.'

'No, it's OK.' I shake my head and climb into bed, relieved when Rupert finally turns out the lamp. Maybe Rupert is right and I'm just being silly. Maybe there is nothing to worry about.

The next morning, I watch through the living-room window as Rupert chases down the last bits of recycling from behind the two small stone lions that flank the porch – plastic wrapping that has blown round the side of the house – and stuffs them deep down into the black bin. In the cold light of day, I feel ridiculous for getting worked up over the bin toppling over – and Amanda was keeping an eye on the house; she must have opened the window upstairs to air out the bedroom a little. Either that or I really did forget to close it before we left. That's what I'm telling myself anyway. It was such a busy week, after all, the week before the wedding, maybe I only *thought* about closing the window. An icy finger crawls up my spine, making me shudder and I pull my cardigan tightly around my body. It did feel as though someone had been in the house though; the air had that disturbed feeling about it, and I am sure I wasn't imagining the faint hint of perfume, the light scent of something that might have been nectarines on the air.

A few days later, I still haven't shaken the uneasy feeling that settled on me the night we arrived home from Barbados, although Rupert seems to be back to his usual self. He grabs a piece of toast, shoving it into his mouth while searching for his car keys, as I sit quietly at the kitchen table, still in my dressing gown. I'm finding it strange to be sitting here, with nowhere to go and nothing to do, while Rupert rushes around frantically. I nurse the dregs of a cup of tea, as I wait for him to leave the house so I can start getting ready myself, although ready to do what exactly I don't know.

The days are different, now Rupert has taken on a cleaner – a Polish woman named Anya, who seems to spend a lot of her time scowling at me – and taking care of the house is no longer my responsibility. It turns out that I'm not as brilliant at keeping house as I thought I would be, and after I used neat bleach to clean the marble floor tiles in the main bathroom (damaging them beyond repair, much to my horror), Rupert insisted on getting a profes-sional in to take over. So now, instead of spending my days tidying and cleaning, I watch someone else do it. And do a better job of it, too. I pop the tiny bubble of boredom that grows in the pit of my stomach, telling myself that this is what I want.

'What are your plans for today?' Rupert asks, as he shoves papers into his briefcase. He's asked me the same question every morning since we got home.

'Probably nothing, the same as yesterday,' I say, feeling prickly and scratchy. I get up and put my arms around him. It's not his fault that I am irritable this morning.

'I spoke to Sadie last night,' Rupert's chin rests on my hair, 'she said she's going to a yoga class this morning, if you'd like to join her. She's going to text you.'

'Oh. OK.' That would be nice, I think. I haven't been to a yoga class for months, not since I left Harry. It'll keep me busy, stop me from worrying about whether someone – some unknown identity – has been in the house, whether someone is watching me. Watching *us*. I have to keep busy, to stop myself from worrying about things. Rupert says he'll get the security cameras fixed outside so I won't feel quite so jumpy at being alone in the house anymore, but right now, every time I think I am OK, that I have got over things, I see the letter on the kitchen table, **BITCH** etched onto the paper.

'I've put Find My iPhone on your phone, by the way,' Rupert says as he takes a mouthful of coffee, almost spilling it down his tie.

'Oh. Isn't that like a tracker type thing?' I reach for my phone. I don't know when Rupert had the time to download it.

'Kind of.' Rupert tips the rest of his coffee into the sink, his back to me. 'I thought it might make you feel safer. I know you've been worried about things, and at least this way you know I can find you if something happens. Which it *won't*,' he says, tugging on his jacket as I look up in alarm.

'Right. No, of course it won't. It's just me being silly.

134

OK, then. Well, I won't be going far today, only meeting Sadie.' As if on cue, my phone buzzes with a text message from her.

'That'll be nice,' Rupert says absently, and I get the feeling that although he mentioned the yoga, he's already moved on his head. Not for the first time I wonder if he was the same with Caro, or if Caro demanded his attention. 'I'll see you tonight.' He kisses the top of my head as he passes, leaving me to another day on my own.

I take my time getting dressed, and Sadie is waiting outside the gym when I walk round the corner in my leggings, her yoga mat rolled up under her arm.

'Emily!' Sadie leans in and kisses my cheek, before holding me at arm's length and looking me up and down. 'Look at the tan on you! You wouldn't think you'd go so brown, being blonde the way you are. You'll have to tell me all about the honeymoon, quick, before the class starts. I can't believe you two have been back for days already and we haven't seen you.'

I'm a little taken aback by Sadie's enthusiasm. I've never really had the kind of friends that you see immediately you get back from holiday, thanks to my mum carting us all over the country in her quest for perfection, so it hadn't really crossed my mind to check in with Sadie. 'Sorry, I…'

'Oh, darling, Rupert told me you've been a bit worried about things at home.' Sadie lays a hand on my arm, and I don't know what to say at first. I hadn't realized that Rupert would have discussed my feelings with anyone, least of all Sadie.

'It's not a big deal, not really,' I say, as we turn and walk into the swanky gym that Sadie is a member of. 'I think I just let my imagination get the better of me. Seeing things that aren't really there, you know.' The photo of myself, gripping my bride-to-be sash, fear etched onto my face, swims in front of my eyes, and I shake it away. 'Anyway, I've got a morning of yoga with you, so things can't be all bad.' I force a smile and make a show of pulling my hair up into a ponytail.

Sadie gives me a small smile in return. 'Quite. Although…' her face turns serious, and her voice lowers, 'Rupert did also tell me about the letter you got. He said something about an ex-boyfriend… are you OK?'

'Oh.' I didn't realize that Rupert had told anyone about that, and I don't know how I feel about it. It's hard to write something off as nothing when other people know about it. 'Yes. Things ended badly between us… it was, well, it wasn't a very healthy relationship, if I'm honest, and I was a bit concerned.' I blink away the image of Harry's hands looming towards my throat, his face twisted and ugly. 'But I'm sure it's fine. Probably just… I don't know. A mistake. Or a prank. Hopefully.' My face clouds over and I search for something to say to change the subject.

'OK,' Sadie eyes me closely, 'well, if you want to talk about anything – I've had my fair share of relationship troubles, let me tell you – you know I'm always here. Me and Amanda. Although Amanda can be a bit prickly at times, so maybe don't go to her if you want any sympathy. She literally is dead inside.' Sadie laughs, a shrill tinkle, and I try to, but it sticks in my throat a little. I'm not sure I want to talk about it with anyone, if I'm honest.

The yoga class is busier than I was expecting, and I have to wedge myself into a tiny corner of the overheated room, behind Sadie. The other women all seem to have their own space that they occupy every week, so I try to slide in unobtrusively, not wanting to draw any attention to myself.

'Do we have any new members today?' the instructor calls out, a tiny woman with ropy arms and big calf muscles. I keep my head down, avoiding eye contact, but Sadie points to me with an, 'Over here!' and I sigh inwardly as I see the instructor start making her way across the floor, stepping over mats and bare feet.

'Hi. I'm Sorcha. Have you done yoga before?' The woman crouches down to where I sit cross-legged on my mat, as Sadie hovers in the background, stretching her arms over her head and bending down to touch her toes. *Show-off*, I think, feeling stiff and creaky in my own body.

'Yes, I have a little.' I turn my attention back to Sorcha. 'I've done it a few times, actually. But not for a while. I'm a bit rusty, I should think.'

'Have I taught you before?' Sorcha looks at me quizzically.

'No, I don't think so.'

I can almost feel Sadie's ears prick up, as she swings into an upright position and beams at Sorcha. 'No, Emily hasn't been here before. She used to go to one in the centre of town, didn't you, Em?'

'Oh, only a couple of times.' Feeling awkward under

the scrutiny of Sorcha's gaze, I tug the sleeves of my thin cardigan over my hands, against the chill of the air conditioning.

'Maybe I did see you once or twice? You do look familiar. I filled in a few times at a class over that way. You know, Sadie, the one that Caro used to like?'

I freeze, as my cheeks start to burn. I didn't realize that this class was going to be taught by someone who knew Caro, someone who had taught Caro yoga. I throw Sadie a panicky look, to let her know that I don't feel at all comfortable with things, but Sadie is chattering away to the woman on the mat next to her and doesn't notice.

'I don't think so,' I manage to stutter, my fingers fluttering to my sleeves again, 'I only went once or twice. Like I say, I'm a bit rusty.'

Sorcha smiles and says something about loosening me up, but I can't keep my focus on her. I feel more than a little furious with Sadie for drawing attention to me, and also for bringing me to a class where the instructor knows Caro. Embarrassment makes my cheeks burn hot and red, as if everyone knows that I am the second Mrs Milligan, and they are all comparing me to Caro. I lean down and fuss with my mat, making sure it's straight before turning my attention to my feet.

An hour later, I am too sweaty and exhausted to be annoyed at Sadie anymore, and the thinking time the yoga class has afforded me has made me realize that if I fall out with Sadie then I really will be lonely, especially now that Mags and I are barely on speaking terms – I called

Mags when we got back from our honeymoon, hoping to make amends for not inviting her to the wedding, but Mags cut me off and when I called back the phone was switched off.

'How about lunch back at mine in an hour? I'll text Amanda and see if she wants to join us,' I suggest to Sadie as we leave the class. Nervous, the words tumble out, leaving me slightly breathless. I've never invited Sadie to do anything with me before, aware as I am that she was Caro's friend, but I'm not quite ready to be on my own yet today, and the idea of stepping through the front door knowing that I have company for the afternoon gives me a lift.

'Oh. That sounds… lovely. OK,' Sadie says, as if surprised that I would want to have lunch with her. Surprised, and pleased, I think. 'I'll give you a bit of time to freshen up, shall I?' She casts her eye over me, and I am aware of my sweaty hairline, and the way my T-shirt sticks to my back and shoulders.

I hurry past the line of cabs waiting for their next fare, opting to walk instead. I still can't get used to the idea of jumping in a cab for a ten-minute journey, when I could walk home and take in the beauty of where I find myself living now. I've never lived in a village before, and I still get a little shiver of glee as I walk through the main street, shaded by trees, giving little nods to the postman, the woman who works in the local shop. Feeling as though they recognize me as one of them, as though I belong, at last. My smile soon fades as I catch sight of my reflection in the shop window, my face pink and flushed, and I hope that Sadie gives me enough time to spruce myself up properly before she arrives.

The house is still and empty when I let myself in, dust motes swirling as I step towards the stairs. There is a faint scent of something I can't quite place in the air, something sweet and floral. All things I still can't quite get used to. The flat was always noisy, whether Mags was home or not, thanks to the constant buzz of traffic and the banging and shouting of the takeaway guys downstairs, and it never smelled fresh – a combination of kebab meat and Mags's constant weed-smoking made sure of that.

Shedding my sweaty yoga gear, but not quite managing to leave it on the floor for the cleaner to pick up – unlike Rupert, whose trousers and shirt from yesterday still lie in a heap by the laundry basket – I jump into the shower, eager to rinse the sweat – and Sorcha's mention of Caro – out of my hair. As I lather up, I berate myself for being so touchy about Caro. Caro lived round here for years, it's inevitable that I'll meet people who knew her, go to places that she went to. It's hardly Caro's fault that she was married to Rupert first. I have to remember that I am the one married to Rupert now, Rupert *chose* me. I turn off the shower and am just stepping out onto the mat, wrapping myself in a huge, fluffy bath towel, when I think I hear something.

My heart starts to race in my chest, and I step off the mat, padding silently across the tiled en-suite floor to the carpet of the bedroom. There it is – the snick of a door closing shut. Grabbing a robe from the back of the door with shaking hands, I quickly knot the belt and start to make my way downstairs, my breath coming fast and loud in my ears. *I'm not imagining it now*, I think, my hands shaking as I cling onto the polished oak bannister, my knuckles turning white. *There is someone in the house, someone who shouldn't be here.*

On legs like jelly, I tiptoe as quickly as I can to the huge fireplace in the sitting room, snatching up the poker from the set that sits on the huge marble hearth. Feeling safer now I have something in my hand to fend off whoever it is, I pause for a moment, straining to hear the slightest noise, but there is nothing except the rapid thud of my pulse beating at my temples. Dabbing at the sweat that beads my upper lip, the poker falls to my side and the doubts creep in. *Did I really hear something? Or did I just imagine it, caught up as I was in thoughts about Caro?*

I close my eyes, willing my heart rate to return to normal, for my breath to come evenly and steadily. I stand still, not moving a muscle until the adrenaline has faded away and I feel as though I can move on my shaking legs without falling over. Slowly, I open my eyes just in time to see a shadow flit past the stained-glass panes of the front door.

'Arrrghhh!' I shriek a war cry, yanking the front door open with the poker held high above my head, only to see Sadie on the doorstep. 'Shit. Fuck. Oh God, Sadie, I'm so sorry.' Panting, I slouch against the doorframe, hot tears stinging my eyes.

'Oh my God, Emily! Are you OK? What the hell is going on?' Sadie peers past me into the hallway. 'You terrified me!'

'Sadie, I'm so sorry. I was in the shower, and I thought I heard something, like the sound of a door clicking shut… I thought someone was in the house.' An ugly heat starts to spread across my chest and up my neck, and I pull my robe tightly closed at the top. 'You'd better come in.'

'It was probably your cleaner woman… what's her name?' Amanda appears behind Sadie, immaculate in very expensive loungewear. 'I thought I saw someone walk out of your drive as I turned into the road.'

'Yes, that's probably it,' Sadie says, but her brows tug together in a deep V of concern, and I wish I hadn't told her about Harry. 'Amanda was just walking up the driveway when I arrived.'

I stand to one side to let both women in, feeling under-dressed and smarting with embarrassment. 'Yes. It probably was just Anya, now that I think about it. I don't know why I overreacted so badly. Look, let yourselves through into the kitchen and I'll go and get dressed. Won't be a moment.'

Sadie and Amanda head into the kitchen and I scurry upstairs, feeling like a stranger in my own home. I shrug off the robe, grateful for the cool air on my hot skin before reaching for a pair of leggings and a soft, grey cashmere jumper – another gift from Rupert, I never would have been able to afford it myself – and as I turn to leave the bedroom, something catches my eye on the bedside table. Frowning, I scoop it up, turning it over in my hands, its weight a small pebble in my palm. A lipstick. The ruffled gold casing of a Charlotte Tilbury lipstick, so familiar that at first, I think it must be mine, but when I open it it's not my usual nude pink, but the distinctive orangey-red colour that I've only ever seen one woman wearing: Caro, in the photographs dotted across Sadie's piano, the red her signature shade. With a shiver, I ram the lid back on and shove it into the bathroom bin.

'So, what will you do with yourself now you're no longer a working woman? I mean, you have a cleaner now, so it's not like you still have your old job,' Sadie asks with a raised eyebrow, as she sips at a glass of wine, pushing her salad around her plate. I've yet to see Sadie eat anything of real substance in all the time I've known her, and I feel a sharp pang as I think of Mags, stuffing in macaroni cheese as she watches *Masterchef* on the battered old sofa in the flat.

'I'm not sure,' I say, resisting the urge to shovel the last of my quiche into my mouth. Maybe if I eat like Sadie, I'll have collarbones like her too, one day. 'Probably some charity work? I don't just want to sit around at home all day, I think I'll go mad.'

'So why not try and get another job?' Amanda asks, as she lays her knife and fork down, half the food still left on her plate. I lay my own cutlery down, looking regret-fully at the last piece of quiche on the serving plate. Mags and I would have split it, and the thought of collarbones wouldn't have even crossed my mind.

'Well, I did think maybe I could, but Rupert doesn't

seem too keen. He's quite insistent that he's happy for me to stay home and look after him. I'm just not sure that I would be cut out for it.'

'I bet,' Amanda says. 'Caro would never have stayed home like a good little wifey.'

'I suppose it's a bit different now you have someone in to do all that stuff for you. And even if you didn't, it's not like you'd still be getting paid to do it,' Sadie says, her voice edged with something I can't place. Before I can think of the best way to reply, she speaks again. 'Emily, you have to do what's right for the two of you. Although I do think that charity work might be a good thing for you – it'll keep you busy, but you can still be about for Rupert, if that's what he wants.'

Amanda snorts and reaches for the half-empty bottle of rosé on the table. 'Well, if Rupert isn't happy about you going out to a full-time job – although honestly, Emily, I wouldn't let Will dictate to me like that – charity work is better than nothing, I suppose. Caro did charity work, so I don't really see how Rupert can be against you doing something similar. Until you have a baby, at least.'

Heat creeps up my neck and I feel a blush stain my cheeks as I open and close my mouth uselessly, the words not there when I need them. Eventually, I hold out my glass for Amanda to fill it. 'I'm sure I'll find something,' I say, brushing away Amanda's comment about babies. 'I have plenty of time.'

It's not until later, once Sadie and Amanda have finished the bottle of rosé, and we've spent the afternoon discussing the honeymoon and how I am going to fill my time now that I'm not working, that I remember what Amanda said when she first arrived. *It was probably your cleaner woman.* My mind flits back to the bedroom earlier today, stepping over Rupert's dirty laundry to get to the bathroom. The thing is, I am pretty sure that Anya wasn't supposed to be working today.

Chapter Fourteen

Rupert is exhausted when he gets home on Friday night – this week has flown by and it feels like the honeymoon was months ago, although to be fair, he carried on working from his sun lounger for most of it. He felt less relaxed when he got back than he did before he left.

'Honey, I'm home!' He chuckles to himself under his breath, as he lets himself in through the front door. He always used to call the same thing out to Caro, and she would call back with some witty remark, but now there is only silence. 'Em? Are you about?' He drops his laptop bag by the front door and peers into the sitting room, where he sees Emily tucked up in the huge armchair, her feet curled up underneath her. 'Are you OK?'

Emily has lit the candles that line the mantelpiece, and switched on the tiny Tiffany lamp that Caro bagged at a flea market in Brooklyn years ago, but the dim lighting does nothing to hide the dark circles under her eyes. She looks up at him, almost as though she hasn't realized he was there. 'Oh, you're home.' Her eyes wander to the clock on the wall and then back to his face. 'Yes, I'm fine. I didn't hear you come in.' She gets to her feet, and as she goes to pass by him, he pulls her into his arms.

'I missed you today. What did you get up to?' He nuzzles her hair and she leans against him, her arms loosely round his waist.

'I had a bit of a day, actually.' Emily sighs, pushing her shoulder-length, blonde hair behind her ears as she wriggles out of his grasp and heads towards the kitchen.

'Oh, why's that?' Rupert follows her, watching as she opens the fridge door and pulls out a bottle of Sauvignon.

'Just silly things, really.' She blinks, as if to hold back tears, and shakes her head. 'I went to the yoga class today with Sadie. It was kind of her to invite me. It must be hard for her to see you move on after Caro.'

'Yes, Sadie is lovely. So, what was the problem with the yoga class?' Rupert reaches over to take the wine bottle from Emily's hand as she struggles with the corkscrew.

'Oh, it's stupid.' Emily shakes her head, tugging a tissue out of her sleeve and blowing her nose. 'I feel ridiculous even mentioning it.'

'Try me.'

'Well… the instructor knew Caro. I know, I know, I shouldn't feel weird about it, but I did. It just made me feel a little out of place, that's all. Like, everyone is comparing me to Caro.'

'Don't be silly, no one is doing that. It's just a coincidence – surely there are only so many yoga teachers in the area? And Caro did do a lot of yoga, so she was probably taught by most of them at one point or another. But if it makes you feel uncomfortable, maybe no more yoga, eh?'

'Maybe.' A cloud crosses Emily's face and she opens her mouth as if to speak before closing it abruptly again.

'Was there something else?'

'You're really going to think I'm daft if I tell you.' Emily lets out a little half laugh, but Rupert can tell there is something on her mind that's bothering her.

'Tell me.'

'Well, I thought I heard someone in the house today, and I almost thumped Sadie over the head with a poker, but it turned out it was just Anya.' She tries to smile. 'I told you it was silly.'

'You almost thumped Sadie over the head with a poker?' Rupert gapes at her, as he wonders how on earth Sadie coped with *that*.

'*Almost*. I didn't actually do it. See, I told you you'd think I was an idiot. I thought she was an intruder, I was trying to defend myself.' Emily folds her arms across her chest.

'Well, if you thought you heard something…' Rupert says, trying to keep the doubt from his voice. He doesn't want to tell Emily that she was probably imagining it, not when she'd told him she's received horrible letters and strange text messages, but he's been through this stuff with Caro before. 'Who could blame you, eh? I bet you gave Sadie a right old fright.' He gives a huff of laughter, trying to show Emily that there was nothing to worry about, but when he looks at her, her mouth is turned down, and there is a faint shimmer at the corner of her eye.

'Sod it,' he says, throwing down the corkscrew next to the still unopened wine, 'let's go out for dinner, just the two of us. Go and get changed.'

'Tonight?' Emily looks towards the chopping board, where two delicate sea bass fillets are sat waiting to be prepared. 'You know what? That would be lovely. Really lovely. I feel as though I've barely seen you all week.' She moves past him quickly, shoving the fish into the fridge and giving him a fleeting kiss on the cheek. He lets out a sigh once he's alone. He'd forgotten how complicated it was, keeping a wife happy.

They get a cab into town before walking the short distance towards the restaurant, meandering along the streets with their arms linked together under a clear, dusky purple sky. Despite the slight chill in the air, there is still that faint sense of the last vestiges of summer thanks to the fact that the clocks haven't yet gone back, and that people are still braving the outside areas of the few pubs that they walk past, some huddling under patio heaters but still in T-shirts, reluctant to let autumn kick in properly. Emily seems to have relaxed now that they are out of the house, her forehead no longer tightly creased with a frown, the dark circles under her eyes hidden by concealer. Rupert is pleased that he thought to bring her out to dinner, he should have realized that she needed to get out after being at home on her own all week.

They reach the door of the Italian restaurant that Rupert has frequented for years. A tiny, family-run affair, Rupert and Caro used to come here regularly, but Rupert hasn't been since Caro died. He didn't feel ready before, the place awash with memories of past nights out, that nagging guilt heavy in the pit of his stomach, but he's missed the excellent food, the friendly service. Tonight, he can't think of a better place to spend his Friday evening.

Rupert pushes open the door, leaning out of the way so that Emily can duck under his arm and enter the restaurant first. The familiar smell of garlic on the air makes his stomach rumble, making Emily laugh as she hears it behind her. A laugh that quickly fades as Gino, the restaurant owner, bears down on Rupert, arms spread open in welcome.

'Ahhh, Mr Osbourne-Milligan! How lovely to see you, but where is the delightful Mrs Caro?' He peers over Rupert's shoulder out into the street, and then back to Rupert with a questioning look on his face. Rupert's mouth goes dry, and he can't find the words to speak.

Emily looks up at him, her face stricken. 'Rupert?'

His face burning, Rupert tucks his arm around her, 'Gino, this is Emily. I'm afraid…' He has to cough, to push the words past the lump in his throat. 'Caro passed away. Emily and I were very recently married, and I wanted to bring her to my favourite restaurant. Could we possibly have a table for two, please?'

Rupert slides the light jacket from Emily's shoulders and holds it out for the restaurant owner to take, even though the place is crowded, and Rupert can't see any vacant tables.

'Oh… of course, I apologize for my…' Gino breaks off, turning to survey the room. 'This way, please.'

Rupert and Emily follow him through the crowded restaurant to a table tucked away in the corner that Rupert hasn't seen. It's perfect – completely private, the best place for a romantic meal for two – Gino obviously wants to make things up to them. Gino scurries away to get menus as Emily and Rupert take their seats.

'Em, I'm so sorry. I haven't been here for… God, months and months. Way before Caro died. I just didn't think.' Rupert is being deadly honest – he really hadn't thought about it, he'd just fancied a meal out at one of his favourite restaurants. It hadn't even crossed his mind that the restaurant owner wouldn't have known that Caro had passed away.

'It's fine.' Emily gives a tight smile and fusses with her napkin, seemingly fully absorbed in making sure that it is spread over her lap perfectly.

'No, it's not. I should have thought about it. I'll explain to the owner what happened to Caro… I feel awful, especially after what happened at yoga today with the instructor.' Rupert wants to make it up to her, but if he's honest he doesn't really know how to even start. Nothing like this ever happened between him and Caro, obviously.

'Really, Rupert, I'd rather you left it.' Emily takes a deep breath, exhaling slowly and forcing her mouth into a smile. 'Let's just have a nice dinner, like we planned. Ahh, here we go, menus.' She turns the full-watt smile onto Gino who hands over the menus and discreetly backs away.

Rupert eyes her carefully as she reads the menu, her face serious. Is that really all she's going to say about his giant fuck-up? If it had been Caro then he would have been in serious shit, and they probably would have rowed for days. Emily must feel his eyes on her, as she looks up and smiles. 'Are you ready to order?'

'Yes.' Rupert smiles back. She really does seem to be OK about things. He waves Gino over. 'We'll both have the veal, please, Gino. That's OK with you, Em, isn't it? It's the best dish on the menu, I have it whenever I come here.' Too late, he realizes he probably shouldn't have said that last part.

'Um, I quite fancy…'

'It's really, really good. We'll have a bottle of Chianti to go with it, Gino.' Rupert snaps the menu shut and hands it back, before turning to Emily. 'Now, let's concentrate on us. How was your first week as a lady of leisure?'

'If I'm honest with you, Rupert, I'm not sure I'm cut out for this housewife lark,' Emily says, tapping lightly on the table with her fork. 'I'm not really enjoying being at home on my own.' She looks as though she'd like to say more but doesn't.

'Em, it's only been a week! Once you get in the swing of things, you'll be OK. There's always plenty of stuff to do at home; Sadie and Amanda are always busy.'

'Well, Amanda still works, so of course she is.' Rupert had forgotten about Amanda's little interior design company she'd set up after marrying Will.

'Sadie, then. Sadie always has stuff to do – I'm sure she can give you some ideas on how to keep busy. I mean, if you really want to work then of course you can, but I won't lie to you, I am quite old-fashioned about things like that. I loved coming home to you tonight, seeing you curled up in the armchair waiting for me.' Rupert reaches across the table and grasps her hands in his.

'Well, Sadie has given me a few things to think about.' Emily pauses as Gino brings over the wine and Rupert is made to taste it and approve it. She waits until Gino leaves. 'We were talking about charity work and I know you have one that you like to donate to regularly… it might be something to consider.'

'Hmmm,' Rupert says, sipping at the wine. It really is excellent – he's sure Gino has brought them over a better vintage than they ordered. Presumably to make up for the faux pas when they arrived.

'I think if I have things to do then perhaps I won't have time to dwell on things so much… you know—' Emily looks at him from under her lashes '—the feeling that someone is… *there* all the time.'

'Yes, of course I understand. Look, Em, I just want you to be happy.' And he does, but more than that Rupert just wants to eat, his veal has arrived, and the smell is driving him mad.

'I *am* happy. I don't want you to think I'm not, it's just that I need to keep myself occupied. So, you'll be OK if I contact the charity and see if there's something I can do for them?'

'Hmmm?' Rupert looks up, his mouth full of food. 'No, I don't mind. You go for it. Have you tried this yet? It's fantastic.'

The mood lightens for the rest of the meal, both of them enjoying the spark of electricity that still leaps between them every time their hands accidentally meet, although Emily doesn't manage to finish her veal, meaning Rupert gets to eat the rest. It's an unexpected pleasure – Caro would only ever order a Caesar salad, and while she would never finish it, Rupert doesn't find leftover salad quite so appealing. They talk about Sadie and Miles, about how Emily must meet the children properly soon (a statement that Emily admits makes her nervous – she has zero experience when it comes to entertaining children), and Emily asks about Rupert's job, but he changes the subject. He really doesn't want to talk about work on a Friday evening, even leaving his phone in his jacket pocket so he can't check his emails.

'I could get used to this married life lark,' Emily says with a grin, nudging him in the side as they head back home, and Rupert thinks that maybe, just maybe, he's won her over on staying at home instead of working. They are both a little tipsy, after the wine, some grappa, and Rupert's bright idea of an Irish coffee to finish the evening off. The walk back to the taxi rank takes longer than anticipated as they keep stopping to kiss under the streetlamps, like teenagers, unable to keep their hands off each other.

As they step out of the taxi, Emily sighs and leans against Rupert's shoulder. 'Are you going to take me out for dinner every Friday night?'

'I don't know about that,' Rupert laughs, 'what will I get in return?' He leers at her and she shrieks, kicking up gravel as she runs up the driveway towards the front door, before he catches her and they crash against the solid oak door, kissing, bodies pressed hard together. Emily breaks away, her cheeks flushed and pink as she fumbles for her key.

'Come on, it's bloody freezing out here now.' She shoves open the door, kicking off her shoes and making her way towards the sitting room. 'I forgot to tell you,' she calls out as Rupert takes off his jacket and moves to follow her. Maybe they can go straight upstairs and finish what they started on the doorstep? 'Your mother left a message. Something about Christmas… Oh.'

'What is it?' Rupert stands behind Emily, where she is frozen in front of the fireplace. He follows her gaze, to where, on a mantelpiece that Rupert is sure held only candles and a tiny Tiffany lamp earlier this evening, Caro's face beams out from a photograph. Not just any photograph – framed in heavy silver, it's Rupert and Caro's wedding photo.

Chapter Fifteen

'Did you put that there?' My voice is strangled, and I rest my hand lightly at the base of my throat, my pulse jumping wildly under my fingers. The shock of seeing Caro's face staring out at me from above the fireplace has made my chest tighten, my throat close over.

'Me? No, I didn't put it there.' Rupert steps past me and I catch a whiff of his aftershave. *Hugo Boss*. I bought him a bottle of some swanky Tom Ford aftershave before the wedding, but he rarely seems to use it, instead reaching for the bottles of Hugo Boss that Caro bought him, left in the bathroom cabinet. Habit, I hope, but part of me wants to smash every bottle in the cabinet.

'I'd rather you were just honest with me, Rupert. If you want a photograph of Caro on display, then that's fine. You don't have to sneak it onto the mantelpiece while I'm upstairs changing for dinner.'

'I didn't put it there, Emily! Do you really think that I'd put up a photograph of my dead first wife without speaking to you about it? Did you not notice that there are no photographs of Caro *anywhere* on display in this house?' Rupert marches the few steps across the room to the fireplace and snatches the silver frame up, shaking it in my face.

I take a step back, unnerved by how quickly Rupert has lost his temper. We've gone from pressed against one another, heat drawing us together, to icy cold within a few seconds. I've never seen him like this before; he's always calm and laidback, nothing ever really seems to faze him. A thought flashes through my mind that maybe I don't know him as well as I think I do.

'I'm sorry!' I almost shout the words, splaying my hands in a gesture of apology. Adrenaline makes my legs feel wobbly as I am back there in an instant, and it's Harry's voice I hear shouting at me, just before he lays his hands on me, leaving big, purple bruises on the pale skin of my arms. I draw in a ragged breath, trying to compose myself. *This is Rupert, not Harry.* 'I'm sorry, OK? But Rupert, if you didn't put the picture up there and I didn't put that picture up there, then who did?'

Rupert stares down at Caro's face and I am unsettled by the look that crosses his face as he takes in Caro's features as if recommitting them to memory. 'I don't know. Didn't you say Anya came today? Maybe she put it up?'

'No. That's just it.' Exhausted, I sink into the huge, squashy armchair. 'I don't think she did come today. Amanda said she thought she saw someone leaving at lunchtime and assumed it was her, around the time I was about to crack Sadie's head open with a poker. But if she did work today, then why were your clothes still left all over the floor when I came home?' I scrub my hands tiredly over my face. Any good feeling from our evening out has been washed away in a tide of mistrust and anxiety, and I feel the irresistible urge to fight to get it back.

'Maybe she had to leave suddenly?' Rupert frowns. 'I *don't know*, Emily. But I swear to you that I didn't put that picture up there.'

'What if it wasn't Anya? What if someone else *did* get in the house? Because someone put it up, Rupert. I found a lipstick on the bedside table today… and it matches that shade.' I can feel a mildly hysterical note creeping into my voice as I gesture towards Caro's face, trying to push away the panic at the thought of someone breaking into the house, while at the same time I feel an overwhelming sense of relief that I wasn't imagining things.

'A lipstick?' Rupert looks confused. 'It probably is Caro's; she did live here.'

There is something sharp underlying his tone and I have to blink hard, his words pricking my skin like tiny darts. 'I know that, Rupert, believe me I am fully aware of how Caro lived in this house before me, but I still feel as though someone was in the house.' I can't help the bitter note that sours my tongue, my words coming out with a serrated edge.

'Please, Emily, not this again.' Rupert lays the photo down on the coffee table and comes to sit beside me. 'Em, I've told you there's nothing to worry about. Have you had anything else come to the house? Letters, texts, anything at all?'

I shake my head, avoiding his gaze. 'No. But that doesn't mean...'

'It *does*, Emily,' Rupert says softly. 'No one wants to ruin things between us. I hate to say it, but you are being a bit paranoid – I went through all of this with Caro and I don't think I can do it again, do you understand?'

'What are you saying,' I turn to face him, a sick feeling building in my stomach, 'that you'll leave me?'

'What? No, Emily, God, no.' He takes my hands in his, his palms warm against my icy fingers. 'I think you're a bit overwhelmed, that's all. I think you had a tough time with Harry, you told me that yourself, that he was violent towards you, that he threatened you, and I think maybe you're anxious now that you're finally happy, that someone will find some way to ruin it. I promise you, they won't.'

'That doesn't explain how Caro's photograph suddenly appeared on the mantelpiece though, does it?' Rupert's hand is stroking my hair and I have to fight down the urge to wriggle away from his touch. I can't help feeling as though he is trivialising this. This isn't about Harry; this is about *us*.

'Well, who else was here today, who could have done it?'

'Only Sadie and Amanda,' I say, quietly. 'They both came over for lunch, after the yoga class. That's when Amanda said she thought she saw Anya leaving.'

'Well,' Rupert gets to his feet, picking up the photo frame. 'It definitely wouldn't be either of them.'

'Are you sure?'

'What?'

'Are you sure? That neither Sadie nor Amanda would have put that photograph on display? Because at the end of the day, Rupert, between the letter calling me a bitch and this – not to mention someone changing our wedding song – it feels as though someone is trying to come between us. Why not one of them? Sadie was Caro's best friend, and Amanda was her sister-in-law.'

'Out of the question,' Rupert says, and there is a hint of finality in his tone, 'you're being ridiculous, Emily. Sadie *was* Caro's best friend, now she's yours. Amanda *was* Caro's sister-in-law, and now she's yours. No one is trying to come between us; the only thing that's going to come between us is you thinking that everyone is out to get us.'

I say nothing, blinking back hot tears as I try to process Rupert's words. His reaction is not what I was expecting, and I don't know how to respond. In the end, once I am sure I have my tears under control, I get to my feet trying not to let him see how he's made me feel. How *little* and *pathetic*. 'Of course, you're right. I'm just being silly. I think I'd better go to bed. I've had a bit of a long day.' I brush past him, pausing as I get to the bottom of the stairs. 'If it's OK with you, I'd prefer it you could put the photograph away, or at least display it somewhere a little less… prominent.' Then I turn and hurry up the stairs, without waiting for an answer.

I think about feigning sleep on Monday morning as I hear Rupert up and moving around, getting ready for work, but when he leans over and kisses me, I open my eyes.

'Sorry, I didn't mean to wake you. And I'm sorry about this weekend.' We have barely spoken since Friday night, Rupert busy on Saturday with rugby, and then meeting Will for a few pints after, and me borrowing the car to spend Sunday in Salisbury, browsing the artisan market alone. It would have been that way regardless of whether we had argued on Friday night, our plans already made, but *because* we had argued, I'd felt as though I'd moved through the weekend under a thick black cloud. Rupert's kiss is like a chink of sunlight on a grey day.

'Me too.' I give him a sleepy smile. Part of me does want to stay cross with him, at the way he just seems to brush my concerns aside, but I've been through so much to get where I am – to be with him – that I can't. Rupert kisses me again properly this time, not even minding about morning breath, and I wait until I hear the door snick closed before I get out of bed. Heading straight for the bathroom, I shower quickly and brush my teeth. It sounds ridiculous, but it doesn't seem to matter how many times I brush them, I still think I can taste Friday night's veal at the back of my throat. I managed to mask my horror as Rupert ordered it for me, but I couldn't eat it. I try to drown it out downstairs by making a large mug of coffee, and then heading upstairs to brush my teeth again, but it's still there, coating my tongue and making me feel slightly nauseous. Or maybe that's just nerves.

I'm excited, my stomach fluttering at the thought of what I am about to do today. No more drifting around the house with nothing to do; I'm going to follow Caro's lead. My mouth twists a little at the thought of Caro. Rupert and I didn't discuss the photograph again after Friday night. I don't know where he's put it, and I don't want to know either. All I *do* know is that it isn't on display anywhere, and on Sunday evening when I got back from Salisbury, our own wedding photo was on display in the sitting room. Still, the very fact that Caro's picture somehow found its way onto the fireplace makes me feel unnerved, as though Caro's ghost floats through every room in the house. I wonder briefly whether to ask Sadie or Amanda about it but push the thought away. Like Rupert said, they are my friends now, even if I do feel as though I have only a tenuous grip on the friendship. I'm just starting to feel accepted, and I don't want to accuse them of something and potentially rock the boat. I scoop up my bag and grab my scarf, realizing as I check my watch that I'm going to be late, and that wouldn't do, not today.

Half an hour later I am rushing along the pavement, head down and mindful of what I am about to do, when I collide with someone, losing my grip on my bag – tampons, pens and make-up tumbling out across the pavement as it hits the floor.

'Oh, shit!' I exclaim, as the guilty party, a man in a suit apologizes profusely before dashing away down the street without even offering to give me a hand to pick my things up. Sighing, I crouch down, biting my lip hard in frustration.

'Em? Is that you? Are you all right?'

On hearing a familiar voice, I look up from where I am

scrabbling in the gutter for my favourite mascara, aware of the soggy, blackened leaves perilously close to the hems of my designer jeans, to see Mags standing over me. 'Oh, Mags.' I swallow hard, suddenly caught off-guard. Mags is the last person I was expecting to see. 'Hi. Yes, I'm fine, that… idiot just knocked me flying.'

'Let me help you.' Mags bends down and I am assaulted by that old familiar scent of patchouli oil and weed.

'It's fine, Mags, honestly,' I say as Mags grabs the last of the detritus from the filthy pavement and slides it with a grimace into my bag. 'I should…'

'It's been ages,' Mags interrupts, 'I haven't seen you since you came and got your things. How was the wedding?' Her voice is cool.

I cringe inside a little, guilt making me feel hot and prickly. 'It was lovely, thank you, I'm sorry I…' I break off. *I'm sorry I didn't invite you*, were the words on the tip of my tongue, but it seems too cruel to say it so bluntly. I had had every intention of inviting Mags to the wedding, had even started to write her name on an invitation, but when I thought about the way people – new friends like Sadie and Amanda – would look at Mags, the way Rupert had said, 'Are you *sure* you want her there?', I had torn the invitation in two and stuck it deep down into the kitchen bin. 'I'm sorry.'

'No problem. I was probably busy that day.' Mags sounds hurt, but she hides it with a cool smile, nothing like her usual wide grin. 'Your new life seems to be suiting you, anyway.' She looks me up and down, taking in the expensive jeans, the silk top, the Hermès bag that now swings from my forearm, a honeymoon present from Rupert.

'Look, Mags, I really do have to dash, I'm sorry.' Discreetly, I check my watch again, 'I know I should have called, or come over, or something, but we've only been back from our honeymoon for a few days and things have been kind of manic.'

'Right. Kind of manic, going to that posh leisure centre down the road to do yoga with that girl. What's her name? Sadie.'

I pause, my heart doing a funny stutter in my chest. 'Mags...'

'No, no. It's fine. I only put you back together again after the whole Harry thing. But you know, as long as you have time for yoga with your new friends, that's the most important thing, right?' Mags pulls out a crumpled hand-rolled cigarette and lights it with a flourish. 'Don't worry about it, Em.'

'There's no need to be like that,' I say, but I would feel the same way, I think to myself. Mags has every right to be annoyed with me. 'I'll come and see you next week, shall I? We can have lunch or something.'

'What, you'll invite me over to your big house, with your stone lions, and your big driveway, like you do all your other, new friends? I don't think so, Emily, that's not really my style is it?' Mags turns and starts to walk away, but not before I see the hurt flash across her face. She turns back. 'You've got some post, at the flat, by the way. I'll send it on, shall I?'

I watch silently as Mags strolls away, an unsettled feeling sitting heavy in my stomach. I feel bad about neglecting Mags, of course I do; Mags was the one who gave me somewhere to live and helped me get back on my feet when everything went wrong with Harry. I've been a shit friend, I know that, but Mags was never perfect. I think of the way she wore my clothes without asking, the messages that never reached me, the way I woke up to find her standing at the end of my bed, apparently asleep. And now there's something about the way Mags was with me that has left me feeling a little rattled, but I'm late and shaking the thought from my mind, I hurry up the road to a building on the corner.

I've timed it perfectly. Angus Beaton, head of children's charity The Children's Trust, is juggling his briefcase, hot coffee, a bagel and trying to get the door open with one hand.

'Here, let me—' I push gently past him, holding the door open and then cheekily sliding in after him.

'Thank you.' Angus is walking towards the lift, about to not give me another thought, but I follow him, the heels of my boots clacking across the tiled floor.

'Mr Beaton, isn't it?' When he nods, I stick out a hand for him to shake before I laugh, nodding at the coffee in his left hand and the bagel in his right. No sign of the butterflies that are currently swarming in my stomach. 'Maybe no handshake… I'm Emily Milligan.'

'Pleased to meet you, Miss… Milligan.' Frowning,

Angus punches at the lift button with his thumb. 'Was there something I could help you with? Do you have an appointment with me?'

'It's *Mrs* Milligan. Sorry, I don't have an appointment, and I know I'm being a bit cheeky just turning up like this... although I prefer to say, motivated and acting on my own initiative,' I give another tinkling laugh, as I follow him into the lift, 'but it's about your fundraising and communication department... my husband donates to you quite a lot, and from your literature you've sent to him, I understand you currently have a vacancy?'

It's only later, when I have taken myself out for a celebratory lunch of sushi and Sauvignon, congratulating myself on taking the initiative and bagging myself what did – in the end – turn out to be a sort of job interview, although it is of course a voluntary position to begin with, just like Caro's, that I remember about Mags, and the chill that settled on me when she left. It's only now, when I've had a chance to sit and relax for five minutes, to process the whole conversation, that I realize what made me feel so rattled. How did Mags specifically know that I was doing a yoga class at the leisure centre? Even I didn't know until that morning. I sip at my cold wine as I think, but the icy finger that runs down my back has nothing to do with the ice in my glass as another thought strikes me. *How does Mags know where I live, when I've never given her the address?*

Chapter Sixteen

Rupert and I are back on track after our rocky weekend, and I am trying to keep things that way. I haven't mentioned seeing Mags, or the strange unsettled feeling that comes over me when I replay our conversation in my head, the way she knew where I lived, and where I had been. I've also pushed away the way Rupert's face changed that night, contorted into some ugly expression of anger and something that almost looked like fear. If I close my eyes, Harry's face replaces Rupert's and I see him coming for me, spittle flying from his mouth as he shouts, vicious words pouring from his lips as he calls me a bitch and his outstretched hands close around my throat. *Rupert is nothing like Harry*, I tell myself as we snuggle onto the sofa together each evening, my head on his chest, his fingers entangled in my hair, our hearts beating in rhythm. Maybe Rupert is right; I am so worried about someone wrecking this happy place I've found myself in that I keep finding things that point to everything going wrong. There have been no more letters, no more texts, no more disturbances that make me feel watched, hunted. All I need now to make everything perfect is for Angus Beaton to call and offer me a job.

I am sat in bed, reluctant to start my Friday even though it's nearly ten o'clock and Anya will be here at any minute to start cleaning the house, when my mobile rings. I check the screen, expecting it to be either Sadie or Rupert – after all, they are the only people who call me these days; Mags doesn't have my new number and I haven't heard from my mum since before the wedding, despite emailing her the photos – and when I see who it is my heart does a little leap in my chest. It's Angus Beaton, calling from The Children's Trust. I give a tiny yelp of excitement, pressing my hand to my mouth before smoothing back my curls, even though I know Angus can't see me.

'Hello?' I inject a question into my voice, even though I have Angus's number memorized, and I feel like I've been waiting forever for him to call me.

'Ahhh… Mrs Milligan? Emily?' He sounds different on the phone to how he does in real life, almost nervous.

'Yes, this is Emily. Angus, how lovely to hear from you.' I shift slightly in the bed, before pushing back the duvet and swinging my legs out, a shiver of anticipation running down my spine. I feel as though I've been waiting weeks for Angus to call, spending hours walking in the park, and doing class after class of yoga (although not at the one Sadie goes to) in an effort to pass the time every day. It feels wrong now to be lounging in bed when I hear whether Angus will let me come and work for him. I stand, pulling my long T-shirt down over my knickers, a faint chill about my legs where the heating has gone off.

'Sorry it's taken me a while to get back to you, I had a number of factors to consider, you understand?' He sounds more confident now, more like the man I met in the office.

'Of course, it's no problem. I understand. I know I don't have a lot of experience, but I am willing to learn, and as I said to you before, my husband is very committed to The Children's Trust.' I hold my breath, waiting for his response. I'm still not too sure why this charity is so important to Rupert, why he donates such a large amount to them every month; all I know is that if I can tell him I'm going to be working there I'm sure he'll be pleased. He'll understand that I'm doing the very best I can to fit in with what is important to him.

'Listen, Emily, you were very impressive when you came to see me. Very impressive indeed...'

'Thank you,' I blurt out, wanting him to just say yes or no, to get to the point and stop beating around the bush.

'But unfortunately, in this instance, we won't be able to offer you the vacancy in our fundraising department.'

'What?' Pressing the phone hard against my ear, I want him to repeat it, sure that I have misheard him.

'I'm really sorry, Emily. It's vital that we get the right person.' Angus is quiet, apologetic.

'But it's a *voluntary* position at first,' I say, still not quite sure I have heard Angus correctly. If I'm honest, I thought I had it in the bag, and I was looking forward to having some sense of purpose back in my day. 'I'm offering you my time and my skills for nothing. I would have thought that that would be enough.'

'Well, of course we appreciate that, but like I said, I had a number of factors to consider. I'm very sorry to disappoint you. We have events throughout the year – you're more than welcome to come along and support us at these.'

I murmur something – I'm not even sure what I've said – into the phone and then hang up, sinking onto the chaise longue under the window sill. I can't understand what has gone so wrong. Angus and I got along famously when I went to his office. Maybe that was the problem? Maybe I came on too strong? Perhaps I should have called him, rather than just turn up there, but I thought if I called, he might have hung up on me or I might not have even been able to get through to him at all. There must have been *something* I did wrong – I was offering my time for no pay – so why on earth would he turn that down? I get up from the chaise longue – *Caro's* chaise longue – and move towards the bathroom, disappointment bitter on my tongue. There is that old familiar feeling of somehow failing, of somehow not being enough, lurking over my shoulder and I stare into the bathroom mirror, taking in every inch of my face. *How would Caro have reacted to this?* I think, pulling at the skin around my eyes, dismayed by the way it crinkles slightly under my fingertip, *she'd probably have taken to her bed. You're better than that,* I tell myself.

★

I am already dressed, ready to go out for Miles's birthday dinner when Rupert arrives home from work that evening. I perch on the chaise, smiling prettily at Rupert as he emerges from the en suite in a cloud of aftershave and scented steam, a small towel round his waist.

'Come here.' He pulls me to my feet, twirling me in my tight-fitting dress. 'God, do we have to go out? Miles won't even notice if we don't turn up.' He nibbles at my neck and my knees go weak.

'Yes, we do. Miles has booked some place in town, and the cab will be here any minute.' I kiss him back, already feeling better now that he's home, and spin away towards the mirror to fix my hair. I watch him in the mirror as he smooths his hair down, fastens his shirt buttons and think again how lucky I am to be here, in this house, with him.

My good feeling doesn't last too long, though. I don't mention the call from Angus until we are in the cab on the way to the restaurant, and only then because he asks if I am OK.

'Em, is everything OK? You're very quiet.' Rupert reaches for my hand, fiddling with the pair of diamond cut rings – one for engagement, one for wedding – that adorn my third finger.

'Not really,' I turn and give him a thin smile. I thought I had managed to convince myself that it didn't matter, but clearly it does. To me, anyway. 'I heard from Angus Beaton today.'

'Angus Beaton?' Rupert says, pulling his fingers away. 'What are you doing talking to Angus Beaton?'

'The Children's Trust?' I say hesitantly. 'You donate to them every month, their letters are always sitting in the post pile. I went to see Angus, to see if I could start volunteering with him, but for some weird reason he said no. I did mention it to you when we went out for dinner. You said it was OK.'

Rupert is silent for a long moment, and I can feel the beginnings of a headache thumping at my temples. 'Well,' he says, eventually, 'it's not like you need to work anyway, is it? Probably for the best.'

'It's not about *working*, Rupert,' I say testily, a buzz of irritation vibrating under my skin. 'I just don't understand *why* he turned me down. I mean, I'm offering him my time and my skills, *for free* – at first anyway – and they are a charity, for goodness' sake. You'd think that they'd snap my hand off for offering, especially since…' I stop, turning to look out of the window. 'I thought Angus and I got on really well, the interview was excellent. I'm just disappointed, I suppose. I was looking forward to having something to do every day.'

Rupert says nothing for a moment. 'I'm sure something else will come up,' he says eventually, the relief when our cab pulls up outside the restaurant and he can avoid talking about it anymore evident on his face. He helps me from the car, pulling me to his side as we step over a large puddle. 'Come on,' he says, squeezing my shoulder a bit too tightly, 'it's not the end of the world. I'm sure, if you really, really want to volunteer then there will be somewhere else that could make good use of you.'

I can't help feeling as though Rupert has just brushed the whole thing away like it's nothing. *Again.* And it's not nothing, not to me anyway. I can't help believing that he wouldn't have reacted that way if Caro had been upset. I have to force myself not to think like that, and I sneak a glance at Rupert, as we enter the upmarket Chinese restaurant Miles has chosen, reminding myself that he's *my* husband now.

I shake the feeling off, determined not to spoil the evening and soon feel better once we get inside. The others are already here and are seated with the men at one end of the table and the wives at the other, and I won't lie, I feel a little relieved by this seating arrangement. At least I can relax and have a drink with Sadie and Amanda without having to pretend I'm not annoyed with Rupert. I hope they will be a little more sympathetic to my disappointment.

'You look gorgeous, I love how you've done your hair.' Sadie sits down next to me and passes me a pisco sour. I have never had one before, not that I'm going to admit that to Sadie, and the combination of pisco and lime dances on my tongue.

'Thanks. I'm looking forward to having a drink tonight, if you must know.' I raise my cocktail glass, the foam from the egg white running over the top, making my fingers sticky.

'Bad day?' Sadie puts her head on one side and pouts. I get the feeling that maybe this cocktail isn't Sadie's first drink of the day.

'Ugh. You could say that. I got a phone call from the guy at The Children's Trust.'

'Oh?' A look crosses Sadie's face, her brows drawing tightly together. 'What about?'

'After we talked about doing charity work at lunch the other week, I went to see him about volunteering in their fundraising department – basically he called me today and turned me down.' I make a face and sip at my drink, the alcohol buzzing straight to my head.

'Perhaps it's for the best. Everything happens for a reason and all that.' Sadie is brisk, brushing it aside in much the same way Rupert did, although this time there is an underlying edge to her voice as if I have said something wrong.

'Maybe.' I eye her closely, as she looks down the table to where Rupert, Miles and Will are all talking animatedly. 'Sadie, did I do something wrong? You seem a little… I don't know. Is it something about Angus and the trust?'

'Look, if you must know…' Sadie folds her napkin into tiny squares, her immaculate nail polish catching the light. 'The Children's Trust… it's where Caro used to work. You caught me by surprise, mentioning the name of it, mentioning Angus.'

'Oh my God.' I sit back, my hand covering my mouth. The pisco sour is a heavy, sticky mass in my stomach. 'The vacancy in the fundraising department isn't Caro's job, is it? I had no idea.'

'Well, why would you? I mean, it's not like we talk about it, is it? And Angus probably had no idea who you are. Don't take it to heart, him saying you weren't right for the job. He always was a fussy old bugger, according to Caro.' Sadie rests her hand on mine, patting it as if to comfort me.

'No, of course. I feel like a fool… Rupert never mentioned it when I told him I'd been speaking with Angus.' A bloom of hurt bursts in my chest and I have to swallow hard. No wonder Rupert has been donating so much money for all this time. It was all for Caro. I feel sick as I picture his face when I mentioned Angus's name.

'He probably didn't want to upset you. Like I said, Em, don't take it to heart.'

'Here you are, ladies—' Amanda appears beside us, a waiter stood next to her with a tray full of more pisco sours. 'Emily, nice to see you.' She gives me a kiss on the cheek, the overwhelming scent of her perfume tickling the back of my throat. She slides into the seat next to me and starts talking about her latest design project. When I look up the table at Rupert, he is engaged in conversation with Miles, so I reach for another cocktail, trying to push Sadie's comments from my mind, feeling like the biggest kind of idiot.

We order food, and the conversation turns to more general things – work, holidays, what everyone will be doing for Christmas. The food is fancy – not the Chinese food I am used to, slumped on the overstuffed sofa at the flat with Mags – there are fat, plump dim sum crammed full of seafood and chicken, thinly sliced duck, bowls of fragrant rice. I struggle with the chopsticks, having never learnt to use them properly, and my cheeks burn as Sadie whispers to a waiter and he returns a few minutes later with a knife and fork, laying them carefully on the table next to me. It doesn't take long for the conversation to turn into a game of 'remember when', and I paste a smile on my face as they all talk about things that happened long before I met Rupert.

'Remember the Norway flight, Rupert?' Sadie gives a ladylike snort of laughter as Rupert grins and covers his face with his hands.

'Never been on a flight like it, before or since,' he laughs. 'It was so rough even I was throwing up, and I always say I've a cast-iron stomach.'

'Caro was the only one who didn't look like she'd been run over,' Amanda says, turning to me. 'It was horrendous, Emily, the worst flight we've ever been on.'

'I can imagine,' I say, wishing desperately that the conversation would turn back to things we can all discuss.

'Or that time we went to the college wrestling, and Miles got given an atomic wedgie.' Will can barely get the words out he's laughing so hard, which sets the others off as Miles bangs the table in protest.

'No, no, I gave *him* an atomic wedgie!'

They all erupt into hysterics, as I sit there forcing out laughter, feeling alone and adrift as they reminisce about things that I have no idea about. I finish my drink and wait, staring into my empty glass with its sticky egg foam wash around the rim, trying not to make my discomfort evident until finally Will says, 'Come on, guys, let's not forget about Emily, she wasn't around for this stuff, remember? Sorry, Em.'

'It's OK,' I say, injecting amusement into my tone, 'it's very interesting to hear what Rupert got up before I was on the scene.'

Rupert gives me a small smile and a wink, and says, 'Nothing as interesting as the things I get up to now you *are* on the scene.'

The table falls silent, and I feel it again, the ghost of Caro filling the room as clearly as if she were sat at the table next to me.

'Let's go dancing,' Will says, jumping up from the table, and the thick silence is broken. 'Girls, are you up for a night of wild clubbing?'

Sadie bursts out laughing. 'Bloody hell, Will, I don't know about that, I've got to be up at the crack of dawn with the twins.'

'Don't you mean the nanny has to be up at the crack of dawn with the twins?' Amanda says, laughing as Sadie looks at her in mock horror. 'How about Salamander's?'

They all murmur their agreement, and as we walk outside to catch a cab – we could walk, but Sadie is already bitching about her heels – I loop my arm through Rupert's, wanting to be close to him after feeling so out in the cold.

'I've never been to Salamander's,' I say, trying to ease the worry from my face. I've found the evening overwhelming and I am floundering a little, out of my depth. To now have to go to the most exclusive club in the county makes my stomach swoop, and a thick nausea rise in my throat; I don't know if it is nerves or pisco. I'm not sure I am ready for Salamander's. Part of me longs for our big, cosy bed, the blinds closed against the outside world, just the two of us together. 'Do I look OK?'

'Absolutely.' Rupert leans down and kisses me, making my heart skip a beat. Whatever happens between us, nothing seems to kill that flame that he sparks in me. 'You look perfect.'

'I didn't even know you were a member there.'

'Yes, for years. How was your meal? You girls looked thick as thieves down that end of the table.'

'Oh. It was lovely.' I keep my eyes on the pavement, careful not to trip on the uneven slabs, as I wonder whether to tell him that I know about Caro and Angus Beaton. 'It was nice to talk properly with Amanda, too. I think that's the first time we've had a proper conversation.'

'Right. Well, that's good. It's nice to see all you ladies getting along together.' Rupert sticks his hand out and a black cab glides to the edge of the kerb, and my opportunity to speak frankly to him is lost. 'Here.' He opens the door for me, Sadie appearing by my side. 'You girls jump in. We'll meet you there.'

Salamander's is like nothing I have ever experienced before. I watch Sadie and Amanda closely, making sure that I don't slip up and do anything to embarrass myself, always conscious that fitting in is a full-time job by itself. Feeling myself getting tipsy, I excuse myself from the dance floor and head to the bar, asking the barman for a soda water. As I slide onto a barstool, trying not to gawp at the lizard-inspired décor now that I have a moment to myself, I notice Rupert and Amanda at the far end of the bar, heads angled close together as they talk. I feel remarkably less annoyed at Rupert now – I haven't forgiven him for not mentioning that Caro worked at The Children's Trust, not by a long shot – but the booze has settled in my veins, making me feel less spiky. He probably didn't say anything because, like Sadie said, he knew it would make me feel awkward. I feel a sudden rush of love for him, and slide from the bar stool. I totter along towards them, careful not to spill my drink, until I am standing close enough to catch the odd word of their conversation.

'. . . Angus Beaton,' Amanda is saying. Her mouth is downturned, and she raises her glass in a jabbing motion towards Rupert. Rupert is replying, and I step forward, my hand poised to tap him on the shoulder.

'. . . and wrong, somehow. Em isn't Caro, she never will be.' Rupert's words reach my ears and it's like I've been drenched with a bucket of cold water. I step forward, my stomach churning.

'Everything OK, you two?' I say brightly, looking from one to the other.

'Absolutely dandy,' Rupert says, in that fake posh way he puts on sometimes in front of his friends. His hand slides around my waist and then down to rest on my bum and I resist the urge to pull away.

'Amanda, is everything OK?' I press, as Amanda knocks

179

back the rest of her drink and avoids my eye. 'You two looked very intense, you weren't arguing, were you?'

'No. God, no, of course not,' Rupert says, 'just catching up. Are you OK, darling?'

'I need another drink. Excuse me, Emily, won't you?' Amanda turns, swaying slightly on her heels, before heading towards the bar, her empty glass clutched tightly in one hand. I look up at Rupert, drinking in his features, my heart lurching in my chest as I hear his words again. That I'm not Caro and never will be.

'Rupert, is that true? Is everything all right between you two? It looked as though… well, Amanda didn't look very happy.'

'Ahh, you know how she is…' Rupert leans down, his lips searching for mine, but I place my hand on his chest to stop him and his mouth twists in irritation. 'Em, please. You must know what she's like by now. She loves a drink, doesn't know when to stop. Sometimes her mouth runs away with her. She just pissed me off a bit and I was telling her to give it a rest.'

'Right.' I don't know what to think. I didn't hear the full conversation, I don't know why Rupert said that about me not being Caro, but maybe he was standing up for me if Amanda had said something out of order. She doesn't keep it a secret that she idolized Caro, but I had thought that she and I were becoming friendlier, if not quite properly friends.

'Come on—' Rupert drags me towards the dance floor, wrapping his arms around me and I breathe in the familiar scent of him, let him press his body against mine, and try to forget Amanda, standing watching us from the bar.

★

Rupert passes me a large mug of coffee as we sit at the breakfast table the next morning, my head fuzzy and my temples thumping from too much alcohol and a distinct lack of sleep. I was exhausted by the time we fell in the door at 3 a.m., but as I lay in our huge bed, Rupert's arm around my waist as his breath whistled softly in my ear, I couldn't sleep, my mind going over and over the words I had heard exchanged between Rupert and Amanda. Now, I am hot and prickly, my brain feeling foggy, and I jump when my mobile beeps. It's a text message from an unknown number. I glance at Rupert, where he stands at the stove attempting to make pancakes, before my gaze drifts back to the screen and with a thumping heart I swipe to open it.

Ask your husband why Angus Beaton didn't take you on.

A sharp intake of breath, and my throat thickens as I look up to see Rupert frowning over me.

'Em? What's the matter?' His brow is creased with concern, and his hair sticks up on one side. His cheeks are dark with a day's worth of stubble, and as I look at his familiar face I think for a moment, *Do I know you? Do I even really know you?* I don't speak, instead I just hand him my phone.

181

'Oh shit, Em,' he sighs, laying the phone on the table and pulling out the chair next to me. 'Who sent you this?'

'I don't know, it's from an unknown number,' I say, 'but aren't you going to say something? Explain it?'

He scrubs his hand though his hair, and I feel a surge of anger. 'Explain, Rupert. What the hell is going on?'

'Look—' He reaches for my hand and I pull away, hurt smarting my insides. 'It wasn't meant to be anything… I didn't want to upset you.'

'Rupert, for fuck sakes just explain yourself.' My tone is cold, and I wrap my arms across my body, not wanting him to touch me.

'Yes, OK,' he says eventually, 'yes, I did have something to do with Angus not taking you on but let me explain. I didn't realize at first that The Children's Trust was where you were looking at volunteering, but then I saw a message on your phone from Angus thanking you for coming in and I freaked out. I called him and told him not to take you on.'

'But why, Rupert? I don't understand. I wanted to do something with my time, and I chose Angus because I knew his charity was important to you. I wanted to do it for you.'

'Because of Caro, OK?' Rupert shoves his chair back and starts pacing the kitchen. 'Because Caro worked there, and it was *bad* for her. She saw such awful things, heard such awful stories, and it really affected her mental health.' He pauses for a moment, takes a minute to steady his breathing. 'I am pretty sure that the things she saw, the things she

182

heard about there were partly to blame for why she did what she did and I didn't want the same to happen to you.'

'Oh, Rupert!' I get to my feet and go to him, wrapping my arms around his waist. 'I'm not like Caro.' His words from the previous evening ring in my ears and I let go of any residual anger. 'You don't need to worry about me, but you should have spoken to me, not gone behind my back.'

'I know that now.' Rupert looks down at me, and my heart breaks at the expression in his eyes. 'I'm so sorry, Em, it's just… all that stuff about people watching you, horrid messages… Caro said the same things to me and it was all in her head and I just got so… frightened that I reacted without thinking. I can't lose you, too. I love you so much.'

Tears spill over my cheeks as I lift my face, reaching up to kiss him. 'I love you too, I understand now. I don't need to volunteer there; I can find something else.'

It's only later, after we have abandoned the cold, flabby pancakes and gone back to bed, taking our time over making love, my skin on fire as he trails his fingers over my stomach, and down my inner thighs, that it comes to me. Later, once he is asleep and I am laid awake, fingers of sunlight creeping through the gaps in the blinds as the street below hums with the sound of a hedge trimmer somewhere further down the lane, that someone sent that text message. Someone knew what Rupert had done and had deliberately sent me that text in order to bring uncertainty and mistrust into our lives. If Rupert has lied to me about this, what else has he lied to me about?

Chapter Seventeen

'Ready to go *proper* shopping?' Sadie is standing on the doorstep, her car – complete with driver – idling at the kerb waiting to whisk us away to London for the day.

'Ready.' I flash her a quick smile, as I slide my new black American Express card into my bag. Rupert presented me with it a few days after I found out about his role in Angus turning me down, and although it feels like a guilt present, I accepted it without an argument.

'Ooh, fancy,' Sadie says as she watches me tuck my purse into my bag. 'Rupert had some making up to do by the looks of things.'

I give her a look; not sure quite how much Rupert has told her about our argument the day after Miles's birthday dinner. 'No, not at all. He just knows I need to do some Christmas shopping, that's all.'

Fatigue tugs at my bones, as I turn and scan the hallway, as if committing it to memory. Rupert has been home late every night for the past few weeks, and several times the phone has rung late in the evening, only for there to be no one there when I answer it. Every time I answer with a brisk hello, without giving my name, I am met with a yawning chasm of dead air, punctuated only by the sound of the other person's breathing. Breathing that I have convinced myself sounds like Harry, although of course I can't be sure of it. It never happens when Rupert is in the house, only when I am alone, and I have found myself lying awake at night, willing the phone to ring so that Rupert can answer it and I won't sound mad when I tell him it's been happening regularly. The idea that Harry knows where I am, that he knows when I am alone... that all he has to do is pick up the phone and dial a number and he is there, battering his way into this safe haven I have created for myself, makes my heart race and my skin prickle with fear and anxiety.

Satisfied that everything is as it should be, that if I came home and something was out of place I would know, I usher Sadie out and tug the front door closed, checking it twice, then again that the door is double locked.

'All set?' Sadie asks, as I turn and look over the front of the house, making sure all the front windows are closed.

'All set,' I say with a small smile, as the telephone starts to ring behind the tightly locked door.

Hours later, we are in the café at Harrods, a superfood salad in front of each of us, along with a glass of champagne. I would rather have had the cinnamon apple braffle – a Harrods speciality – but when Sadie ordered a salad, I felt I had to do the same. I pick at it listlessly, not enjoying the combination of beetroot and goat's cheese. I realize that

Sadie has picked out her goat's cheese and left it to one side, so I don't feel so guilty about doing the same. My feet are throbbing, my Am Ex has taken a beating, but I would still rather be sitting here, with a lunch I don't want to eat, than be at home on my own.

'Is everything all right, Emily?' Sadie takes a sip of her champagne, still looking as immaculate as she did when she picked me up. Her black bob is still sleek and her make-up perfect, whereas when I went to the Ladies I had to smooth down my curls and lick my finger to get rid of the slight smudge of mascara that was under my eyes. 'You seem a little… I don't know – subdued, maybe? Not your usual bubbly self.'

I take a deep breath and fork a mouthful of salad into my mouth to buy myself a few seconds before I respond. Do I really want to confide in Sadie? She has been a lot nicer to me recently than she was at first, but I am still aware that she has been friends with Rupert for a long time. 'Yes, of course. I'm fine.' But as I speak my eyes fill with tears and a wave of tiredness washes over me.

'Oh?' Sadie raises an eyebrow, before she reaches over and scoops up my hand, holding it tightly. 'Your face rather says otherwise. Darling, you can tell me. I'm always here if you need to talk. Caro and I always used to talk about things, get them off our chests. What seems to be the matter?'

'I think I'm just being silly,' I say, blinking rapidly. 'Things have happened since the wedding that feel a little… off. I don't know, I think maybe I'm going mad.' I force out a breath that could be taken for a huff of laughter.

'Try me,' Sadie says, pushing her plate to one side. 'And you never know, it might help to get things off your chest.'

'I keep feeling as though someone has been in the house,' I say bluntly, the words tumbling out in a rush. 'I first felt it when we came home from honeymoon, but Rupert just put it down to Amanda taking care of the house. Of course, it felt as though someone had been in there.' I carry on, seeing Caro's face smiling out from her wedding photo in pride of place on the mantelpiece.

'Perhaps the cleaner put it out? She might not have realized what she was doing.'

'Really?' I look at her incredulously. 'No, it wasn't Anya. And it definitely felt as though someone had been in the house that day. I was showering and I just got that feeling that I wasn't alone.' I wait a moment, before deciding to tell Sadie everything. I might as well, now she knows this much. 'And there have been calls.'

'What do you mean, *calls*?' Sadie asks.

'Dropped calls, calls where nobody speaks, just breaths down the line. It never happens when Rupert is there, only when I'm on my own, and always late at night. I'm so on edge, I jump out of my skin every time the telephone rings. And then there are the text messages.'

'Text messages?'

I reel off the messages, knotting my fingers together as I picture the photograph of me, my sash loose around my body as I rush fearfully down a deserted street in Bristol.

'Oh my God, Em. Have you told Rupert about it?'

'I tried,' I sigh, fiddling with my wedding ring, aware

that it is looser on my finger than it was three months ago. 'I told him how I felt and he just kind of… brushed it aside. Said I was imagining things. He said he'd been through it all before with Caro.'

'Oh. I see.' Sadie waves over the waiter and orders another two glasses of champagne. 'Listen, I can sort of see his point. Caro was… He had some difficult times with Caro, and it's probably hard for him to deal with it. Maybe you shouldn't tell him about it, not unless you have proof that you can show him. Do you still have the text messages?'

'No, I deleted them. I should have kept them, shouldn't I? I feel like such an idiot, but honestly, Sadie, it made me feel ill just to know that they were on my phone.'

'Look, without actual proof it's going to be hard to make Rupert listen. I'm not dismissing it, Emily, you know I would never do that, but I think perhaps you are reading a little too much into things, when there are perfectly reasonable explanations. The calls could just be a wrong number… the photo could have been put up by the cleaner—' she holds up a hand before I can speak, 'no, I know you disagree, but you haven't actually asked her, have you? How are you sleeping?'

'I'm barely sleeping at all at the moment, and not just because I'm worried about things.' I swat at my cheeks, at the tear that runs slowly down my face. 'It's just so *hard*, Sadie. The whole marriage thing. I don't mean to sound cruel, but it's difficult for us to make a life together when Caro is everywhere. I feel like I'm constantly battling her ghost.'

'But Rupert doesn't talk about her that much, does he?' Sadie leans in close, her perfectly groomed eyebrows meeting in concern.

'It's not that. She's just left reminders everywhere. Like, on our honeymoon, I know he'd been to the island before, but I'm sure he'd been to the restaurant we ate at, too, presumably with Caro. Just from a few little things that he let slip... the maître d' seemed to know him, and he commented that the menu was amazing before we'd even seen it.'

'He could have googled it, to be fair.'

'He could, but I just got the feeling that he was familiar with the place. I waited and waited for him to say something and he didn't. And he's just a bit distant sometimes, I suppose, compared to when we were first dating.'

Sadie looks as though she'd like to say something before she smiles and moves on. 'Look, marriage is difficult. It wasn't all plain sailing for Rupert and Caro either, you know.'

'No?' I raise my tear-stained face to meet Sadie's eyes.

'No, of course not. They argued like any other couple.'

'About what?'

'Well, that isn't for me to say,' Sadie says primly, and I feel like a klutz, putting my foot in it. Of course, Sadie isn't going to tell me things that Caro told her in confidence. 'All I will say is that life is never perfect, Emily. Now, come on, let's go and fix that make-up.'

I let Sadie lead me into the Ladies, where she disappears into a cubicle and I delve into my handbag to pull out a lipstick. Only, when I slide off the lid, instead of the almost nude pink I'm expecting to see, it's Caro's distinctive orangey-red and the blood in my veins turns to ice.

The night sky is clear and dotted with stars as we drive along the lane that leads to the house, the glow of the single streetlamp across the street making things feel sinister rather than comforting, and I find myself anxiously scanning the darkened windows for signs of movement as we pull up. Sadie marches inside and goes straight to the fridge to open a bottle of wine, as if she owns the place, leaving me to slide reluctantly out of the warm, luxurious car, smiling at the driver, before I walk across the gravelled drive to the front door. My steps are heavy, my feet reluctant to move towards the house. There is a tiny tug of fear as I step inside, a knot of worry that picks at my insides as I wonder whether I'm walking into yet another surprise – another photo of Caro, the faint scent of her perfume staining the air in my bedroom. Stepping into the kitchen where Sadie is pouring two huge glasses of Sancerre, I let out a long breath in relief at everything seemingly undisturbed.

'Here. You look like you could do with this.' Sadie hands me a glass and I take a healthy swig. 'It's not just the shopping that's got you looking so washed out, is it? You really are worried about things?'

'Yeah,' I admit, nodding slowly, 'yes, I am worried. A bit. But maybe it just feels worse because I'm tired.'

I do feel better after talking to Sadie today, and standing in the kitchen, the bright lights overhead adding to the warmth of the centrally heated room, I think that maybe I have let things become bigger in my own mind than they really are.

'Darling, perhaps you should consider calling the police,' Sadie says, but she is frowning as if even though she has suggested it, she doesn't really think it's a good idea.

'Do you think?'

'Well… you could, if you were really worried. But in all honesty, darling, I don't think they'll do very much.' Sadie gives a shrug. 'When Will and Amanda had all those problems with the gypsies that moved in at the bottom of their garden, the police didn't want anything to do with it.'

I don't know anything about that, but I do know that Will and Amanda's house backs onto a country park, so I'm pretty sure Sadie is exaggerating things when she says 'back garden'.

'And anyway,' Sadie goes on, 'you two are rock solid – it doesn't matter what anyone says or does – you two are happy, even if you are feeling a bit strained at the moment.'

'Hmmm.' I sip at my wine, pretty sure that Sadie only hears what she wants to hear.

'You are happy, aren't you? Leaving Caro out of it for a moment – the two of you are OK?' Frowning, Sadie lays a hand on mine, her fake-tanned skin a warm orange against the pale white of my fingers, my honeymoon tan long gone.

'Yes,' I stare down at our hands, feeling a little disloyal to Rupert, 'but like I said earlier at lunch… things are a little harder than I thought they would be. Rupert isn't quite like I thought.'

'Oh?' Sadie raises an eyebrow and I feel a flutter of panic, remembering that Sadie has been Rupert's friend for a lot longer than she's been mine.

'I don't mean that in a horrid way!' I backtrack. 'I just mean things like… well, he ordered my meal for me the last time we went out, and he ordered veal. I hate veal, and I tried to tell him, but he just ignored me and ordered it anyway. And he always asks me every morning what I'm doing that day. It's not a problem, but it just feels a little controlling.' I fiddle with my glass, feeling heat creep into my cheeks. 'He has more of a temper than I realized.'

Sadie reaches for the wine bottle and tops her glass up. 'Do you know what I think?' she says in the end. 'I think perhaps you're a little sensitive to things like that after what happened with Harry. Rupert isn't trying to control you; he's trying to look after you.'

'He's the reason why Angus Beaton didn't want me volunteering at the charity,' I blurt out, a twist of hurt digging in my chest.

'Rupert is?' Sadie frowns.

'He basically told Angus he didn't want me there because of Caro. I wished I'd known before that Caro had worked there.'

Sadie blushes, a pink bloom bursting over her cheeks. 'If I'd known you were going to apply there, then of course I would have told you. Like I said, Emily, I don't think he's trying to control you, he just wants what is best for you. For both of you.'

'I'm sure you're probably right,' I say with a sigh, 'I'm

just being an ungrateful brat, aren't I? God, I bet Caro was never like this.'

Sadie doesn't reply, instead checking her watch and pushing her chair back. 'I'll just nip to the loo before I get off. And yes,' Sadie grins, 'you're being an ungrateful brat.'

I sit in silence as I wait for Sadie to come back from the bathroom, our conversation buzzing around in my head. Sadie is right, I am just being silly. It was never going to be easy, Rupert and I adjusting to married life after dating for such a short time, and I'm glad I plucked up the courage to talk to Sadie. Married life is never plain sailing, and Sadie hinted at the fact that things weren't perfect between Rupert and Caro. I frown as I mull over Sadie's words, wondering exactly what it was that wasn't perfect between them. Rupert has only mentioned one or two things about Caro – mainly about her mental health – and given the choice doesn't really talk about Caro, not to me anyway. In fact, I'd go so far as to say I've felt a little fobbed off at times when I have asked about her. I pick up my phone, toying with the idea of texting my mum and asking her advice, but then I remember that she still hasn't replied to the last text I sent her, and I lay my phone back on the table, pressing the side button to turn the screen black.

Em is not Caro, she never will be. Rupert's words to Amanda come back to me and I take another sip of my wine, now warm and sour on my tongue, the beginnings of a headache starting to thump at my temples. I'm not sure whether the fact that Rupert said I'm not Caro is a good thing or bad thing now, after what Sadie said earlier.

Sadie enters the kitchen, rubbing her hands together, her huge handbag already over her shoulder. 'Thank you for a lovely day, darling. I hope I haven't upset you, talking about Caro. You and Rupert are wonderful together, despite what some people think.' I get to my feet and Sadie flaps a hand in my direction. 'Darling, I have to go. I haven't seen the children all day, and I wasn't there to put them to bed last night either; they'll be a nightmare for the nanny tonight if I don't get back. Don't get up, you look exhausted.'

'Thank you for today, Sadie, sorry if I…'

'Oh, don't be silly. Nothing to be sorry for, we all have our ups and downs. Just so long as you know I'm always here if you want to chat.' Sadie puts her head on one side. 'We'll go to yoga next week, shall we? That might help.'

'Oh no,' I say, almost knocking my wine glass over in my haste to stand up, 'I can't. We're going to Rupert's parents for Christmas and to be honest, Rupert isn't too keen on me going there again.'

'Oh.' Sadie looks away, fiddling with the strap of her bag. 'Well, no problem. You two have a lovely Christmas together, won't you? I'm assuming Will and Amanda are going to be there too?'

'Yes. Everyone will be there.' I'm looking forward to it. It's been a very long time since I got to experience a proper family Christmas. Although if I'm really honest, I'm not sure the Christmases I spent fighting with other kids who weren't my siblings after my mother remarried really count as proper Christmases. *See?* A voice says at the back of my mind, *You don't know how lucky you are. Rupert is giving you something you've never had before – he's not just given you a safe place to live, he's given you a family.*

Sadie leans over and kisses me on the cheek, her thick floral scent making me want to cough as she gives me a hug. 'Don't see me out, you look utterly exhausted. Go and have a hot bath before your handsome husband comes home.' With a wink, Sadie floats out of the kitchen on a cloud of perfume and wine, leaving me at the table alone.

I am sticking the receipts from my day out with Sadie into my scrapbook, alongside a perfume sample and a picture of the two of us together at Salamander's, printed from my phone – a record of happy memories, I tell myself – when the doorbell makes me jump. I pause, my heart thudding in my chest as I glance towards the window automatically, despite the inky blackness outside making it impossible to see who is there, just my own shocked face reflected back at me in the glass. Slowly I close the scrapbook, stuffing it under a sofa cushion to be retrieved later, and walk towards the oak front door, my fingers trembling slightly as I reach for the lock. *Sadie just forgot something,* I tell myself as I take a deep breath, preparing to pull the heavy door open, *Rupert forgot his keys, that's all it is.* But I know Rupert won't be home for hours, and Sadie left nothing behind. I yank the door open, but the figure on the doorstep is the last person I was expecting to see.

'Mags.' I hear the note of delight in my voice, and I realize that I've missed Mags more than I have admitted to myself.

'Glad you're pleased to see me,' Mags says, and I am relieved to see the old grin on her face, not that cold, chilly smile she gave me in the street.

'I am. Of course I am. It's been ages.'

'Aren't you going to let me in?' Mags takes a step forward and Tiny appears from behind her legs. I have to forcibly squash down the groan that rises in my throat.

'It's not really a good time,' I check behind me, as if seeing if something is burning, or someone is calling to me. I don't think Rupert would be very happy to know Mags came over. Ever since she upset me at the flat, he's had no time for her. 'I'm just in the middle of something.'

'Right. Too busy, eh? Thought you might be.' Mags yanks at the dog's lead, pulling her away from the front door. Tiny responds by pissing up the stone lion that flanks the right-hand side of the porch, and I feel a bubble of annoyance popping in my belly. 'She's forgotten all about her old friends, Tiny.'

'Mags, come on for goodness' sake, I didn't mean it like that,' I say, pointing at the lion, 'but you can't just turn up here unannounced and then let that bloody dog piss all over my house.'

'Your house, eh? Don't forget your roots, Em.' Mags raises an eyebrow, that familiar grin replaced by a quirky, lopsided smile that I haven't seen before. 'I came over because I told you I had mail for you and you still didn't bother to come and collect it.' It's only now that I remember Mags telling me that, and I notice a small card and a package in Mags's hand.

'It won't be anything important, that's why I didn't bother with it,' I say cautiously. The stark white paper, the word **BITCH** etched into it in inky black, angry letters floats in front of my eyes.

'Well, it is nearly Christmas and it looks like a card. I was hoping you'd come and visit and when you didn't I thought maybe you wouldn't mind if I came to you. The parcel isn't from the flat, by the way. It was in your porch,' Mags says, holding it out as she peers past me into the hallway.

'Oh. Thank you. Look, Mags, I'm sorry I didn't come over, things just got away from me, you know.' I hold my hand out for the package, a flutter of nerves making my skin sing as I take it. *Hand delivered* is written in tiny letters in the corner. 'I didn't realize you knew where I lived.' I did, of course I did, ever since she mentioned the stone lions that day, but I want to see how she knows. If she has told Harry.

'God, Em, you're not that hard to find, you know,' Mags snorts. 'All I had to do was google Rupert. Before he married you, him and the first wife were all over the media. Glitzy society bits, you know. It didn't take me long to find out where you lived.'

My mouth goes dry and I find I can't swallow, the weight of the gift like a stone in my hand. I picture Mags as I saw her last, in the street, bending to pick up my things as they rolled into the gutter. 'It was that easy?'

'Yep.' Mags fumbles in her pocket and pulls out a battered hand-rolled cigarette, lighting up on the front porch and blowing a stream of cigarette smoke in my direction. I flap a hand irritably.

'Mags, you haven't heard from Harry, have you? You haven't told him anything about where I live?' I can hear the panicky undertone in my voice, and I can't help peering past Mags into the darkness, sure I can see a shadowy figure lurking under the streetlight. 'You saw him in the pub, and I thought... maybe you might have seen him again?'

'No.' Mags is insulted, her nose turning up at the thought of it. 'I might be a lot of things, Em, but you might want to remember that I was – am – your friend. I know what he did to you, remember? I saw the bruises he left on you; I saw how terrified you were when you first moved into the flat. I thought I was doing you a favour, coming here, but clearly you don't need me now you have *Rupert*...' She spits out his name like it tastes of dog shit.

There is a sharp tug of annoyance in my chest and I open my mouth to defend Rupert, but before I can speak, I realize that there *is* a shadowy figure coming up the driveway, and my heart starts to beat double time in my chest. 'Mags...'

'*Hello* there.' A hearty voice booms out, and I slump against the doorframe in relief, as Rupert appears next to Mags out of the shadowy gloom. 'Em? Who's this?'

'Rupert, darling.' I try to keep my breathing under control, not wanting Rupert to know how much he alarmed me. 'This is Mags. You remember, my old flatmate. Mags is just leaving.'

Rupert turns to look Mags up and down a little, and I want nothing more than for her to leave without another word. I don't want her to bring me mail, I don't want her to stand on my doorstep and speak about Rupert in that tone. 'Oh, of course.' Rupert reaches down to pet Tiny, who gives a low growl and backs away. 'Oh dear, someone clearly doesn't like me.' Rupert lets out a laugh that I am ninety per cent sure is fake, as Mags and I look at each other over the top of his head. 'Nice to meet you, Mags. Come on inside, Em, it's freezing out here.' With a charming smile, Rupert whisks me back inside and closes the door before Mags can say another word.

'Wow. What was she doing here?' Rupert asks, as I stand shell-shocked in the hallway, the parcel still in my hand.

'I don't really know.' I glance down at the package, wrapped neatly in green paper, my name written across it in swirly gold pen. 'She said she came to deliver a card that had been sent to the flat in my name. I saw her in town a while ago and she mentioned it, but I just ignored it. Didn't think it was important.'

'How did she know to come here?' Rupert turns to look at me, a frown on his face.

'I don't know, I never told her.' I feel as though I have to make Rupert aware that none of this is down to me. 'She said we weren't that difficult to find.' I stop short of mentioning Caro and the society pages.

'Well, probably best if she doesn't come here again, eh?' Rupert brushes past me towards the staircase, dropping a kiss on my head as he passes by. 'Every time you see her, she seems to upset you, Em. I did tell you it's best to stay away from her.'

I say nothing, waiting for him to go upstairs before

I switch my attention back to the parcel. I turn it over in my hands, a chilly hand stroking my spine. Whatever it is, whoever it's from, I don't want it. I should have asked Mags if she saw who had left it and I wish for a brief second that I hadn't opened the door at all. Another part of me wishes, just for a moment, that I had invited her in for a cup of tea, before I remember how suffocating she can be, how clingy, and how much easier life is without her in it. I turn on my heel and head into the kitchen, where I stuff the parcel behind the bin, and pour myself a fresh glass of wine, trying to shake the image of Mags on the doorstep from my mind.

Chapter Eighteen

Christmas Eve. As a kid, Christmas Eve was my favourite day of the whole year, even more so than Christmas Day. The anticipation of what would be at the foot of the bed when I woke up, the smell of ginger and cinnamon on the air as my mum stirred, and mixed, and baked in the kitchen. We didn't have a lot of money, but it hadn't seemed to matter; right up until I was about twelve anyway, when my mum remarried for the first time and everything became about him. Turns out my first stepfather wasn't as keen on children as he'd made out. The first time she left me behind at Christmas – leaving me with an aunt who I don't actually think was really my aunt, fighting for attention with kids who weren't even related to me – she and my stepfather spent it on the beach in Lanzarote, and I cried for days. By the time I left home I didn't celebrate Christmas anymore. Today though, some of that old magic has been recaptured and I shiver in the passenger seat of Rupert's car, not sure if it's the chill in the air, or excitement.

'Cold?' Rupert turns up the heater, and I snuggle into my scarf. 'You're not too nervous, are you?'

We are on our way to Rupert's family home by the coast in Norfolk, where we will spend three nights with his whole family. I am a little nervous, a ripple of butterfly wings fluttering in my belly when I picture it, but I'm excited more than anything. Excited to get away from the house, the dead air on the end of the telephone line, the feeling of dread that sits on my shoulders every time I turn into the driveway.

'A little. Excited, though, to spend time with your family.' I smile at him, refusing to think about the house anymore. 'Do you always spend Christmas together?'

'Ahhh… we didn't really used to,' Rupert says, not taking his eyes off the road, 'Caro and I just used to go for the day usually. My mother is looking forward to spending time getting to know you.'

He smoothly changes the subject and I don't press him for further information. Caro's parents had invited him to a church service this evening, a tradition they had held when Caro was alive apparently, and I had let out a sigh of relief when he had firmly but gently turned them down. I don't want to spend the holidays thinking about Caro – Rupert has been working ridiculous hours, and I feel as though Christmas is the perfect time for us to get things back on track.

Rupert's mother is waiting on the doorstep when we arrive, wrapped up in a thick grey jumper against the cold. A battered old Land Rover sits on the drive, next to a gleaming Jag, which I assume belongs to Will and Amanda. A brisk, icy wind, laden with the scent of the sea cuts across me as I step out of the car, and I am relieved to see smoke pouring from the chimney. Rupert's mum – 'Diana, darling, call me Diana, you're family now' – bustles us into the house, calling to his father, and to Will and Amanda. The afternoon is spent catching up, drinking pot after pot of tea, as Diana stirs, and bakes, and chops in preparation for tomorrow's big lunch, before we move onto wine, a deep, spicy red that complements the beef stew Diana has prepared beautifully.

'Having a good time?' Amanda appears beside me at the sink as I wash the dinner pots. We have packed Diana, Eamonn – Rupert's father – and the husbands off into the living room, while we clean up. I had offered after Diana had done all the cooking, and to my surprise Amanda joined me.

'Yes, brilliant, thank you.' I scour at the burnt-on gravy in the casserole dish. 'It's been a long time since I had anything like this to look forward to on Christmas Eve.'

'Oh?' Amanda looks at me questioningly as I scrub. 'It feels a bit different this year for us too, if you must know.'

I lift the heavy pan from the soapy water and set it on the draining board, not sure what Amanda is getting at. Different good, or different bad? 'Why's that?'

'Just... everyone here, together. It's what Diana loves, and we didn't really do it when Caro was alive.'

'I suppose she had to spend time with her family too.'

'Hmmm.' Amanda doesn't look at me, as she starts to stack plates in the ancient dishwasher. 'She liked to go away at Christmas, most times anyway. She and Rupert would go to the Caribbean, or Malta, or Africa, somewhere where it was hot. It would just be me and Will and the parents most years.'

'Oh.' Spraying cleaning solution, I start to wipe over the battered, pockmarked oak table, with its stains of paint and slashes of biro, where Eamonn sits to do the crossword every morning, and where, once, Rupert and Will sat to do their homework. 'I don't have anyone to spend Christmas with here, so I was just happy to do what Rupert wanted.'

Amanda tucks the tea towel into the handle of the warm Aga and turns to stand in front of me. 'It's nice,' she says quietly, reaching out to rub the top of my arm. 'I mean, it's nice that we're all together. Diana is happy, so everyone is happy.'

She gives me a crooked smile, and walks out into the living room, leaving me standing in the kitchen, pretty sure that the warmth I'm feeling is from her words, not the Aga.

We spend the evening playing Trivial Pursuit, finishing off the rest of the red wine, and laughing until my sides hurt. There is something sweet, something intimate, about hearing the stories of Rupert and Will growing up together, the scrapes they got into, and I hang on every word as more and more of him is revealed to me. Finally, just before midnight Diana gets to her feet and claps her hands.

'Right, bedtime, children. It's almost Christmas Day.'

Rupert and Will both groan. 'Mum,' Will says, 'we're both over forty years old, I think we know what time we can go to bed.'

'Not on Christmas Eve,' Diana says, as Amanda and I slide a glance towards each other, our mouths curving into twin smiles.

'Come on.' Amanda pulls Will to his feet, and they slip from the room with a wave, Will blowing kisses at his mother as Rupert and I follow behind them, slipping into Rupert's childhood bedroom that still has his swimming trophies on a shelf above the bed. It makes my heart give a little squeeze, the idea of spending the night in Rupert's old bedroom.

'Come here.' Rupert reaches for me, his fingers cold on my skin, and the taste of red wine on his lips as he kisses me.

I shiver, and not just from the chill of his hands. 'No, Rupert, your brother is right next door and your parents are across the hall.' I laugh softly, pressing my mouth to his bare shoulder to quiet myself.

'I got you something.' He jumps off the bed and starts to rummage in the holdall he packed before we left.

'I thought we were doing gifts in the morning?'

'This is something extra. Close your eyes.'

I close my eyes and tentatively hold out my hands. When I feel him place something there, I open them, and there is a deep blue velvet box on my palm.

'Rupert?'

'Just open it,' he says with a grin, and my heart turns over in my chest.

'OK.' Slowly I lift the lid, to reveal a silver brooch in the shape of a dragonfly, two tiny sapphires glinting in the corners of the wings. 'Oh, Rupert. It's beautiful.'

'The sapphires represent us,' Rupert says, tracing a finger along the stones. 'Sapphire is the birthstone for September, and I know neither of us were born in September, but we did get married then so…' He gives a tiny, embarrassed shrug and I launch myself across the bed, kissing him all over his face.

'I love it,' I breathe, as I sit astride him looking into his dark blue eyes – eyes the colour of sapphires – before one thing leads to another.

Later, as Rupert snores softly and I start to drift off, reliving what has been the best day I've had in a long, long time, I chide myself for thinking that Rupert was anything other than the perfect man I saw when I first came to be interviewed as his housekeeper.

Christmas morning, and I wake up with a mild red wine hangover, to see Rupert leaning over me, an excited smile on his face. *Honestly*, I think, *he's worse than a child*, but that doesn't stop me from grinning back at him, my limbs aching from the previous evening.

'Merry Christmas,' he whispers, keeping the noise down so as not to wake his brother and Amanda in the next room.

'Merry Christmas,' I whisper back, forgetting to hold in my morning breath. I jump out of bed and hurry for the small en suite (imagine, growing up in a house where you have your own bathroom attached – I was lucky to get a space in the family bathroom at all when I was growing up) quickly showering and brushing my teeth before we head downstairs for breakfast.

Christmas is definitely as traditional as it comes in the Milligan household – Diana stirs a vat of scrambled eggs on the Aga, as Will butters toast and Amanda shreds smoked salmon, all while Eamonn sits at the table drinking coffee. We toast ourselves with Buck's Fizz, and I am touched when Diana hands out tiny stockings to each of us, including me, that contain chocolate, small bottles of perfume or aftershave, a pair of socks each and an orange. I have to blink back tears as I accept it, retreating to the downstairs loo to blow my nose.

Staring at my reflection in the mirror, my cheeks flushed with the early morning alcohol and the heat of the kitchen, I think about my mum, and about Mags, and wonder what they are doing, whether they are thinking of me this morning. I'd like to think they are, but the truth is they probably haven't given me a second thought. I push away the image of Harry that creeps into my mind, unable to see him any other way than when I saw him last, as he squeezed my throat hard and I struggled for breath, and I thank God that I found Rupert. I think about Caro, and how selfish she was to throw herself off a bridge and leave this wonderful family behind. And then I think about how lucky I am, that she did do what she did, leaving this wonderful family for me to be part of.

Mid-afternoon, once we have eaten lunch and Eamonn has refused to turn on the Queen's Speech, Rupert's father claps his hands together and starts chivvying everyone along.

'What are we doing?' I ask Rupert in confusion, as we

all pile up in the back hallway and Diana hands out pairs of wellies.

'Here, these should fit you.' Diana hands me a pair of black wellies with a jazzy silver glitter running through them and I wonder briefly if perhaps they belonged to Caro before shoving my socked feet into them.

'Dad has a tradition,' Rupert explains as he steps into his own wellies. 'Every year we walk along to the beach to collect coal for the Christmas fire.'

'Coal? On a beach?'

Rupert laughs at the expression on my face. 'You'll see. We don't find a lot, less than we did when we were kids, but Dad loves it, so we all go along with it. It's nice to be able to do it with you. I haven't done it for years.'

I follow him through the back garden, out onto the little path that leads to the beach. Will calls to Rupert and he walks ahead to catch up with Will and Eamonn, the three of them all so similar I can see an older Rupert in Eamonn, a Rupert with grandchildren, and grey hair. Amanda leads the way, her wild curly hair tangled in the sea breeze and I find myself stepping in time with Diana, the two of us bringing up the rear.

'I was worried about you, you know,' she says, tucking her arm into mine.

'Worried? What about?' My heart skitters in my chest and for a moment I get a panicky feeling that maybe all of this was a ruse, that there is no happy family.

'Well, it was quick wasn't it? The courtship, the wedding.' She watches me closely, her feet slowing to a stop.

'Rupert closed himself off after Caro died. I didn't think I'd ever see him happy again. He hid himself away in that big, old house she bought, and I thought he'd never get back on his feet again. He drank heavily for a while, you know. Called me, rambling on about guilt, and how he had failed Caroline.'

I didn't know that. Rupert has never told me about how things were after Caro died. I flounder for a moment, 'Diana, I…'

'Thank you, Emily.' Diana lays a cold hand against my cheek. 'You brought him back to us.' She starts walking again, the rest of the family already off the path and onto the sand. I can hear Rupert shouting to Will from the rocks that litter the edge of the landscape. 'Caro would never have done this, you know.'

'Amanda said she didn't spend much time here.' I am careful what I say, anxious about saying the wrong thing.

'No. It was always her way. Never Rupert's. She certainly wouldn't have indulged Eamonn in his coal hunting; that definitely wasn't her thing.'

I say nothing, just smile and tuck my arm back into Diana's, ready to comb the beach with the rest of them. I've just found my first piece of coal, a tiny piece that probably is best left on the beach, but I am triumphant nonetheless, when my mobile buzzes in my pocket. I pull it out, hoping that perhaps my mum has read my message to her and replied – it's just gone ten o'clock in Florida now, after all – but my heart sinks as I see it is from an unknown number. My eyes flick towards Rupert, but he is too far away for me to call to him without drawing attention to myself. I swipe the screen.

Your first Christmas together. And your last.

I raise my eyes and scan the horizon, sure I can feel eyes on the back of my neck, my skin starting to prickle uncomfortably, but there is no one there, no shadowy figure watching for my reaction. There is only Rupert, and his perfect family.

Rupert perches on a footstool in front of the tree, as we all sit in the living room ready to exchange presents. Rupert's brooch glints at my lapel in the light from the fire, the coal we collected fizzing damply on the wood beneath it, and the scent of pine and cinnamon is on the air. It should be the perfect end to a perfect day, but instead all I can think about is the message on my phone and the fear that spiked in my veins as I read it.

'This one is yours, Mum,' Rupert is saying, as he passes her a neatly wrapped gift in red paper. It's the scarf I chose for her, and she is thrilled with it. I paste a smile on as she thanks me, barely even aware of what is going on. I don't miss the shared look between Rupert and Will though as Rupert gets to his feet. 'There's a special present I need to go and get… hang on.' He gives me a wink and I force that smile back onto my face.

Rupert returns a few moments later with a large cardboard box, gaudily wrapped, the top loosely closed, and hands it to me. 'Here. This is for you, so you won't be on your own anymore.'

I take it, setting it in my lap before I carefully lift the flaps of the box open. Inside sits a tiny tortoiseshell kitten, her face turned up to mine. She lets out a tiny meow as Amanda presses her hands to her mouth.

'A kitten? Oh, Rupert, you got her a kitten!' she cries, rushing to sit beside me as I look up at Rupert, shock etched onto my face.

'Well? Aren't you going to say something?' Rupert asks, uncertainty passing over his features and I gently lift the kitten from the box. Immediately she snuggles into me, letting out a rumbly purr as she kneads at my jumper.

'Rupert, she's lovely. I don't know what to say.' No one has ever given me a gift like this before. 'I already love her. And you.' Rupert crouches down to kiss me, his hand rubbing over the kitten's tiny head.

'Her name is Lola. That's what the breeder called her, but if you want to change it, we can.'

'No,' I say, my fingers running over her silky fur, the tiny pads of her feet. 'Lola is perfect. Thank you.'

'There's another present under here,' Will calls out. He has taken Rupert's place on the footstool and is rummaging under the tree. 'It says it's for Emily.' He holds out a gift, the firelight making the gold writing of my name glint.

My stomach drops as I take it from him, the kitten making her escape onto Amanda's lap. *Hand delivered.* Familiar words scrawled onto a familiar parcel.

'Where did this come from?' I say, my voice cracking

on the last word. Rupert is frowning, a deep V etched between his eyebrows.

'Under the tree,' Will laughs, 'it was tucked at the back there.'

'It was in the bag of presents that you left by the front door,' Rupert says finally. 'Didn't you put it there?'

'*No,*' I say testily, 'I didn't put it there. Rupert, I put this behind the bin.'

'Why would you do that?' Amanda pauses in her stroking of Lola.

'Who put it in the bag? Did you, Rupert? Please just tell me if you did.' I can feel the panic rising, the tightness of my chest reaching up into my throat.

'No, I didn't. I thought you did,' Rupert says, 'Anya probably put it in there, you know how she is. She probably saw it was a present and thought you'd forgotten to pack it.'

I stare at him incredulously, my fingers shaking as I run my hand over my name. 'No…'

'Emily, why don't you just open it?' Will says, smiling, although there is confusion on his face. 'Does it matter how it got into the bag? Just open it and see who it's from.'

I nod, taking a deep breath. It's probably nothing. Just a gift, it is Christmas after all. *Your first Christmas together. And your last.* Forcing the words from my mind, I strip off the wrapping paper, gasping as I tear off the tissue paper underneath to reveal the present. It is a photo, in a silver frame, last seen on my mantelpiece and one that I hoped never to see again. It's Rupert and Caro's wedding photo.

Chapter Nineteen

'I don't know what you want me to do, Emily.' Rupert keeps his eyes on the road as the glow from the streetlamps lights his face in strips of black and orange. We are travelling back from his parents a day early, after a tense Boxing Day, the two of us barely speaking.

I huddle against the car door, watching the verge of the motorway speed past. 'I want you to believe me,' I say eventually. 'I told you someone was… harassing me, I suppose. That's the only way I can describe it. I showed you that text message I received on Christmas Day.'

And I had. After I had unwrapped the photograph of Rupert and Caro on their wedding day, Christmas had been ruined. Diana had swooped down and scooped it up, as I had rushed from the room in tears. Rupert had found me sitting on the edge of his childhood bed, my phone in my hand.

'Here,' I say, thrusting it towards him, 'I got this earlier while we were on the beach.' I watch his face as he reads it.

'Who is it from?'

'I don't know, Rupert. An unknown number, just like

the ones before. The other ones I told you about that you just brushed under the carpet.' Bitterness leaches into my voice and I shake my head, tears dripping off the end of my nose.

'It could be a wrong number.'

'Jesus, Rupert.' I get to my feet and start pacing. 'What do I have to do to show you that someone is trying to get to us? To me? This is proof – how can I be exaggerating, or misreading something when it's right there in front of you?'

I had snatched the phone back and refused to discuss it with him again.

Now, he says, 'It's not that I don't believe you. I do. I saw the message. I was just trying to… I don't know, make you feel better, I guess.' He blows out a long breath and flicks on the indicator to come off the motorway.

'We could call the police,' I say, thinking of how Sadie suggested it before the holidays. 'Tell them someone is harassing me.'

'Really?' He glances towards me but looks back at the road before I can read his expression. 'I'm not saying this to brush it away, Em, but it's just a couple of text messages. I don't think they'll do anything.'

'But someone was in the house, Rupert, I heard someone when I was in the shower.' Irritation makes me snap, and I bite the inside of my cheek hard in frustration.

'I don't doubt that, Em, but we don't have any proof. Trust me, I had enough dealings with the police when Caro was alive – she'd get herself into a state, saying people were watching her. She called the police multiple times and they never did a thing.'

'Oh.' The kitten stirs on my lap, maybe reacting to the tension that makes my nerve endings sing, and I scratch behind her ears to soothe her back to sleep.

'How about I get a couple of extra security cameras? Ones that I can link to your phone. And I'll get one of those doorbells with the camera in it, too, so you don't even have to answer the door if you don't want to.'

It's not as good as Rupert rushing to my defence, telling me that of course he believes me and that we'll slay this particular dragon together, but I guess it will have to do.

Once we are home, Rupert disappears into the small spare bedroom to get some work done, despite the fact that the construction industry mostly shuts down for the last two weeks in December. I potter around downstairs, finding homes for the gifts we received, the kitten winding her way around my feet. Everything feels OK – I don't get the feeling that someone has been in the house, and the telephone has stayed silent, although that doesn't surprise me as Rupert is still home.

Feeling at a loose end I wander upstairs to see if Rupert wants a cup of tea. Pushing open the door to the spare room, I realize it is empty, the chair behind the small desk he's put in there shoved back towards the wall. He said he was coming up here to work, but although there is a faint blueish glow from his laptop screen, his desk is clear of paper, an empty coffee cup the only thing on the desk besides his computer. Moving quietly, I slip behind the desk, crouching over the keyboard of his laptop. The whirling motion of his screensaver casts light across my face and I nudge the mouse. *If there's a password, I'll leave it*, I think, even though I know I could probably get past it, thanks to my years in IT. But there is no password and the screen comes to life.

It's Caro's Facebook page. Rupert has been looking at Caro's Facebook page. I feel sick as I run my eyes over the screen, over her face pressed against his in the top photo. He has clicked onto her photo albums and her face dominates the screen over and over again, tiny pictures of the woman who came before me. I press my hand to my mouth, pulling in a shaky breath. *Eavesdroppers never hear good of themselves*. My mother's voice rings in my ears, and I can almost feel her grip on my arm as she marched me back to bed after she had caught me sitting on the stairs one night, listening to her spin lies to her latest flame. Clearly snoopers never see good things either. I hear the faint flush of the toilet, and jab at the top right-hand button to send the computer back into sleep mode.

'Em? Are you OK?' Rupert's face is flushed as he rubs his hands together, his socked feet silent on the carpet.

'Just seeing if you wanted a coffee?' I say brightly, waving the empty coffee mug at him from the desk.

'Err… yeah, OK. Thanks. I won't be too long.' He kisses the top of my head as I squeeze past him, and he takes his seat at the desk, not touching the keyboard until I leave the room.

I wrap my fingers around my mug, letting the warmth soak into my cold hands as I stare out of the kitchen window. Despite what Rupert says, he's not over Caro, and I have to face up to the fact that perhaps he never will be. Why else would he be looking at her Facebook photos? I move towards the double doors to the orangery. We don't use this room, and as I push open the doors I am struck by the light that fills it. There is a faint hint of dust on the air, which tells me that Anya doesn't clean in here regularly, and underneath that is the tiniest hint of nectarines. I know why we don't use this room. It's Caro's room. She wanted it, and Rupert built it for her just before she died. She never even got to use it, not properly. After she died Rupert closed it off and we have an unspoken agreement that the room doesn't get used.

Not anymore. The words come to me as I move towards the huge windows, looking out onto the garden. Maybe we should use it, lay Caro's ghost to rest a little. I stare into the garden, Caro's other domain. It would have looked amazing once, when Caro was here and tending to it regularly, but now, although Rupert cuts the lawn, the bushes have been allowed to run riot and brambles fill large patches of the borders at the end of the garden.

I gently open the door to the garden and walk out, the damp grass seeping into the end of my shoes, wetting my toes. I wander along the borders, pulling at leaves, poking into bushes trying to figure out what is supposed to be there and which is an intruder. *Like me and Caro,* I think. I dig my toe into the soil, enjoying the earthy scent that rises. I can do this. I can bring the garden back to life. I scan the plot, excitement fizzing in my veins. There's a lot of work to do, and there are a couple of dead patches in the grass that I maybe need to reseed, but I can bring this garden back to its former glory. We could put in a pool, like Sadie and Miles have. I imagine the garden in the summer, a riot of colour and heady scents, as Rupert and I spread open the doors to the orangery and let the sunshine back into the house. I picture myself, bringing out trays of drinks, champagne maybe, to Will, Amanda, Sadie and Miles, just like at Sadie's party, as Rupert flips high-end burgers on a barbecue – I look around, and there doesn't seem to be one, but I can buy one – and we'll all drink, and laugh, and make memories together. I imagine Sadie and I laid out on sun loungers, letting the warm summer air brush over our tanned bodies as Miles and Rupert splash with the children in the pool… maybe even mine and Rupert's children, one day. I imagine Rupert and I sitting out on the grass on a hot summer's evening, watching the stars come out. I imagine no more messages, no more phone calls, no more feeling as though eyes are on me. I imagine belonging.

Chapter Twenty

Rupert is back at work following his short Christmas break, and if he's honest, despite the heavy work load he's under, he's almost relieved to be out of the house. Every time he's been asked if he had a nice break, he's just nodded and said how lovely it was, but in all fairness, things have been so strained between him and Emily since she opened the present on Christmas Day evening, he's glad to escape the atmosphere at home. It doesn't help that in a week's time it will be a year exactly since Caro's memorial and he's sure Caro's mother will be in contact.

He hadn't realized when he married Emily quite how different things would be compared to his life with Caro – after all, marriage is marriage, right? Wrong. Emily is completely different to Caro, and that comes as something of a relief to him. He knows he didn't react very well on Christmas Day to the photograph appearing again, and then when Emily showed him the text message on her phone. How can he tell her that the last thing he wants is to get the police involved? The stress he felt when they descended on him after Caro died, the way they looked at him, asking questions about the most intimate parts of his life with Caro. Rupert isn't sure he could go through that again, and he's pretty sure that his relationship with Emily would suffer if they had to deal with the police as well. Thankfully, Emily hasn't mentioned it again, and he's hoping now that she has the kitten to keep her occupied, it will be enough to shed this (irrational – there, he's said it) fear that someone is out to get them.

Rupert had spent an hour looking over Caro's old Facebook photos on their return home after Christmas, telling Emily that he'd had work to do. It's been a long time since he's allowed himself to look at Caro's pictures, guilt punching him in the stomach every time he looks at her, the curve of her jaw, the way her hair falls over one eye. The way she looked the last time he ever set eyes on her. He needed to do it, though, to remind himself that the life he's making with Emily is the right one. She is what he was looking for, his missing piece after Caro died.

Since they've been home from his parents', the atmosphere has been strained, with both of them on their best behaviour, as if they are roommates, not a married couple. The breathing space that has been afforded to Rupert by his return to work has given him a chance to think about things, and he's come to a decision. He can't let things with Emily go the way they did with Caro. By the time Caro died things were far from perfect between them, and he knows that a lot of it was his fault. Emily is his second chance, his chance to put right all the things that went wrong before. Looking down at the notepad on the desk in front of him, he realizes he has doodled a picture in biro of two hands joined together. A sign, surely, that deep down he knows he must make things work with Emily.

Suddenly decisive, he snatches up the phone and dials the home telephone, drumming his fingers impatiently as he waits for Emily to answer. The voicemail kicks in and it gives him a jolt, even now, to hear Emily's voice on the recorded message instead of Caro's. 'Darling, it's me.' He pauses a second, wondering what to say for the best. 'Listen, I know things have been a bit… you know, but I wanted to tell you I am on your side. I'm sorry. I hate arguing with you. Let's start again from the beginning and forget about all of this, the messages, and the photograph. I'll come home early tonight, and we can get dinner or something. I love you.'

Rupert keeps his word and – fending off his colleague who wants to see him for 'five minutes' in his office before he goes – feigns an urgent appointment as he prepares to close down his computer, bang on five o'clock. He's just about to leave when his phone buzzes and he scrambles in his pocket for it, thinking that perhaps it is a message from Emily. He hasn't heard back from her, so he's assuming she got his message, and all is OK. Either that, or she's still furious with him and her bags are packed. It isn't a message from Emily. It is a message request on his Facebook account. Curious, Rupert sinks back down into his office chair, with a quick glance over his shoulder to make sure his boss is nowhere in sight and opens the message.

Sorry for the intrusion. I understand you recently married
Emily Beaumont. I would like to meet with you urgently
to discuss a few things – it really is in your best interest.
Regards, Henry Carpenter.

Henry Carpenter. Rupert isn't one hundred per cent sure,
but he thinks perhaps this might be Emily's Harry – after all,
Harry and Henry are interchangeable, aren't they? But Emily
Beaumont? Emily's maiden name is Belrose. Rupert has seen
her birth certificate, and it definitely doesn't say Beaumont.
He toys with replying for a moment, but he can't think what
to say. He gets up and pushes his office door shut, suddenly
convinced that his boss or one of his colleagues will make
an appearance and he just needs quiet for a moment so he
can think about this. The message is intriguing, but only if
it really is for him, and given that he doesn't know Harry's
surname, and that Emily's maiden name is wrong, he has to
assume it isn't for him. *And*, a voice whispers at the back of
his mind, *Emily is your second chance to get things right, remember?
You're building a new life together, moving on from what happened
with Caro. You're starting over. Be honest with yourself Rupert,
you don't want this message to be for you.* Decision made, he
brings up the message and taps out a quick reply.

Sorry, I think you have the wrong person. I don't know
anybody called Emily Beaumont.

Satisfied that the message has been dealt with, Rupert
snatches up his phone and wallet and shrugs on his coat.

He's already decided that he won't mention the message to Emily – he truly does want a fresh start, and if he's honest, a protective streak has kicked in. Emily has been through enough with her ex-boyfriend, she doesn't need anything else to get paranoid about, and anyway, the more he thinks about it, the more he thinks that Henry Carpenter must have contacted him by mistake. The more he *wants* to think it's a mistake.

When he leaves the building, it is dark, the weather squally with sheets of rain being blown across the pavement by the strong north-westerly wind. A storm is on its way, and Rupert hurries along the pavement towards the tube station, his head down to avoid getting poked in the eye by wayward inside-out umbrellas that some commuters insist on carrying despite the fact they don't do a jot of good. He battles his way inside the tube station, remembering now why he doesn't usually leave work this early – the rush hour is in full swing and he has to force his way onto the platform.

As he stands waiting for the train, he swears he can feel the prickle of eyes on the back of his neck. A bead of sweat inches its way down under his collar and he rubs his hand over the back of his neck. *Paranoid*, he thinks, with a little internal laugh. Emily's jumpiness is rubbing off on him. Or maybe it's the Facebook message. Rupert fumbles in his coat pocket, squeezing the phone out in the tiny space between him and the commuter next to him, but the screen is blank and shows no signal. Of course, there's no signal, not this far underground.

He feels the prickle of eyes on him again, and he turns slightly, craning his neck to see over the swarm of people that crowd the platform. No one is looking at him, all eyes are on phones, or peering down the tunnel to see the tell-tale light of the approaching train. He shakes himself, tutting under his breath at his idiocy, as the rumble of the tracks and the rush of warm air tells him that a train is approaching. He steps neatly one step to the left and front, to squeeze into a tiny gap between a tall man who is sweating profusely under a bowler hat, and an overweight woman with a large bag slung over one arm, in the perfect position to rush the open doors as soon as possible.

Definitely a mistake. And Rupert shrugs the message from his mind, instead thinking only of Emily.

Chapter Twenty-One

As Rupert goes back to work and we settle into our normal everyday routine, I try to push away the thought of Caro, and the image of Rupert sitting upstairs scrolling through her pictures. Lola has also settled well into the house, and Rupert was right, having a tiny little furry body following me around all day has definitely made me feel less lonely.

Today, I'm following through on my promise to myself and starting on the garden. I've spent hours sketching up plans of how I want it to look, and it's been good to exercise my brain. *Maybe*, I think, *I could go back into IT.* Now everything has died down between me and Harry, maybe I could do something from home. I'd be working under a different name, so there's a chance people wouldn't even realize I'm back.

Humming to myself, I change into old clothes and head downstairs to make a start outside with the plants I picked up from the garden centre yesterday, all stacked neatly to one side on the drive. Yanking the front door open, I step out and shriek, as my foot almost lands in a sticky, congealed mess.

'Jesus.' I press my hand against my chest, feeling my heart thudding frantically beneath my thin flannel shirt. Leaning down, I examine the bundle of blood and gore, deducing from the ragged feathers and remains of a beak that it was once a bird. Nausea washes over me, and I have to swallow back the saliva that fills my mouth. *Don't puke, Emily.* I hold my hand over my mouth, anxiously peering up the drive and out onto the road to see if someone is loitering. The road is empty, and there is a chirrupy purr as Lola saunters around the corner looking very pleased with herself. She sits next to the mangled mess and starts to wash.

'Lola, you naughty thing.' My heart rate slows to its usual rate as I realize it's nothing sinister, just the cat acting on her instincts. I scoop up the bird between two pieces of cardboard and throw it in the bin, stopping to pick up Lola on my way back into the house. 'You gave me a fright.' The cat yawns and struggles against my shoulder so I set her down and she pads off on silent paws and heads to her bed in the living room.

I work solidly for hours, lugging the heavy boxes of plants down the side path into the garden, weeding and hacking at the bushes until everything starts to resemble more of a garden than a jungle. I sing along to a Spotify playlist as I work, old songs that remind me of my mum, when it was just the two of us. Before husband number two, then three, four, five… you get the picture. I leave one headphone dangling loose, so I am not completely cut off – I still feel a little jumpy, and to have my hearing blocked completely makes me feel vulnerable – but I still jump and utter a sharp shriek, dropping a trowel on my toes as I glimpse movement out the corner of my eye.

'What on earth are you doing?' Sadie appears, immaculate in a silk jumpsuit and jacket, completely inappropriate for the damp winter chill. 'I tried the front door, but no one answered so I let myself in the side gate. I hope that's OK.'

'Of course. Sorry, I had these in.' I gesture to the head-phones and get to my feet, my knees creaking from being stuck in one position all morning. 'I'm just sorting the garden out. I thought it might be nice to get it ready in time for the spring.'

'You could get a gardener to do that.' Sadie eyes my muddy leggings distastefully and I feel a hot flush working its way to my cheeks.

'I could… but I wanted to do it myself, for Rupert. Caro kept a nice garden apparently, so I thought he might be missing it.' I toe one of the patches of dead grass, remind-ing myself that I need to see to it. 'I was thinking maybe we could put a pool in? Not a huge one, but somewhere here…' I wave my arms in a vague circle, 'it's not too far from the orangery, and I thought it would be relaxing for Rupe, especially in the summer when he's cooped up in the office all day. What do you think?'

'Well, if that's what you want.' Sadie shrugs. The idea of a swimming pool is clearly not a big deal to her. 'If you can handle them digging up the garden when you've just planted all this… but yes, I suppose Rupert does love using our pool. And you have the space.' She shivers dramatically in her thin jumpsuit and scrubs her hands over her arms.

'Do you want to go in and put the kettle on? I just need to seed these bits where the grass doesn't seem to grow properly and then I'll be in.'

Sadie looks relieved to have a reason to get inside, and she scurries in through the orangery door with only the slightest of pauses. I sprinkle the seeds and then stand back to survey my work. *Not bad for a first day*, I think, a tug of pride nudging a smile onto my face. I can't wait to see Rupert's face when he gets home.

Warmth hits my face as I enter the kitchen and I let out a sigh of satisfaction. I hadn't realized how cold it was out there. I strip off my gloves and take the coffee mug Sadie holds out to me, sinking my aching bones gratefully into the kitchen chair.

'I can't believe you're going to redo that garden all on your own. You must be mad,' Sadie says, as she eyes me over her coffee cup.

'It's not that bad. Once I've cleared the overgrown stuff and planted in the gaps it'll take care of itself. You didn't used to help Caro with the garden then?'

'Ha. No, definitely not. And Caro didn't do *that* much. She had a gardener who did most of it, up until Rupert started the extension, and then after that… well, you know what happened after that. Rupert left the garden to go wild. It might be a good idea to put a pool in. Change it up a bit out there.'

I pause, my gaze wandering to the open doors of the orangery. I saw Sadie pause, just as she stepped over the threshold, and I know that she is aware that Rupert closed it off after Caro died. 'Rupert built the orangery for Caro, didn't he?' I know he did, but this is my chance to learn more about Caro and what happened.

'Yes.' Sadie follows my gaze and lets out a long breath. 'She was so thrilled with it when it was finished. The light, the view, everything. Just thrilled. Her face when she showed us…'

A memory swims to the surface of my mind – something about a party – and I grope for the words used, before remembering it was at the wedding, those bitchy women talking about a party. 'Was that the night of the party?'

'The party?' Sadie says sharply. 'Did Rupert tell you about the party?'

I shrug noncommittally and sip my coffee.

'Yes,' she goes on eventually, 'the party was to celebrate the orangery being finished. Caro was so excited, but there was definitely something in the air that night. She looked fantastic, as always.'

'She did?' I am thirsty for knowledge; I want to know every little detail. Looking at Caro's Facebook or reading articles about her online just isn't the same. I don't push to know what Sadie means by 'something in the air that night', but instead let her speak, her words tumbling out as though someone has pulled a cork.

'Caro always looked amazing.' Sadie runs her eyes over me, and I feel every speck of dirt grained into my leggings, the sweat that has beaded and dried at my temples. 'That night she wore a red, ruffled Givenchy gown – it was too much for a house party, especially in January, but that was Caro all over – with matching kitten heels, and her favourite diamond earrings, ones Rupert had bought her when they got married. Her hair all swept up in some fancy bun. You should have seen Rupert's face as she came into the room.'

I swallow, her words a sharp dig in my side, but Sadie doesn't seem to notice, and she carries on talking. 'It was an… odd night. It was mild for the time of year – there was a storm later that week, I think – and the orangery was warm… too warm, I had to ask Caro to open the door. People drank too much too quickly. I know I did.' She looks down at her cup. 'Speaking of which, shall we open some wine? The sun's over the yardarm somewhere.' Without waiting for a response, she pushes back her chair and goes to the fridge, helping herself to an unopened bottle of Sancerre. Reminding me that she's known this house for longer than I have.

I wait until she has poured us both a glass, even though I don't really want one. 'What happened, Sadie?'

'I don't know. They argued, Caro and Rupert.' She blinks. 'They tried not to let it show but everyone knew what was going on – you know the kind of row, where you're trying to keep a smile on your face as you're hissing at each other – and then Caro stormed out. Rupert called me in the morning to see if she was at mine, which she obviously wasn't, and said that if she wasn't home by night-time he'd call the police. None of us were overly worried – she'd done it before. Three days later I got the call to say they'd found her car and that she was gone.'

'Sadie, I'm so sorry.' I reach out and lay my hand over hers. 'I shouldn't have asked you about it.'

Sadie looks down at the table and sniffs, before she tugs her hand away and gives me a brisk smile. 'I'm OK. And now look, Rupert has you, and you're going to fix the garden, and everything will be as it should be.'

I smile uncertainly, not sure if I am imagining the bite to Sadie's words, and then Lola strolls into the room.

'Oh! Rupert said he was getting you a special present for Christmas!' Sadie leans down and rubs a hand over Lola's back, before tucking the trousers of her silk jumpsuit out of the way so Lola can't brush against her and leave cat hairs. 'Isn't he lovely?'

'She. She'd be even lovelier if she hadn't left me a dead bird on the doorstep.' I wrinkle my nose and Sadie laughs, and by the time she gets up to leave I have convinced myself that she didn't mean anything by her earlier comment. It's just how she is, I think, but as I close the door behind her all I can see in my mind's eye is Caro, dressed up to the nines in an expensive gown, excited to show off her new orangery, and then later, Rupert's face when he realized she was never coming home.

Hours later, the light outside is dimming, and I stretch from where I have been curled into the corner of the sofa, Rupert's spare laptop on my knees. He gave it to me after we were married, seeing as I didn't have one, and I don't think he realized just how much stuff he's left on there, which is simple enough for the wrong person to access if they wanted.

Unable to help myself, I have spent hours scrolling through Caro's Facebook page, a wealth of information at my fingertips. Her profile isn't private – although I probably could have hacked in to it if necessary – and her statuses are generally upbeat, some inspirational quotes that relate to mental health, and photos of her life. There are some blank spaces – days, sometimes a couple of weeks – where she posts nothing at all, and I assume that these must coincide with her dark patches. They seem to be more frequent in the last six months of her life.

Even though it is like digging my nail under a scab that isn't ready to be picked, I can't stop myself from obsessively scrolling through the photographs. There are hundreds – Caro and Sadie with a drink in their hands, at a festival with flowers in their hair; Caro, Will and Amanda crowded together around a church font, clearly at a child's christening, and then there is photo after photo of Rupert and Caro together. Holiday photos – I feel a sharp pang as I recognize Bridgetown in one – Christmas photos, charity balls, evenings out. In every picture she is clear-eyed and smiling, sometimes facing him, sometimes looking away or into the camera, but every time I am struck by the way Rupert looks at her. I don't think he's ever looked at me that way.

I get up from the sofa, wincing at the pins and needles

that shoot through my foot, and pace the floor. Finding Rupert scrolling through Caro's pictures means there is a chink in our closeness – a tiny gap, which if I don't get control of, could spiral into a huge chasm, and I couldn't bear to let that happen. I glance towards the now black laptop screen, wondering if it's not me after all that is the problem. Maybe I need to become more like Caro. A *better* version of Caro. I can't lose Rupert, not after everything that has happened. I love my life with him, and I won't let it go without a fight, and certainly not because someone is trying to scare me off. I need to find out exactly what happened when Caro died, and do whatever it takes to lay Caro's ghost to rest.

Chapter Twenty-Two

Excited, I spring my idea on Rupert as soon as he arrives home, but not before I guide him out into the garden. It's dark, and mist is starting to roll in across the fields behind the house, but I'm hoping the bright glow from the security lights Rupert has installed will be enough.

'Ta-da!' I push him out through the back door onto the York stone patio. 'What do you think?'

Rupert takes a moment before he answers. I suppose I should have given him a chance to get his coat off and pour a drink before I bundled him back out into the cold. 'Wow,' he says eventually, before slinging an arm over my shoulder.

'Do you like it?' A grin bursts across my face and I squeeze his waist tightly. 'I've still got more to do, but just think once the summer comes…'

'I love it,' he interrupts, leaning down and smashing his lips against mine, his teeth bruising against my top lip. 'You don't need to do any more, this is perfect. I had forgotten how good it could look.' A look I can't read drifts across his face, and I frown up at him.

'Are you sure you like it?'

'I love it, Em. You've done a brilliant job.' He kisses me again, gently this time, his tongue flicking against mine as his hand moves to my breast. I sigh, relaxing against him for a moment before I pull away.

'There's more, though,' I say, excitement fizzing in my veins. 'I was thinking, what if we put a pool in?' Stepping away from him, I mark out the position of where I imagine the pool to go. 'We could put it here. Just think, when it's hot and you've been in the office all day you can come home and we can jump in the water together.' Waggling my eyebrows at him, I step closer, reaching out to pull him back into my arms.

'No,' he says shortly, turning away and walking back into the kitchen, leaving me standing open-mouthed for a moment before I follow him.

'What do you mean, *no*?' I can't understand why he's being like this. 'It would finish the garden off perfectly, and we have the space.'

'I don't want a pool, Emily.' His voice is cold, and he keeps his back to me as he wrenches the lid from a bottle of whisky, before pouring himself a generous measure. 'Don't even think about discussing it any further, I don't want a pool out there.'

'But Sadie said…' Hot tears spring to my eyes, tears of frustration and anger.

'Sadie? Since when does Sadie live here? Since when does Sadie pay the bills? It's a waste of money, Emily – *my money*. I don't want a pool – I don't need a pool. If I want to swim, I'll go over to Miles's and use the pool, or I'll go to the gym. The garden is fine as it is.'

'OK,' I say quietly, 'I just thought…' I swallow down the thick lump in my throat. 'I just thought it would be nice, that's all. I saw your swimming trophies at your parents' house and I… oh, I don't know.'

'Em,' Rupert turns, whisky in hand. 'Oh God, Em, don't cry.' He reaches for me now, and I have to force myself not to pull away. 'Look, it's a lovely thought. I do love swimming, you're right, and I do miss it, but not enough to shell out thirty grand on a swanky swimming pool, OK?'

I nod my head and smile, swiping at the damp tracks on my face, before I make a show of starting dinner. All my hard work today in the garden, and still it seems I can't get things right.

The shrill ring of the telephone makes me jump, as I sit at the kitchen table paying bills online. I have taken over this household duty from Rupert, and I still get a tiny shiver down my spine at the figures that sit at the top of the banking page, still not quite believing they are real. *Rupert could afford to put the pool in*, I think, *if I scaled it down a little*. Part of me wonders if he feels strange knowing that it would be Caro's money he would be spending. But Caro isn't here anymore. Anya pokes her head around the doorframe, a bottle of bleach in one hand.

'I get it?' she asks, a frown distorting her features. She is always frowning, a permanent look of disapproval.

236

'No,' I breathe out, 'I'll get it.' I snatch up the phone and jab at the answer button. 'Hello?'

Nothing. My heart stutters in my chest. Dead air again.

'Hello? Hello? Listen, if you're not going to say anything then just fuck right off, OK?' Apprehension makes my words weaker than I had hoped for but calling in the daytime is new. I've come to expect it on the cold, lonely evenings when Rupert is working late, but not now, when the sun is streaming in through the orangery windows, and I am feeling if not safe, then less threatened at least. Anya's face appears back in the kitchen doorway, her dark eyes wide.

'Bitch.' I hear the faintest hiss, the word floating down the line and I click the off button. Less satisfying than slamming down the receiver, but at least I cut whoever it is off.

'Is wrong number?' Anya asks.

'Yes,' I say shortly, slamming the lid of the laptop. 'I have to go out now.' Another day, another lunch, this time at Amanda's. 'If the phone rings, just… don't bother to answer it, OK?'

I step out into the bright, chilly sunshine, relieved to be out of the house. I am more shaken by the phone call this morning than I care to admit, and I am glad to be headed out for the afternoon, out of reach of that hissing, vitriolic voice. Walking quickly, the back of my neck itches where the wool of my scarf meets it, and as I reach up to loosen it, I think, from the corner of my eye, I see someone behind me. Pausing, I turn, scanning the pavement behind me.

There are plenty of people there, all going about their day, but no one is looking at me. Following me.

I let out a breath I don't realize I am holding, and then start to walk again, conscious of the heels of my ankle boots as they strike the concrete. My heart sinks as I approach the underpass that leads to Amanda's house. I could walk round the long way, up and over the dual carriageway, but it's busy and there isn't much of a footpath. Turning, I can see that the path behind me is empty. There is only me, and the long tunnel in front of me.

Don't be ridiculous, Emily, I chide myself, *it was a voice at the end of the phone. There's no one following you. Just walk.*

Tentatively I take a step forward, pulling my hat off my head and pushing my hair away from my ears. Nothing. It's fine. I step forward again, my shoulders easing down, my breath coming a little easier in my chest. *Idiot.* I allow myself a little breath of laughter as I fix my eyes on the white, cloudy sky, rimmed by bare tree branches at the end of the underpass. A faint smell of piss and something musty hits my nose, and I speed up, my heels striking the concrete with a dull thud.

And then I do hear it. A second footstep in time with mine, then faster than mine, and muffling a shriek into my scarf I start to run, too frightened to look over my shoulder at whoever is chasing me, too scared to slow down even though my chest is hurting through lack of oxygen. I tear through the tunnel and out the other side, only slowing when I am out into the daylight. A burly man walking an

English bull terrier gives me a curious glance as I bend at the waist sucking in gasping lungfuls of air.

I raise my eyes to the tunnel, but it is dark. No one comes running from the mouth of it, and after a few seconds a cyclist whizzes through, legs pumping, eyes hidden by sunglasses.

Idiot, I think again, *there wasn't anyone chasing you, you didn't even hear footsteps. It was a bloody cyclist.*

Straightening up, I start to walk again, a thick, hard lump in my throat. Maybe Rupert is right. Maybe I am just imagining it all.

'Emily!' Amanda opens the door with a grin, ushering me through into the huge kitchen, where I take off my coat and sink gratefully into a chair, my body still sticky with sweat from my impromptu run.

'Sorry, I'm a bit early,' I say, glancing at the clock. Sadie isn't here yet. 'It didn't take me quite as long as I thought it would to walk over.'

'Oh God, you didn't go through that dodgy underpass, did you? I'm always terrified walking through there; I'm convinced that someone is following me every time I walk through it.'

'It was fine,' I lie, saved by the sound of the front door slamming closed, as Sadie makes an appearance, dramatically kissing Amanda on the cheek and complaining about the traffic.

'Emily—' she kisses my cheek too, leaving a jammy red lipstick stain on my skin, 'gosh, you are keen, aren't you?

I thought I was the early one! Still, I suppose you didn't have much to do this morning, did you? Amanda, please tell me you got some of those gorgeous little macarons. We have to let Emily try them!'

I smile, though the thought of eating anything right now, even 'gorgeous little macarons', makes me want to heave.

'Ladies, it feels like ages since we were all together,' Sadie announces, as she pops the cork on a bottle of champagne. I groan inwardly – Sadie is only ever concerned with every event being a party – and I am too exhausted to try and battle the headache that is sure to follow drinking champagne at one o'clock in the afternoon. Amanda also doesn't look too thrilled by Sadie's decision to get the booze out.

'I'm not sure I fancy it, to be honest,' I say to Sadie. 'I've got a bit of a headache already and you know that champagne doesn't agree with me.' Not strictly true, and Sadie knows it but as I suspect, she doesn't challenge me.

'You do look a little bit peaky,' Sadie says, lowering the bottle. 'Are you feeling OK? Look at her, Amanda. Doesn't Emily look a bit pale?'

'I suppose so. A bit tired, maybe.' Amanda shrugs, before she turns to the oven to pull out the macaroni cheese. 'Sorry, ladies, it's only something simple I threw together.'

It doesn't look thrown together. It actually looks quite fancy, if macaroni cheese can look fancy. 'Looks delicious,' I say, even though the heavy smell of cheese is turning my stomach.

Amanda gently puts the steaming hot dish of pasta on the table, rips off her immaculately clean oven gloves and slides into her chair with a sigh. 'Gosh, I'm starving. Dig in, ladies.' She raises a hand as Sadie goes to pour her a glass of champagne. 'Oh no, Sadie, not for me. I'm with Emily today, I'm afraid.' Sadie pouts, but reaches for the glass jug of fruit-infused water on the table and fills both our glasses up, before pouring champagne for herself. As Amanda spoons the cheesy pasta onto my plate, I have to fight back a wave of nausea.

'Will you excuse me for just a moment?' I shove my chair back, startling both women. 'I just need to use the bathroom.'

Rushing from the room, I press my hand against my stomach as it swoops and swirls, slamming the lock home on the bathroom door. I lean on the sink and take a deep breath before running the cold tap and splashing water on my face and wrists to cool myself down. I raise my eyes to the mirror, to my reflection staring back at me. Sadie is right, I do look awful. I think of Rupert and I together in Sadie's downstairs loo at her Easter party, my face flushed, my eyes sparkling as I watched us in the mirror. Today, by contrast, my face is pale, dark circles smudge the skin under my eyes, despite the caking on of concealer, showing the lack of sleep I've had. I flush the toilet for effect and splash my face with water once more, drying my cheeks on the soft, almost linen-feel paper towels that Amanda has left out for her guests. As I step on the pedal to raise the lid of the bin, something catches my eye. Leaning down,

I pick it up, careful not to touch the end, and look back at myself in the mirror. This explains why Amanda doesn't want a glass of champagne.

When I return to the table the two women are a little flushed and giggly. I sit back down, apologizing for rushing off so quickly, as I try to shake off the feeling that perhaps they have been talking about me.

'Are you all right?' Sadie asks. There is concern in her eyes, but she still reaches for her champagne glass.

'Yes, sorry. I just needed to cool off for a moment.' I laugh and mime fanning myself.

'Well. As long as you're OK,' Sadie says, a slight tinge of suspicion in her tone. 'Sorry, I don't mean to be a mother hen,' she tries to smile but it doesn't quite work, 'Caro kept dashing off like that before she died.'

I open my mouth to ask why, but Amanda breaks in, clearly unable to wait to tell us her news.

'Girls, I have something I need to tell you.' Her face glows as she struggles to hold in a smile, pushing her plate away. When Sadie does the same, I lay down my fork, my food untouched, grateful for an excuse to leave it.

'I'm pregnant!' Amanda announces, and Sadie lets out an ear-splitting squeal, shoving her chair back and running round to squeeze Amanda tightly.

'Oh, darling, this is *wonderful* news!' Sadie beams, turning to me, as I smile and whisper my congratulations. 'Em, it's taken Will and Amanda simply *ages* to get pregnant, hasn't it, darling?' She squeezes Amanda's hand tightly.

'Lovely news,' I say, unsure of how to react – after all,

although I don't know Amanda terribly well, this child will be my niece or nephew. 'How far along are you, Amanda?'

'Only six weeks,' Amanda says, her joy evident on her face. 'To be honest, I only did the test last night. Will is the only one who knows – apart from you two now – so please, *please* don't say anything just yet. I'm feeling a little superstitious. Plus, you know, Will wants to tell his parents before anyone else.' Amanda's hand goes almost unconsciously to her belly to stroke her still flat stomach.

'Oh, Diana and Eamonn will be *over the moon*,' Sadie cries, 'especially after…' She falls silent and Amanda says nothing, leaving me to look at them both questioningly.

'After what?' I say, a confused smile tugging at my mouth. Amanda gets up and takes the plates from the table, moving to the sink, her back turned to me. 'Sadie? What do you mean, *especially after*? And what were you saying about Caro rushing off earlier?'

'Caro was…' Sadie lays her hands flat on the table, looks down at them. 'Caro was pregnant when she died.'

'Pregnant?' My mouth is dry, and I reach for my water, condensation making the glass slick under my fingers.

'Didn't you know?' Amanda turns from where she stands at the sink, her hand still cradling her non-existent bump. 'Did Rupert not tell you?'

'No. No, he didn't.' *Why didn't he tell me?* 'I had no idea. How… how many weeks was she?'

'Eight, ten. Something like that. Not many, but still. It made everything even harder.' Sadie sniffs, knocks back the rest of her champagne. 'I'm sure Rupert had his reasons for not telling you.'

'Yes. I'm sure he did.'

I don't know what to think. If Caro hadn't died, Rupert would be a father. His child – a little boy with his cowlick and his dark blue eyes, or a girl, with Caro's smile – would be a toddler, starting to walk, to talk, to be a little person in their own right. *How could she do that to Rupert? To her own child?*

Marching back up the drive, my head down and lost in thoughts of Caro, and Rupert, and the baby that never was, I am on top of it – of her – before I realize what it is. A bundle of fur curled up at the entrance to the drive. At first I think she is sleeping, although why Lola would be sleeping on the cold block paving instead of her warm bed is a mystery, and it's only as I scoop her up that I spot the blood on her head, the way she is limp in my arms.

'Oh no,' I whisper, tears starting to fall as I begin to process what has happened. My tiny kitten, my little companion, dead. I stumble inside with her in my arms, calling to Anya even though I know she has left for the day. Wrapping Lola's tiny, cold body in a towel, I rush upstairs for an empty shoebox to bury her in, my feet slowing as I reach the top of the stairs and the scent of nectarines fills my nose. My heart starts to hammer in my chest as I inch forward, pushing open the door to the spare bedroom. The perfume is stronger in here, and my stomach does a slow roll. I think for a horrid moment that I am going to be sick, right there on the carpet, and I suck in a deep, shaky breath, grabbing at the shoebox and hurrying back downstairs. Once Lola is tucked safely in the box, the splash of blood on her fur the only sign that she isn't just sleeping, I call Rupert.

'Rupert? Something awful has happened.' I blurt out the words as soon as he answers.

'Em? What is it? What's happened?'

'It's…' My throat is thick, and I have to push the words past the lump there. 'Lola is dead. I came home and she was curled up at the end of the drive. I think… someone hurt her.'

'What? Em, are you sure?' Rupert's voice is quiet, and I have to strain to hear him.

'Of course, I'm sure! There's blood on her head, she was definitely hurt by something. She didn't die naturally. Rupert, listen, someone called the house this morning. They called me a bitch, they whispered it down the line. What if someone deliberately did this to her?'

As the words leave my mouth I start to shake, and I have to sit down before my legs give way.

'Emily, please. We live on the main road into the village; the chances are that she was hit by a car. Please don't freak out about it. I'm sorry, of course I am, I know how much you loved her.'

'She was hit by a car that just so happened to be outside our house?' I snap. 'Can't you see, someone did this deliberately. To hurt me.'

'Em,' Rupert lets out a long breath, 'OK. I can see that

245

maybe it could look that way, but – be honest, it could just as easily have been a car that hit her. Do you want me to come home?'

I think about Sadie's expression as she tells me that Caro was pregnant. About Lola's tiny face, and how she'll never wind her way round my feet again. 'No,' I say, 'it's fine.'

I arrange with the vet to take Lola in for cremation, and then head upstairs, a bone-aching fatigue tugging at my entire body. Lola might have only been in our lives for a short while, but I was attached to her, and I'll miss her winding her way round my feet all day. As I reach the top of the stairs, that nectarine-scented perfume hits my senses and I see Caro's Facebook page in my mind's eye, her face smiling up at Rupert as he gazes down at her in adoration. Enough is enough, I tell myself, opening the door to the spare room and heading straight to the wardrobe. It's coming up to the second anniversary of her death, so maybe the time is finally right. Maybe if her things aren't here, I won't smell her on the air anymore, and the house will finally start to feel as though it belongs to Rupert and me. Maybe I'll start to feel as though I belong. Maybe by getting rid of every trace of Caro, I'll let whoever it is that is calling me – that shadow that follows me everywhere I go – that I'm not taking it anymore. That they can send me all the text messages, and call me as many times as they like, I am here to stay. I run my fingers over the fabric of her clothes and start to pull out the hangers sorting them into piles.

'What the hell are you doing?'

I jump, catching my hair in the empty hangers that dangle above my head. 'Shit, Rupert, you scared me.'

I manage to disentangle myself and stand, tired and aching, as Rupert surveys the spare room, the piles of clothes that lie on the bed, the dressing table, the floor.

'I asked what you were doing.' He doesn't step forward to kiss me hello, like he usually does.

'I'm sorting Caro's things out,' I say, heat making my cheeks flush pink. Maybe I should have checked with him first. 'I don't want to upset you, Rupert, but I live here now. It's hard for me to live in a house where your first wife's clothes still hang in the spare wardrobe.'

'Of course. I'm sorry. You just caught me unawares, I wasn't expecting it.' Rupert steps over a pile of high-heeled sandals and pulls me into his arms. 'And you've had a horrible day too.'

'Pretty shit,' I say into his shirt, as he kisses the top of my head. 'Amanda's pregnant.'

'Oh?' Rupert slides a hand under my shirt, as he traces a line of kisses along my jaw and down to my neck. Despite the shot of desire that makes my knees weak, I place a hand on his elbow to stop him. It feels weirdly wrong, when we are surrounded by Caro's things, her perfume staining the air.

'We've never talked about it, have we? About starting a family. I don't even know how you feel about children.' Now is his chance to tell me about Caro. I wait, turning to the clothes on the bed, pretending to fold them.

'I, ahh…' Rupert runs a hand through his hair. 'I don't know how I feel really, I haven't ever thought about it much.'

'Really?' I turn back to him, my arms folded across my chest. 'Not once? You never thought about maybe turning this room into a nursery?'

'No. Emily, what is this about? Have you suddenly decided you desperately want a baby or something? Because, not being funny, you've never mentioned it either.'

He's not going to mention it. 'Sadie told me about Caro.' I watch his face as a whole range of emotions flicker across it; fear, anger, and then finally sadness. 'Why didn't you tell me she was pregnant when she died, Rupert?'

'What was I supposed to say?' He finally raises his eyes to mine. 'Don't you think it was hard enough to tell you how she died? I wanted to tell you but…'

'But you didn't,' I say, flatly. 'I had to find out from Sadie like some sort of idiot, who doesn't even know who she's married to.'

'God, Em, please don't be like that.' Rupert moves towards me, but I hold up a hand.

'I felt like a fool, Rupert. I'm sorry, but I did. You should have told me.'

'It was too hard, OK?' Rupert almost shouts the words, and I feel something in me crumple. Maybe I'm being unreasonable. Cruel, even. 'I couldn't tell you because it was too hard. It was bad enough telling you she killed herself – what would you have thought of me if I told you that life with me was so unbearable she took our child with her?'

A single tear tracks its way down his cheek before he walks from the room, slamming the door closed behind him leaving me standing alone in a room filled with his dead wife's things, wishing I had just kept my mouth shut.

Chapter Twenty-Three

I apologize to Rupert again in the morning, pressing my body against him before the alarm clock goes off and he has the chance to slide out of bed to go to work. He rolls over and kisses me hard, pulling himself on top of me, knotting his fingers through my hair until I wince.

'I'm sorry,' I whisper, tracing my fingers over his cheeks, following the track his tear made. *Lying by omission isn't really lying, is it?* That's what I tell myself – that Rupert didn't really lie; he just didn't tell me.

'Let's not talk about it.' His voice is gruff, his face scratchy with stubble, and I let him move on top of me, biting against his shoulder to stifle my cries. Later, as I watch him knot his tie and slide his feet into fancy loafers, I push myself up on my pillows and say it again. 'I really am sorry, Rupert. I didn't think before I spoke, but you know you can talk about Caro to me. I won't be upset.'

'I know.' Rupert leans over and kisses my forehead. 'We'll talk about it later, OK? I'm late. And don't forget we have that dinner tonight.' And then he is gone in a cloud of aftershave. At least he's wearing the Tom Ford now.

I slump back against the pillows. I had forgotten about the charity dinner tonight. It's being hosted, as it is every year, by an important client of the company Rupert works for. Caro's father's company. I didn't want to go, but Rupert told me it was expected. Rupert has to attend, and therefore I have to as his wife. I go cold at the thought of Caro's social media photos, the pictures showing her and Rupert at this event in previous years. At the thought of running into her parents.

I spend the day running errands and working on the garden, even though Rupert said it was fine as it is. I haven't given up all hope of the pool just yet, and I could maybe even see about getting rid of the old shed at the bottom of the garden, and putting in a new one as a pool house for changing in, if I could get it for a good price. I let my mind wander as I burn the piles of dead wood, bushes and leaves that I have cleared and plant a rose bush in memory of Lola. The grass seeds have taken, and the lawn is looking more lush than scraggly in places at long last, and I prune and weed, all the while trying not to think about tonight's event. Rupert isn't best pleased when he arrives home to find me sipping brandy, watching the bonfire as the flames leap high into the sky.

'Sorry,' I pass him what's left in the brandy glass, 'I lost track of time. What do you think?'

'It's great.' Rupert gives me a thin smile, and I think how tired he looks. 'You don't have to though; I'm happy living with it like a jungle, I told you that.'

'Ha. I'd never have guessed.' I check my watch. 'Yikes. I really am going to make us late.'

I hurry upstairs and into the shower, relaxing at last now that Rupert is home and any last remnants of our argument seem to have been forgotten. Riffling through my wardrobe I take great care with the dress I choose. I did do some shopping with my black Am Ex, choosing three dresses, and now I select the one that is least like any of Caro's, no longer hanging in the wardrobe next door but bagged up and delivered to the local charity shop. I deliberately delivered it to one of Angus Beaton's shops, sure that Caro would have been pleased with the idea.

I pick out a slinky, midnight blue dress, cut much lower than anything Caro owned. I twist my hair up into a chignon, a few strands falling artfully around my face. As I push tiny gold hoops into my ears, my gaze falls on Caro's jewellery box, still sitting at the very back of the dressing table, behind the huge mirror. I pull it towards me, noticing the light sprinkling of dust on the top. Glancing towards the en-suite door, where steam escapes and I can hear the hiss of the shower running, reassuring myself that Rupert is not going to walk in on me, I open the lid, letting out a small gasp as I drink in what lies there.

Gold necklaces, earrings, a fat, glistening ruby on a square gold setting – I pick that one up and slide it onto my finger where it spins, far too big for my slender hand – a brooch, not dissimilar to the one Rupert bought me for Christmas, only instead of a dragonfly it is a bee, the white of its stripes made from diamonds. These things must be worth a fortune, and I imagine, just for a moment, being a woman who owns thousands of pounds' worth of jewellery. I imagine my mother's face if I rocked up at her house wearing this ruby ring, the bee brooch attached to my coat.

'Em?' Rupert's voice shouts to me through the door of the en suite and I hear the shower switch off.

'Shit,' I whisper to myself, thrusting the brooch back into the jewellery box, knocking the whole thing from the table in my haste to put it all back where it was. Gold and silver spills from the box and I scramble onto my hands and knees, scooping up rings and earrings, tumbling them all back into the box, reaching right under the dressing table to pull out an expensive-looking diamond stud earring that has rolled almost out of arm's reach. I fumble under the dressing table, looking for the other one but it's no good, I can't find it. Flushed and panting, I shove the box to the back, behind the mirror, and am sitting fixing my hair, which has escaped its grips, by the time Rupert comes out.

'Mmmm,' he kisses the back of my neck as he passes, 'you look fabulous.'

I give him a smile and slide a secret glance towards the box, making sure it's exactly as it was, hoping that by the time we get into the cab to go to dinner, my heart rate will be back to normal.

Amanda has cried off the dinner, citing extreme morning sickness, so I am sitting with Sadie, according to the table plan. Rupert sits opposite me, next to Miles, and another couple I've never met before also are seated with us.

'Hi,' I whisper, sliding into the seat next to Sadie. We are slightly late – it turns out Rupert really did think I looked wonderful, and I ended up taking my dress off before the cab arrived. 'Sorry we're a bit late.'

'How are you?' Sadie asks, head on one side as she lays her hand on mine. 'I'm so sorry about the other day, at Amanda's. I just assumed that Rupert would have told you. You didn't have a frightful row, did you?'

'No,' I lie, picking up the small menu in front of me. I have no idea what half the items on it are, so I lay it straight back down. 'Of course not. It's fine, nothing to worry about.'

'Oh, thank goodness,' Sadie presses her hand to her chest, 'I'd hate to think that I'd caused any trouble between the two of you. He's so happy since you came on the scene and we see so much more of him.' She looks across the table and I follow her gaze to where Rupert is listening to something Miles says, before tipping his head back and letting out a huge belly laugh.

I scan the room anxiously, looking for Caro's parents. 'Have you seen the Osbournes? I'm a bit worried about bumping into them.'

Sadie looks around before discreetly inclining her head towards a table at the front of the room, next to a small stage. 'Over there. But honestly, darling, don't worry. They understand. They know Rupert needed to move on, no one expected him to be a lonely widower forever.' There is something in her voice, sadness maybe, before she pins on a bright smile.

'Thank you,' I say, reaching out and squeezing her hand in a warm burst of appreciation. 'I've never… no one I've ever been out with before has had a wife who passed on, so I just don't know what to expect or how to react sometimes. I'm constantly worried that I'll put my foot in it.'

'Oh, no need,' Sadie says, 'everyone understands people have to move on. I was the one who told Rupert it was about time he sorted himself out, after all. You're one of us now. Anyway,' she smiles brightly and changes the subject, 'what did Rupert think about your plans for the garden?'

'He wasn't as pleased as I hoped,' I say, glancing along the table to make sure he is still occupied with Miles. 'He shouted at me a bit about the pool, saying he doesn't need one.'

The memory of his harsh words makes the back of my throat feel thick and I blink rapidly.

'Oh God, really?' Sadie rolls her eyes and reaches for my hand. 'I suppose he came out with some old crap about not spending the money? That's what Rupe does, I'm afraid.'

'What do you mean?'

'Oh, he's got such a chip on his shoulder about Caro's family being so much more well off than his. He won't want to pay for the pool because he'll feel guilty that it's Caro's money, which is just plain *ridiculous,* if you ask me. If I were you, I'd just get the plans drawn up anyway. Once he sees it, he'll come around. In fact, I'd go so far as to say he'd be thrilled.' Sadie shrugs, and takes a huge sip from her glass. 'You didn't let him upset you, did you? The rotter. Honestly, darling, I'll defend you to the ends of the Earth if he shouts at you again. I told you, you're one of us now.'

I want to cry; I feel so pathetically grateful. Sadie is an important person in Rupert's life and to have her approval means so much. I raise my glass to her, and we drink, and finally I begin to relax.

Sadie gets more and more drunk as the evening wears on, taking full advantage of the free wine. I, however, am trying to be on my best behaviour, conscious as I am that Caro's parents are here. And I'm glad I did keep my wits, as I bump into Mrs Osbourne in the Ladies. I'm not sure she knows who I am, and I avoid eye contact, concentrating instead on washing my hands and scarpering back to our table. I slink into my seat, telling Sadie that I saw Caro's mother.

'Did she say anything?' Sadie's eyes are wide as I tell her. 'The last time I saw her was at Caro's memorial. She didn't speak to us then, and I thought it was because she was upset but, in all truth, she never really liked me.'

'Really?' An auction has begun, and I sneak a glance at Rupert, who is already bidding on things with Miles. 'Why not?'

Sadie shrugs, a sloppy gesture now she is three sheets to the wind. 'Who knows? She's a funny old woman. Wouldn't leave Rupert alone until he held the memorial.'

'Why?' I lean in close, so no one can overhear our conversation. 'Why did she want to have a memorial? Surely the funeral would have been enough?'

Sadie blinks. 'There was no funeral.'

'No funeral?' I frown, the alcohol in my veins making everything feel a little muddy and blurred. 'What do you mean there was no funeral? Everybody has a funeral.'

'Not if there's no body.'

Not if there's no body. Sadie's words are at the forefront of my mind as I swim up into consciousness after a ragged few hours' sleep. My mouth is dry, and my tongue feels too big. A persistent banging thuds at my temples and my eyes ache, although from tiredness or alcohol I'm not sure. I didn't imagine it – Sadie definitely said there was no funeral for Caro. I close my eyes again, thinking on how I had pressed her on it as she stumbled over the words, slurring and mumbling.

'They never found her,' Sadie says, a tiny hiccup escaping her mouth as she speaks. 'They found her car, and her purse was in it and she'd left a note saying she was sorry.'

'Oh my God, that's awful.' I press my hand to my mouth, imagining Caro's body being dragged out to sea, crashing against rocks, being nibbled by tiny fish. 'Poor Rupert.'

'Poor all of us,' Sadie says, 'it took us a long time to accept that she was gone. I mean, there was never any doubt that she meant to do it, not with the note and her state of mind at the time. The police said she never would have survived the fall, and that with the current she might never… wash up.'

I have barely slept, her face, underwater, hair drifting across wide, staring eyes, floating into my mind every time

I try to sleep. I glance to my left, where Rupert lies snoring, oblivious to the bombshell that Sadie dropped last night. Rupert never told me that they had never found Caro's body. Another lie by omission. I lie unblinking, staring at the ceiling as another thought strikes me. *Who's to say that Caro is even dead?*

Chapter Twenty-Four

The image of Caro, broken and bloated, appears to me when I least expect it – every time I close my eyes, as I tackle the mountain of ironing that Anya has left, as I walk around the supermarket, picking up food items and putting them down again, unable to keep my mind from wandering. Rupert must know that something is up, by the number of times I've opened my mouth to ask him things, abruptly changing my mind and pressing my lips closed before the words have a chance to tumble out.

I haven't slept since Sadie told me they never found Caro's body, and I feel weirdly disconnected, moving through life as if on autopilot. Finally, after a week of sleepless nights, the final straw comes as I stand in the kitchen, holding an envelope with Caro's name on it. It's nothing important, a circular from some charity that she must have donated to before she died, her name still on some list somewhere, but as I stand there staring at her name in bold, black font, the phone rings and I shriek, my frayed nerves jangling. Crushing the envelope deep into the bin, I glance at the clock and see that if I'm quick I can probably catch Rupert as he goes on his lunch break. He's not on site today, working out of the Swindon office instead, his hi-vis and hard hat still tucked into the cupboard under the stairs as I grab my coat.

The air is damp as I wait outside Rupert's office, the cold mist settling on my chest as I pull my scarf closer around my neck. It feels as though spring will never come, the days still holding the dark gloom of winter. I long for sunshine, the warmth of the sun's rays on my back, Rupert's strong fingers rubbing sunscreen into my skin as we lounged on the beach in Barbados. *I wonder how many times he did that with Caro*, I think, my eyes filling with unexpected tears. I almost miss him, so busy am I rummaging in my coat pocket for a tissue, as Rupert strides past me with his head down, lost in thought.

'Hey!' I run after him, my fingers catching on the sleeve of his thin jacket. 'Rupert.'

He stops abruptly, a frown etched deep into his forehead before he smiles a puzzled smile. 'Em? What are you doing here?' He leans down to kiss me, his breath scented with coffee, warm on my cheek.

'I thought maybe we could have lunch together.' I tuck my arm into his, and we start to walk along the street, dodging the rubbish that spills from an overflowing bin as we pass.

'Oh. We can do, I only have half an hour, though. Are you all right?' He stops and turns to study me closely. 'You look awful.'

'Thanks.'

'I didn't mean it like that, I just meant… you're pale, and you look exhausted.'

'I am a bit tired,' I say, 'I just wanted some company. Surely you can spare a lunch hour for your old lady?' I nudge him, and give a laugh, showing him that I am *just fine*.

'Of course, come on.' Rupert leads me to a pub tucked down a small alley. It's a proper pub, the kind I imagine my dad used to go to. Not that I would know. He left before I was old enough to remember him. We order drinks – a pint of IPA for him, a large white wine for me – and both of us order steak and chips.

'Rupert,' I say, once the food has been delivered and we're halfway through our drinks. 'I wanted to talk to you about some things.'

'Oh?' He pauses, his last few chips crammed tightly on his fork, almost at his mouth. 'What things?'

'Well… about Caro. I feel as though you haven't been entirely honest with me about what happened.'

Rupert sighs, laying his fork down beside his plate. 'Emily, look, I told you before…'

'I know,' I interrupt, 'I know it's painful for you to talk about. I do understand that. But to hear from Sadie that Caro was pregnant when she died, I mean… I just felt…'

'Sadie needs to mind her own business. What happens between you and I is nothing to do with her, nor is my relationship with Caro. Look, I wasn't going to show you this until tonight.' He digs deep into his jacket pocket, pulling out a piece of white paper, carefully folded in half. 'Here, look at this.'

I reach across the table for the paper, uncertainty making my heart skip a little in my chest. Slowly, I unfold it and scan the words written there, as Rupert's eyes never leave my face.

'Well?'

'I don't know what to say.' I smile, folding the paper again. It's a three-night stay at a luxury cottage in the Cotswolds. I mentioned to Rupert that it looked lovely after I saw it in one of Sadie's glossy, upmarket magazines, but I never expected him to book it. I press my hands to my cheeks, trying to hold back my grin. 'Thank you. This is incredible.'

'You deserve it,' Rupert says, taking my hands in his. 'Listen, I know things have been tough for you, it's not been an easy few months, has it? I know that it's difficult to step into someone else's shoes.'

I shake my head, blinking rapidly. He's right, it hasn't been easy at all. In fact, it's been a hundred times harder than I ever imagined it would be. Maybe he *was* paying attention to me when I said things weren't right after all.

'I can see that you're exhausted – let's go to the cottage, have an amazing weekend, just the two of us, and then I'll get my Emily back… the Emily I know and love. A fresh start for both of us.' He gets up and pulls me to my feet, wrapping his arms around me. *The Emily I know and love.* I let myself smile into his shoulder.

Later that afternoon, I mull things over. By booking the cottage, Rupert clearly wants to make amends for all the arguments we've had recently. I let my gaze fall on our wedding photo, the two of us smiling at each other as if no one else existed. I love Rupert, and I love my life with him. He's made mistakes when it comes to telling me about Caro, I can see that, but how would I react if my loved one had died? Wouldn't I find it hard to talk about things?

Reading over the booking again, I smile to myself. We've had a stressful few months since the wedding, and Rupert is clearly making an effort. Maybe I should too. Sadie's words ring my ears. *I'd get the plans drawn up anyway.* A spark of excitement lights in my belly. I should do it, as a surprise. And then Rupert will be thrilled, just like Sadie said, and he'll know that I care about him, that I'm committed to the relationship and to making him happy.

I run upstairs into the spare room that Rupert uses as an office, riffling through the filing cabinet until I find the folder marked 'Orangery'. Holding my breath, worried in case the plans aren't there for whatever reason, I slide out the paperwork, shuffling through until I find it.

'Bingo.' I unroll the plans and see the garden area marked out. It could work. We could put in a small pool close to the house, with a cute little cabin alongside for a changing room. We would still have room for the borders and shrubs, and even a barbecue area. I could sell it to Rupert that it'll save us money on holidays in the long run, as we won't need to go away, and anyway, like Sadie said, he'll be happy once I take the initiative and show him how lovely it could be.

On impulse, I dial the number on the business card in the file for the building company.

'Hi,' I say, excitement making my breath come short as a gruff voice answers, 'I wondered if you could help me? I'm looking at getting a quote for a swimming pool…'

The builder remembers the house, and Caro (not such a surprise, really), and he asks me to send over my ideas via email. It's not long before he gets back to me.

'Yeah, your idea isn't going to work, I'm afraid.' He sounds apologetic and I try not to let my disappointment come through.

'Really? What's the problem?'

'It's too close to the house, to be honest. The site you've marked out is where the first soakaway is. The second soakaway is next to it, which means you don't really have the space to fit a pool in there. You could do it further down the garden, but that makes access to the site a bit difficult. It'll cost you.'

'Oh. OK. Thank you for your help anyway.' Despondent, I hang up, and re-roll the drawings. I tidy the file away, not wanting Rupert to know I've been in his office. I had been so thrilled by the idea, and so excited when Sadie had said that despite Rupert's response, he would have loved it, and now it's not going to work anyway. I'll just have to find some other way to make things up to Rupert.

'Bloody hell, Rupert, this is gorgeous.' I crane my neck to peer out of the car window at the yellow stone cottage, as he pulls onto the wide drive.

'Come on.' Rupert hops out of the car and I race him to the front door, letting him catch me and kiss me until

I am breathless and panting on the doorstep. 'Let's check out the bedroom.' He waggles his eyebrows at me as he unlocks the heavy front door and pushes it open, and I follow him inside.

The 'cottage' – if you ask me, it's more of a mansion than a cottage – is stunning. Flagstone floors lead into a country-style kitchen, the kind I can imagine myself bringing up a huge brood of children in, and then out onto a terraced area, with a pool and a hot tub tucked away in the corner for privacy. I trail my fingers over the sharp, marble kitchen counters, slide off my shoe and dip my toe in the icy cold water of the pool, run my fingers over the fronds of the thick ferns that line the garden borders, eager to soak up every part of this stunning house. It's not the sunshiny, scorching heat of Morocco or the Caribbean that I was craving, but this will definitely do. I turn to Rupert as he stands at the kitchen counter, wrestling the foil from a bottle of vintage champagne, and let a knowing smirk play across my lips.

'Come on, then. You'd better show me what this bedroom looks like.'

The weekend is perfect. That's the only way I can describe it. Away from the threat of the ringing telephone, the nectarine-scented air of the house, the memory of Lola's tiny, broken body curled up in the driveway, I can push away the thought that Rupert lied to me, even if it was by omission. I tell myself that to keep this life we are living, I can look past the secrets he's kept – that we all have things we don't want others to know about – and I begin to relax, realizing that this is exactly how I wanted my married life to be. Rupert cooking breakfast as I sip coffee at the breakfast bar, a post-coital glow making both our cheeks turn pink, long walks in the damp, drizzly rain into pubs with roaring open log fires, good ale and hearty lunches, sitting in the hot tub under the stars, champagne glasses in hand as our breath streams out into the cold night air, matching the steam that rises from the water. It's as we sit in the hot tub, Rupert's thigh pressed against mine, that I broach the subject one last time.

'We never did finish that conversation, you know.' I sip at my champagne, the bubbles going to my head as the water heats me from my core.

'Which conversation?' Rupert leans his head against the padded cushion on the moulded seat and closes his eyes. Sweat trickles from his temple, running down the side of his face. It's too hot in the water, but frost is already starting to glint on the surface of the terrace, and I can't face getting out just yet.

'The one about children.'

Rupert opens one eye to look at me, and then closes it again. 'What about them?'

'Well, do you want them?' I sit forward, raising my shoulders out of the water. I resist the urge to hiss in a breath as the cold night air hits my skin. 'I'm not asking about Caro, or anything, I'm just asking if one day in the future you want to have kids.' I let out a small laugh, a tiny shrug. 'We are married, we should probably talk about it at some point, so why not now?' I am feeling much more like my old self, like the old Emily, thanks to this weekend. The old Emily would never have hesitated to ask Rupert what he wanted.

'I think I would always have the concern that something might go wrong, if we were to get pregnant, after what happened with Caro,' Rupert says finally, 'even though I know you and Caro are not the same.'

Em isn't Caro, and she never will be. I splash water over my face as the words float through my mind, holding my hot palms over my eyes.

'But I wouldn't say never,' Rupert says, sitting up. 'One day it would be nice to have a family. For there to be three of us, instead of two.'

'That's all I've ever wanted,' I say quietly, and I let him untie my bikini top, and we don't leave the hot tub until much, much later.

Rupert is relieved that Emily seems to have forgiven him for being economical with the truth. He didn't lie to her, he would never do that, but he admits that he didn't quite tell her the whole truth about what happened with Caro. And now thanks to Sadie, Emily knows more than he wanted her to. He glances across at her as she snoozes in the passenger seat next to him. It's been the perfect weekend – he must remember to thank Will for suggesting it – the only blot on the landscape is Emily's mention of children. It's not that he doesn't ever want them, he didn't lie about that, it's just that every time he thinks about babies, he thinks of his child that never was. He hadn't handled things very well when Caro had told him they were going to have a baby.

'Aren't you pleased?' Caro is perched on the edge of the expensive sofa, the only comfortable seat in the house, the pregnancy test in her hand. The other hand lays protectively against her still flat stomach.

'Pleased?' *Are you mad?* he nearly says, but doesn't, because no one ever mentions the word *mad* in front of Caro. 'God, Caro, it's not that I'm not pleased, but it's a hell of a shock, and let's be honest, is it really the right time?' He scrubs his hands tiredly over his face, and lets his words sink in for a moment. Rupert had come home just a month before to Caro locked in the bathroom, threatening to slash her wrists. He's not sure he could cope with her mood swings *and* a baby.

'Darling, it's never the right time.' Caro gets to her feet and comes to him, laying her hand flat on his chest. She fiddles with the buttons on his shirt, a smile tugging at the corners of her mouth. 'Everyone agrees on that. But just think, a little me or a little you. How lovely would it be?'

'It wouldn't be lovely, Caro,' he pushes her hand away, panic overwhelming him, 'it would be hard, and I don't know that your… that your mental health could take it. You've been ill, Caro, a baby might just be too much for you.'

'Oh, just fuck off, Rupert.' Caro pulls her hand back, snatching up the pregnancy test. 'Who says you'll get to make the decision anyway? It's my body.' And she flounces from the room, leaving Rupert feeling like the bad guy, even though he's just worried about her. It's what she does. Manipulates the situation so he is the one in the wrong.

Now, he pulls up at the house, nudging Emily awake and carrying their things indoors. Emily will understand that he wants to wait a while, he thinks, as he fills the kettle, pulls out the bag of fancy tea that Emily insists on buying. But he won't talk to her about Caro. He can't.

'Rupert!' Emily's cry from upstairs is a piercing shriek, and Rupert drops the mug he is holding, shattering it into a million pieces over the tiled floor. He eyes it for a moment, before stepping to the bottom of the staircase as Emily calls him again, a panicky edge to her voice. Rupert steps on the bottom stair with leaden feet, his heart sinking in his chest. Emily was back to her old self at the cottage, but from the sound of her tone now, the relaxed, funny, laughing Emily of the past three days is gone.

'What is it? Em, are you all right?' Heading upstairs, Rupert peers into their bedroom but it is empty.

'In here.' Tears make her voice sound thick and clumsy. 'Look.'

Rupert pushes open the door to the spare bedroom, the room he found Emily in just a little while ago, surrounded by his dead wife's clothes. 'What is it?'

'I came in here to see about redesigning it into a nursery...' Rupert says nothing as Emily swipes at her eyes.

He didn't think they'd agreed to start a family yet. 'And look.' She gestures towards the wardrobes, the closets that should be standing empty. The hangers are full, crammed with silks, satin, dresses, coats and other clothes. *Caro's clothes.*

Chapter Twenty-Five

So much for a fresh start. The door to the spare room is firmly shut, and I hurry past it, the urge to go in and check the wardrobe, to see Caro's things hanging there neatly after I dropped them at the charity shop – and I did, I remember doing it – almost a compulsion.

In the kitchen, I make myself a cup of Earl Grey and pull my mobile from my pocket, scrolling down until I reach Mags's name. I need to talk to someone, a person I can trust. A friend. Rupert won't talk about it. I picture his face as he looked into the wardrobe last night, the way he had gone a grey, waxy colour before he made an excuse, just like he had before.

'Are you sure you dropped these things off at the charity shop?' he says, stumbling slightly over the words. That's how I know that he's shaken too.

'Yes,' I snap, my sharp tone belying the fact that my hands are shaking, 'I'm not an idiot, Rupert. I dropped them off at The Children's Trust. I thought that was the best place for them, given Caro's connection to them.'

'Well, that explains it then.' Rupert visibly brightens,

and my heart sinks as I realize that he's still not going to see this the way I do. 'If you took them *there*, that explains everything.'

'How? How does it explain the way your dead wife's clothes got back into our house?'

'Obviously, Angus visited the shop and saw them and thought that they had been donated in error. I…' he looks at me sheepishly, 'I did once say that I wasn't sure I'd ever be able to get rid of Caro's things.'

'Right.' A pulse flickers at my temple and I have to hold in a deep breath in order to keep my temper. 'So, say that Angus *did* return the clothes to the house – which, to be honest, just sounds like a complete fantasy to me – then how did the clothes end up hanging neatly back in the closet?'

'Anya hung them up, of course. While we were away.' Rupert looks completely satisfied with this answer. 'She didn't know Caro, she didn't start working for us until after we were married, so she probably assumed they were yours and hung them all back up. She probably thought she was doing you a favour. I don't see what part of this is a fantasy,' he snaps.

'Jesus, Rupert…'

'No, tell me. What makes more sense? That Angus returned the clothes and Anya hung them up, or your latest paranoid idea? Presumably you think that some mysterious someone broke into our house and put all the clothes back. It's ridiculous, Emily, and you know it.' He storms from the room leaving me standing there, open-mouthed, because he's right. I do think that someone got those things back from the charity shop and put them back in our house. And now I know that they never found Caro's body, the whole thing doesn't feel as imagined as Rupert is making out.

I click on Mags's name, praying that the call will connect. I imagine myself sitting on the threadbare, overstuffed, leaking sofa, eating custard creams and letting Mags make cup after cup of hot, sweet tea with two sugars, as I pour my heart out to her. She'll know the right thing to say to make things better, she always does. It's only now I've been away from her overbearing, suffocating brand of caring that I realize how much I miss it.

The phone beeps in my ear and cuts off without connecting. I'm debating whether to just head over to the flat – I don't know if Mags still has my number blocked or if she hasn't paid her bill again – when the doorbell rings and I see Sadie's outline through the glass in the front door.

'Darling!' Sadie barges her way into the house, much the same as she did that first time I opened the door to her, what feels like a hundred years ago. 'Rupert called me.'

'He did?' I follow her into the sitting room, where she is already sitting in the corner of the sofa that is my usual spot. 'What did he say?'

'He's worried about you…' She pauses, cocking her head to one side. 'He's worried about your health. Physical and mental. You do look dreadful, Emily.'

'Oh, for God's sake,' I mutter, unable to rein in the irritation that fizzes in my veins, 'there is nothing wrong with my health, mental or physical.' I pause. This is my chance to get Sadie to tell me everything she knows about what happened the night Caro died, before Rupert has a chance to tell her that he thinks I'm probably going mad. I realize she's talking at me again.

'. . . And Rupert can't cope with more... mental instability. After everything he went through with Caro, he needs someone to be there for *him*...'

'Yes,' I interrupt, 'Caro. Let's talk about Caro. Sadie, I want you to tell me everything you remember about that night.'

'What?' Sadie looks taken aback. 'Are you even listening to me?'

'Yes, of course I am. But I need you to go over things one more time. Tell me everything that you can remember from that night.'

'OK,' Sadie says slowly, and she starts to repeat the story of how there was a storm brewing, both weather-wise and at the party, that Caro was wearing a red, ruffled dress with exquisite diamond stud earrings, that she and Rupert had rowed.

'What about?' I say, leaning forward and resting my chin on my hand. 'What was the row about?'

'Well, I don't know.' Sadie blinks. 'No one could actually hear them arguing, it was all hisses and whispers.'

'Didn't you ask Rupert?'

'Well, I might have mentioned it to him afterwards, before we realized what she had done. He couldn't really remember, he said it was just about nothing really. It's what Caro was like – part of her liked the drama.'

I sit back, piecing together what Sadie has told me so far. 'So, Rupert and Caro rowed about something – something insignificant, according to Rupert – and Caro stormed out of the house. Then… what? No one saw her alive again?'

'Yes.' Sadie looks away, rummaging in her handbag for a tissue that she holds to the corner of her eye. 'Rupert called me the next morning to say she hadn't come home, that her car was still gone from the garage. We were all worried, of course we were, but she'd done it before, flounced off and then come home days later as if nothing had happened. She'd tried to commit suicide before too, but only ever at home.' She raises her eyes to mine and grief is etched deep into her features. 'None of us realized that she would… that she had done it for real this time.'

'I'm sorry, Sadie,' I say, reaching forward to squeeze her hand, 'I'm just trying to get things straight in my head. So, after a few days Rupert called you to tell you what the police had found?'

'Yes.' She blows her nose delicately and sits up straighter, shaking her fringe out of her eyes. 'Rupert called and said that the police had found her car close to the Severn Bridge. There was a note on the passenger seat that just said "Sorry". It was clear that she'd gone through with it this time. It was utterly devastating, but I'm afraid to say it wasn't really a shock to those of us who knew her well.'

'But they never found her body?'

Sadie stiffens slightly. 'No. They never found her. The police told us she would never have survived the fall, and that the currents can be so strong that she might never wash up. We held a memorial in her honour a little while before Rupert met you. She'd been gone for a year by then.'

I nod slowly, trying to match the puzzle pieces in my mind. A flicker of excitement burns in my belly and I have to think through what I am about to say, conscious that I might make things worse.

'Sadie?' I take a deep breath. 'I've been thinking, and I have an idea, only I think it might be upsetting, so I'll apologize now before I say it, OK?'

Sadie frowns but doesn't say no.

'What if… what if the reason they never found Caro's body is because Caro never died? What if she's still alive?'

'What?' Sadie goes white, her hand flying to her mouth. 'What do you know?'

'Nothing – not really,' I say. 'Please, Sadie, don't say anything to anyone. You know everything that has been happening to me – the letter calling me a bitch, Rupert and Caro's wedding photo appearing on the mantelpiece… it's been getting worse. I found Lola on the driveway. She was dead.'

'Oh my God.'

'And I gave all Caro's clothes away to the charity shop, but when Rupert and I came home from our weekend away they were all hanging back in the wardrobe.' Now I have started talking I can't stop, the relief at being able to potentially have an explanation for all that has happened making my words tumble out. 'At first, in the very beginning I thought maybe it was my ex – we had a really nasty break-up and he's not the kind to let things go – but everything that has happened has been related to Caro. As if someone is trying to scare me off Rupert, to get me to leave him. What if it's Caro? What if she isn't really dead?'

'Oh my God, Emily.' Sadie stares at me, her face pale. 'I don't know… I mean, it *could*. I suppose. It's not impossible.'

'Thank you.' I smile at her, relieved that her first reaction isn't to call me bonkers. 'You don't think I'm crazy?'

'No,' she says quietly, 'but what are you going to do? Are you going to leave Rupert?'

'What? No, of course not. I'm going to find out as much about Caro as I possibly can. If there's even the slightest chance that she is still alive then I'm going to find her.'

Sadie leaves, and I make her promise not to tell Rupert what I've said to her. I want to tell him myself, knowing that he might be devastated to think that Caro is still alive – that she chose to live a life without him. Fear beats in my chest too, at the knowledge that once this is out there, Rupert might try to find her himself, and that if he does, there's every chance that he'll pick her over me, and our time together will be up. But at the moment, he thinks I'm mentally fragile, just like Caro was, and if there's the slightest chance that this can prove to him that I'm not, that there is a reason for these things happening to me, then maybe he'll realize that I haven't imagined it all. When he comes home, I am waiting for him.

'Rupert, I need to talk to you.' I pass him a glass of the good red that he keeps in the basement, hoping to soften him up a little.

'About your hare-brained theory?' He snatches the glass out of my hand. 'Sadie called me at work. She told me what you said. She's worried about you.'

'What? I told her not to say anything!' The bitter sting of deception makes my eyes smart. 'I wanted to talk to you about it myself.'

'About the way you think Caro is still alive?' Throwing back the wine, seemingly without even tasting it, Rupert pours himself another leaving my glass empty. 'Jesus, Em, I don't know what to say to you.'

'But it's a possibility,' I cry, tugging at his sleeve as he turns to leave the room. 'Don't you agree? They never found Caro's body… what's to say that she isn't still alive? She could be doing all of this to scare me off, to get rid of me.' Desperation claws at my throat and I swallow, trying to get rid of the lump there.

'She's *dead*, Emily,' Rupert roars, spittle flying in my face, and I jump back in fright, my heart hammering in my chest. I think for a moment he's going to hit me – the image of Harry flying at me, the way he pulled me naked and crying from his bed, throwing me to the floor, as fresh in my mind as if it had happened yesterday – and I raise my hand to ward him off. Rupert slumps against the wall, rubbing his hand over his face. 'She's dead, Em. I know she's dead. She walked out of that party and she drove to the bridge and she threw herself into the water. And I let her go. Please. Can you just stop now? I can't take any more of this.'

I watch him walk slowly up the stairs, his feet dragging,

and his shoulders hunched and rounded and feel a hot spurt of shame. I did this to him. I reach for my scarf and coat, and tug open the front door, stepping out onto a mess of blood and guts. *Another dead bird.* Only this one has a note attached to it. It reads,

BITCH

Chapter Twenty-Six

In the morning, in a rare twist, Emily is up before him and Rupert comes downstairs to hot coffee and a bacon roll, even though it is barely seven o'clock. He kisses her on the cheek and smiles his thanks, even though he's not sure his stomach can take bacon at such an early hour.

'Will you be home for dinner?' Emily asks, her hands knotted together in front of her. Her knuckles are white, and Rupert can see the way her wedding ring digs into her finger.

'I'll try.' Rupert stoops to pick up his briefcase, as Emily lays a hand on his arm.

'It would be nice,' she says hesitantly. 'I'm sorry for what I said last night. I know I hurt you, but I really didn't mean to. Rupert, I'd be devastated if things went wrong between us.'

Rupert stops fiddling with his tie for a moment, not sure how to respond. 'I know. I probably overreacted, but honestly, Em, you need to stop this, OK?' His eyes search her face, but she looks down, scrubbing at something stuck onto the table. 'Em, I mean it. I love you, and I want to spend the rest of my life with you, but I can't deal with all this stuff you keep raking up. Caro is dead. Please, can we just focus on us?'

Emily finally looks at him, her face pale and her eyes ringed with dark circles where she hasn't slept. Rupert feels an unshakeable sense of déjà vu, as he manages to lean down and peck Emily on her pale, cold cheek.

'I'll call you later, let you know about dinner.' He picks up his briefcase and dashes for the front door, as if trying to outrun the claustrophobic feeling that he has been here before. That, despite his best efforts, things with Emily are going much the way they went with Caro. That this second chance to get things right, to get things exactly as he wanted them to be, is all going horribly wrong.

There is a knock at Rupert's office door a little before lunchtime, and his heart sinks as Sadie is shown in by his secretary. Much as he loves Sadie, he knows that she is only here today to talk about the events of yesterday, about Emily's revelation, and if he's honest, he just wants to get on with his work and forget about it all for a few hours.

'Darling, how are things?' Sadie looks concerned, but Rupert notices how she arranges herself artfully in the chair across from him so that her legs are on full display, in typical Sadie fashion.

'Fine,' he says, shortly. 'I'm quite busy, though, Sadie, so if that was all you wanted…'

'Oh Rupert,' she sighs, 'can't you even spare me five minutes? I just wanted to check in on you, that's all. I'll probably go and see Emily later as well, just to make sure she's OK. She was terribly worked up yesterday when I left her.'

'I'm sure she was,' Rupert sighs, putting his pen down. He won't get anything done now until Sadie leaves.

'It must have been a terrible shock, Emily coming out with something like that. Are you sure you're OK, Rupert? You look dreadful.' Flirty Sadie is gone, now it's just his old university friend in front of him and Rupert feels himself relax.

'Oh God, Sadie, I don't know.' He pushes his hand through his hair and then scrubs both palms over his face. 'I thought meeting Emily, *marrying* Emily was a second chance for me. A chance to put everything right that went wrong with Caro, but it just doesn't seem to be happening like that. Emily is convinced that someone wants to split us up – I still don't know what to think – and her saying last night that she thinks Caro is still alive… If I could go back to that night, the night Caro died and change it all then I would.' He stops talking abruptly, as if shocked at his own words.

'Oh, Rupert,' Sadie says, 'what happened to Caro wasn't your fault.'

'What if it was?' Rupert asks, getting to his feet, 'I argued with her, after all, and it was about something silly, nothing that warranted what happened after. I just want Emily and I to get back on track.'

Sadie says nothing for a moment, her lips pressed tightly together. 'Look, Rupert…' She pauses as the door opens and Rupert's secretary pokes her head in with a curious glance at Sadie.

'Sorry, Rupert, Michael just wants to see you in his office for a second. Could you possibly spare him a few minutes?'

Rupert nods. 'Tell him I'll be along in a second. Sadie, are you OK to wait here for a moment while I just speak to Michael?'

Ten minutes later Rupert returns to his office to see Sadie collecting up her things and getting ready to leave.

'I'm sorry, darling,' she says, kissing his cheek and leaving a smear of her trademark red lipstick, 'I have to dash, something at school for the twins that I simply cannot miss. But Rupert, what happened to Caro wasn't your fault, and you know where I am if you need anything – *anything* – at all, OK?'

Rupert lets her go without an argument, almost relieved to see her leave. It was bad enough when Caro's parents contacted him a few weeks ago, around the time of Caro's anniversary, without having Sadie in his office, dredging up more painful memories. He can't spend any more time today thinking about Caro, or Emily. A worm of guilt squirms in his stomach. He lied to Sadie, when he said he couldn't remember what he and Caro argued about – of course he can remember. It would be impossible for him to forget. He pushes the thought away and tries to focus on the spreadsheet in front of him. He is about to ring through to his secretary to ask her if she'll make him a coffee when his mobile buzzes on the desk next to him. It's another message request on his Facebook account.

Rupert, please meet me at Paulo's coffee house this afternoon. It's about Emily. If you'll just meet me then I'll explain everything. Henry Carpenter.

At four o'clock Rupert finds himself waiting anxiously in Paulo's for Henry Carpenter to show up. On receiving the message his instinct had been to ignore it or refuse to come but then he remembers his promise to himself, that he would meet Henry if he contacted him again. Despite his reluctance to get involved, he needs to set this guy straight – and if he is the guy that Emily has been running from, then he needs to protect her and see him off once and for all.

Now, he fiddles with his empty sugar packet as he waits for him, half expecting him to not turn up. He'll listen to Henry, he decides, he'll warn him off and then he'll go home to Emily, make sure he's back in time for dinner like she wanted. They'll talk, and get things sorted out, and everything can go back to normal. It can be like it was at the cottage for the weekend. Maybe he'll book something else, something a little more fancy to take Emily's mind off it all.

He looks up as the ping of the bell above the door tells him someone has just walked in. A tall, slightly dishevelled man enters, looking around the dimly lit café until his gaze lands on Rupert. He starts to make his way over and Rupert feels his pulse increase. This must be him.

'Rupert?' The man stands in front of him, his dark hair falling over one eye, a hand outstretched to shake. 'I'm Henry Carpenter. You can call me Harry.'

Harry. Rupert's stomach swoops as he shakes Harry's surprisingly firm handshake, and Rupert gestures for him to sit down. 'Harry. I'm not sure I'm the person you think I am…' Rupert starts to say, even though now he thinks maybe he is.

'You are,' Harry says shortly. 'You married Emily, didn't you? Crazy bitch.'

'Hey,' Rupert says, a spark of anger flaring, 'don't speak about her like that.'

'So, you did marry Emily Beaumont then?' Harry forces his eyes up to Rupert's face, and Rupert can't fail to notice that his hands shake slightly as he pulls out the chair and sits down.

'No, I didn't,' Rupert says, 'I married a girl called Emily Belrose. I've seen her birth certificate, her passport. That's definitely her name.'

Harry fumbles in his pocket and brings out an older generation iPhone. He flicks at the screen before turning it to Rupert. 'Emily. See?' Rupert peers at the screen, swallowing as he sees a photo of Emily, his Emily, smiling back at him. It's a photo he's never seen before, but it's her all the same. Emily as she looked before all the trouble started.

'Look, Rupert, I know it's difficult, but I came here to warn you.'

'What do you mean *warn me*?'

'About what she's really like.' Henry – *Harry* – sits back as the waitress brings him over a foamy cappuccino. 'I bet she's all sweetness and light, isn't she? It won't last like that, though. Before long she'll show you what she's really like. I was married before Emily came along. Happily married, or so I thought. And then she wormed her way into our lives, and I lost everything.'

'That's not the way she tells it,' Rupert says, thinking of the fear on Emily's face as she told him what Harry had done to her.

'Oh? Whatever her story is, let me tell you the truth.' Harry drags a hand through his unruly hair before sipping at the coffee in front of him. *A delaying tactic*, Rupert thinks. 'Emily and I worked together in IT. It sounds like a cliché, and it was I suppose. I was the boss, the director, and she was the new girl. Emily was – she was talented, enthusiastic, like a breath of fresh air. It was like she cast a spell on all of us, and yeah, I'm guilty of letting her get under my skin.'

Harry stops for a moment, as if catching his breath. 'We started an affair… It was only a couple of times, but then I broke it off. I loved Liv, my wife. Emily was a mistake. Emily wouldn't accept it. She hounded me day and night, broke into our house, things went missing – silly things like Liv's necklace that I bought her for her birthday, my favourite tie. Emily reported me to the police for stalking *her* – as if I couldn't get away from her if I tried. Obviously, Liv found out, and she was devastated. She took the children and left. Emily thought that meant that we would be together, and I came home to find her in my bed.'

Rupert says nothing, waiting for Harry to finish.

'That was the final straw. I'd lost my wife, my children,

and that day I'd found out I had lost my job because I had taken so much time off with the stress of dealing with Emily's behaviour. I dragged her out of the bed and threw her out of the house. I'm not proud of myself, I behaved in an appalling manner. I grabbed her by the throat, and I told her if I ever saw her again, I would kill her.'

Harry presses his fingers to his lips, as if pushing the words back inside. 'She hacked into my bank accounts and stole every penny Liv and I had saved together for the children. I tried to get her arrested, but she'd covered her tracks so well she'd made it look like I had taken the money myself. I haven't seen her since, but neither have I seen Liv or the children.'

Rupert doesn't know what to say. 'Harry, I'm sorry, I really am, but this doesn't sound like Emily. She's nothing like that.'

'Don't you get it, Rupert? I've lost everything because of that woman. *Everything.*' Spittle flies from Harry's mouth as his face contorts in anger and he slams a fist down on the table making Rupert jump. 'I'm trying to warn you – to help you – and you're so infatuated with her you can't see what she's like! I know where you live, Rupert, I know exactly where she is, and I could destroy her anytime I wanted to.'

'So, why haven't you then?' Rupert says, starting to get his things together. It looks like Emily was right after all about Harry, he is mad. 'Why haven't you come to our house and demanded that she repay you every penny?'

Rupert leans down and touches Harry's badly knotted tie, a tiny threat.

A look crosses Harry's face that Rupert can only describe as fear, and a shot of adrenaline pumps through him. He pushes the knot further up the tie.

'Why, Harry? Why haven't you come after her?'

'Because…' Harry swallows, and Rupert realizes the fear isn't aimed at him, it's because of Emily. 'She… she's fucking crazy. I don't ever want to see her again.'

Rupert shoves him back into his chair and snatches up his jacket. He doesn't need to sit here and listen to Harry's lies. Emily was right to be afraid of him, the man is insane.

'Bullshit. I don't believe a word you've said – stay away, Harry. If it's you that's been sending her letters and trying to frighten her then just stay away. Because if you don't, I'll come after you, understand? I'll kill you.'

Harry scrambles to his feet, his face flushed a bright, unhealthy pink. 'You're welcome to her. I tried to tell you, but you're just as crazy as she is. Don't say I didn't warn you, when the truth comes out about her.'

Rupert sits motionless, his heart thundering in his chest as he watches Harry leave, waiting a few moments before he makes his exit.

As Rupert strides towards the train station, he keeps seeing Harry's face change as anger consumes him and he shakes his head. He's never seen any sign of Emily behaving the way Harry has just described. In fact, he can't marry up the Emily presented by Harry to the Emily he knows at all. The Emily he knows is fragile, loving, maybe even a tiny bit broken by what has happened to her in the past, and yes, they have their problems at the moment, but his

Emily is nothing like the woman Harry has described. What he can picture though, is Emily cowering in fright as Harry's meaty fist comes down on her body. Emily's face, fear written all over it, as she tells Rupert that someone is watching her, she's sure of it.

Rupert pushes back his chair and pulls out his phone. 'Emily, it's me. I will be back for dinner after all. Meet me at the Italian on the corner, you know, the one… where we went last time.'

Chapter Twenty-Seven

I clear away the dead bird, without any mention of it to Rupert, and I fix a smile on my face and make sure my handsome husband's shirt is ironed for work, without any mention of his possibly not-dead wife, and I make sure to be as sparkly and normal as I possibly can, while all the time in the back of my mind is the possibility that Caro is behind everything.

When Rupert goes to work, I watch him walk briskly along the street in the direction of the train station, his coat pulled up around his ears against the March chill. In a few weeks it will be Easter, and I think back to last year, to Rupert getting down on one knee in front of everyone and the way I had felt just the tiniest flutter of panic before I said yes. *Premonition, maybe?* I wait until he is out of sight and then scan the road both ways, double-checking that no one (Caro) is lurking outside. The street outside is empty, but I close the blinds anyway before I head upstairs, my feet slowing as I approach the door to the spare room.

It makes sense to start in here, as Rupert had moved Caro's things in before I'd even met him. Sitting on my feet, I pull out the shoeboxes that line the bottom of the closet, riffling through each one, but none of them contain anything other than shoes. I pull out drawers, dig beneath mattresses and even try Rupert's desk, but there is nothing. There is no trace in the house, other than the wardrobe full of clothes, that Caro ever even existed, let alone lived here.

Sweaty and dusty – I did a much better job of cleaning the house than Anya has, that's for sure, despite wrecking the marble tiles – I head downstairs for a glass of water, pausing as I reach the orangery doors. Rupert has closed them back up again, despite my leaving them open. Could there be anything in there? I push the doors open, marvelling again at the light that floods the room. Such a waste, not to use it.

The only thing in the orangery that could possibly hold any answers to Caro's secrets is a large footstool, with storage inside. Even though I'm ninety per cent sure it won't contain anything of interest, I pull up the lid, to reveal a half-sewn cross-stitch pattern, the H and O of HOME embroidered in navy blue, and two photo albums. The sight of the half-finished needlework gives me a pang in my chest as I lift it to one side, imagining Caro sitting in here, stitching it for the house, only for it to be left unfinished. Lifting the albums, I dust off the covers and open one up. The first picture is of Caro and Rupert in a dingy pub. They are young, barely in their twenties and it must have been taken in the Nineties as Rupert is holding a cigarette. I didn't even know he'd ever smoked. Flicking through, I chart their progress together – graduation days, fancy dress parties, other people's weddings, their own wedding, and then finally the last photo – a grainy black and white scan picture, Caro's name and the date at the top. I slam the album closed, not expecting the sharp fingers of hurt that ripple through me. I knew Caro was pregnant when she died, but I just hadn't ever imagined a real baby.

As I get to my feet, writing off this whole search as a waste of time, I catch sight of the shed at the bottom of the garden. *Could there be something in there?* It was Caro's, after all, and she might have left something. Rupert doesn't go in there, and I've never bothered, apart from to fetch the gardening things. Shoving my feet into my trainers I snatch up the key to the padlock and hurry across the damp lawn, not noticing the chill in the air.

As I slide the key into the padlock it turns easily, and I shove my way in through the door, sticking and swollen with damp. The shed is tidy, with the garden tools hanging on nails on the wall, and racking against the far end filled with boxes, all slightly musty-smelling. Brushing aside cobwebs, I reach for the first box and open the flaps, only to find it full of damp, mouldy card beer mats. I vaguely remember Rupert telling me his dad used to collect them for him, so I close the box and place it on the floor and pull the box behind it towards me. This box is newer, with no sign of the damp that has infected the others. A tingle works its way up my spine, and I shiver, tugging the box down and opening it before I can change my mind.

★

Pay dirt. That's what runs through my mind as I reach in and pull out a sheaf of envelopes and paperwork. Ignoring the spiders that run out from under the racking, I scan the envelopes first – they are unopened, all in Caro's name and appear to have come from the bank. I pause for a moment, listening hard, and once I'm sure I am alone, I run my fingernail under the flap and slide out the sheet of paper inside. It's a bank statement, for an account in Caro's name only, dated June last year. Rupert must have taken it from the pile of post and hidden it out here. I run my eyes down the columns, gasping when I see the balance. There is a vast amount of money in the account, but no transactions have taken place.

I turn to the pile of papers and start to flick through them. They are bank statements too, some for Caro's account, and some for an account that is in both Rupert's and Caro's names. This account has a significant amount of money in it, too, but it's not an account I recognize as Rupert using regularly. I start to organize them into date order, and I see that occasionally a lump sum will leave the joint account, transferred into an account I recognize as Rupert's sole account. Nothing has left Caro's account since the day of the party. I check every single one painstakingly, going through over two years' worth of statements but there is nothing. Caro hasn't touched her bank account since the day she walked out of the house. Rupert, however, has topped up his personal account – the one without my name on it – several times using their joint account.

Frowning, I lay the statements to one side, a flicker of

doubt stirring low in my belly. *Maybe I have it all wrong after all? But then who, if not Caro, has been doing all this?* I dig deeper into the pile of paperwork, determined to leave no stone unturned. Just because she hasn't used that bank account doesn't mean she doesn't have another one, one that she had been siphoning money into. Maybe, despite Rupert's adamance that Caro would never have left him, she was planning to leave all along. The box seems to be never-ending, full of receipts, theatre tickets, formal correspondence and handwritten letters, that appear to be from a friend to Caro, written while they were at university. I resist the temptation to read them, not sure if my heart can take written descriptions of Rupert and Caro's love affair, and I am ready to bundle everything back into the box when I see there is one final envelope at the bottom, the first spots of mildew starting to discolour it.

I slide it out and pull out the contents. It's only a couple of pages long, and is on headed paper, from a solicitor in West London. As I scan the words, realization dawns, and only because my mother had been up in arms the day her third husband to be (who never became her third husband in the end) asked her to sign a similar document. It's a pre-nuptial agreement between Rupert and Caro. It states that in the event of a divorce Rupert would not be entitled to half of Caro's estate, and would only be entitled to certain amounts on prior agreement. However, if Caro died before Rupert, he would inherit everything, with a clause stating that on Rupert's death, any inheritance shall be divided between any children born to him and

Caro, and not to children born by a subsequent partner. All pretty straightforward. I pull out the bank statements and run my eye down the column again, disappointed in my failure to prove what I was so convinced was right.

Shoving the paper back into the box, I square the corners neatly and put it back on the shelf, placing the mildewed box in front of it, before surveying the shed to make sure everything has been left as it was. A wave of tiredness washes over me, and for a moment I feel sick and dizzy, nausea making my mouth fill with saliva.

If Caro hasn't been in the house, leaving dead animals on the doorstep and filling her wardrobe with her clothes then who has?

Chapter Twenty-Eight

Rupert is home early, catching me unawares as I stand at the stove, stirring a big pot of chilli, a glass of red wine in my hand. My mind is still ticking over everything that I uncovered today, and something isn't sitting quite right, but I can't put my finger on what it is.

'Something smells good.'

I jump, a slosh of red wine jumping out of my glass and running over my fingers as Rupert enters the kitchen silently. I haven't even heard the front door open, and I feel my shoulders tense. Anyone could have let themselves in and I wouldn't have heard. I need to start putting the chain across.

'Rupert, you made me jump. Good day?'

'Eventful.' He leans over and kisses me on the cheek. 'Didn't you get my message? I rang and said I'd take you out for dinner.'

'No, sorry.' I glance towards the telephone and hope he can't see the cord that has been pulled from the wall. 'I was outside in the garden for most of the day.'

'I told you to just leave it. It looks fine for now.' There

is something snippy in his tone and he moves towards the wine bottle. 'Do you mind if we stay at home after all?'

'I don't mind,' I say, ever the peacemaker. Rupert seems to be in an odd mood, not his usual self. He hasn't pulled me into his arms, or kissed me properly, just a dry peck on the cheek. There is an aura about him, something fizzing and volatile. 'Why don't you go up and have a shower? Dinner will be ready soon.'

I give him a winning smile and feel myself relax as he smiles back. Maybe I'm reading too much into things. It's hard to know how to respond after being with Harry and his unpredictable reactions.

'Emily, I think we need to talk.' Rupert's voice is grave, and I feel the smile slide right off my face as I pass him the rice. I look down at the tablecloth, straightening my knife and fork so they are the exact same distance apart.

'Yes,' I say eventually, 'I think we probably do. Listen, Rupert, I'm sorry for what I said about Caro… about Caro still being here. I was wrong. I know I shouldn't have but I—'

'It's not about Caro,' Rupert says, talking over me before I can confess to rummaging through the paperwork in the shed.

I reach for my wine, my eyes never leaving his face as my pulse starts to increase, a steady beat I can feel in my temple.

'I had a visitor today. Well, no, that's not strictly right. I agreed to meet with someone today,' Rupert says.

'Who?'

'A man called Henry Carpenter. Harry.'

Rupert waits for a moment, as I sit there unable to speak. A wave of dizziness washes over me and I swear I can feel the blood drain from my face.

'Harry?' I whisper. My hand goes to my throat and I massage the skin there, hoping to ease the lump that rises. 'What did he say to you, Rupert?'

'Some pretty vile stuff, to be honest.' Rupert stalls, taking a sip of his wine. He watches me as I reach for the glass of water on the table next to me, my wedding ring spinning on my finger as I do so. I've lost so much weight without even trying, thanks to the stress I've been under.

'Please, Rupert, don't just look at me like that,' hot tears burn my eyes, 'will you just tell me what he said?' I blink, and a fat tear slides over my bottom lashes.

'He said that the two of you had an affair. That you worked for him, seduced him, and then when he told you he didn't want you anymore you turned into a psychopath. Stalking him, breaking into his house.'

'Oh my God.' My heart is pounding fit to burst out of my chest, and that old familiar sick feeling that I will always associate with Harry makes my stomach roll. 'Do you believe him?'

Rupert says nothing for a moment.

'Rupert, do you believe him?' My voice rises and Rupert leans forward, grasping both my hands in his. 'Do you honestly believe that I am capable of that?'

'I told him that that isn't the Emily I know,' Rupert says,

squeezing my hands so tightly I can feel the sharp ridge of my diamond engagement ring cutting into my skin. 'I didn't even want to meet with him, but I wanted to tell him to back off, if it is him who has been hassling you.' He pauses. 'Do you want to tell me the full story? I think I deserve to know.'

I nod, swiping at the tears on my cheeks. Maybe once I have told Rupert the full story we can move on, and Harry won't hold any sort of threat anymore. 'I should have told you before, I'm sorry. It was just too painful to talk about. Harry's right – I did know he was married when I met him.'

'OK,' Rupert says, but I can see the look of disappointment on his face, and I feel a hot dart of shame.

'He told me about Liv, his wife. He told me that they were getting a divorce, that he didn't love her anymore. He was a gentleman at first. He took me to nice places, treated me well. I'd never really had that before, he dazzled me, I guess. He was the big boss, the man everyone in the company looked up to, and here he was, giving all his attention to me.

'Everything changed after a few months. He became secretive, argumentative. I was walking on eggshells around him all the time. It started small, just harsh words and a light slap every now and again, but as time went on, it got worse, more violent. I had to hide the bruises at work, pretend that I had fallen over again… clumsy old Emily. The day I told him I was leaving him was the day it all came to a head properly. He accused me of taking everything from him – Liv, the kids… even though he hadn't seen them at all in all the time we were together – and then he dragged me out of bed and put his hands around my throat, and he strangled me until I passed out.' I let the tears run freely down my cheeks now, and Rupert's face is filled with horror.

'I got out as soon as I came round. I found a room with Mags and she helped me put myself back together again. And then I met you.' I give him a watery smile, the emotion of telling him making me feel wrung out and drained.

'Jesus, Emily. You should have told me before.'

'Can you believe I didn't want to tell you, because I knew Harry was married? I didn't want you to get the wrong idea about me.'

'The wrong idea? It's not 1945, Emily. I'm not a complete tyrant. I can't believe you didn't tell me the truth.'

'I know, I should have told you. Will you forgive me?' I turn to him, my eyes wide and after a moment's pause he finally nods.

'Of course I will. It's hardly your fault that you were in an abusive relationship. But I need you to be honest with me, always? After Caro…'

'I don't want to talk about Caro,' I say, getting to my feet and moving to his side of the table. 'I was wrong, the other day. I don't want to talk about her anymore, this is just about you and me now.'

Rupert gets to his feet, and I wrap my arms around him, raising my mouth to his, moaning softly against his lips as he slides his tongue into my mouth. I can feel him hard against my thigh, and I fumble for his zip as he hikes up my skirt, pushing me back onto the table. I'll make Rupert forget about Caro, and Harry, and anything that went before.

Later, I am curled up in my usual spot on the sofa reading a crime thriller, as Rupert sits across from me watching some inane TV show with lots of canned laughter. The blinds are closed, the lamp is lit, and for the first time in weeks I feel safe. No one can see in, there is no scent of nectarines hanging in the air. I snuggle into the sofa, rereading the page I've already read twice, when my phone buzzes next to me.

Glancing towards Rupert, whose eyes are still fixed on the television screen, I pick up my phone and see I have a message from an unknown number. Instantly, I go cold and any feeling of safety vanishes. I raise my eyes to the blinds, double-checking they are still tightly closed. I debate for a moment whether to just delete the message without reading, but the last time I did that the message was just resent a few minutes later. Rupert looks up in confusion as I get up from the sofa.

'Just popping to the loo,' I say, brightly. I hurry into the downstairs loo, flicking on every light as I go and lock the door, perching on the closed loo seat. Finally, I swipe to open the message. It's a video. Against my better judgement I press play, the sharp metallic taste of fear in my mouth.

It's a recording on a mobile phone by the looks of it, the angle of the screen showing that it has been propped against something, I think. I recognize it as Sadie's house – her kitchen to be precise, and I hold my breath as two people come into view – Sadie and Rupert – Sadie leaning against the kitchen counter, Rupert standing close to her. She's wearing the dress she wore to her garden party, and my breath sticks in my throat as I realize it is the night of Sadie and Miles's Easter party. The night Rupert proposed to me. The night Rupert told me that he hadn't seen anyone when he went downstairs.

Sadie has her arms around Rupert's neck, and they are talking, but the sound is muted. I turn up the volume on the phone as high as it will go, but it's difficult to make out the words. It sounds as though Sadie says to Rupert, 'It should have been me,' but I can't make out Rupert's reply and his back is to the screen so I can't even lip read. Adrenaline pumps through my veins as I watch them both on the screen, still talking quietly, before Rupert raises his voice and finally, I am able to hear what Rupert says.

'Sadie, I love you.' His words are clear, and I feel them as sharply as if Rupert had stabbed me himself. The video ends.

I lay in bed all night, stewing over the video. I replay it three times in the privacy of the downstairs toilet, until Rupert bangs on the door to check if I am OK. Now, in the darkest hours of the early morning, I slide out from under the covers to peer out into the street below, straining my eyes to see if there is a shadowy figure watching the house. Now I know that Caro is dead, I know she can't have sent the video, so who did?

Rupert snuffles in his sleep, rolling over onto his back and I hold my breath for a moment, until I am sure he won't wake up. The cold from the oak floor is seeping into my toes, and I shiver, although I don't feel cold. I feel as though I am burning up from the inside out, the way you do when you have the flu. Clicking my phone onto silent, I replay the video again, the screen casting a blue glow across my features.

Without the sound, I can focus on their body language and I'm sure it's not my imagination that Rupert doesn't look entirely comfortable as Sadie latches her arms around his neck. She, on the other hand, looks as though she is enjoying it far too much, although her eyes are half closed and she looks as though she's had far too much to drink. I am trying to be generous.

Sighing, I pad silently across the room and slip back into bed, the warmth from Rupert's body raising goosebumps on my skin. He throws his arm over my waist and mumbles 'love you' into my ear. I close my eyes, the words he said to Sadie printed indelibly on my mind. I picture myself, standing at the bottom of the stairs that night, seeing the two of them together, and then Rupert telling me the next morning that he hadn't seen anyone when he went downstairs. *Lies by omission.* I wriggle out from under his arm, my skin burning. I know what I need to do. I'll go and see Sadie first thing tomorrow morning and find out exactly what the hell went on that night.

Chapter Twenty-Nine

It's my turn to lie by omission as I don't mention to Rupert the video sent to my phone, instead waiting until he has left for the office before I snatch up my keys and my bag and walk the twenty minutes to Sadie's house. I could have taken the bus, but that intense heat still burns me from the inside out, so I try to walk it off before I arrive.

When I arrive at Sadie's twenty minutes later, my anger has cooled ever so slightly, no longer white hot, but a fierce red that bubbles and rages in my veins. It's been a long time since I felt this angry about anything, which tells me my relationship with Rupert is worth fighting for. We might have had our problems lately, but I'm certainly not ready to give up, not by a long shot.

'Emily! What a surprise!' Sadie looks immaculate in designer loungewear, her hair tied up in an artfully messy bun – the type that when I tried it before, I looked as though I'd just woken up, and not in a good way. I don't bother with pleasantries, instead I shove my way into the house, the way Sadie has done to me so many times before.

Sadie's twins gawp at me from where they sit on the living room floor, surrounded by expensive toys.

'Kids, out of here. Tallulah!' Sadie shouts for the nanny to come and get the children. 'Emily, is there a problem?' Sadie's porcelain white cheeks are stained with a red flush, and she looks nervous.

'You could say that.' I brandish the phone at Sadie. 'I think you've got some explaining to do.'

Sadie is silent as she watches the video, the red flush on her cheeks creeping down to stain her neck in an ugly rash. Finally, with shaking hands, she hands the phone back to me. 'Really, Emily, this isn't what you think it is.'

'Then what is it?' A note of steel has crept into my voice, and I feel a flicker of the old Emily coming back to life. The Emily who wasn't too afraid to go out and get what she wanted. The Emily who wasn't scared of her own shadow. 'Because from where I'm standing it looks as though you and Rupert were… getting close to each other on the day I accepted his proposal.' My voice breaks on the last word, and I swallow hastily.

'I was drunk…' Sadie says, rubbing her hands over her face. 'I know it's no excuse, but I was upset about Caro and I said some things I probably shouldn't.'

'So did Rupert from what I can see.' Steely Emily is back, and I eye Sadie closely, scrutinising her face as if to check for clues that she is lying. 'I want to know the whole conversation.'

'I told you, this isn't what you think. Rupert loves you. This is just…' Sadie waves a hand towards the phone, before

305

she turns and walks into the kitchen. 'Emily, please listen to me. This is not what you think. You said yourself that someone has it in for you and Rupert.'

'And I seem to recall both of you telling me that I was overreacting, that I was just being ridiculous.'

'Well, I was wrong, I'm sorry,' Sadie says, sharply. 'Someone clearly does have it in for the two of you. Clearly, someone doesn't think that you and Rupert should be together.' Sadie lets her eyes fill with tears and takes a huge gulp from the glass in front of her. It looks like a Bloody Mary, and I watch as she swallows it down, before going to the fridge and pouring herself another one.

'I think it's pretty obvious that they do. And neither you nor Rupert would believe me when I told you that. You told me I was overreacting, that I was mad. This is real—' I wave the mobile phone, 'I know what I saw and what I heard.'

'Taken out of context,' Sadie says, 'Emily, I am your friend. I've known Rupert for years, of course we love each other – as friends. Someone is trying to cause trouble, that's all this is, and by reacting this way you've given them exactly what they want.'

I pause for a moment. Sadie does have a point – reacting this way gives whoever sent the video the response they were after – but I can still hear Rupert's voice telling Sadie he loves her.

'Maybe if you find it so easy to believe that Rupert would cheat on you, then perhaps your relationship isn't as secure as you believe it to be,' Sadie says gently, and I begin to feel the fight go out of me.

'I don't believe that for a second. Rupert and I are strong together, we love each other, but whoever is doing this…' I break off, distracted by a shriek from upstairs.

'Excuse me a moment.' Sadie strides from the room, shouting the nanny's name. I wait, sniffing at Sadie's glass – it definitely is a Bloody Mary – and running my fingers over the shiny, black marble counter tops. I pause as I look over the vast American-style fridge, with magnets stuck all over it. I never would have put Sadie down as a woman who would stick magnets all over her fridge. There are pictures drawn by the children stuck on with magnetic letters, scribbles all showing 'my family', 'my house', 'my dog' – wishful thinking on someone's part, as Sadie would never have a dog – and a shopping list, written in familiar handwriting.

I peer at the slip of paper, an unsettling feeling resting on my shoulders. The writing is familiar, but I just can't place it; all I know is that it has awoken a creeping sense of dread. I close my eyes and breathe deeply, letting the scrawl sit in my mind's eye, and then it comes to me.

The Christmas gift. The one that was left on the doorstep, the photograph of Rupert and Caro on their wedding day. Mags had come over to deliver my post, but Sadie had been there that day too. My name was written in gold pen across the top of the gift in this very handwriting, I am sure of it.

Shock makes my eyes ping open, and my heart starts to race. I slide my gaze across to the key hooks that are fixed to the wall next to the fridge. I step closer, reaching out, looping my fingers around the one at the very end. It's my key – the spare key to my (*our*) house. I tug it from the hook, as things start to slowly, gradually click into place. *The handwriting. The key.* All this time Sadie has had access to our house. She knows what perfume Caro wore; what's to stop her from walking in when no one is home and spritzing it around the bedroom, making me think that someone – Caro, even – had been in there? I think of the day I had found Lola lying broken in the driveway, my heart twisting as I picture her tiny face. That was the day we'd been invited to Amanda's for lunch, the day she announced her pregnancy. Sadie had arrived late to the lunch, making some bitchy comment about how I had been early. Couldn't she have waited for me to leave before hurting Lola, and then coming to lunch as if nothing had happened? I want to kick myself – she practically told me herself in the video, her arms looped around Rupert's neck – '*it should have been me*'. I feel sick, hot, the room starting to spin a little and I sink into the nearest chair.

'Darling, are you OK?' I look up to see Sadie's concerned face looming over me. I'm not sure if I am imagining it, but I think I see the corner of her mouth tug up into a little smile.

'It was you, wasn't it?' I say after a moment, raising my eyes to her. 'You did all of this.'

'All of what? You haven't been sipping out of my glass, have you? That's for grown-ups only.' Sadie smirks and I know for certain then.

'How could you?' I get to my feet, shaky now the shock

has set in. 'Rupert was supposed to be your friend, but you did all of this. Sneaking into the house, making me think that someone had been there. Sending me vile messages and Lola… oh my God, you did that to Lola.'

'I fucking hate cats. And so does Rupert, believe it or not.' Sadie smirks as she pulls out a packet of cigarettes and lights one, blowing the smoke in my face.

'And you sent that video message. What were you going to do, delete it so that when I showed Rupert it was gone, and I look mad?'

'Clever girl. Who do you think Rupert is going to believe when you run to him and tell him that Sadie is the big, bad wolf? Me – his oldest friend? Or you? Some little tart he's married to but barely knows. Who's been accusing people of all sorts of things practically from day one? Calm down, Emily, you'll only be making a fool of yourself. Although, I suppose that's the best way for things to go.'

'He'll believe me.'

'No, Emily, he won't. I've made sure of that, haven't I? Don't you realize that you've fucked everything up by appearing on the scene?'

'You wanted Rupert for yourself.' Realization dawns as I watch the hatred settle on her face. She never liked me. All those times that she 'let me in' it was all fake. 'You wanted Rupert all for yourself. What did you do? Drive Caro to it?' I can't resist taunting her a little. 'You drove Caro to it, and then your plan backfired?'

Sadie is silent for a moment, shock written all over her face. 'What kind of person do you think I am? Of course,

309

I had nothing to do with Caro dying, you sick bitch. But when Rupert was all alone, I knew it was our chance to be together. It should have been me all along – it would have been if I hadn't introduced him to Caro at university.'

'That's what you told Rupert, that night of your Easter party, wasn't it? And he rejected you.'

'I told him he needed to sort himself out after the memorial. I meant it was time to move on, with me. I was always the right one for him, and I thought after Caro died, he would see sense, finally. I didn't mean for him to settle down with some…' Her mouth twists as she spits the words at me.

'Some… what?' Fury makes me bold. 'You wanted me to think I was going mad – you wanted *Rupert* to think I was going mad. That way, Rupert would leave me of his own accord, and then you could step in, and no one would think badly of you, they'd all be relieved that Rupert had someone who could take proper care of him.' I let out a harsh bark of laughter. 'I think you might have severely underestimated me, Sadie.'

Sadie blinks, and takes another drag on her cigarette. 'The way you underestimated me, you mean? *Oh, thank you Sadie, for including me, thank you for being so kind to me, Sadie.* You're pathetic. And now Rupert thinks you're bonkers, he'll be glad to be rid of you.'

'I doubt that very much,' I say, as I hold up my phone, the screen showing that our entire conversation has been recorded.

Chapter Thirty

Sadie sits shell-shocked at the table, as I scoop up my bag and turn to face her.

'I think it's best if Rupert doesn't see you for a while,' I say.

'All you have to do is leave,' Sadie says finally, quietly from where she sits at the kitchen table. 'That's all I ever wanted to do was to make you leave. You're like a cuckoo, forcing your way into the nest.'

'I'm not the cuckoo, Sadie,' I say, 'you need to look a lot closer to home for that. Don't contact Rupert – don't call him, don't try to see him. I'm warning you.'

Without waiting for her to reply, I slam my way out before she can get to her feet. Once away from the house I start to run, heart racing, my feet slamming against the pavement sending shooting pains into my knees. I wait until I am around the corner before I stick my arm out and hail a passing cab. I give the driver the address of Rupert's office and slump back in the seat, my breath coming in painful gasps. I am sure that Sadie will be on the phone to Rupert before I've even made it to the end of the road, but it doesn't matter, I have the recording.

We pull up outside Rupert's building and I pay the driver, before taking a deep breath and approaching the glass-fronted space where my husband spends every day. A receptionist is on the phone as I enter, and she holds up one finger in my direction as I walk up to the desk.

'Rupert Milligan, please,' I say, as an older gentleman passes by, giving me a quick double take before he gets into the lift. There is something familiar about him and it's only as I take my own place in the lift up to Rupert's floor that I realize it is Michael Osbourne, Caro's father and the owner of the large construction company Rupert works for. I offer him a tiny smile, the back of my neck prickling uncomfortably, and I am relieved when I step out of the lift and he stays on.

Rupert is sitting at his desk, engrossed in whatever is on his screen when I tap lightly on the door to his office. He glances up, irritation on his face at being interrupted before he realizes it is me.

'Emily—' His tone is cautious, and he peers behind me as if expecting someone else to be there. 'What are you doing here? Is everything OK?'

It seems that Sadie hasn't called him – although what exactly could she say, knowing that I had recorded our entire conversation? 'I'm sorry to come here unannounced. Have you got a few minutes? I really, really need to talk to you.'

'I've got a meeting in half an hour, but yes, I guess I can take a break now. Do you want to go out and get some coffee?'

He's already reaching for his jacket, and I think about Michael Osbourne and the way his eyes flickered over me. I think I'd prefer to talk to Rupert outside, away from any connection to Caro, so I nod and follow him back into the lift and out into the street. We enter a tiny coffee shop set back from the main street and Rupert gets us both a drink.

'What's all this about, Em?' Rupert looks at me warily, and tips sugar into his coffee.

'All these things that have been happening at home… the notes, the phone calls, what happened to Lola… I know who's behind it.'

Rupert lets out a long stream of air, his cheeks flushing a dark pink. 'For God's sake, Emily, we've talked about this! I don't want to hear any more about it! No one – I repeat – no one is out to get you. No one is trying to scare you away. No one has been in the house, no one is watching you. *Caro is dead.* Please, Emily, just leave it because I don't know how much more I can take.'

I blink and wait for a moment, a little shocked by the way his anger rises to the surface so easily, before I pull out my mobile and slide it across the table towards him.

'Like I said, Rupert, I know who's behind it all. Just watch the video.'

He picks up the phone and presses play, and my voice filters out from the speaker. '*It was you, wasn't it?*' I watch the emotions play out across his face as he watches the video from start to finish, the blood draining from his face as he hears me accuse Sadie of pushing Caro over the edge.

'Oh my God.' Rupert slides the phone back to me, his

hands visibly shaking. 'Emily, I'm so sorry. I should have believed you.'

I shrug, as if it's not that important, but part of me wants to get up and shout, '*Good! You should be sorry; you should have taken my word for it.*' But if there's one thing my mother did teach me, is that it's sometimes best to hold your tongue.

'Caro said the same things, sometimes, you know.' Rupert speaks again, stirring at the remains of the coffee in his cup. 'That things had been moved, that she thought someone was following her, but there was never anything concrete, nothing solid. It was exhausting, that constant act of reassuring her. I thought it was just the same thing happening again with you. I thought you were just…' He puts his head in his hands. 'You accused her of pushing Caro too far?' When he raises his eyes to mine, they are bloodshot and watery.

'It just slipped out. She denied it, but she admitted that she'd done all those things to me. That she wanted you for herself. Well, you know what she said, you watched the video. I haven't been lying, or making things up, and I'm definitely not going mad.'

'I'm just a bit stunned by it all,' Rupert says, as he takes up the phone and watches the video again. 'Part of me can't believe that Sadie would behave as aggressively as that – I've known her for over twenty years! We went to uni together, I was best man when she and Miles got married and I never realized… I mean, she said stuff when she was drunk, like the night of the Easter party but she never meant it.'

I direct him on my phone to the video message that Sadie sent to me last night, watching the shock on his face as he sees himself and Sadie on the night of the party. 'What did you say to her, that night?'

'She was drunk,' Rupert says, 'she was saying something about how it should have been her, we were a good team, something like that. She always says stuff like that when she's pissed... I always just brushed it away as a joke. I know she's not one hundred per cent happy with Miles, but whoever is one hundred per cent happy?' He reaches over and squeezes my hand, as if to reassure me that this doesn't apply to him. 'I said something to her about how I love her, but as a friend. I didn't tell you I saw her when you asked the next morning because I didn't want to upset you. You were already a bit down about the fact that someone had called you Caro by mistake.'

'You should have told me,' I say quietly, 'and you should have believed me.'

'I'm so sorry, Em,' he picks up my hand, kisses the back of it, 'and I should have known. I should have known that Sadie would be jealous, that she would cause trouble between us. I feel like an idiot for not seeing it, for just seeing her as good old Sadie, friends for years.'

'What do you mean? Why should you have seen it?'

I certainly hadn't – I'd been desperate for her acceptance. I remember how I had felt that day when she'd said I was 'one of us', how pathetically grateful I'd been.

'Sadie was always on at Caro... she always wanted whatever Caro had; I just didn't realize that that extended to me.

If Caro bought a new bag, Sadie would turn up with the same one the next day. If Caro was wearing a new dress, sure enough a few days later Sadie would be wearing it.'

I think back to the first time I went to Sadie's house, how it had struck me that her furniture and the décor in the sitting room had been remarkably similar to the sitting room at Rupert's house. 'What did Caro think about it?'

'She didn't mind,' Rupert says, 'most of the time anyway. I got more annoyed about it than her, I think. She took it as a form of flattery most of the time.'

I don't know whether to feel offended or relieved that Sadie clearly doesn't think my style is worth copying. 'Most of the time?'

'Yeah, there were some times when it did really get to Caro. I mean, Sadie can be a bit overbearing, you know that. Sometimes Caro didn't want her to copy her. I remember Caro being pissed off about a pair of earrings – she was wearing them for the party…' he breaks off for a moment, brushing at sugar that has spilled across the table, 'she was wearing a pair of diamond earrings that I'd bought her for our wedding day and Sadie had wanted to borrow them. Most of the time Caro was quite relaxed about lending her things to Sadie, even though half the time she wouldn't get them back, but this time she said no, and Sadie got the hump about it.' Rupert shrugs, and finally meets my eyes again. 'Can you ever forgive me for not believing you? Can we get back to how things were?'

I stare at him, his deep, navy blue eyes, the way his hair falls over his forehead, the light stubble that grazes his

cheeks, even though he shaved this morning. It wasn't supposed to be like this. I was supposed to be his housekeeper,
to come in, do what I needed to do, and go. There was
never meant to be any emotional attachment. I was never
meant to fall in love with him.

'Em?'

I smile, realizing he's still waiting for a reply. 'Yes,' I say,
even though as I say it there is something nagging at the
very recesses of my mind, that unnerving feeling that I had
before that something is not quite right. 'Of course we can.
But I think it's best if we don't see Sadie for a little while.
I just feel as though everything will be too awkward.'

'Obviously.' Rupert gives me a relieved smile. 'I'll do
whatever you want to do. I'm just glad you're OK. We're
OK.' Checking his watch, he pulls a regretful face and slides
out from where he's sitting. 'I'm sorry, Em, I have to go.
I can't miss this meeting. Are you sure you'll be all right?'

I nod and let him kiss me, watching him walk the few
feet back to the office before I turn and walk in the opposite
direction, back towards the house, finally feeling for the
first time in a long while as though I don't need to dread
going home.

It's only much, much later, after Rupert has arrived
home early with a bouquet of flowers, and we've been
out to our favourite Italian for dinner and then made
love, quietly and urgently as if that will patch up the last
of the holes between us, that it comes to me and I realize
exactly what it is that didn't feel quite right, and my heart
goes cold.

Chapter Thirty-One

Feigning sleep as I hear Rupert get up and get ready for work, I wait until I hear the front door slam closed before I open my eyes. I haven't slept a wink, not since I realized what it was that didn't fit, the thing that was making me feel off kilter. I lay there, rigid, all night, afraid to move a muscle in case I woke Rupert up and he asked me what the matter was, as I tried to fit all the pieces together and come up with something that added up.

Feeling stiff and sore, and almost foggy with tiredness, I slip out of bed and pull on some sweatpants and a jumper – cashmere, both of them, and both bought by Rupert – and tying my hair up into an untidy bun, I sit down at the dressing table and reach behind the mirror for Caro's jewellery box. Remembering how everything had skittered out across the floor and table the last time I opened it, this time I gently lift the lid with care. The light catches the gold and silver trinkets as the sun streams in through the open blinds and I feel a sharp pang of envy that Caro had all of this, before I mentally slap myself – Caro might have had all of this but it doesn't mean she was happy.

Carefully I sift through the jewellery, pulling out gold chains and larger earrings, laying them gently on the dressing table as I search for the tiny item I'm looking for. Finally, I find it, tucked into the corner of the velvet lining, and I pull it out and hold it up to the light. A single, solitary diamond earring, .31 carat, by the looks of things and remarkably similar to ones that I have eyed on the Tiffany website many times before. Large enough to be expensive. Large enough that you wouldn't be so careless as to just lose one.

I slide to the floor and sweep my arm under the dressing table – that's where I dropped it before, so it stands to reason that the other would be somewhere near by – but there's nothing under there but dust. I check all around, sweeping my arm under the wardrobe, and under the bed but there is no sign of a matching earring.

I hear Rupert's words as he sits across the table from me yesterday – '*She was wearing a pair of diamond earrings that I bought her for our wedding day*' – and Sadie telling me that on the night she disappeared, Caro was wearing a ruffled red gown and diamond earrings. My stomach rolls as I finally start to accept the implications of what finding this earring might mean.

Maybe she had other pairs? I return to the jewellery box and rummage through it closely, and although there are plenty of earrings, none of them are diamonds. *Amanda will know.* I head downstairs, needing coffee and something to settle my roiling stomach, and as I wait for the kettle to boil, I dial Amanda's number. It's not as if I can call Sadie, not after yesterday.

'Hello?' She sounds blurry, groggy, and I glance at the clock, realizing it's barely eight o'clock.

'Amanda? I'm so sorry to wake you, it's Emily.'

'Emily? It's early... sorry, I was awake half the night; this baby is going to be a gymnast, I think.' She pauses for a moment and sounds as though she is stifling a yawn. 'Are you OK?'

'I think so.' I dump water into a mug with coffee granules and give it a half-hearted stir before I move to the kitchen table. My legs feel wobbly, and I am dizzy and nauseous, but I am not sure if it's from lack of sleep or fear of having my thoughts confirmed. 'Listen, I wanted to ask you about the night Caro disappeared.'

'What about it?' A cautious note creeps into her tone and I hear a slight rustling, as though Amanda is propping herself up in bed.

'Sadie said Caro was excited about the party, but then she and Rupert had an argument and Caro stormed out.'

'Yes, that's what happened. What exactly is it that you want to know, Emily? Do you really need to bring all this up again?'

'She was wearing a red, ruffled designer gown, heels and a pair of diamond earrings, is that right?'

'Yes,' Amanda sighs, 'but I don't really see why you need to know all of this. And if Sadie has already told you this, why aren't you asking her to confirm it all? I have to get ready for work in a little while.'

'I know, I'm sorry, I promise I'll be quick,' I say, crossing my fingers, 'I would have called Sadie only we had a little bit of a… set-to yesterday.'

'Oh?' Amanda sounds interested now.

'I'll tell you when I see you,' I say hastily, not wanting to be distracted from the difficult questions that I need to ask. 'Listen, it's about Caro's earrings. Was she wearing the ones that Rupert gave her as a wedding gift?'

'Yes, that's right. Diamond studs. Big ones,' Amanda sighs enviously, 'from Tiffany. I remember Sadie wanted to borrow them that night, but Caro wouldn't let her.'

'Did she have any other pairs? Of diamond earrings, I mean.' My heart stutters in my chest as I ask the question.

'No,' Amanda says after a pause, 'no, I don't think she did. She had plenty of earrings, don't get me wrong, tons of jewellery, but that was her only pair of diamond earrings. That's why she was a bit precious about them.'

The wedding photo pops into my mind, Caro's face smiling out at me, the earrings catching the light as they sit in her ear lobes, her hair twisted up. 'And after she and Rupert argued, Caro just stormed out of the house, leaving all her guests there?' I have to get all of this straight in my head before I can let myself form the thought that is buzzing at the base of my brain.

'Yes,' Amanda says, and it sounds as though she is going to cry. 'I wish now more than anything that I had gone after her. We all just stood around, not really knowing what to do. It wasn't an uncommon thing, Caro storming out, so we sort of just finished our drinks, and then Rupert made an excuse and basically told everyone to leave.'

'Did Caro come back to the house?'

'No. She never came back to the house, and Rupert called us in the morning to say that she hadn't come home and to ask if we had seen her, which of course we hadn't. We offered to help look for her, but she'd done it before. None of us realized quite how serious it was this time. The police found her car three days later...' Amanda breaks off and I hear her blow her nose. 'If there's one thing I do feel guilty about, it's that I never even noticed that she had taken her car from the garage, none of us did. If I'd realized she was driving after drinking so much, I would have gone after her, all of us would.'

'I'm sorry I've made you go through it all again, Amanda,' I say, and I mean it. I like Amanda, even if she did take a while to get used to me. Maybe in another life we would have been friends, close friends, like her and Caro.

'Why are you even asking me this though, Emily?' Amanda says, and there is a sharp edge to her voice now.

'I just wanted to get things straight,' I say. 'I've only ever heard bits and pieces from different people about that night and I wanted to know what happened. How it could happen, that one day she was there and the next she wasn't.'

'Sadie told me that you thought she might still be alive.'

Of course she did, I think, and I am glad that I no longer have to deal with Sadie.

'I did,' I might as well admit it, 'but I was wrong. You understand why I couldn't talk to Rupert about it?'

'Yes, but…'

I butt in before Amanda can finish her sentence, 'Gosh, I'm so sorry – you'll be late, won't you? Thank you for talking to me, Amanda, we'll catch up soon!' and I hang up before she can respond.

Biro and Post-it notes in front of me, I write out a note for every piece of information that I have about the night Caro died. It doesn't matter how many times I move the pieces around, I still keep coming to the same question. If Caro was wearing the earrings the night of the party – the night she disappeared – then why is one of them sitting in the jewellery box upstairs?

I get up and start to pace the floor, trying my hardest to find a solution that doesn't lead to the worst possible scenario. It's been confirmed that both Amanda and Sadie saw her wearing them as she was arguing with Rupert, only Rupert says that once Caro stormed out of the house, she never returned. The only possible way the earring – which I now think must have been under the dressing table the entire time, until I found it when I dropped the contents of the jewellery box – could have got back into the house is if Caro returned after everyone had left the party. Which means Rupert has lied about the fact that she never returned. *And why would he lie about that, and all the other things he's hidden from me unless he has something to hide?*

I scrub my hands over my face, before throwing open the doors to the orangery, trying to imagine the scene as Rupert and Caro hissed at each other, and the guests tried to look as though nothing was happening. I feel sick, shaky with the knowledge that if Rupert has lied about the fact that Caro returned to the house after everyone had left, then he potentially could have had something to do with Caro's disappearance. Why else would he say that she never came back?

I step towards the window, to the light that streams into the room, and try to imagine the room that night, lit by fairy lights, music playing softly in the background – something jazz-like, I think Caro would have chosen. I look onto the garden, to the borders and shrubs, before my gaze snags on the lush patches of grass to the left of the orangery. Pushing open the doors I step into the fresh spring sunshine, and press my toe into the thick grass, wondering if I am imagining the slight dip there in the earth.

I look back to the extension, newly finished when Caro disappeared. *Ridiculous,* I think, *you're being ridiculous.* But something in my gut tells me that I'm not. *The site you've marked out is where the first soakaway is. The second soakaway is next to it, which means you don't really have the space to fit a pool in there.* The words of the builder ring in my ears, as I realize that this is another thing that doesn't add up. The house isn't on a flood plain that I know of, so why would it need a second soakaway? Surely one is enough? Why go to the expense of adding an extra one?

I need to speak to the builder – it could be nothing, in which case maybe I'll ask Rupert about that night one more time. I'll show him the earring and see if he has a valid explanation for why it is in the house after Caro supposedly disappeared wearing it. *And the money,* I think with a shiver, as if someone has walked over my grave, *Rupert was adamant that he didn't want to use Caro's money on a pool… but he's been making transfers into his own bank account regularly from her funds.*

Suddenly chilly, I hurry back into the house, closing the blinds in the orangery and slamming the door closed. As I head back upstairs to put Caro's jewellery away, I think of Rupert and my heart turns over. Things had got bad between me and Harry, violent and out of control, but this time – I pause as I reach the bedroom, our wedding photo on display on the nightstand – this time, I think I have bitten off more than I can chew.

Chapter Thirty-Two

Jittery with nerves, it's hard to act normally when Rupert comes home from work, knowing what I think I know. I have to keep reminding myself that I don't actually know *anything* as yet – all I have is an idea, a suspicion, but still the temptation to call the whole thing a day and shove my things in a bag and run back to the flat, to Mags, is strong. Not that Mags would probably let me in, not after the way I've treated her. Instead I paste on a smile, and let Rupert pull me down onto the sofa, laying my head in his lap after dinner.

He runs his fingers through my hair, making my scalp tingle, and if I close my eyes, I can almost pretend that nothing has changed, that Rupert hasn't lied and everything is perfect, just as it was.

'Rupert, what's the worst thing you've ever done?' I ask, from my position lying prone on the sofa, as his fingers massage my scalp. I open my eyes a fraction, enough to see his reaction. His fingers pause for a tiny second, before he rakes them through my hair.

'Gosh, I don't know. Nothing excitingly bad.' He lets

out a laugh, but I can feel the way his chest strains as he forces it out. 'There was that time I paid a guy ten quid to give Miles a wedgie, and then obviously Will's stag do, when we tied him to a lamppost, naked, which is something he's never forgiven me for... that's as dark as I get, I'm afraid. What's brought this on, anyway?' He shifts so that I have no option other than to sit up.

'I was just thinking about Sadie,' I say, tucking my legs up underneath me. I let my fingers mingle with his. 'How we both thought she couldn't possibly behave that way. It must have been more shocking for you than it was for me. After all, you've known her for years.'

'Yes,' Rupert says quietly, 'I suppose it was shocking. Although not entirely surprising. People only show you the façade that they want you to see. Everyone does it. We all show our best faces to the others around us.'

Goosebumps rise on my arms and I rub at my skin through the thin material of my cardigan, as a prickle of unease runs down my back. I can't have expected him to just admit to me that he had something to do with Caro's disappearance, and now I'm starting to wish I hadn't asked the question. 'Yes. I suppose you're right. Still shocking, though.'

'What about you?' Rupert says suddenly, his mouth twisting into a smile. 'What's the worst thing you've ever done?'

'Oh, I don't know,' I say, breezily, trying to make light of things. 'Probably the way I treated Mags. I shouldn't have cut her off when I met you. She did a lot for me, and I feel bad that I didn't keep in contact with her. That I dropped her.'

'Hmmm, she wasn't really your friend, Em,' Rupert says. 'She was obsessed with you, standing over your bed at night, always wanting to know where you were, what you were doing.'

I nod noncommittally, thinking of how best to turn the conversation to the things I really want to ask him about. I get to my feet, under the pretence of stoking the fire he lit earlier, throwing another log on and standing for a moment, my hands outstretched to feel the warmth of the flames. I let my gaze wander to the doors that lead to the orangery. *People only show you the façade that they want you to see.*

'Rupert, are you sure you want to keep the orangery locked up?' My pulse speeds up as I finally get up the nerve to turn the conversation to the extension, wondering what his reaction will be to me mentioning the builder. Surely if I have jumped to the wrong conclusion, Rupert won't have any issue with me speaking to him.

'Hmmm?' He looks up from the television, seemingly distracted by whatever TV show is on, but I get the impression he's buying himself a few seconds.

'I know I've said it a million times, but I think it's such a shame to waste the light in that room, it's such a gorgeous space. We could redecorate it…'

'No, Emily.' Rupert's tone is sharp. 'I told you the reason why I don't want to use that room. We've already talked about this.'

'Well, maybe… and this is just an idea… but perhaps if the memory of Caro is so strong in there that you don't want to use it, perhaps we should consider knocking it down and starting over.'

'Absolutely not.'

'But why? We could knock the existing orangery down and rebuild it, change it slightly so it's ours. We could even build it double-storey so there is more room for when we have a family.' I hold my breath, waiting for him to respond.

'I said no, Emily. I don't want to use the orangery – maybe in the future I'll change my mind. And I certainly don't want to knock it down. I can't believe you'd even suggest something like that.'

'OK, I'm sorry, I didn't mean to upset you.' I go to him on shaking legs, curling into where he sits on the sofa and lay my head on his shoulder, breathing in the scent of him. *It still doesn't mean anything,* I try to tell myself, but as I sit there, fake laughing at some stupid TV show, pretending that everything is all right, the same questions keep revolving in my mind. Why, when I said that Caro could still be alive, was Rupert so insistent, so *adamant* that she was dead? They never found her body, but Rupert is convinced that she is dead – is that because he knows something we don't? And is that the real reason why he neither wants to use the orangery nor tear it down? Because he feels guilty? Or for some other, more sinister reason?

Chapter Thirty-Three

A man in his late forties, with a closely shaved head and tidy beard, wearing dirty Levi's and work boots, is loading stuff into a pick-up truck, as I approach the address I've found online for the builder Rupert used to build the orangery. I thought Rupert would never leave this morning, as I sat and sipped at my tea, pretending that nothing was wrong, that my heart wasn't beating so hard in my chest that I was worried I might pass out. Half of me still hopes that I have jumped to the wrong conclusion, that Caro took her earrings out before she stormed off, that Rupert really just doesn't want to spend the money Caro left him, but the other half of me – the half that believes in instinct and that more than one coincidence is too many – believes that Rupert could have done this. Now, today, if the builder tells me that there was a legitimate reason for building the second soakaway, then maybe I can give Rupert the benefit of the doubt and find another explanation for why Caro's earring lay hidden beneath the dressing table.

'Excuse me?' I catch the builder just as he is about to hop into the truck. 'Are you Nick Williams?'

He pauses, his hand on the door handle and frowns. 'Yes? Can I help you?'

'I hope so.' I pull the rolled-up plans from under my arm. 'Do you have a few minutes? You built an extension for my husband a little while ago and I wondered if I could chat to you about it.'

Nick looks wary. 'Why? I give everything a guarantee, but if there's a problem…'

'No, there's no problem.' *At least, not with the building.* At my words he visibly relaxes, and I swoop. 'Do you think we could maybe go inside for a few minutes? I won't keep you long, I promise.' It's starting to rain, and I shield the plans with my jacket.

Nick makes a show of checking his watch. 'It'll have to be quick. I'm already late for a job.' He bangs on the driver's window and a young lad looks up from his phone. 'Tom, I just need a word with this lady. Go up the road and get us a bacon roll each, yeah?' He turns to me. 'Come on then, you'd better come inside.'

I follow him into the house, through to a small but airy kitchen. A woman, presumably his wife, looks up in confusion from where she sits at a breakfast bar feeding a chubby baby.

'Sorry, love,' Nick stoops to kiss her head, 'this lady just wants a quick word about her extension. Can you give us a minute?' With a curious glance between us, Nick's wife wipes the baby's face and scoops him from the highchair, leaving Nick and I alone. 'Right, what did you want to know?'

I lay out the plans, and as Nick looks them over, he nods his head. 'Yep, I remember this one well. Lovely, light airy room, and a nice couple to work with. The architect did a brilliant job on the design.' He frowns. 'You're not the lady I did the work for, though, did they move already? Seems a shame to spend all that money and then move away. Wait… didn't we speak about a swimming pool?'

'We did, and no, they didn't move,' I say, my cheeks flushing warm and pink, 'Caro, the lady you did the work for, isn't around anymore. Her husband got remarried… err, to me.' I give him a small smile and he just nods again.

'So, what's the problem?'

I flounder for a moment, not sure what to say, everything I've prepared melting out of my head. 'The pool. I wanted to get some more clarification on the pool. Make sure there won't be any surprises if I go ahead with it.' Tucking my fingers into my sleeves to hide their shaking, I incline my head towards the plans.

'What? Like dead bodies being unearthed?' I feel my eyes go wide, as Nick grins. 'Just joking, love! No, no surprises. It was a quite straightforward job, actually. One of those rare jobs where everything seems to go smoothly. Even the bricklayers turned up every day.' He gives a laugh, deep and infectious, and I get the feeling that maybe the bricklayers don't always turn up.

There is a pang of *something* deep in my chest and I can't figure out what it is. I don't want to call it disappointment, because obviously I don't want Rupert to have done something terrible, but equally it isn't quite relief either.

Maybe I have got things all wrong after all, maybe Rupert was right, and I do see things that aren't really there. I reach for the plans, but Nick lays his hand flat on them.

'Why are you asking? Is there a problem with the build?'

'No. Not a problem,' I smooth my hand over the drawings, 'it's only that you said that I couldn't put the pool where I wanted it because of the second soakaway. Is it usual to have a second soakaway? It seems a shame, that's all,' I say hastily.

'Well, originally there was only one. You only really need one,' Nick says, happy to explain, 'but I got a call from the home owner – the gentleman, not the wife – asking me to come out and see about putting in another one. You could always put the pool in further down the garden, but like I said, it'll cost you.'

'But why? Why would he need a second one?'

'He was concerned about flooding – the land is partially clay there, so there is potentially a very small risk of flooding, seeing as you're not miles from the river, and the weather was shocking, if I remember it correctly. It was a wet winter and there'd been storms, some real torrential rain. He was worried that the original soakaway wouldn't be able to cope – bit overcautious, really, but you know how it is, the customer is always right. He was quite panicky really, he wanted it done as a rush job. Luckily we weren't too busy.'

'When was this?' That creeping sense of unease is back, prickling its way along my spine and round towards my heart, a cold fist closing over it. 'I mean, how soon after the build was finished?'

'Maybe a week or so?' Nick rubs a hand over his forehead. 'I'm pretty sure it wasn't very long because we'd just had everything signed off. She – Caroline? Christina? Sorry, I can't remember her name – she said she wanted to have a party to celebrate. She invited us, me and the wife.' He laughs, as if embarrassed by the thought. 'We didn't go, though. They were all a bit too upmarket for us, and anyway I don't mix business with pleasure.' Dropping a lazy wink, he grins to show he doesn't mean any offence.

'So, you went back after the party and put the second soakaway in?'

'That's right. A couple of days after the party, if that. It took us a couple of days, but the fella said he'd pay us double if we could fit him in and get it done ASAP.' He looks at me quizzically. 'Are you all right? You look a bit peaky.'

I swallow, unable to take my eyes off the spot on the drawing where the soakaway lies. 'Yes,' I manage, 'I'm fine. Thank you so much for your help. That explains a lot.'

'Well, if you want me to come back and see about where you can put the pool in without digging up the drainage then I'd be happy to help.' Nick is guiding me towards the front door, and I am only too happy to leave, keen to get out into the fresh air and process what I've discovered.

'No, it's OK. Honestly. I won't keep you anymore.' I wait as he jumps into his truck and gives me a wave as he drives off, before I turn towards the bus station and head back to the house.

★

I stand in the garden, almost mesmerised by the thick, lush grass that marks where the soakaways are, my stomach swirling uncomfortably at the idea that Caro has never been far from the house this entire time. I turn back towards the house, slowly walking through and letting my eyes roam over the large kitchen with Caro's fancy American fridge and the Aga that I can never get to work as I'd like it to, the sitting room with its designer furniture and cosy feel, up the stairs to the bedrooms, all such a contrast to the damp, dingy flat I shared with Mags.

I should have done what I was meant to do, that first time I came to the house for a job interview. I wasn't supposed to get attached to Rupert. I never get attached, not after growing up with a mother like mine. I walk into the spare room, the one Rupert uses as a study, and lay the plans on his desk before turning my attention to the safe. Poor Caro. It feels strange to be feeling sympathy for a woman who, not so long ago, I was convinced was still alive and tormenting me. Now, I am certain that Caro is dead, that she died the night of the party, but only after she had returned to the house – to Rupert – and I wonder how Sadie will react when all of this comes out. And Will and Amanda, and Rupert's lovely parents who did nothing but make me feel welcome. Sitting back on my haunches I pause for a moment, as something like grief washes over me. Shame and the humiliation of being duped burns as if I have been branded. How could I, of all people, not seen Rupert for what he really was?

Chapter Thirty-Four

Rupert is distracted as he waits in line at Pret to pay for a soggy, overpriced sandwich and a coffee. His mind is full of thoughts of Sadie, and how appallingly she has behaved, and Emily, who he is starting to think he really does need to worry about. He swipes his card, and doesn't realize for a moment, until the barista says, '*Sir*' a little too loudly that it has been declined. He hands over a tenner and makes his way to a table where Sadie sits waiting for him.

'I'm so sorry, Rupert,' Sadie is tearful as he takes his seat, 'thank you so much for agreeing to see me.'

'You didn't really give me a choice, did you?' Rupert is curt with her, not taken in by her crocodile tears. 'Why did you do it, Sadie?'

'I was concerned for you...' she heaves in a dramatic breath. 'Everything happened so quickly, how could you be sure that Emily was the real deal? Call it a test, if you like.'

'It wasn't your place to "test" anything,' Rupert says, pushing the sandwich away from him. He has no appetite.

'I just wanted to protect you, Rupert. After Caro died you pushed us all away, you refused to see me for months.

I was worried that things were moving too fast with Emily, that's all. I didn't mean for things to get so out of hand, and of course I didn't realize how mentally fragile she is, I mean, talking about Caro as if Caro could still be alive…'

'I don't want to talk about Caro,' Rupert snaps. 'This isn't about Caro, it's about you. I'm sorry, Sadie, I can't see you for a while, not until I get my head straight. I'm finding it all a bit hard to process, to be honest.'

He is blunt with her. Rupert has only agreed to see her today because she hasn't stopped calling since the day Emily came home and told him it was Sadie who had done all of these things, things he had written off as Emily being a bit paranoid, to his shame. Now, he shoves back his chair and snatches up his jacket. He hasn't told Emily that he's taken today off work, wanting some time to himself to process everything, but now he feels the urge to go home and tell her he's sorry. For everything.

Rupert stops in the upmarket supermarket on the High Street on the way home and picks up a fancy meal for two that he will prepare this evening, along with two bottles of decent red wine. Emily is worrying him, with all her talk of Caro, and knocking down the orangery. Tonight, he will put any negative thoughts out of her head, once and for all. He can't afford for her to keep pecking away at him about Caro, he'll snap if she does. Maybe he'll stop thinking about booking that holiday in the sun and actually book it – that should take her mind off of everything. The self-service checkout beeps at him and spits his bank card out, and he looks around in frustration for a member of staff.

'There's something wrong with this till,' Rupert says, as he picks up the bag of groceries.

'I'm sorry, sir, it's not the till,' the girl says, 'your card has been declined. Do you want to try it again?'

Rupert pushes his card back into the machine and once again it is declined. He shoves the bag of groceries back at the cashier and storms out of the store, his face burning as he calls the bank from his mobile.

'I'm sorry, Mr Milligan, your card was declined due to insufficient funds.' The woman on the other end of the line is aloof, bored almost.

'No, that's not right,' Rupert feels his blood pressure rising, 'can you just check them again, please? All of them?' He waits a moment, before the woman tells him the exact same thing. Insufficient funds. On every bank account he holds. 'There must be some sort of glitch your end. I hope you're going to pay out compensation for the inconvenience.'

Rupert hangs up, his mood not improved. *It's OK*, he thinks, a short time later as he walks down the driveway to the house, Emily has her black Am Ex. They can use that to go out for dinner later, and then he'll speak to her about booking that romantic getaway, and things can go back to how they were.

As he lets himself in, the first thing he notices is that the house is silent. Emily must be out shopping. Hopefully that will have taken her mind off rebuilding the orangery – at least she's abandoned all talk of putting in a pool. As he pushes open the door to his study, the second thing he notices are the plans to the orangery, laid out on his desk. Frowning, he steps forward, a ring of blue pen on the plan glowing like a beacon and his stomach drops away.

He closes his eyes, fighting a wave of nausea as everything about that night comes back to him, engulfing him and he presses his hands onto the desk, leaning into them in order to stay on his feet.

'Rupert, darling, please let's just tell everyone tonight.' Caro is manic, her eyes glittering in the glow of the fairy lights as people mill around, drinks in hand, all there to admire the new orangery that has cost Rupert a fortune. An orangery that Caro wanted and neither of them needed. 'It's a double celebration – our beautiful home and a beautiful baby.' She lays a hand on her stomach and Rupert grips her by the wrist, pulling her to one side.

'No, Caro, we're not telling anybody, not tonight.' He fixes a smile on his face as Sadie walks past with a drink in her hand, aware that he is hissing the words. 'I thought we agreed that we haven't even made a decision yet about what we're going to do?'

'I've made *my* decision,' Caro hisses back, before she pastes on a brilliant smile as Will brushes by them. 'Will, darling, would you mind grabbing me a drink – just a soda water for now.' She beams at him, but her eyes glitter with tears and Rupert feels the first flicker of fear. Caro in this state is wildly unpredictable. She turns back to him. 'How dare you be so fucking selfish?'

Rupert glances around, convinced that all their guests know there is a row going on, has been since before the party even started. 'Caro, all I'm saying is that we need to think things through properly before we make a final decision. It's not fair for you to call me selfish.' He leans in closer. 'Don't you think you're being a little selfish?'

'*How fucking dare you!*' Caro forgets their guests, forgets that this row is supposed to hissed and whispered, forgets that they are supposed to be putting on a façade to the rest of the world. She throws what remains of her soda water in his face and turns on her heel, slamming her way out of the house. Rupert stands there, face dripping wet and aflame with embarrassment as their guests turn to stare.

'Rupert, darling, are you OK?' Sadie is by his side in an instant, dabbing at his face with the bell sleeve of her dress. He brushes her aside, her attention only serving to irritate him.

'Sorry, folks, it looks like the party is over.' Rupert claps his hands together. 'Thank you for coming everyone, but yeah… it's time to leave. Thank you for your time.' He starts to usher people towards the door, many of them too embarrassed on his behalf to say anything.

Sadie loiters, and Rupert lets Miles call her to the door. 'Sorry, old chap,' Miles gives him a sheepish grin, 'I'm sure she'll calm down soon.'

'Call me if you need to.' Sadie presses her lips to Rupert's cheek, and he is relieved when finally, everyone has left. He's cleared away the glasses and bottles and is upstairs listening to Caro's mobile ring downstairs when he hears the slam of the front door. He ends the call and waits as her footsteps march up the stairs and she throws open the bedroom door, clearly still unhappy.

'So, you decided the party was over as well, did you?' She stands there, her chest heaving, her eye make-up a dirty smudge around her eyes.

'Caro, you didn't give me much option. You stormed out. You threw a drink over me in front of everyone.'

'You want to abort our baby. You think you get to make the decision, but it's mine, Rupert, do you understand? It's my decision, it's my body.'

There is a tinge of hysteria in her voice and Rupert struggles to squash down a sigh. It's going to be another of those nights, of Caro repeating herself, and Rupert trying to explain and then reassure her, until finally, probably in the grey dawn hours, she will be so exhausted she'll fall asleep and he'll have to go to work on no sleep, with the very real fear that he'll come home to blood in the bath, or an empty pill bottle.

'That's not what I said, Caro.' Rupert feels the uphill battle start, already weary at the thought of the climb. 'I said we need to talk about it, think things through properly.'

'There is nothing to talk about.' Caro's words are bumpy and hitched as she forces them out between heavy, hysterical sobs. 'Why don't you want a baby with me? Because you don't love me? Is that why? Is that why you have people watching me all the time, moving my things? Is that your lover, the one you cheat on me with?'

'I don't have a lover,' Rupert says, for the millionth time.

He feels something inside him snap. 'I don't want a baby with you, Caro, because I don't want to bring a child into *this*.' The release is like a dam being broken and he couldn't stop the words if he tried. 'You drain me, Caro, your moods, the way you are tonight, I don't ever want a baby with you because of *how you are*.'

He knows he's hurting her, but he hurts too, and he doesn't expect it when she flies at him, her hands going for his face, the rake of her nails along his neck. He tries to push her off, his hand catching her ear as she grabs for his throat and she's just so *strong*. Panic and rage and fear – yes, rage that she could be such a *bitch, a goddamn fucking bitch* and fear that *she's going to really do something bad, really hurt him this time* – overwhelm him and Rupert grabs her, his hands closing around her throat and there's something just so *satisfying* about the give of her skin under his fingers and the way she finally, *finally*, stops shouting, as they both sink to the floor.

Rupert takes his hands from her throat, panting, his breath hurting in his chest as he looks down at Caro, her face pale and her eyes wide, the purple marks of his fingers already standing out against the alabaster white of her skin.

'Caro?' He whispers it, as if worried he'll wake her and he waits a moment for her to blink, to ask him what the hell he thought he was doing. But she doesn't. And Rupert feels a sick sense of dread start somewhere around his stomach, a whispered '*fuck*' escaping his lips as he presses his fingers against her already cooling skin in search of a pulse.

The third thing Rupert sees as he stands in his study is the safe door, wide open and swinging. In two strides he is across the room, peering into the now empty safe, and realization begins to dawn. There was no glitch at the bank, there will be no compensation for inconvenience. He pulls out his phone and opens the app. Every bank account is empty. He covers his face with his hands as he remembers Emily, sitting at the kitchen table as he rushes around getting ready for work, waving a utility bill in his face.

'Just give me the log on and I'll do it online,' she says, a trace of irritation in her voice. 'You did say you'd do it last week, Rupert, and I'm worried they'll cut us off. Give me the bank login and I'll sort it out before you forget, set up a direct debit so it's done for the future.'

And because he was busy, stressed with work, because she made his heart flip over when he looked at her and sometimes – most of the time – he felt the blood shoot to his groin when she smiled at him, he gave it to her.

Rupert goes into their bedroom, but he can see before he's even looked properly that she is gone. Caro's jewellery box stands empty on the dressing table, the en suite is cleared of cleanser and make-up, her hangers swing empty in the wardrobe. Groaning, Rupert slams the wardrobe door closed, blaming himself before a wave of fury washes over him. How dare she do this to him? He swipes the phone screen, dials a number and waits for it to connect.

Pacing the floor downstairs in the sitting room, Rupert tries and fails to see the signs that Emily wasn't who she said she was. That he was taken in so completely. He is lost in thought, when just ten minutes after making the call, the doorbell rings and with a looming sense of déjà vu, Rupert opens the door to the police.

'Mr Rupert Milligan?'

'Yes, that's right. Come in.' Rupert stands to one side to let them through. 'Thank you so much for coming out to me so quickly. I can give you a list of everything taken, I'll do anything I can to help you catch her.'

The two officers exchange a quizzical look before the taller one, an officer that Rupert realizes with a sinking feeling that he has seen before, says, 'Mr Milligan, we are arresting you on suspicion of the murder of Mrs Caroline Osbourne-Milligan.'

Chapter Thirty-Five

Early September, and it's been six months since I fled Rupert's house, taking everything I could and putting in a call to the police before I turned my back on the house for good. Today is our one-year wedding anniversary. I should have been spending it somewhere warm, having let Rupert pay for some extravagant holiday to celebrate. Instead, he is languishing in a cell and I am sitting on the beach in Devon, the home of my new life, enjoying the early autumn sunshine.

It didn't take me long to piece together what I thought had happened to Caro, and it took me even less time to pack my stuff and get out, clearing Rupert's bank accounts on the way. I picture him now, hefting Caro's dead weight into the soakaway, watching as Nick and his men piled on the topsoil. Driving Caro's car away in the dead of night to leave at that notorious spot near the bridge, while she cooled back at the house. His hand shaking as he forged her one-word suicide note. I should have known that letting myself get attached was a mistake, but there was something about Rupert that I couldn't resist. My plan on getting the job was to make him fall for me, take the money and go, like I have so many times before, but he crawled under my skin and I let myself fall for him. Things got a bit sticky with Harry, especially at the end, when I broke into the house and waited in his bed, and he lost it completely... but this time I *definitely* bit off more than I could chew.

People only show you the façade that they want you to see. Everyone does it. We all show our best faces to the others around us.

Rupert's words come back to me, from the night I realized that he wasn't who I thought he was. I've spent my life putting on a façade in order to drag myself up from nothing to where I am today, thanks to my mother's training and the hefty bank balances of Rupert, and Harry, and a guy called Justin before them, back when I was calling myself Ellie.

Now, sitting in my little corner of paradise, I watch the man playing with his children, running in and out of the surf even though it's too chilly for that. I smile as the youngest, a girl, kicks up a spray that soaks his trouser legs and he laughs, his curly blond hair blowing wildly in the breeze. Thanks to the nanny who looks after his children – a round, rosy-cheeked woman who spends a lot of time discussing her employer in the local coffee shop – I know that his name is Patrick, and his wife died five years ago, when the youngest child was barely a few weeks old. He runs his own business, and is very successful at it, winning awards. He likes fishing, hiking, good ale and on top of all that, he is practical, with hands the size of shovels. I also know from the nanny that he is lonely, that he longs for a partner to share the vast amounts of money he has made. For someone to be a proper mother to his children.

I get to my feet as they start to walk away from me, Patrick engaged with the older of the two children, trying to untangle a snag in the line of the kite they're trying to fly. Following their footprints in the sand, I see the girl take a tumble as she runs through the surf, trying to get to her feet before the waves wash over her legs and I see my chance.

'Oopsadaisy.' I slide my hands under her arms and lift her to her feet with a smile.

'That's *my* name,' she shrieks in delight, 'Daddy, Daddy...'

Patrick turns and I am relieved to see he is as good-looking as I had hoped. Daisy is brushing the sand from her bottom, telling him how I saved her from being washed away, enjoying the attention as she ramps up the tension in her story, to punish him for not watching her.

'Thanks,' Patrick says, as Daisy finally takes a breath, 'I think she's making it sound a little more dramatic than it probably was.' He laughs, a deep, rumbling laugh and I feel that familiar tingle that tells me I was right.

'That's five-year-olds for you,' I smile back, aware of his gaze as it travels over my face, down my neck to the slight hint of cleavage that peeps from my shirt. 'Hi, I'm Emma.' And I hold my hand out for him to shake, and it starts all over again.

Acknowledgements

As always it took an entire army to get this book from first draft to the finished article. Thank you to Lisa Moylett, Zoe Apostolides and Elena Langtry at CMM for all your support and guidance. I am so lucky to have such strong, amazing women behind me.

Thank you to my editor, Kate Mills, who always knows the right thing to say, and always encourages me to go that little bit darker. Thanks also to Vikki Moynes and Becky Heeley for all your hard work, and to the incredible Lisa Milton.

Caroline Brownsell, I am so eternally grateful that you let me kill you on paper … sorry it was a bit more horrific than I originally planned. Cocktails on me to make up for it. And thank you to Rob, for loaning me his tradition of collecting coal on the beaches of Norfolk.

Thank you to all the bloggers, reviewers and readers – I can't even tell you how grateful I am for all the support I have received from the reading community. I am still pinching myself that people pay to read and enjoy my work. You are all wonderful.

Finally, thanks to Nick, George, Missy and Mo for everything. Sorry I am sometimes a bit rubbish at cooking dinner/cleaning the house/remembering appointments. I promise you it'll be worth it in the end...

Loved *The Perfect Couple*? Read...

HAVE YOU SEEN HER

...another gripping thriller from Lisa Hall.
Available now!

ONE PLACE. MANY STORIES

Bold, innovative and
empowering publishing.

FOLLOW US ON:

@HQStories